The
Delivery
Room

SYLVIA BROWNRIGG

The
Delivery
Room

PICADOR

First published 2006 by Picador
an imprint of Pan Macmillan Ltd
Pan Macmillan, 20 New Wharf Road, London N1 9RR
Basingstoke and Oxford
Associated companies throughout the world
www.panmacmillan.com

ISBN-13: 978-0-330-44242-8
ISBN-10: 0-330-44242-2

1 3 5 7 9 8 6 4 2

A CIP catalogue record for this book is available from
the British Library.

Typeset by IntypeLibra, London
Printed and bound in Great Britain by
Mackays of Chatham, Chatham, Kent

For Sedge

PART ONE

The Children

For to exist on the earth is beyond any power to name.

Czesław Miłosz

One

March, 1998

Everybody that spring seemed to be talking about children. Having them, not having them. How to have them, whether it was possible to have them, how to have them the right way, what the right way might be.

'Everybody has been talking about children,' Mira told Peter one night over dinner. (Sausages and potatoes: lazy, she chided herself, a child's meal.) 'To have them, not to have them. How to. Why.'

'*How to?*' Peter raised a brow. 'Do you really have to tell them that?'

Mira nodded towards the joke. 'Yes – they should pay more for that, shouldn't they? But everybody has difficulty with it now. One kind or another. It is not as easy as it was, apparently.'

'Does "everybody" include the Bigot?'

'The Bigot talks of children he already has.' Mira took a plump bite of sausage and eyed Peter's. He was not eating much. Was eating very slowly. 'He doesn't much like them. Perhaps would have been happier without them. One of them particularly – the son.'

3

'Ah. The *son*.' Peter closed his eyes as if to ward off his surroundings: their narrow wood-panelled dining room, a cooling, unappetizing dinner, a television in the next room waiting with unsavoury information if they cared to watch. The word 'son' was complicated for Peter, Mira knew. Dear man. Eyes closed, he had the exalted look of a priest. 'And what is the son of the Bigot like, do you know? A kettle of rage, like his father, or rather gentle and tolerant? Children do sometimes go the other way.'

'Angry,' she said. 'Angry, like his father. They are too alike. He created a child in his own image; a kind of revenge against the mother, I think. They loathe each other.' Mira paused. 'I shouldn't tell you more, probably.'

'No, of course.' Peter opened his eyes, and there she was before him: confessor, magician, wife. His beloved Mira. Gatherer of stories. He would hear as much as she was willing to tell him about the Bigot's son or anyone else. It was only recently, since the so-called peace of the past few years, that Mira was able to sound as though she found her work compelling again. In the bleaker, bloodier years she had all but stopped telling Peter about her people. But: how long would this peace hold?

Mira's voice changed register. Doctor to wife, Peter could hear the lowering tone.

'Peter, love,' Mira said, and however often she said his name – she said it often, she loved saying it – it never sounded English, altogether. Always in that short music some mention, the slightest, of another country, a different history, a foreign landscape. She leaned forward, for emphasis. 'Why aren't you eating?'

Mira started her work early on a Tuesday; not with the Bigot, fortunately, but the American. By the time the American came round Peter had not yet left for the Poly. (His employer had renamed itself Brookes University, in the fashion of polytechnics, but Peter said he thought it a nonsense; 'Oxford Poly' still sounded to his ear far more adventurous and egalitarian, containing all that seventies optimism.)

At times Peter's scuffles and grumbles were audible even through the various closed doors. It was not a large flat. Some patients did not mind the ambient noise, indeed welcomed it, as it afforded the chance to ask Mira about her life, out of projection, or as a means of escaping reflection on their own. She would not allow enquiry, however. She met all such questions – 'Is that your husband?' 'Did you have a nice weekend?' – with a nod and a silent smile, sometimes accompanied by the simple phrase a colleague had once suggested to her: 'Thank you.' It was an effective smothering blanket.

Others were disturbed by the flat's emissions, and Mira thought she knew why: such sounds violated the patient's fantasy that the therapist had no life outside of their sessions together, no husband or family or concerns of her own. The American was such a patient. She asked nothing of Mira, and always wore a slightly hunted expression when she heard Peter off in the wilderness distance. Now for example, twitching and distracted, the girl tapped her feet against one another and furrowed her brow, as if trying to rid her ears of Peter's gentle clattering, a muted bark that Mira recognized as a half-stifled cough.

How to start? Jess wondered. That was always the problem. You walked through a muffling fog to get there, only a few blocks in her case but that didn't make it an easy journey, there was traffic always, it was London, there was nothing but traffic and bossy road surfaces telling you to LOOK RIGHT or LOOK LEFT as if looking anywhere would be any protection, finally, against the accelerating white vans and suicidal motorbike couriers, the red leering buses and gas-masked androgynes on bicycles. They were all out for blood, Jess felt – and sometimes, on a bad morning, specifically hers. They were out to get *her*.

'I've been feeling a little paranoid lately,' she started now, looking up at Mira's round, weathered face for signs of encouragement. Or tolerance. Or wisdom. Sometimes Jess suspected she went to see Mira chiefly for the latter, diamond-rare commodity the older woman seemed to stash about herself. Wisdom.

'Yes?' the therapist offered with her distinctive head-tilt, and the cluttered consonants or blunt vowels that gave her speech that remarkable sound. More than anything else about Mira, Jess loved her voice, old, slow, other – a voice from some culture distinct from Jess's own, that had had plenty of time (hundreds of years, and a dozen or more wars) to think about humanity and the world and the relationship between the two. An Eastern European country, that was clear, but Jess had never asked which. Czechoslovakia, she sometimes thought. Possibly Romania. She liked the odd blind fact of not knowing.

'Not paranoid, exactly.' Jess gazed at the picture on the wall – vaguely Japanese, vaguely a body. It had always irritated her, that picture. 'More – I don't know – marked for death. I keep thinking I'm about to die. If I'm on a busy street corner, I imagine a bus hitting me. If I pass a hospital, I imagine I'm in there dying of cancer, or that I soon will be. If I see some horrible news coverage on TV, you know, massacres in Bosnia or wherever—' She looked out the window at the familiar squirrel darting up and down the railing outside the window. Was it always the same one? Or did they take turns? 'Well, it's not as though I think I'll get killed in those situations, obviously, but I imagine what it would be like to be there, wondering if you were going to get killed.'

The art of the profession – one of its more delicate arts, that required reserves of resilience – was in not responding to provocation. Mira's hands instinctively tightened around each other. She knew the American was attentive, though, so made sure to busy the hands elsewhere, using them to rustle the folds of her skirt, to shift slightly, distractingly, in her chair. Just at that moment – bless him! – Peter sneezed. It was terribly loud, elephant-like, a surprise in such a quiet, placid man. Mira once commented that Peter seemed to reserve all his private noise and need for attention for his boldly declarative sneezes.

Perfect. It did rattle the American's nerves and dampen her awareness. The young woman had been speaking her death thoughts, as she often did. Self-mutilation fantasies; suicidal ideation, occasionally; mostly a leaning towards the morbid and self-destructive. Mira was crafting the right question to prompt her when the American continued on her own.

'I guess that's why I keep thinking about having a baby.' She sat back in the chair, her face unusually smooth and unguarded.

'What is the connection?'

'I feel I'd like to embrace life, not death. Having a child might be my way of fending off mortality. I don't know.' The American tried to put language to what was wordless within her, this desire. Usually she was so assured verbally, crafting sentences with care and precision, but this subject seemed almost to mute her. 'I'm tired of being shut out of life. My future begins to seem so arid . . . If I don't become a mother I'll have failed, somehow. I'll be empty, it will be an empty life.' She paused and shrugged, an apologetic gesture. 'And then also it's that clichéd thing – if I die, I want to leave someone behind me. You know, I'd live on through my child. I know that's vain and narcissistic, but I'm sure that's part of what I imagine. Why I'm obsessing about it.'

Difficult not to notice the complacency, though, even amidst the pain. As if she were a god, wondering whether or not to make the world. That was the nationality, Mira reflected. She watched

Jess, a wealthy American in her thirties, journalist, dressed as usual in morose jeans – dark shrouding clothes, death rags, gloomwear. (Her socks, particularly, were terrible. They seldom matched her shoes or trousers and on occasion did not even match each other.) Yet Mira had a fondness for this girl. The American had a sense of humour about herself. She could make Mira laugh, with her broad, hyperbolic gestures and deadpan observations. And she was not English. This was a source of alliance between them.

'Who would be the father of this child?' Mira never hesitated to ask direct questions.

'I don't know. That's the thing.' Jess screwed up her face like a little girl. 'I'm working on it.' She looked back at Mira. 'Do you have any suggestions?'

Just then the phone rang from within the flat. Almost, Mira thought, as if a kind male friend was calling to volunteer his services.

Peter took the coach to work. It gave him a particular pleasure never to drive. Standing in the elements down near Baker Street twice or three times a week, waiting for the bright yellow-and-blue colours to lumber along and collect him into the warm, soft-clothed interior. Little reds would pass, greens, locals, Lutons, airports, and finally his: Oxford. It had a soothing, rolling rhythm, the coach, more nowadays than the trains did – gone were the trains that rocked one *ch-ch-ch-chhhh, ch-ch-ch-chhhh*, all the British Rails of his locomotive youth. They used toy trains to Oxford now, two- or three-carriaged, over-bright confections that looked like they'd been built quickly from a kit and pestered the traveller with an unending stream of red-lettered information, unnecessary and distracting. Crowded now with bicycles and children and Japanese tourists, waiting to be delivered to the western end of the University city and the soulless new station there. Though 'new' dated Peter, as it wasn't especially new any more, it simply wasn't old, wasn't the old station, with the Menzies stand out on the platform, from where all those years ago he had left on journeys up to London (for filial duties, theatre, friends). Introduced at a dinner given by the Epsteins, who were analysts, to a shy, moon-faced woman with eyes that had seen things other than Peter had, and a voice so thick he wanted to stroke it. They had traded sartorial commentaries: he had admired a colourful scarf Mira wore (given to her by her father, she said with seeming ruefulness) and she had nodded towards his thick red pullover, making a joke about communist threads, surprising in a person new to the language. Peter had known immediately he wanted to meet her again (he didn't think of Graham). Mira had been living in London, training in Hampstead at the Tavistock in a self-imposed exile from her difficult country. And he became terribly, sentimentally fond of the Oxford train station then as it was the means by which he could visit his new friend, Mira. And she could come to visit him in Oxford.

Nevertheless. Peter did not move as easily onto the coach as he once had. There was no way to pretend otherwise. Something in his back, was it? Or a low ache – hard to pinpoint. Something in him didn't move as easily it used to. Age, he supposed. Just age. The indignities kept coming. Just as one accepted some new phenomenon – hair in the wrong places, and it undoubtedly being harder to hear, and the digestion making more voluble and embarrassing protests than formerly – another part of the body would show a leak or tear, and one's basic system of coping had to be realigned, redesigned. It was a bit like the apartment block he and Mira lived in. Seemed so modern when they first moved there, just after marrying, in the seventies – bricks, sleek glass,

9

that blocky sixties style – and now every week a notice from the landlords: subsidence a problem, plumbing works to be examined, inadequate roofing. He himself had inadequate roofing today. Should have worn a hat. It was spring now, nominally, but dim and damp and would be damper in Oxford, as it always was. A hat: he had not thought of it in his usual rush to leave the flat. (He knew some of the patients muttered and minded when he was about; he felt something like Anne Frank when he was at home with them, that he must on no account reveal by noise or tremor that he lived there. Had he made that analogy to Mira? It might amuse her. Though the notion of patients as Nazis was complicated, perhaps, in light of her past.) The phone had rung this morning, Clare setting up a time for her and Graham to come visit in a few weeks, and after that he had hastily left. Hat-less.

The coach left behind the rubble and grime of the outer sprawl – Hillingdon, other unknowns – and Peter found himself with England, just England to look at: the green and pleasant lands that rolled along as the bus did, freeing Peter's mind to thought or sleep. He should think. He should think about the course, he had returned to *Oblomov* this year, felt he had neglected the idle aristocrat and should pay him some mind again, so had reorganized Russian Literature Before the Soviets to include it. And *War and Peace* this time over *Anna Karenina*: the meanings of death and life over the agonies of adultery. Or Peter could think about Andrew, his Victorianist colleague, with whom he was having lunch later that day. Andrew was dying, perhaps. Some strange remarks he had made lately on ash-scattering and other funeraries, together with a general pallor, suggested it as a possibility, but Peter did not know how to ask him directly what was wrong. (Would Andrew tell him if he were dying? Or was it the kind of thing he would keep private? Peter

10

was not sure of the degree of closeness in their relationship.) It might be an illness brought on by his (presumed) homosexuality . . . Aids, obviously. All the stories one read. A single, chance encounter – a random night – followed by slow and certain death. Haunting. Then again, Andrew might not be ill at all. Perhaps this was a darkening effect the great conflict-at-a-distance had had on Peter's imagination, living all these years under the constant, if remote, shadow of the Balkan wars. He tended to sketch the worst ends to everyone's stories.

As his thoughts grew heavy, his lids heavier, it was another figure who came to mind. Neither Oblomov nor Andrew, nor for that matter his good, whole good, whole Mira. No, it was Graham's face Peter saw as he closed his eyes. A face a little like his own, so people said; both had blunt noses and greyish complexions, a propensity to bristle at the chin. There was a belligerence about the eyes in Graham that had its echo in Peter's own face and had made people ask him from time to time, comically enough, if he had ever boxed. The only athletic period of Peter's largely sedentary life had been a late-teen spell of race-walking, training in joyful, swaying loops around Regent's Park with a man who once race-walked, so he claimed, for Britain. Peter had briefly entertained fantasies of competition until his hip swayed too wide one day and a sharp pain intervened, and interrupted. Peter recalled those looping race-walking days, wondering, before he fell into a thick public-transportation doze, if it was a story he had ever thought to tell his son.

At two o'clock, someone new. Mira sat in the kitchen sipping soup. There was no space for a table, the room was a clotted box of hob, refrigerator, sink, and counter – but often when she was home alone she pulled a chair across to the kitchen window and sat drinking in a little of what passed for light in this country.

Watching the polluted skies of Camden Town. How had she ended here, she often wondered, in Camden Town? And: would she end here, in fact? Or should she go back? But the time she had thought most seriously about going back, perversely perhaps, had been at the beginning of this end, just as many there thought of leaving. 1991, 1992. Watching from a distance as her former country worried itself into separate bloodied pieces, raw parts and limbs, had in turn worried Mira into a diminished rendition of herself, leeched her of her ease and humour. She had spoken frequently, near feverishly, of her need to return, though as Peter had rightly said there was nothing to be gained by such a move, and no practical way her presence there would help her family through the country's dissolution. So Mira had not gone, had listened and watched, helpless, like so many others. And now, a lull; two and a half years into a slowness named after a meaningless American city – *Dayton* – which Mira felt did not have the ring about it of a place with authority, such as Berlin or Versailles. This 'Dayton' had smothered the flames of the worst conflagrations and reined in some of the period's brasher brutes and war-frenziers; but Mira didn't trust it – *Dayton* – and as every day and headline passed it was ever clearer that new hells lay ahead. There was a place still unresolved. There was Kosovo. Should she go back?

If Peter were to die – not to indulge in morbidities, but he would die, so would she, it had to be considered, planned for – Mira thought she might go back then. What would keep her here? Certainly not the American or the Aristocrat or the Bigot, or any of them. Her friends? Her colleagues? Perhaps, but. There was no family. Mira felt this differently as she got older, she felt it in her bones, this absence of family. Of course there was Graham, and there was Clare (with whom she got on better, that was no secret) – but, again. *But*. Not family, truly. She felt it in her bones, the absence.

The buzzer rang. Already? Mira looked at the clock. Almost ten minutes early. That was generally a bad sign. She slowed, deliberately spooning the last of the chicken broth and its potatoes and carrots into her mouth. An internal steeling: someone new. Referred by the Aristocrat – the daughter of one of her mother's friends. Mira would have to find an empty file drawer in her storied, busy mind for a new collection of names, events, terrors, dreams, anxieties, jokes. She hoped this one had a few jokes.

Mira got up, heavy as a horse, and buzzed her in, then waited to hear footsteps on the outer hallway's tiles. She opened the door to a terrible sight. A white-faced woman already deep into crying, in the seize of crisis, tissues held to mouth, eyes red with drear and dread. *Oh dear.*

'Come in,' Mira said to her, thinking *This girl needs to be held*, knowing it was not her place to hold her. 'Please. Are you all right?'

The figure nodded into her tissues, apologized, 'I'm sorry – I thought – I was all right a minute ago,' followed Mira up the short stairway into the therapy room. (Peter had various joking names for it – the Confessional, the Hold, the Delivery Room.) Once inside, the woman sat down on a wide chair, still hat-and-coated. She seemed to want to keep her layers about her.

Mira sat on her own familiar chair and waited. And watched. She made sure the woman had a box of tissues. She could see more of the woman now, even if she was folded into herself, wrapped in her coat and her apologies. She was how old, with that face? Late thirties; early forties. An uncomfortable age. She had not reached some point in her life she had hoped to reach. Her body expressed not just despair but disappointment.

13

She came, from the sliver of voice Mira had heard so far, from the upper classes. Mira's ear had been schooled enough now to know the difference in tones. It was a necessary talent for working in England, like being able to distinguish safe mushrooms from poisonous in her own country – there were distinctions one had to have the confidence to make. The vowels and manner gave this woman away. She evidently felt she should be able to speak normally despite whatever tore at her. She had tried again once or twice – 'Sorry – Sorry, I'm just—' but could only weep. Mira waited. She could wait as long as was necessary. She would wait for the entire near hour, if necessary.

And when would she be able to speak again? Surely, Kate thought, she could *speak*. She had narrated the events before to people, knew that if she could just calm down, arrive at the place where what had happened to them was a story, a terrible story, but not – not – it was all around her, here, there was something about being in this room with a kind face and knowing it was all right to break down in this violent way, even if the woman thought she was mad, that was all right too, she'd seen mad people, she knew how to deal with them, that was the whole point presumably, that was precisely her professional role, to look after the mad and the distressed, and no amount of hysteria, no coughing sobs, however embarrassing, however excessive – *Jesus, God* – no amount of wanting to die, or not being able to go on, would surprise her. Would overwhelm her. Kate was permitted to do this here. Wasn't she? She wanted to look up and into the doctor's face again – it had looked kind for the instant Kate had seen it, the woman, Braverman she was called though the accent certainly wasn't English, looked old and kind and long-suffering, as if she knew as much as anyone might need her to know about dreadful things happening, about pain. But Kate could not look up just then. A spasm seized her and instead she covered her eyes with her hand. She could not look at the world just now. Could not see it, did not want to see it. And at the same time she had to block the doctor's view of her, since she did not want to be seen either, she wanted to be buried, she wanted to wrap herself in her coat and lie down and die, she did not want to have to face light or conversation or William or this woman or anything about being alive, about going *on*. She did not want to go on. 'You'll have to find a way to go on,' her mother had said to her, trying, Kate supposed, to be helpful. And she had wanted, when she heard her mother say that, to throttle her; she had the first genuinely murderous thoughts she had ever had in her life. It was a friend of her mother's who had found the name of this doctor for her to see, it was absurd really, to trek all the way to Camden Town from Kensington, the journey itself had nearly killed her. Why had she felt compelled to come by Tube? Some false stoicism. She had stayed tear-free on the journey, couldn't bear to break down on the train itself, there were some humiliations she was not willing to allow, and no doubt that facing of humanity, of people with their coughs and their novels and their miseries and complacencies and their wretched children, their wretched *babies*, their wretched fat and pregnant bellies – that was what had wrecked Kate probably, why she had arrived at this woman's door with nothing but weeping left within her. The moment Kate had rung the buzzer and not heard a prompt response, it had started. She could not help herself.

It was getting better now, though. The sobs were turning to hiccups. That was a sign she would be able to speak soon. She would speak soon.

She used several more tissues, tried to tidy up her face a little. She did not look at the woman sitting in the chair just across from her but tried to focus instead on the print hanging on the wall. It was some sort of flooded, abstract image. A blurred horizon. A bluish wash.

'My name is Kate,' Kate said in a voice thinned by its wordless exertions. 'Last week – just over a week ago – we lost our baby.' She said this much, but it was no use, it was impossible. The waters broke again, and her head dipped forward, and her shoulders resumed their customary, helpless heave.

The poor woman. It had taken her twenty minutes to speak. When she did, finally, the story had poured from her, as crisis does. She spoke lines she clearly had before – not yet often enough that they were toothless and unvenomous as she uttered them, but travelling a groove of familiar detail so that she didn't have to draw each moment anew, sketch it for the first time on an empty page.

Everything had been trotting along, she said smoothly at last, while Mira listened. It had all been going fine. It had been a bit of an ordeal to get pregnant, she was older, William and she had married late. They had been trying for a little over a year and had eventually resorted to those depressing charts and calendars and finally, one day, she had thought of it as one of the happiest days—

And here the salt rose to her eyes, and she coughed, and paused.

'Perhaps I can tell you another time about that. But I did get pregnant, finally. And here we were, eight months along, nearly there. The baby – she was a girl – had been moving, and we'd gone through all the scans, everything looked wonderful. I could feel her kicking . . .' She paused again; then pushed forward. 'And then I couldn't. I noticed that I hadn't felt very much movement. For a few days. This was – we were eight months along. Did I say that? We rang the doctor, who told us it was probably fine, she

16

was probably just "having a kip", he said, but they'd be able to reassure us at the hospital, we should just go to have our minds put to rest. He didn't sound worried, so we weren't, you know? He sounded perfectly calm. So William and I went to the hospital, and we saw nurse after nurse – they kept trying to find the heartbeat, and they couldn't. And then finally another doctor came up and examined me and told us that Cassandra had died.' She swallowed. 'And I had to stay in the hospital then and give birth to her, even though she was no longer alive. They gave me masses of drugs to induce labour and block the pain and I think somehow make me forget what was happening, that I had to deliver my baby, though she was already dead.' She stopped. She made herself take a different direction. 'We named her Cassandra, for one of William's grandmothers. She was beautiful.' Another pause. 'There was no explanation of what had happened. They don't know why. She just – she just . . .'

It had not been the time for clinical niceties.

'I'm so sorry for you and your husband,' Mira said from her safe chair. She had remained solid, warm in the telling, a reminder of life, making it clear that she could house, and would, however much grief this terribly distraught woman might find within herself. Depression, anger, dissatisfaction, anxiety – those were very different states to allow room for, and Mira had the key to rooms and rooms of each, for her various patients. She had not known to expect this, the shriek and shred of grief, with the new patient. She thought of Francis Bacon: his wide, silent screaming mouths. They were the most eloquent expressions Mira knew of pain of this kind.

What had the Aristocrat told her, in referring this woman Kate to Mira? 'She's a daughter of one of my mother's friends and has gone through some horrible trauma.' Ignorance, or discretion, not to tell Mira more? Impossible to say. The Aristocrat was caught (wasn't everyone?) in her own web of distress. The Aristocrat, married miserably, fearful of leaving her husband, fearful of being left, flagrantly betrayed as she had been (the husband had made little effort to cover his traces), unable, thus far, to have a child, and ever more coiled in obsession with that lack and that difficulty – for her to hear of a woman whose much-wanted and desired baby had died would perhaps have been too much to admit or to bear. There are times when others' losses are a ghoulish source of comfort – *Misery loves company*, the English acidly and correctly said (Peter had taught her the phrase with some pride). But Mira knew that misery can love solitude, too – can love its own uniqueness. The Aristocrat might not have had the patience to hear of this woman's terrible mourning. The Aristocrat was thoroughly, anciently English – a race that had the unnatural religion of evasion, worshiping as they did at the altar of Carrying On, Making Do, not so much the 'stiff upper lip' of the cliché as learning to say, 'Yes it was *dreadful; horrible*' – and then turning away. The Aristocrat showed a face weathered to a hard, edgy humour about the indignities of her marriage and even her fertility problems. Mira remembered her lovely, lemonish mouth saying, 'I've been probed and injected like a pig – I've far more sympathy with farm animals now than I used to. Increasingly I see a likeness between Hugo and the furious, uncooperative stallion Daddy used to loan out for stud duties – you know, breathing an enormous sigh and saying, *God*, not this again, all right, bring me my magazine and my sugar beets and a small plastic vial and I'll do the best I can.' Mira could not imagine such a person taking in the tear-stained reality of this bereaved woman, the Madonna manqué.

When the new patient finished her recitation that morning Mira told her she could come back if she liked; or, if she preferred, Mira could refer her to another psychotherapist. The woman looked stricken at this suggestion. 'No, *please*,' she had said, 'I couldn't bear to tell the story again. I'd like to see you, if that's all right.' Her voice had such leaning in it, the knock on the door in the middle of the night, *Take me in, please, please give me safe haven* – Mira knew she would have to find room for her, too. For this new voice from the wilderness, and her flat sea of infinite grief.

And just after she left, the Bigot. Sometimes, Peter said this to her, Mira might try to place more of a buffer between one horror and the next, it wasn't what others did but Peter loyally insisted she was not like the others, that she felt these distresses more deeply. It was dear of Peter to say so but it was not true. Mira had the same protective mechanism as any of her colleagues, the ability to hear and collect pain and store it away from herself, outside of the main house of herself, in a back patio, a back area like the sheltered area behind the house she had been in as a child, her grandparents', where there was a store of firewood and boots and spiders and shovels. A tin of paraffin for the lamps – *be careful, Mira, be careful of the paraffin.*

Still, sometimes they did come too close together. Mira had never felt that when she was younger, closer to the rigours and certainties of her training and less far into her own particular peopled territory of fear and disaster. There were the patients one liked, and even looked forward to seeing, or at least didn't mind seeing. There were surprises – like that last poor girl, the Mourner she might call her to Peter. (Mira always found an alias to give them, perhaps this one might be the Mourning Madonna, for she had seemed so ready to be a mother, so poised on the edge of that sanctified rite. It helped assuage Mira's conscience about telling more than she ought to to Peter, if she assigned each patient an alias, which then became how she thought of them in her mind. Each had his place, not Howard or Jess, Caroline or Kate, but the Bigot, the American, the Aristocrat, the Mourning Madonna.) The patients one liked, the surprises – and then there were the patients one did not like, the patients one dreaded. The Bigot. Mira would have referred him to someone else months ago, she could see the problem from the start, but he himself had been referred to her by Marjorie, who thought Mira strong enough for him, and Mira did not want lose Marjorie's good opinion by admitting that she too had been unable to stomach the man, his aggressive provocations, his divorce acids, his suave sarcasms. That was his finger on the buzzer now and Mira's whole body tensed in a spring action, like a trigger.

And she only got uglier, it seemed. The psychotherapist. Fat in her big skirts like a peasant, like a Serbian peasant. She probably had a passel of soup-sipping relatives still in Serbia and they were probably all torturing Croats and Muslims at this moment, or had been until the UN came in to stop their savageries – rendering people legless with mortars and shelling, raping their wives and destroying the future for their children. Brutes. It was why she kept such a low profile about her nationality, though Howard had learned some time ago that she was a Serb. He had made her tell him. 'It seems ironic,' he had said to her in response, 'to be lectured at on how to live properly by someone whose nation is the scourge of Europe.' 'Do I lecture you?' she had asked with one of those annoying half-smiles they used to taunt you. 'It's implied,' he answered. 'You're on the right side, there. I'm on the wrong.'

Ever since then, Howard had delighted in lighting small fuses under the flammable subject. 'Worrying stories in the news,' he said today, during a lull. 'Things unravelling in Kosovo. Milošović has more horrors up his sleeve, I've no doubt.'

Mira remained impassive. Look at her. She probably revered

Milošović, probably thought he had been misrepresented in the Western press, was really a hero who had helped restore pride to her people.

'I was thinking,' he said, sitting back and opening his arms as if he were about to make some broad, inclusive point, 'that people focus so often on one individual, right, *Milošović*, he's a monster, he's a Hitler, so what can anyone do? But Hitler, or Milošović, they need a whole country of willing followers. Couldn't do it if the people weren't with them. They need a country full of Nazis – or Serbs – to do their bidding. To guard the camps, fire the bullets, dig the mass graves . . .'

She tensed, which was gratifying. He thought he saw her jaw clench. But he knew what was next. She would turn the tables back on him as she always did. It was part of the game they played with one another.

'What makes you think about the Nazis?'

'I should think anyone does who's followed the Balkan disaster over the years.'

An expensive game, certainly. But he enjoyed fending her off.

'But why Nazis? What does Hitler mean to you?'

'The same as to anyone.' Sometimes her questions were absurd. He vibrated with impatience. 'Man at his most evil. Man's brutality to man. A psychopath. A psychopath with power – a sociopath – with a people to follow him.'

She drew a breath. 'And have you ever felt brutality in yourself?'

'What, do you mean on a bad day do I see myself as a Nazi?'

She made a brisk noise of impatience, a bit like a cow in a field, breathing out through her wide nose with some vehemence. *Ha*. She was not supposed to let him see that he had managed to wind her up. One point to you, Howard.

'I wonder why you think about brutality. Why you're interested in it.'

He waved an impatient hand in the direction of the print on the wall. Supposed to be soothing, he supposed: gentle, flowing colours of no significance. The picture irked him. Some joker's idea of Art. 'Because it's on the bloody television every time you switch it on. Serbs behaving like barbarians. Locking people in camps, mass executions, all that. And as I'm sure you're aware, Mrs Braverman, it is about to erupt again now. In Kosovo. You must be worried.'

'An accord was signed for peace. Why do you choose to ignore that?'

'Peace! I don't believe Dayton will hold, not for another bloody minute. And nor do you, I imagine. Not as long as Milošović is sending his men out to terrify the Albanians. That doesn't strike me as much like peace. Or am I missing something?'

She paused. She was going to try a different line of attack, he could see that.

'What about your relation with Richard in this regard?'

'Richard?'

'Yes.'

'What relation? What does Richard have to do with it?'

'I wondered about the dream you had about him.'

'Ah yes, the famous Richard dream. Months of material there. What of it?'

'In the dream, at the park, Richard talked of visiting you among the brutes.'

'Yes, animals, he meant. Creatures. I don't know what word it was—'

'You said "brutes".'

'Did I?'

'Yes. You speculated that perhaps he thought you were rather

22

"brutish" towards his girlfriend, Joelle. That the dream was perhaps a reference to that.'

Their fucking *memories*. That was one reason he hated her. She could remember every bloody thing he had ever said to her. This single dream of his – a dream, for God's sake – was forever being used as a damning reflection of his entire personality.

'You seemed to think that Richard views you as in some measure wild,' the therapist continued mildly. 'Not tame.'

'Yes, well, he's a self-righteous arsehole, my son, if you'll pardon the expression.' All right, might as well give it to her. This is what she wanted, after all. 'Not what you're supposed to say about your own son, is it? And his girlfriend, Joelle, is an insufferable nag, and I may have told him so once, and he may have taken offence. He may have felt I was a *brute* to say so. Truthtellers are never appreciated as they should be. Are they?'

Mira said nothing. But he was sure he could see her shoulders loosen, relax.

'I don't really hold with your view that that bloody dream, with the park and the shit on my hands and the fact that my son called me a brute or something like it, tells us everything we need to know about myself and my son. More to the point, I'd say, is that Richard has recently been offered some *frightfully* good job – siphoning off people's life savings, or some such – in Kent. Where, as you may remember, his mother lives. Sheer coincidence? Or Oedipal inevitability? I don't know, Mira, you tell me.'

'You are telling yourself, Howard.' She sat straighter. 'And that's where we have to finish for today, I'm afraid.'

He started to say something, 'Fuck,' or 'Oh, for fuck's sake,' but stopped himself. His eyes were hot with loathing. He tried to control his voice so as not to give her the thrill of victory.

'Just as it was getting interesting. What a shame.'

But she had won, in any case. He wanted to hit her. How

polite these bloody stupid rooms were, like tea parties. Sitting civilized and polite when really what he wanted to do was to stand up and smack that slight Serbian smirk off her wide, unriled, peasant-doctor face. Give her a taste of what her people had been doing to everyone else.

Now that it was March there was beginning to be a sense that the darkness would retreat. One could imagine the longer evenings again, one could imagine – fragrant streams of daffodils and narcissi helped one to imagine – the stretching of light and blankets on the grass for picnics. Not that Mira and Peter ever picnicked, though they were a short walk from the park. Mira found Regent's Park oddly forbidding, with its dogs and its toddlers and its lone readers of Marx or McEwan. Packs of children on weekends colonizing the broad expanse of lawn for their sports games, or enjoying an unpaid portion of the zoo, glimpsing the bored, cold elephants and smartly housed penguins. Mira preferred the green of the countryside near Clare and Graham's home to this tidied greenery – Avon, a place that had sheep and hills and farms that reminded her, by some scent or creature-bleat, of the countryside she had known as a child.

Peter felt otherwise, Mira knew. He was quite passionate about Regent's Park, had been coming since he was a young Londoner. The place was his childhood and adolescence: these tended many acres were Peter's forests and rivers, his cool orchard evenings and flower-lit hillsides. If Peter had not had frogsong over black ponds or chickens in the backyard scratching and chuckling, wolves on occasion and the folk memory of bears, he had at least known the park's birdchoir at dawn and its scuttling rabies-free squirrels, a hundred varieties of dog and the great colourful splash of the waterfowl. Peter loved the manufactured waters of Regent's Park and the birdlife they nurtured,

quite found room for. He had had Graham, of course, but that had not been a planned adventure. Peter felt a failure with regard to Graham, Mira sensed – he did not know how much he had given the boy, still lived in subdued fear of him. When Mira and Peter visited their friends with children, or now grandchildren, Mira saw and wondered at Peter's fatherly knack, his ability to climb down and experience the world from that height of three or four feet. He was able to understand children's small and searing concerns: to speak, to be heard, to be recognized, to have cake. He gave them cake and recognition. He would beam, showing the ducks to a child. The child would listen to his recitation of names. Peter would be wonderfully content, she suspected, to show a child the vast plain of Regent Park's upper stretch, pretending that herds of elephants had once grazed there, that the direct descendants from that once wild herd now stood nearby, in the zoo.

Mira could not follow Peter into such a conversation. There were many imaginative areas they shared (Beckett, Dostoevsky, Florence, certain rooms at the National Gallery – plenty of it, acres) and others that remained distinct and private. It was how they both wanted it to be. Happiest together, in many ways, reading in the living room, each looking up from time to time, sharing a joke or a line or a patch of light from a given page with the other.

And so often in these recent years Mira had gone somewhere Peter could not go. He knew the faces – they had travelled to Beograd perhaps half a dozen times over the years, he had met the important people, her sister Svetlana, the children Jasna and Josip, Mira's mother while she lived, a scattering of cousins. But Peter could never hear them as she did, their voices in her head asking her unanswerable questions, demanding impossible responses. Mira contained within her their fear and their disgust, their flares of rage and their sense of onslaught; a catastrophe unasked for, unwanted, transforming every single person in what had been a beautiful if complicated landscape into a martyr, a coward, a monster, a hypocrite. There were no good choices and there was nobody left uncut or unscarred. It was Svetlana Mira spoke to mostly, and she told Peter of these conversations in abbreviated, English versions, never in her own tongue. He did not have more than a smattering of Serbo-Croat; if sometimes she spoke a paragraph or two in her schoolgirl Russian he would follow her, but she could not tell him fully what she thought. And what point was there in dragging Peter into everything that was most wretched about the wars when it was not his family or his country that had been tearing at itself like a dog gnawing its own leg to escape from the trap? Mira did not want to poison him with it. She wanted to protect him, not that he asked for protection.

Peter, for his part, urged her to think of other things. He could see how the news corroded her, and though he did not blame her, he tried to nose her out of such thoughts (perhaps, yes, as a dog might). It made her feel more than ever that the English were an alien citizenry, washed up on the shore of her life like some blunt, opaque sea glass. The English neither loved nor hated with the rooted, historic passion she had grown up knowing – they hated rather with a slow, sly simmer (although if drunk, one football fan could pummel another into a bloody mass and not much regret it in the morning). That phlegmatism may have been one of the reasons she had made her home with them, yet it was a reason now that they could seem, on a bad day, a damp people, never on fire. The English were lizards, Mira had once declared to Peter. Their blood ran cold. Yet she treated them; they were her patients. They came to her for solace. Whatever colour or temperature their blood, she must not lose hold of her work – Peter said it often and it was true, it was the ballast, it was the one fixed place other than her love for her own Englishman, for Peter. And her work was to hold and soothe their particular pains. She must get on with it. She must keep listening. And if all that mattered to a person was the birth or not of their beloved, wanted child – if that was what all war and famine and blood-poured violence reduced to, and nothing was important about vengeful religious hatreds and lustful grabs for power and a century or three of colonizers and tyrants and on and on into the darker ages – well then, her job, Mira's, was to sit still in herself and listen. A doctor, a wise German woman Mira had encountered in her training, who had helped persuade her that this was work worth doing – this Dr Baum had told Mira always to find within her the answering voice to that of the patient. It was a constant challenge. The task was what made this work, if one did it properly, extraordinarily demanding. Thank God she did not have children; a person could not, Mira believed, have children and patients both. The best doctors, Baum had told her, were those with quiet lives whose noise and fury were expended in the engagement with their patients.

And so. If someone came to her eaten alive by the pain of losing her baby, Mira must find an answering pain, unspoken of course, that would give her voice or even her silence some resonance. Some truth. Mira was not a mother. She never had been. She had decided early in her life that she did not want a child: early, in Yugoslavia, for a complexity of reasons, after she had seen how the experience changed her sister. Mira would not lose herself to another as Svetlana had lost herself to that dear tiny daughter, Jasna, and later to her son Josip. Mira would work, and study, and move to England. She would choose a different course, one hard to find a picture of in the rooms and streets she had grown up in. She would not have a child.

Which was not to say there had not once been that possibility; that there had not once stepped a sequence of days in which a new life had tentatively resided inside her.

Two

April

It had fallen to Clare to set up this visit, as it often did. She had become the keeper of the familial calendar.

If you married someone, you married his family as well. To have and to hold. For better, for worse, for richer, for poorer, in sickness and in health. Till death relieved you of the burden. Clare believed this. Her own childhood had been perforated by sharp disagreements between her mother and the Harrogate grandmother, Granny Alice; she remembered bitter, furtive exchanges about bedtimes and clothing, religion and manners. Furtive, as if Clare and Sara hadn't been aware of the bottled antipathy between their mother and her mother-in-law. Their father taking newspaperish shelter from the battle, or settling stolid-shouldered in front of the television as the women boiled and troubled among themselves.

In her own marriage Clare wanted peace across in-law lines. She hoped never to issue the phrase, 'Your *mother –* ' with that particular threatening lilt.

She had married Graham knowing his family situation was irregular. This was part of his appeal to Clare, that beneath his competent, shirt-and-tied exterior, Graham Thomas shielded some fundamental uncertainties. Smoothly, fluently, he might discuss properties and contracts, and dates for taking possession – there was something in the solicitors' language that was deeply foreign and masculine to Clare – but there was a corollary swagger that he lacked. He lacked the solidity of a man who knows his father.

She had seen this during the very first lunch they had together. A surprise, to be asked by one of the solicitors for lunch. Clare had been working in the Bath office as a temp, planning to stay only until she found a more plausible position: working in such a hushed and proper environment was a mistake for her; she was better suited to work with charities, or children – people who needed her help, who she could feel a bit sorry for. The clients Graham's firm served were, on the whole, comfortable and self-satisfied and she could not always help but dislike them, and could not always help but show it. For this, it seemed, Graham had noticed her.

Over lunch they had traded pocket résumés – university experiences, work histories, geographies of significance. Clare had briefly sketched her family: father a Yorkshireman, chemist by profession, gardener and cricketer by passion; mother an Avon housewife, happier after the family returned to the south from Harrogate, who derived great pleasure from living in a home that had a name rather than a numerical address (The Willows, Lee Lane, Bath); sister a student still, in style and opinions if not in fact. When Clare asked after his family in return, Graham had subtly contracted. He spoke of his mother, Lydia, who worked at the Oxford University Press. His father was an academic who lived in London, but folded under this reference had been a white, stiff silence, an evasion. An ugly divorce between the parents, Clare had assumed, a common enough story, but later, on an evening out together for a film and some Chinese food, Graham had told her that his parents had never been married in the first place. That his mother, unmarried, had decided to 'keep' a child his father had neither anticipated nor desired, a decision his father never even became aware of until Graham himself was seven, and the two were introduced to one another for the first time by a woman who temporarily took on a god-like mantle, creating life where there had been none.

'So technically, I'm a bastard,' Graham said, a practised line obviously meant to diffuse embarrassment or curiosity, though in Clare it inspired both, along with a seedling of pity for the man who had lost his father right at the beginning, when he was too young to know anything or protest. *Before you were born*, she kept thinking. *Your father was gone before you were even born*, and the pathos of the line stirred what became her great if secretly sorrowful passion for Graham. She understood that the father was restored to him later, but surely by then it would have been too late? In the beginning, when it mattered, there had been a blank.

'I see him now,' Graham had told Clare. 'As I say, he lives in London. He's been married for years to a woman from Yugoslavia. A Serbian.' In the year they met – 1995 – Sarajevo was still burning in the collective memory and the word *Serbian* could seem in itself a slap or a curse. She saw Graham's lip curl as he said it. 'A Serbian?' she repeated. But what could Clare say? It had to be true that some were different, it wasn't as though each and every Serb had been shelling innocent children in breadlines. 'Do they have children?' was all she could think of to ask.

'No.'

Graham looked to an upper corner of the room. A dusty speaker dispensed scrapings of some unfamiliar Chinese music, redolent of water chestnuts and ginger and field after field of rice-wet green.

Children. Graham had never imagined it, actually, his father and Mira producing a child between them. The thought had never crossed his mind. He was fifteen when his father, a man whose shape had become familiar but who was still not (never would be) *known*, had told Graham rather sheepishly there was a woman he wanted his son to meet, a woman he planned to marry. All was hormones and exam prep for Graham at the time, though he had watched enough television to entertain a brief fantasy that his father would usher some busty bottled blonde into their lives. (A Yugoslavian group had entered the Eurovision Song Contest that year – Graham had watched the programme with his mother, lobbing continual sarcastic comments at the screen that had made her laugh – and the buxom lead singer had continued to visit him for weeks afterwards in the dark privacy of his room.)

In the event, Graham met an ash-haired, serious woman whose roundness was not of the kind he had wolfishly imagined, whose humour did not correspond to his, whose smell was foreign and whose deep voice off-putting. Her body spoke, it seemed, in an unfriendly way to him, although the words themselves were amiable, if accented. He took some pleasure imitating her speech patterns later to Lydia. *We'll go to cafe. Would you like to take satchel?* Graham sensed that this woman, his father's intended wife, was unwilling to take him in. That was all right. Graham didn't need to be taken in. He had a mother already.

Years later, when the wars came, and he along with everyone watched that compromise country, Yugoslavia, fall into its separate selves, Graham felt vindicated in what he had always suspected about Mira. He saw her determined armies seizing territories, her vicious sons eviscerating those who dared break away from Tito's shattered dream, and he felt all the embittered ire as if he himself were a Croat or Muslim or proud Slovene, sheltering in a rubbled building from merciless mortar fire, hoping desperately that his wife would not be raped, his children not murdered before his eyes.

'No,' he had said again to Clare. 'They didn't have children.' Thank God that they didn't.

The food cooled. The speakers scraped. Graham had taken a risk in talking to her this way, a temp from the office, who might still choose to shrug and retreat. She was, he thought, even now wondering whether to fall back into the suits and properties of their formal relationship or move forward into something else. Another bottle of wine and an exchange of further intimacies, or count the minutes until they asked for the bill, and leave it there? It would be a shame to lose her: the curve of her fair hair, the warm blue of her pooled eyes, the lips he had needed to kiss since he had first met her in that desert-dry office. But he would manage without her, if he had to. Of course he would.

Whereas Clare, for her part, was only trying to stop herself issuing impossible sentences to this man she hardly knew. She wanted to say, 'It's all right,' 'It doesn't matter,' 'I love you any-way.' She could not say any such thing. Clare could not say anything at all. All she could do – and how did she find the bold-ness, ten years younger than this solicitor? – was put her hand over his, a tentative gesture but a noticed one, before pulling it back towards her wine glass and taking a restorative sip.

And for that gentleness, he loved her. For that hand over his. She could see it.

It had fallen to her to set up this visit, and if Clare minded that less than she sometimes did it was because on this occasion she had her own reasons for going to London. It was a campaign stop, a reconnaissance mission. She needed help of a particular sort: she needed help in the project of having children. Graham was reluctant, and they had reached an impasse about it. Yes, eventually, he'd say to her with obvious discomfort, when everything in Clare said, Not eventually but now. Now. *Now.*

It was never easy to persuade Graham to see Peter and Mira, and this she had not expected. Once you had married the family of the person you had chosen, it seemed wrong that it then fell to you to maintain those relations on his behalf. Clare did not ask Graham to remember her sister's birthday or send cards to Granny Alice, now in a home and scarcely able to speak or recognize or remember. Clare wrote the thank-you notes in Graham's name to her father for the books he sometimes sent along to Graham – *The Country Garden*, for example, or *Border Perennials*. (Her father had, charitably, manufactured gardening as a common interest with his son-in-law, whose hands rarely touched the raw earth.)

Graham's mother, Lydia, Clare needn't worry over: Lydia rang, they visited, cards were exchanged on the appropriate occasions and holidays could be spent in one another's company – Christmas last year, crackers and plum pudding and nobody argued. Graham teased his mother, reassured her, gave her advice (cars; money) and kept a conspicuous silence on the subject of her companion of the past several years, a divorced art teacher named Christopher with a drooping moustache and a face like a bloodhound, who painted large moody canvases of people lost, separated, and uncertain.

With Peter and Mira it was far more difficult. Clare generally had to set something up herself, as she had rung Peter to arrange today's lunch with them in London. Clare did not understand the relationship. Even now, married over a year to Graham, together for three, she felt like some bungling diplomat, assigned to a strange country whose methods of negotiation she did not grasp. Months would pass with no contact between them at all, not a telephone call or a postcard. She knew that Graham's father – Graham often referred to him as 'Peter' – travelled often, for academic conferences or to visit Mira's family or just because he and Mira could, and they enjoyed it. Perhaps, they'd mention over lunch, they recently spent a weekend in Amsterdam or had gone to Paris for an art exhibition. But there was never a *postcard*. How hard would it have been for him – or her, for that matter – to write a card? Wasn't that the least they could do? Clare minded that, though she felt narrow, suburban, for minding.

She believed the difficulty had something to do with the Balkans, but she did not altogether understand what. Graham seemed to blame Mira for the war, the wars. But was a person to be held responsible for the policies of a government she had nothing to do with, that was miles away, over which she had no control? Was a person to be reviled for the actions of her fellow countrymen? That wasn't the point, Graham told her crisply, and this had been a conversation in which Clare had felt herself to be younger than Graham, as if he understood more than she did, and she could not decide whether to embrace or resist the feeling. He had a strong argument that people were inescapably the products of their nations, and in the worst years (Srebrenica, Sarajevo), he felt that Mira was somehow on the side of the Serb nationalists. All right, she deplored the fighting and the bloodshed, that was easy enough to do, but Mira also seemed to think there *were* reasons, there *were* causes, and she resolutely rejected the suggestion that unfettered aggression of Milošović or Karadžić's kind was not so far away from that of the Germans during the Second World War. There had been a terrific row between Graham and Mira at the peak of the Bosnia devastation. (*You know nothing about the Nazis*, she had shouted at him, and when he tried to explain what he knew and had studied, she would not listen.) Her blindnesses, Graham explained to Clare, were national blindnesses. And yours aren't? it had occurred to Clare to ask, but the anger on his mouth warned her off the question. Something was wrong or unsaid in Graham's report of this disagreement, Clare suspected, but she was not quite old or brave enough to discover what it was.

The fact was, the car made a hum at high speeds. Graham heard it, dismayed. That's how you knew it wasn't German. Or Swedish. Mark's Saab, for instance, could cruise along at eighty with hardly a whisper. Graham had noticed it when they drove together to speak with one of their clients at her stately home. Mark was very pleased with his Saab. You could take the top down on a good day, and it was sleek and blue and told you everything you might want to know on its high-tech panel – how many miles till you ran out of petrol, outdoor temperature, latest football scores, the FTSE index. (It wouldn't be long, would it: a touch of one of the control-panel buttons and up would pop your e-mails, text messages from the mobile, a line from your wife, perhaps, telling you not to forget to pick up a pint of milk and a loaf of bread on the way home.) Of course, Mark wasn't married; he had the Saab instead. If you were married, you had to make do with a Peugeot. That was apparently how it worked. If you were married you must have a house, and furniture, and everything about living became mysteriously more expensive, and the car had to be tame and easy to keep up and not merely beautiful, an object of desire. And London, that near and distant Mecca towards which the Peugeot was now serviceably speeding, remained several long strides out of reach. One reason Graham so disliked going there was that the city tempted him so, its throngs and languages and intelligences. Its massive, sprawling centrality. He had always wondered whether he was equal to it and had failed to give himself a chance to find out. If they were to have children now – Clare did go on at him about it, making him itch – London and a life of interest would disappear entirely. Graham would be trapped in their nice little house on a quiet street in a south-western city, consigned to years of television and pleasant dinners rather than vibrant nights and sustaining conversations. Sharing his prison quarters with this affectionate, pretty, unexpected woman who now had the right to that strange moniker, *his wife*.

How had it happened? This was a question Graham could not answer. How had it happened that he, a boy who knew nothing of marriage, having not grown up with such a thing over his own head, had taken on the mantle at this mid-thirtyish stage? Once he had done it, married Clare, it seemed the only and obvious thing to have done, but right up to that point he had not imagined having that contract in his life. It seemed unnatural to him, not that people should live alongside one another and love one another, but that the arrangement should be packaged up and bar-coded in the traditional hat-and-champagned fashion. He had attended various friends' weddings, school friends, university friends, as if he were an old lady tottering along to a rugby match, unsure of the rules of the game but wanting to make a good show by going. He had guessed it to be a social convention, like drinking tea in the afternoon or sending out Christmas cards, that he himself would forgo. Then he had seen the curve of Clare's hair, and felt the forgiveness of her hand, and heard the catch in her voice, and he had found himself enquiring whether he might sign on for having her with him indefinitely by issuing certain promises aloud in the company of relatives and mates, people expecting good food, after, and possibly dancing.

And still it occurred to him, as it had almost daily in the past year, how strange it was to be married. He understood now the jokes and clichés of bondage – 'Enjoy the ball and chain, lad,' his father-in-law, admittedly drunk, had said to him that day at the reception, though something a bit lighter, a rope or a tether, was the image that came to Graham's mind. He loved Clare. There was no doubt that he did. But there was something so odd, suddenly, in having a witness and collaborator on hand for all situations, even those one could handle quite adequately on one's own. There was always *company*. No thoughts could move free and uncharted any more. If you had a system for dealing with your parents, for example, their eccentricities and selfishnesses, their irritabilities and irritations, this system was now exposed to scrutiny and interrogation. Graham rolled down the window. It had become rather hot as they approached the capital, with its excesses of vehicles and soot and human complications.

'Will you tell them, Peter and Mira,' Clare said, more or less out the car window, 'that we're driving back to Oxford, after, to spend the night at your mother's?' She was watching a neighbouring car for something, he could not see what. A child's face? A woman's expression?

'I don't know. If it comes up.' Clare seemed to have some quaint idea that it was indelicate to mention either of his parents to the other, but Graham never worried about it. It was, he had always believed, their soap opera, not his – history graduate gets pregnant by too-recent boyfriend, who's child-shy and abortion-friendly; quits studies and decides to keep child, against wishes of boyfriend, who has no interest in marrying her; takes this as reason not to keep in touch with former boyfriend, thus setting the stage for the dramatic encounter several years later in which the existence of father is revealed to son, and vice versa. 'It wouldn't bother them to know,' he said.

'Do they speak at all?'

'Who? Peter and Lydia?'

She nodded.

'No. They don't.' Actually Graham had no idea whether or

not they spoke, but he could not think that they would. His mother and father? What would they talk about? He could not imagine. In fact, he found it hard to imagine, the few times he had tried, what they had ever had to talk about, even thirty-five-odd years earlier. His mother was an anxious, regulated person, concerned with details – shopping and school uniforms, bed linens and bank balances. At the Press, she copy-edited. She made sure the details lined up correctly. (If the war started in 1832 on page 41, with the Turks finally thrown out in 1878, the war must start in 1832 a hundred and fifty pages later, the Turks still exit in 1878.) Lydia was not someone who thought or spoke in the big sweep of ideas. She had worked hard to raise Graham well, he knew. He was her main passion. Otherwise she had a few close friends, was a consumer of biographies, and watched a surprising amount of television (the higher-quality series, and countless documentaries). Peter did not, by contrast, seem to be a man of anxieties: he read passionately and loved calmly. Peter was simply absent, amiable and absent and surrounded by books and friends and gentle comforts and never (or rarely) the effort of looking after someone younger than himself. His son.

'It's a sad story, about your mother,' Clare murmured, keeping her face turned away from Graham. What was she looking at? 'I always feel that.'

And the '*that*' had the flatness, the northern lilt he loved, that allowed him to ignore the sense of the words preceding it.

Peter poked his head around the sitting-room doorway. 'They're coming shortly,' he said to his reading wife. 'It's nearly twelve o'clock.'

She looked up, her eyes luminous with affection. It was a small miracle, the way Mira could look up at him from her pages, a warm, owlish expression on her humoured face. She seemed to know he was nervous, and sought quietly to quench his anxiety. Not that she must not have some too, anticipating lunch with Clare and Graham: four people making their careful, mine-fielded way through conversations not about her country.

'How is the production?' Mira asked, folding up a colleague's volume. Papers and papers. There were always more papers, in both of their professions.

'We won't know till later.' Peter made an exaggerated grimace. 'The reduction did not reduce quite as I was expecting it to. It's a bit *frothy*. And though ED says it's all right to make it an hour ahead, I wonder if ED herself ever actually did.'

Elizabeth David. Always the writer Peter turned to when he was troubled or his hands needed employment. He had taught himself to cook in the bachelor days, the Molly in Oxford days, when he was working to get to know his son on odd weekends, and like a nervous bride-to-be he had thought to win the boy over by appealing to his stomach. If he fed the fellow well, wouldn't some scrap of affection be sure to follow? He had probably picked up the idea from some film one of his helpful female friends had taken him to – single fathers coping with comic aplomb with their children. American, doubtless. The Americans were wonderfully sentimental about the myriad ways families might fragment and then re-gather: it always came right in the end. Anything, in that willed vision, was fixable.

In any case, Peter had hoped that cooking would make a difference as Molly, his other courtship strategy, had singularly failed to entice Graham. The boy did not like dogs. He was rather skittish and fastidious, didn't like the fond tongue or heavily wagging tail or Chum-scented breath. And that had put paid to Peter's single, vivid fantasy of father–son companionship: that they would take long walks through the parks together with his beloved trotting Molly. It was the only clear image that had come to mind when he received the first, shocking telephone call from Lydia.

It had been years since he had seen her. She moved flats shortly after their disputes about the pregnancy, and then hadn't been on the telephone, as far as he could discover; so that he assumed, perhaps lazily, that she had dealt with the situation, as women did. Wouldn't she have told him if she hadn't? But: *You're a father*, the pronouncement from his old and accidental girl-friend – he had preferred her flatmate, but these things didn't always work out – as if someone one hardly knew had the right to issue such a lurching, shape-shifting remark about one's life and self at any arbitrary moment. *He's a lovely boy, he's called Graham* – and all Peter could think was that Molly would help. The idea of a son terrified him, frankly, a son was not a quantity for which he was prepared, but Molly would make him brave and would befriend the little lad. What boy didn't like dogs? She could act as a kind of go-between, the female influence, the soft touch. She was good with children, everyone said so. Whereas in the event Molly ended up sleeping gloomily in corners when Graham visited, nosing as she did the stench of hostility from the child.

With Elizabeth David, Peter fared somewhat better. Not initially: there had been a disastrous Provençal fish that Graham hadn't wanted to eat in the first place, then vomited up tomatoey and white in the avocado-green basin of Peter's cluttered East Oxford flat. 'I *hate* fish,' the boy wept in the bathroom's harsh midnight fluorescence, and Peter had stroked his familiar hair (the texture: he knew it; and how odd that was, that a feature of his should be found here in this boy, this person he did not know). He apologized and soothed as well as he could, noting to himself *Never again cook your son fish. It is wrong to cook your son fish.* But Elizabeth David could also cook you a chicken, and she could make you a soup, and she could show you the way to a gratin that would warm a boy's heart. Melted cheese, of course. He should have known. ED had come through for him, after all.

'I thought I'd put together a salad as well, before they come. It's salad weather by now, I think. Don't you?'

'I'll do the salad.' Mira stood and stretched. They managed this well, their kitchen choreography. The bolthole of a kitchen could scarcely accommodate two, it seemed designed for the lone toiling wife and not the cooking camaraderie of a couple. But they achieved an almost jaunty, syncopated rhythm together, one trading in for another. Mira had been in earlier, making a strudel.

'Here, let me help you, Peter.' She reached around his lean frame to undo the tidy strings at the back. How deeply endearing, this man in an apron. She would like to be twenty again and able to tell her lion-like father, seated in his great chair, *I am going to marry an Englishman and he will wear an apron and cook beautiful dishes inspired by the French. I will love him. In his way, he will save me.* She would so like to have told her father. 'You sit. You need a rest.'

'Yes, I do, actually. All that reducing has left me quite tired.' And he collapsed on the leather sofa they fondly referred to as the 'vinyl nightmare' – a quotation from a neighbour friend who had dropped by one afternoon soon after they'd bought it. So much of the modest furniture Peter and Mira owned was worn and orange and dated from an optimistic Habitat era, the seventies, a decade that like every other proudly considered itself *modern*. The leather sofa was a rare new purchase funded by money Peter had received from his mother on her death, and they both adored its sleekness, its newness, its elegant style. But, 'Gracious, Peter,' Sally had bellowed on entering the sitting room, the voice of a bull in a china shop, 'where on earth did the vinyl nightmare come from? Was it your mother's?' Peter, tactful, not wanting to embarrass Sally, said nothing; it fell to Mira to say, 'We just bought it. Isn't it good?' a line she shuddered to hear herself utter, as it proved that she had come to appreciate the peculiarly English pleasure of catching a social mis-step in someone one did not much like.

Mira's Englishness only went so far, however. She knew that Peter had bled into her, staining her manners, her perceptions, her humour; and since she loved Peter she did not mind these colourings. If some turn of phrase or gesture she borrowed from Peter enabled her to move through social occasions more smoothly, where was the harm? But she could not feel that she owned any Englishness herself, properly. And this, she sometimes told herself, was the problem about Graham.

He was her stepson. Graham Thomas. That made him a relation, didn't it? Stepson. Son of the husband, and as such she should feel close to him, or draw him closer to her. Oughtn't the love she had for Peter to ensure it?

But Mira had never been able to love Graham. He was fundamentally strange to her, this creature who looked like Peter in some lights – had his gait and his chin and something more cantankerous about the mouth that might perhaps have come from the mother. (That mouth had taunted her in the early years, when he was a sarcastic teenager and her mispronunciations or mistakes in grammar bothered him; it was a mouth she had longed to slap, once or twice, after it issued a smug correction.) Mira did not know the mother. Had met her on a handful of occasions only, Lydia stiff and suspicious, Mira retreating tactfully. *Don't worry*, she had wanted to tell the woman, *I don't want Graham. He's yours. You've no competition from me.*

Perfectly understandable, all the myths about stepmothers. They want to boil you in the soup and serve you to the father, not that he'll know till he's had his fill of you, savouring every mouthful. They want you to spend hours cleaning the house and then sleep in a cupboard and not make a peep. They want to send you out at eight years old to sweep chimneys and bring home your wages. They want to eat you up. They want to push you out the window. They want to lock you in a dungeon and throw away the key.

She knew the psychic places these stories came from: the displacement of mother anxiety onto the foreign 'other' of a stepmother (exercising the imaginative possibility that all mothers are at heart voracious and destructive); Oedipal worries about sexual tensions with the mother and the need to project those feelings, too, onto an unrelated outsider. At the same time – Mira tore lettuce leaves, diced cucumbers, sliced carrots as the truth came to her – she also knew herself, somewhere, to be just such a wicked stepmother. In her dreams, it was possible, she might serve Graham up as soup. She could not love him. She had tried. (Had she?) It was a failing of hers, and her shamed hope was that Peter did not know her well enough to see it. To see that she had loved Peter around Graham, trying to avoid the piece of him that was Graham's father.

In more recent years there had been reason enough for the distance. Her stepson had become one of those who could not view Mira other than through a screen of televised horror shots: bloody flung bodies and stray child's limbs, the haunted grief of weary columns of refugees. It happened at the same speed as the collapse of her country: as post-Tito Yugoslavia broke back down into its separately defiant selves, like a large family that frays and argues after the death of its patriarch, so did Mira change in the eyes of those who beheld her. As a foreigner she was used of course to distorted reflections; had often watched a strange and often comic figure, 'a Yugoslavian woman', take shape in the eyes of those who met her. She was a communist, possibly, but freer with it . . . She was a Slav, and weren't they quite earthy and emotional? . . . Perhaps she came from people who raised chickens and sang marvellous songs of folk wisdom . . . But then she must be sophisticated, or different, to have elected to live here . . .

After the wars started, the looks changed. The misapprehensions shifted from comedy to cruelty as 'Yugoslavian' broke necessarily down into 'Serbian' and 'Serbian' became the kind of word a polite person did not wish to say. The Serbs, it emerged, in public conversation at least, were demonic aggressors, and the most generous thing anyone seemed to think they could do was not hold this against her. If at first she tried to explain her country, the power grabs on each side, or protest that it had not been so many years since Croats had tortured Serbs in the most appalling fashion (Jasenovac: how many killed there?) and before them the Turks, the Austrians – soon Mira learned there was no longer room for history or nuance and that people only saw, and wanted, blood. If she spoke too much she would sound as though she were making excuses for slaughters and what did that make her? From a certain point on she had become quiet with all but her closest friends. (The Epsteins. Marjorie. They could listen.) It was not up to Mira to tear down other people's stories of Yugoslavia. She had work to do. And if her stepson was one of those whose versions were particularly rigid, it was not for her to change his mind over it.

The buzzer rang.

'I'll let them in,' Peter called, his voice something high, something eager, and Mira felt that terrible clutch of the heart, that ghastliest sensation – pity for the one you love. He tried so hard, Peter, to be something, he did not know how or what, to this man Graham, his son. It broke something in Mira, each time, to see it.

After lunch, a walk in the park. A brief stretch of fumed frenzy crossing the intervening streets, then into the green, spear-fenced safe haven. Peter and Clare walked ahead as Peter assumed his customary proprietary attitude. He did seem to feel that Regent's Park was his, the Broad Walk and Inner Circle, the rose gardens and paddle boats. He had been the same about Oxford's parks, dragging Graham around them at a young age with that vile flatulent dog, Molly. Graham had frequently made a fuss at the time, he remembered, *I'm tired, I don't want to, can't we do something else?* An imitation of ways he had heard other boys talking to their parents. (He would never have whined like that to Lydia; she was both too stern and too fragile to have borne it.) It was a kind of punishment of the man Graham had thought to be exotically far away only to have him pop up, mysteriously, in a flat off the Cowley Road. A man who clearly filled his mother, lone protector till then, with exasperation and even rage, whom he was nonetheless asked, abruptly, to befriend. It had been a confusing request. Was he supposed to refuse?

The walks with his father had got under his skin, though. Graham found that moving through the air, even if it was only Oxford footpath air along the River Cherwell, or behind some cricket pitch or deer lawn, did something good to him. By the time he was eleven he had stopped complaining about the walks at all and by fourteen, when he began to suspect his dad had a girlfriend, in London possibly (he was secretive about it, but Graham noticed some fumblesome new pleasure in Peter's more distractible face; a schedule that seemed fuller), Graham was taking walks on his own. Longer, more ambitious treks through

46

anyway, the suits had met in Dayton a couple of years ago now and more or less sorted it out, Milošović successfully portraying himself as a man of the peace, irony of ironies, though the Kosovo mess was beginning to rumble dangerously again now. Still, the last time Graham and Clare had come up for a visit, Graham had issued what he felt was a reasonably uncontroversial statement about the pointlessness of all the bloodshed, the destructiveness of Milošović and his cohorts, which had set Mira off on a tirade about Europe's blindness and hypocrisies, America's cowardice, and gross distortions in Britain's media coverage, 'Yes, even including your BBC' – as if Graham were personally responsible for the British Broadcasting Corporation. Graham tried to joke his way out, 'Are you criticizing poor old Auntie, Mira? She's having a hard enough time of it now, justifying the licence fees,' but the joke had passed his stepmother by, she had heard only his tone, hadn't understood the content, and it had riled her further. Peter had stepped in then, almost literally Graham remembered, brandishing cups of tea and making an effort at ceasefire with some extinguishing comment along the lines that it was very difficult, during war, to know who was doing what to whom. 'None of us will know for years what has really gone on in the Balkans,' his father said conclusively, as if that remark might be enough to stanch the flow of unfriendly talk in the meantime.

And Peter's time with Clare was up, apparently. He was suddenly aware of Graham not so subtly jostling the two twos into a different arrangement: father with son, now, and Mira with Clare. Peter had been enjoying himself, leaning in to this smooth-skinned young woman whose face had an openness that made him oddly weak. Had he been bothersome? Was Graham kindly rescuing his wife from the droning father-in-law? Peter didn't think the girl had minded his little disquisition on the waterfowl – she seemed to be enjoying his company. Perhaps she was simply polite, humouring an old fellow. Never mind. It would be easier on Mira this way. She never had much to say to Graham, theirs was at best a detente-like relation: suited, closed, formal. He was aware of the schisms between his wife and his son, though whether they were ideological or merely temperamental he could not say. They had surpassed their mutual jealousies years earlier, surely? And yet there was a hovering, a mistrust, between them that no amount of Elizabeth David or strudel could at this point put right. 'Your son reminds me of someone I knew in Beograd,' Mira had told him once years ago, her face a sealed volume. 'A professor who taught at the University.' – And that was as far as she had gone, leaving Peter to imagine for himself a Yugoslavian lecturer. Croat or Serb? Slivovitz-drinking communist or morose romantic poet? Or both? Chain-smoker, had to be, a man who drank fiercely strong coffee and had a carved, angular face (those were common in Belgrade), with something in him of Graham. A man who had known his Mira when her hair was brighter and her Russian better than her English, when she was first exploring the labyrinths of the psyche and finding in them the fascinations that would lead her to her work, and to himself.

'All right, Dad?' Graham asked. A nice touch, the 'Dad', one he didn't use often. It had a peculiar effect on Peter, making him once again feel weak. When had he become so emotional? 'Would you like to sit down?' They were approaching one of the park's several doll-like teahouses, and Peter must not have looked altogether right as he could see that Graham, now close to him, was concerned, as if he had caught sight of some sinister shadow. Sitting down did suddenly seem quite appealing.

'Yes, perhaps – if you wouldn't mind.' Lightly, trying to disguise his own alarm. He shouldn't be this tired. They hadn't walked far at all. God. Perhaps he would have to see a doctor, after all. 'Rest the weary old bones. One becomes decrepit without even realizing it.'

They looked behind, where the women were deep in conversation. Peter indicated to Mira that he and Graham were going in but she scarcely looked up. Well, that was good. He didn't imagine they were talking politics, and anything else that could have Mira listening so intently had to be a good thing.

Peter sat in the midst of noise, prams, and ice creams and allowed his son to buy him a bit of cake. A cup of tea. He wouldn't touch the cake, in the end, but Graham wouldn't notice. They would talk carelessly of something (Blair, perhaps, or the European Union, or perhaps he would just say something simple and paternal, *What a nice girl Clare is. I'm so pleased for you both*), as the crowds beached and ebbed in the park, and a pain he wanted keenly to ignore made its long, sinuous journey within him.

This had not been her plan. She had had a plan, and this was not it.

Clare had thought, boldly, to speak to Graham's father. She found him easier than Lydia, even if Graham did not. Lydia, Clare knew, was watching her carefully; there was the inevitable, unspoken *Are you good enough for my son?* that was all the more acute given what she and her son had been to one another. (Still were.) She was ever so slightly like a hawk, Graham's mother: that alert, stern gold in the eye, the sharp beak. Clare had no intention of arguing with her ever, and they never had, but she did not feel free to tell Lydia what gnawed at her.

About Peter she felt differently. He was kind, primarily. He was a kind man. And not simply kind in a general, democratic way, though he was that; he had specific reserves of concern and yes, love for Graham, though she suspected her husband did not know how to see it. Just look at what Peter had cooked for them. Roast duck in an elaborate and delicious sauce – he had obviously gone to a good deal of effort. Look at the lines of eagerness around his eyes; look at how he spoke to her, Clare, guessing that she was softer and more likely to let him in than Graham. Peter tried. He wanted, in his way, to make the four of them seem like a family. That business about the birds, for example. He was enthralled by them and wanted Clare to be, too. She could so see him, this rather dear man, if awkward, if an academic, who had never known a small child of his own, holding the tiny hand of a grandson or a granddaughter, giving the child bread to feed, in turn, to his precious ducks.

She had decided to come to him, to Peter. Clare had the sense that he had some feeling for children, in spite of the mangled accident of Graham's birth. (She supposed that was how he thought of it initially, as an accident. *Good heavens*. Do you mean to say I've had a son all this time, and I didn't even know it? There I was, ambling about parks with my dog, seeing little boys playing in swings and on roundabouts, and I didn't even know. I may have seen my own child somewhere, alone in a queue at the newsagent's, eating sweets on the bus, walking with his heavy satchel to school. I would not have known!) How it must have been to discover the news, belatedly, from Lydia, Clare could not imagine. And why had she waited so long to tell him? That was beyond fathoming.

But a blessing, surely? Peter must have felt God had smiled on him, if he believed in God, which of course he did not. All right, but he must have felt lucky to have Graham added, miraculously, to his life. Clare was quite sure he must have felt shocked and blessed, even if that was the pastel-coloured version of the story, as Graham might say. In Graham's rendition Peter Braverman woke up one startled morning to the surreal news that his

51

ex-girlfriend from some years ago would be bringing his offspring for a visit in a few days and he had better hurry up and learn the humours and tastes of a seven-year-old if he wanted to get along with him. The man did his best, probably, but he never quite got the hang of the job. Not, admittedly, helped much in the endeavour by the child's mother.

Clare had wanted to say something to Peter. She wasn't going to make a scene, just drop a line, a reference, a hopeful note or two – perhaps a request. *Please talk to Graham. Can you? He's unwilling – he doesn't seem to understand –* But just as she was gathering courage, preparing the lines that she had rehearsed in the bath, alone, trying to find the right way to express it – along came Graham to fling her and Peter apart. She couldn't think why, unless he was on the verge of another row with Mira.

And now instead of Peter here was Mira, who was Serbian, and what could Clare say to her about grandchildren? Wouldn't the question seem rather trivial to someone whose country had been at war for years? And again, now, in spite of the peace, there were rogue killings and skirmishes on the news, somewhere else – Graham was following it and expected the worst. Clare hoped he hadn't brought it up. Still, the sidestepping seemed wrong to her, as well. Was there another way to ask?

'I don't know much,' she said to Mira as their footsteps fell in pace with one another, 'about your family, your other family . . . Graham hasn't told me much. Do you have brothers, sisters, nephews – back in—?' She couldn't refer to it as 'the former Yugoslavia', as if she were a newscaster, yet Clare felt awkward saying the word 'Serbia'. It seemed almost rude, a synonym for 'Hell' or 'land of the devil'.

'I have a sister, Svetlana, in Belgrade,' Mira said. 'She has two children. They're grown now, a son and a daughter.'

'You must miss them.'

52

'I was very close to my niece, Jasna, when she was a girl.'

'Do they come to England at all? Or did they, before—'

'Once. Years ago now.'

1987. They waited till Mira had been living in England fifteen years. Till that point the country had been unreal to them, the strange northern outpost Mira had claimed for herself. Svetlana had often said she would have understood Italy, or France. But England? A country like a damp cloth. For years she made excuses for not coming, money generally, until finally Mira sent the tickets so they could stop arguing about it. Jasna had been nineteen and mostly spent the visit dancing at West End clubs into the night and sleeping in the day; Josip, seventeen, had requested of Peter only that he take him to underground car parks so he could take a look at the beautiful foreign cars. He had gone drinking in the local Camden pubs and seemed to make, within days, a handful of beer-sodden friends.

'We've gone there, of course,' Mira added. 'Many times. The last time was two years ago.' Jasna had bleached hair when Mira last saw her, and had married hastily and unwisely, like her mother. The echo saddened Mira: the girl seemed determined, like Svetlana, to take her intelligence and fling it into the arms of an unworthy man, and from there into the bottomless demands of motherhood. The man Jasna had married was handsome with a cold eye, a bartender turned soldier. God only knew what kind of soldier. When the news was at its horrifying worst, cataloguing rapes and massacres in Bosnia, Mira could not help scanning the faces or voices for Jasna's Zoran. He was the very model of the BBC's Serb demon, she suspected.

'And do you have plans to visit them again?'

'My sister has asked us to.' Mira was having difficulty sustaining the conversation. 'We haven't been since my niece had a baby. A boy, Marko.' The birth had been hard on Jasna, according to Svetlana. Zoran was almost never there. Jasna was alone, apart from the baby, and the wars and their privations had wreaked havoc on her nerves and her spirit. But Mira did not always hear the news of Jasna, so consumed was Svetlana with the other fear of her life. Her son Josip. He had disappeared. No one had heard from him in over a year.

'You know,' Clare began, haltingly, 'I'm hoping Graham and I will have a baby. That is, I'm not pregnant. I just mean I'd like one. I'd like to have a family with Graham.'

Here. Now. You are in London. You are in Regent's Park. You cannot speak to Svetlana, not now, not today. Tomorrow, Sunday, after the church service. Mira imagined her sister attending the liturgy at one of the larger churches – the beautiful hollow interior of St Mark's, perhaps. Svetlana, who had once mocked Mira for her unobtrusive faith, only to return herself when the skies had darkened. For years now she had gone, she had prayed, she had lit candles, she had asked for light. They went together the last time Mira was in Beograd. *Please, God, don't abandon us. Please, God, bring me back my son.*

'But I'm not sure, you know, that he's ready. He says he isn't.'

'Ah. Yes.' Who wasn't ready? Graham. This was Regent's Park. Someone was speaking to her about family. Another in a seemingly endless series of conversations about having children. How was it that so many people were concerned about bringing more people into the world? Into *this* world? If Clare had been a patient, Mira might have probed the point: why do you feel this need now? But she was in a different role here. She was listening to troubles about Graham. Mira had never felt easy with the name Graham, it was such an Englishness, containing 'grey' as it did, that quintessentially English colour of sky, water, mood. Even now she could not draw the name out to its second syllable and had it closer to *Gram*. What would Peter have called his son had he known enough to name him? Leo, perhaps, one of his heroes. Or Samuel, for Beckett.

'Do you think . . .' The girl was distraught. Mira tried to feel the park around her again. It had receded. But there, through a teashop window, Peter. She recognized her husband. And beside him, Graham. They were talking in a friendly fashion. And alongside Mira, here amidst the roses, a distraught girl, evidently seeking some form of comfort or advice. 'It might make a difference if one of you spoke to him? Perhaps Peter could?'

As she said it, Clare could see how improbable it sounded. Mira looked at her as if she had no idea what she was going on about. As if she must be mad.

'It's just – because of the history, obviously.' No point in mincing words. Mira was a therapist, she must have heard far more outlandish stories. 'Because of Lydia and Peter not marrying, and Peter not knowing about Graham for those years – well all of that, I think Graham just doesn't somehow feel at ease about having a family himself.'

'Has he told you that?'

'Not exactly.' Clare looked away. 'He just keeps saying there's no rush, we can talk about this later, I'm still young, we don't need to think about it for years. But I don't want to wait for years. I am ready now. I am ready to be a mother *now*.'

So Mira would have to listen to this, too. What else could she do? The girl was a sort of family. Mira did not feel it in her bones – she felt some kindness towards Clare, but no kinship – but here she was in distress, and she was asking Mira for help. And that was a bond, wasn't it: the moment someone asked for your help, you became a relation to them. (Save us, give us haven.) You became a Samaritan. That described so much of her life in England, apart from Peter. The helping relation.

'What would you like Peter to do? What would you like him to say?'

'I don't know.' Clare's voice snapped, like hard candy. 'Perhaps – perhaps—'

And here Mira did what she could do with someone who was something like family to her, not a patient. She placed a hand on the girl's shoulder. Then reached down for her hand. She held her hand.

'I'll talk to Peter,' Mira soothed. 'It will be all right.' How much easier, in a sense, when one wasn't in the Delivery Room. Those hearty simplicities one was not allowed in there. Touching someone and saying *It will be all right*. Did Mira believe this? Did it matter? Wasn't it simply the right thing to say?

And Clare laughed, brushing tears from her round blue eyes. They were clear and intelligent and spoke of the wide lakes of Wordsworth, or a shade they called here Wedgwood. 'I'm sorry,' she said, with a smile, an embarrassment – she was English, and for the English embarrassment was as natural as breathing – but she had the grace to keep hold of Mira's generous hand, and give her a clutch in response. In gratitude. A kind of conspiracy, a women's conspiracy, in the touch.

'*Thank you*,' Clare said, and that at least, that *thank you*, reached Mira, beyond the rest.

of having a son, boys were so noisy and dirty and even if they weren't, like Hugo, they had other monstrous qualities, no loyalty or decency or capacity to listen, it was always *them* and their concerns and their discussions of god knows what. Money. Politics (as if it mattered). Computers. But recently, to appease the gods – not that Caroline believed, exactly; it was a feeling, rather, a superstition; in the past few years she had become entirely too superstitious, everything carried secret meaning, a number, a day of the week, a colour worn, a torn headline from the daily news – she had decided quite clearly that she did not *mind* if it was a girl or a boy. She would welcome a boy, too. She was open-minded. Did they hear that, the fickle gods of fertility? She would welcome a boy! She would welcome triplets! She wanted a child. She needed a child. She wanted – *please*, someone, please God, please Dr Beech, please Mira – she wanted someone to hold.

And yet, as she pulled up in the Range Rover – it was absurd in London, on the narrow streets of Hampstead where they lived, but Hugo had to have such a thing for their weekends in the country, it fed some fantasy of his to return with a cluster of pungent, shot-addled pheasant for a late Sunday supper – Caroline *did* feel some shame. Parking across the road from the dreary sixties mansion block to see Mira, she felt as she often did that there must be something wrong with her, to be making these journeys, a year on. A year on from their near divorce and she was still driving to Camden Town one morning a week to sit in a room staring at some odd Chinesey abstraction on the wall. Tell horrible stories about Hugo and issue increasingly distressed bulletins about their failure to have a baby. (As if a baby could make up for that woman, Miranda, Hugo had cavorted with and however many others; and yet, a baby *would* make up for it, Caroline counted on that.) She was beginning to feel rather ashamed about having not yet *sorted it out*. All right, a therapist, perhaps for a small amount of time, just to get you through a rough patch, marriage not exactly what one had hoped for, family not taking shape as it might; but now, surely, by now she should have managed to pull herself together, shouldn't she? What good was it to talk?

There was some shame in the other too, of course, but Caroline had got over that. IVF, like the initials of some splinter terrorist group, the Infertility Victory Front, wageing a busy war against the uncooperative sperm and eggs. They were quite open about it, she and Hugo, or had been in the beginning when they were sure it would work – 'Bacon, sperm, eggs, and sperm,' Hugo had joked at dinners, that was how open they'd been at the beginning. It had seemed science-fictional and almost absurd, a medical gimmick, and they were young(ish) and thought it bound to work, it had for various people they knew. Test-tube babies, there were hundreds of them around these days. That phrase 'test-tube babies', gone now, she remembered it from her childhood – seemed far more direct and graphic than the euphemistic 'IVF'. How old had she been when that first one was in the news? A teenager? The newspapers were full of it, the first Test-Tube Baby (Louise wasn't she called?), it made you think of Bunsen burners and small glass beakers and other antiquated items of equipment in Miss Bellhouse's chemistry class at school. Those funny green aprons they wore for 'lab' work which might or might not involve Petri dishes. *Now, girls*, Miss Bellhouse in her commanding, troops-gathering bray, Today we will be combining cadmium and liquid hydrogen to make *test-tube babies*. Organize yourselves in pairs, please. Any questions? This will be on the exam, so you'd best pay attention. Please write up the results for prep and explain whether you made a girl or a boy, and how. And please name the babies as your heading. (Do use a ruler for underlining, I can't bear wobbly lines on the page.)

Olivia. Or *Sebastian*. Or *Cosmo*. Nothing too silly please, girls, do stay away from *Flavia* or *Bertrand*.

Caroline sighed. She hated to be early, that pathetic minute standing outside the mansion-block door like a tradesman selling magazines, or schoolboys raising money for a half-term trip to the Soviet Union – Russia again now, don't forget. Hugo rolled his eyes in utter exasperation when Caroline issued some cretinism like that. There were times you could see him literally seething with embarrassment to hear her speak. She waited till it was five minutes past the hour, rang the bell, and tripped on in.

And back to the Aristocrat. A long neck, spidery limbs, mouth wide and imperious, dark hair falling about her shoulders like an elegant ermine. Not to Mira's eye attractive; Mira found the fashionable thinness anaemic, and precisely did not associate it with those feminine virtues to be resisted or succumbed to: the desire to feed and nurture, the ability to bear children, the offering of oneself as pillow and solace to men and to children and to those in distress. Thin people seemed to Mira uncomfortable. Who would want to embrace them? Mira accepted that this view set her drastically outside of this culture and its values, its images of beauty, but she could not feel otherwise. She did not consider herself beautiful, of course, simply because she was plump (though she knew that her plumpness was an integral source of Peter's adoration); she'd had a haunting, round-eyed look when she was younger that had been called striking, but as she aged she had become merely wise-looking. Yet she found it hard to see the Aristocrat as beautiful either. Other people apparently did. Or had. The past few years of Hugo's infidelities had keened the edge of the Aristocrat's figure and threatened to turn her thinness into an unhappy spindly spinsterdom.

If you want to have children, Mira sometimes wanted to say to the woman in simple terms, in her own tongue, no prevarications, no circumlocutions – you should eat. *Eat!* Make room in yourself to give the child a home. If your body feels ready for children rather than fashion, perhaps it will understand its new purpose. If Mira could have rewritten the rules for these mea-sured, deliberate exchanges as she occasionally wished to do, she would first have fed the Aristocrat. Started each session with a hot cup of soup: a chicken base, probably, as chicken broth solves everything, and dumplings to give the lean woman some soft-ness and shape.

'Good morning,' the Aristocrat began, and 'Good morning,' Mira replied, awaiting her patient's first significant words, the ones that would launch them into an exchange they had both agreed to, that Mira would be paid for, in which each would attempt to carve out some truths of the kind not found in ordi-nary conversation.

You held names close to you, like blankets, for comfort. They warmed your solitude, gave voice to a place you knew was a fact and not a fiction (though you had turned your back on it) – not a news cartoon or caricature, not a flat map with dots and arrows moving insect-like across it. In the time before all this Mira had kept the names with her loosely, as if in a pouch or bag slung over her shoulder – unobtrusive, but available for refer-ence or anecdote. Few people had reason to think of *Yugoslavia* then with anything but a dim awareness of one year's Winter Olympics (Sarajevo, wasn't it?), those pretty resorts along the Dalmatian coast (lovely Dubrovnik), and the single-word moniker of *Tito*. He had kept the place organized for so many years and had stood up to the Soviets, offering the possibility of a more human communism. The Yugoslavs weren't trapped as other Eastern Europeans were, caged in their countries, and they had seemed (Mira knew this from the way people used to

61

view her) sympathetic, good-humoured, comprehensible – within limits. If they were not *people like us*, neither were they entirely *people like them*.

Then, seven or eight years ago, Yugoslavia had changed. Its sense had ruptured. *Yugoslavia*'s meaning devolved into a synonym for collapse and disintegration, and suddenly this previously docile, ignorable country enacted terrifying reminders of all the bottled hatreds and hostilities of Europe that the EU was supposed to have consigned to oblivion. If Yugoslavia was not Romania, with a killable icon like Ceauşescu to topple, neither did the country recover from its communism with celebrations, as had the good citizens of Czechoslovakia or East Germany, who offered handsome news footage of young people shouting in triumph, bringing tears of sentimental relief to Western European eyes. *Yugoslavia* was ugly and it was difficult and it was baffling, and it spoke in a strange language with two alphabets, its massacres unfolding over a piece of a continent that had considered itself cleverly rid of the anachronism of war.

Mira had seen and heard her country become this. You had only to watch the news or speak to anyone or notice the slant of the newspapers to see how your country had slid into a new identity. In the worst war years, Mira's country became an even more private place than it had been before, one she could not speak of (or only to Peter; perhaps to Marjorie), a place she withdrew to, the country she had known as a child, as a teenager, as a hopeful student, as a young woman. Mira grew used to hearing her places spoken from the television set in the falsifying tones of newscasters bent on mangling their sounds and condemning her countrymen. Names she had not heard in years newly became headlines, excuses, provocations, crises. *Vukovar; Mostar; Srebrenica; Split*.

Some of her names. What were they? A street, Brače Nediča,

brought to her mind a line of gunmetal-grey buildings and the parked row of Fiats and Audis alongside it; a walk with a friend, Lupa, in the acrid Beograd air; the hours of conversation they shared over thick, dark coffee about literature and ideas, when plays and novels were a great source of significance in a city that could seem stark and dreary without them. The name of a play, Ionesco's *Rhinoceros*, a dark hall at the university and cigarette smoke and brandy at the interval, the sense that nothing could matter more than the words and movement of the actors on the stage – and what one said to one's friends about them after.

Voivodina, a northern province, part of Serbia or not depending on who was drawing the map and when – the place where her grandparents had lived through decades of changes. One country after another Mira's grandparents had inhabited without going anywhere: born in Serbia; married in the Kingdom of Yugoslavia, died in the Socialist Federal Republic of Yugoslavia. Places, all, transformed periodically by the vicious, levelling hand of war. Those hills, the standing families of birch and poplar and the wide slate swathe of the Danube – the forests were deep and beautiful there and there were stories within them, stories and bears, or so her grandparents had made her believe. Mira had been small in Voivodina, her father had taken her to a village outside Novi Sad during the war to live with his parents for safety. Too late. Mira's mother already killed in the German assault on Beograd in 1941. A year of darknesses everywhere. (Much later, studying suicides, Mira learned that 1941 was the year Virginia Woolf made her river exit, rocks in her pockets, and Mira always wondered whether part of the motive had been fear of Nazi victory in the war.) In 1941 the Germans had seemed invincible. Certainly omnipotent. They took Mira's mother from her that year, and what greater power can there be than that? As well as an infant brother, tiny Aleksandar, held in his mother's arms as she went out to the streets to help a neighbour look for her wandering child. Mira had been too young to remember it; perhaps. She was two. In her most sinister dreams still she knew what it was like to be besieged by fire and noise, to wake dizzied to blood and grief and an infinitely altered world. 'Punishment' they called it, the Nazis, their code word for that campaign against the obstreperous Slavs, for actions that meant *Let's send the Serbs into metal-toothed hell. They're only half a step up from the Jews, after all.*

Too young then to ask or understand, too young to have known to store images, a holding of her mother. Her father Ivan, no longer the fearless lion (enraged, shredded, impotent, full of blood), took her to his parents in the country. She knew nothing of the travel or her arrival, simply came into consciousness living with *Dedu* and *Babu* and the fear, love and darkness there were at the heart of her still. *Voivodina. Beograd.* At the end of the war they returned to the changed city, a place that had lost so much of itself, and Mira had a new mother-like person to live with, Ružica, her mother's sister who had confusingly become her father's new wife, and there was another new infant as well, not a boy Aleksandar but a girl, Svetlana. And from then on it was Beograd and Tito, *Brotherhood and Unity*, and Babu died as the war ended and animosities were to be put aside in the new Yugoslavia. They were to become a unified people.

Mira continued as an older child to go back to Voivodina as long as her grandmother was still alive, and always there the feeling remained of sanctuary in spite of the darkness, and comfort in spite of the war, and the woods she loved, though they had once harboured soldiers. Terrible things had happened in those woods, probably. Yet in those years after (*Brotherhood and Unity*), the woods were a quiet place where Mira, an older sister now, could escape to by herself, her head full of characters and animals who were in her imagination friendly and not fierce.

that much was understood, and if the name *Ustaše* did not have here the ring of viciousness it had at home (monstrous acts, beyond comprehension), still after the Second World War the Croats were recognized as an unpleasant bunch who had taken the wrong side. And some people she knew here kept some hope for Yugoslavia. Their refugee friends, as many of the Tavistock staff were – Warsaw Magdas and Berlin Evas, who had known well enough the death hand of Hitler and had a native sympathy for Hitler's many other enemies. (*Serbia ist Judenfrei*: the grotesque Nazi boast.) These refugee friends of Peter and Mira's could speak of what had gone on in Yugoslavia before 1989 and understand that countries had layers of meaning beyond the handy media shorthand of *tribal hatreds, ancient blood-feuds*. They knew from their own lives that there had been Germanys and Polands before the holocausts that had earned their grandparents' loyalty.

But her patients. The younger ones, in their thirties or even forties. The Aristocrat. The Mourning Madonna. The American, of course. They knew so little. It was one reason, though she felt flattened each time he left her, that Mira had some respect for the Bigot. He had never been stupid, and he was not ignorant. His bigotry came from his need to hate people, as it always does, but his intelligence required him to come up with an excuse for his bigotry. He had a scheme to explain just why and how the Slavs had this tendency towards self-destruction. He thought the hatred ran in their blood. In that sense they could not help it.

There was one word, one name in particular, surfacing in the news now, and this word more than any other filled Mira with dread. Not one of the people around her knew the meanings of *Kosovo*. Not even Peter. She had tried to explain it to him in analogies, in stories (Hastings, Waterloo, Canterbury – all in one), but you could not take an Englishman to the battlefield of Kosovo Polje in 1389 from his Camden Town flat in 1998. You could not give him legend and myth and deep, song-fed history and expect his heart to beat to them as your own did.

To the newspaper readers around her it was simply a name, yet another one. *Kosovo*. One more lyrical lilt that was beginning to creep into the news. Who knew what it meant this time? More battles, more bloodshed, more camps?

Nobody knew. *Kosovo*: Mira and that name were alone together, expecting the worst.

'My editor thinks I should turn them into a book,' the American was saying. She looked a bit better groomed today: new boots, perhaps, hair more cared for. Her face was clean and marked only with its own peculiar loneliness and anxieties – the thin, scratched writing across it of a person hampered by self-doubt. But under that film, the well-fed mask of the conqueror. Americans: half of them, in Mira's experience, were not even conscious of what they had. Owning the world and its weapons meant not having to know that you did. This woman Jess was well-read and inquisitive in her selected territories, but kept a modest blanket over her nationality, as she did over her body (its curves mostly smothered in long loose pullovers) and her money (the fact of which glittered through, like a guilty diamond, in an occasional reference). 'He says everyone's reading the column now, it's one of the things a lot of people turn to in the paper. And I guess he's right, I get dozens of e-mails about it.' She paused, then clarified, as if that form of technology might not have reached Mira's Camden Town home, 'You know, notes from people, from readers.'

Mira nodded. She was a believer in paper and pen, herself, but Peter faxed and keyboarded. He knew about all that.

'So, I'm surprised – pleased, obviously – but surprised. I thought it was a funny idea, single American woman in London, you know, her dating troubles, her foibles, the prejudices she runs into, the prejudices she *has* – but I wasn't sure other people would find it funny, too. But they seem to.'

Mira had read the columns occasionally. They were well-made meringues: light, sweet, forgettable. Hardly nutritional there.

And what was the point of talking about this? Jess wasn't sure why she had brought up the editor, except that she was pleased about what he had told her, it made her seem less of an emotional fuck-up. (Was she trying to impress Mira? Probably.) Or she might still be a fuck-up, but at least she was getting mileage – a name, money, a modest amount of success – out of being a fuck-up. Didn't that count for something? Still, talking about it was more in the line of a news update than some deep psychological probing. What was Mira supposed to say? 'Well done. Glad you found the right tone – part sarcastic, part self-deprecating, part faux gushing naivety of the kind Americans are thought to have – to lure in bored newspaper readers desperate for distraction or entertainment'?

'Anyway. I don't know why I'm telling you about it. It's just relevant, I guess, in that I have to decide whether to turn the columns into a book.'

'Would you like to write a book?'

Jess shrugged. 'Of course I would. Something that has a possible shelf-life of longer than twenty minutes? Sure I would. You can't help knowing, if you're a journalist, that you may be funny and insightful one day and in the recycling bin the next. Right? The best you can hope for is that someone reads you and then looks up and says, "Honey, listen to this" – reads it to their spouse, they both laugh, and five minutes later it's forgotten. No matter how good you are. Even if you're an important journalist, covering war or something worthwhile.'

Jess looked away for a moment. That was a little glib, wasn't it?

'You know what I mean. Some journalists obviously are doing things much more significant than my little culture roundups and chit-chat. But even with them, their work won't last either. It's all fizz. It all goes flat. Soon – in a day or two.'

'Do you think your work is not worthwhile?'

Oh, right. You silly self-hating woman, can't you value what you do? Come on, Betty Friedan, Marilyn French, Germaine Greer: you matter! Make yourself matter! None of those women were funny, though. People found it funnier if, in print, you called yourself an idiot and a loser. Jess found this easy enough. It was what her internal voices had been saying for years.

'It's not that I think it's worthless, or a waste of time, exactly – I mean, I keep people entertained, I'm smart, they can have a little vicarious glamour through me if I write about bad behaviour at some book party or other—'

Now that did sound worthless. What did Jess really think of what she did? The truth was, *she* found it quite glamorous. And improbable. Her! Jess Carter, a girl from California, who grew up among apricots and eucalyptus trees and geeky millionaires-to-be building the machines of the future in their garages. She who as a teenager used to fill the hours getting high down at the train station with her friends, or driving to San Francisco airport, wandering the over-lit lobbies full of nervous transients – this girl was now going to parties with the literary great and good of the age. Wasn't that something?

'I guess I think of myself as a chronicler, a chronicler of London life in a particular milieu – I know I'm not Pepys or anything, but as a way of showing how people are living now, and from the perspective of an American woman, taking on some of this male world—'

Oh, who was she kidding?

'I don't know. Maybe it is worthless. You're right.'

Wasn't therapy supposed to make you feel better? Wasn't that the point of it? Why spend money to make yourself feel worse? Jess twitched. She wanted to leave. She looked at Mira, whose eyes were unreadable. Wasn't she at least going to contradict her – *I didn't say your work was worthless* – surely that, minimally, was for the therapist to say?

'Then why would your editor be so full of praise?'

Jess waved a hand. 'Because he smells money. He's following the money. Bundle these columns into a book and voila! A "chick-lit" bestseller. Maybe.'

Mira waited. Often she paused at this sort of point, Jess had noticed, as if to prove herself unimpressed by Jess's flashy self-deprecation.

The pause lengthened. Finally:

'And then we would see how much of the book is fact, how much fiction. Do I mention that the main character, i.e. me, is looking for a man to father a child in her desperate quest to create something that will have a longer life than her journalism?' This was sounding worse and worse. 'Do I use the book and its subsequent success as a very elaborate personal ad to try to find the right man to father my child?'

Was Mira even listening to this? No reaction. Nothing. But Jess couldn't stop herself now. She was on a roll.

'Or, on the other hand, does the book become the child? You know, once I become immortal through writing a book I might lose this narcissistic urge to have a baby. Especially if it becomes a bestseller. What could top that?'

Spinning her wheels, spinning and spinning them, for the putative entertainment of the putative Czechoslovakian therapist. It might be time, finally, to find out what she *was*. What nationality, that is. There were wars starting up in various places, and perhaps it wasn't right any longer that Jess didn't know.

'I'm afraid we have to finish for today,' Mira said, and what a good exit line that was. Like the stories Jess used to write as a child: *And then she woke up. It had all been just a dream.* So handy. You could wash your hands of this telling, just like that, without having to come up with a plausible way to get out of the mess you had created.

They all wanted children. Children! Thinking that children would fill or somehow complete a self, a marriage. 'Arid', the American had called her life, as if insensible to its moist richnesses. Learn to look at what you have, Mira sometimes wanted to tell her. Not just at what you want.

These were often the hardest hours in her work and the most important, hours when the patients were gone, when she had to look back at the sessions as if at a term paper, marking her own responses. What were these narratives telling her? And what was she telling their narrators?

They all wanted the child to save them from something within themselves. Was that not it? The infant saviour. Jesus Christ, if you liked. (They wouldn't like: none of them were especially Christian, though the Mourning Madonna had a vibration about her that suggested the possibility.) The child might save them, and it might save their marriage – a common folly. Finally! A conversation topic that will last and last. We will never run out of things to say to one another as we'll have years of their precocities and naughtinesses to report on. Mira sometimes observed their friends with children watching her and Peter, saw them wondering, *What do they talk about? A childless couple. What do they say?* When a great cord tying her and Peter together was their shared, unending curiosity about other people, real or

71

imagined: friends, relations, characters, patients. It was a populated world. There was no shortage.

But these child-seekers must feel that a couple's twosome was not enough. They needed more, felt a deep longing for more. The would-be parents wanted their lives to expand, that was the hope, and Mira had to try to understand this, setting aside her instinctive belief that their lives would contract.

She had seen the transformation most damningly in her own sister. Svetlana had once acted. Greatly. Striking, dark-eyed Svetlana could fling herself into another person's soul with the recklessness of a young genius, risking everything to inhabit a new persona before hundreds of strangers. She had been Hedda Gabler at just twenty-two and with her small frame and volcanic voice had eclipsed all around her. The Parisian audience, when her small troupe travelled there, was thrilled. A small patch of the sixties was becoming hers and some form of international stardom was surely going to follow, when Dušan made his entrance, captivating Svetlana, as he had been captivated by her (so he claimed; and it was romantic, his following her from Belgrade to Paris). Before one blinked – as Mira was still completing her degree and facing her own internal crises to meet, beginning to consider going to England where she might meet the followers of Melanie Klein and Anna Freud – Dušan had turned Svetlana into a wife, and (probably even before that) a future mother. And when the baby was born, beautiful, sweet, disastrous Jasna, Svetlana lost the ability to step out of herself, becoming instead a woman taking refuge, companionship, love, meaning – from her child. Soon: children. Jasna and Josip. And whatever Dušan did thereafter, whatever wanderings he got up to at the University (of course he did; Mira did not try to dispel her sister's suspicions about his infidelities) – Svetlana had beside her her beloved Jasna and golden Josip. They became the characters of her life, of her own narrow – and ever narrowing – theatre. A kitchen sink drama, if ever there was one.

The change frightened Mira. At least as much as what may have happened in those Voivodina woods. It frightened her to see her sister disappear. Not to a bomb and Hitler's 'Punishment' but to paunchy, unpredictable Dušan and his charisma, if one called it that, or tyranny, if one called it that. And, since Dušan himself had become an absent, mythical figure over time, rather like God – or the Devil – Svetlana was on her own with her children. It was an old story. Did they gain from her sacrifice? Did it matter? The children were fine, or when Mira left they were: Josip a small loud puppy, bouncing about and demanding attention; Jasna still sweet but already troubled, suggesting by the lines of her face a problemed future. Mira had held her when she was just born and weighed next to nothing, felt the sensation, like air, of this miraculously small body, and knew for some minutes the unadulterated joy, the blemishless astonishment of new life in her arms. Then she had handed her niece back to a foreign woman (her sister) who bared her breasts and joked about the grey circles around her eyes and flaunted a body suffused with weariness and bliss.

By the time Mira was holding tiny orange-faced Jasna (there was some jaundice), Mira had already decided that she would soon be leaving. She could imagine life alongside this little girl, watching her grow, taking her out for an ice cream or to the cinema, Mira assuming that particular role as the one who spoiled Jasna, the adoring, nearby, childless aunt. For Mira would not have children; the conviction had already been with her some months by the time of Jasna's birth, and watching the erosion of her sister's spirit only deepened it. Someone might say to Mira – Svetlana herself said it on the unhappy occasion they had discussed it – that she was still a woman of courage and imagination, that motherhood required something of the same abandonment of self as had her life on the stage, and if Mira could not see that then her own short-sightedness was at fault. It was simply Svetlana's own two, Jasna and Josip, to whom her resources were now directed, rather than Ophelia or Beatrice, and wasn't that how life was supposed to be? Especially in a country that had known the grief and violence theirs had? Wasn't it the best they could do, to raise their children in this Yugoslavia and raise them well in whatever Yugoslavia would become? *Life*, Mira. That was what you could do for your country; for your people, even. Make life and not death.

Mira fled. She was not planning to set herself up for her country or her people, whoever they were. That was, perhaps, the voice of their father, but it was not her voice. Mira's voice, that she came into as she read and studied at Beograd University, as she watched 1968 work its changes in their city, told her *people*, not *the* people, not *your* people, but people, generally, whose pains were the same though their languages were different. Each person had pains peculiar to them and a history of his or her own, each had been a child who had suffered unfathomable, crucial sadnesses, whose excavation might make easier futures possible. And these excavations were of more interest to Mira than a nation nursing its stories and its wounds within a wider country, a hopeful possibility, *Yugoslavia*.

Mira left. She moved towards a different kind of conversation in her life. She left the nation-building, and mother-sacrificing, to others.

The decision broke her father's heart. And for several years after the move Mira and Svetlana scarcely spoke. When they finally did, it was her sister telling Mira that their father was gravely ill, heart trouble, and Mira should come back to visit him. Mira said that she would be travelling with her new husband. An Englishman named Peter.

Yes, they had married the year before. He was a lovely, gentle man, also as it happened a professor. No, they did not have any children. And, though on this point Mira remained silent, she was quite certain that they never would. The only children in Mira's life would be the children her patients had once been; and the phantoms and fantasies – the children they were, with shared desperation, hoping to have.

It was good to walk. It helped clear the head. He tried telling Mira this, but she was more of a reader than a walker and he couldn't thoroughly convince her that the two were compatible. For himself, it was necessary. When he wasn't teaching, particularly after one of the Poly's rather grim lunches, he often walked. Mira, he knew, sat. Hunched in the kitchen over soup, awaiting Bigots and Aristocrats. Or in the embracing armchair sipping tea, reading poetry and novels and not the newspaper because reading the newspaper drew her into a helpless, gnawing fury. At the newspaper and its lies, and whatever truths lay behind the lies.

He would do the shorter circuit today. Along Gypsy Lane (leaf-trampled and grassy, its name evoking the jangling of bells and telling of fortunes), down the bicycle path and on into his favourite Oxford park, Headington Hill, which greeted one with a postcard sight off to the west, the dreaming spires tastefully framed by the brush of chestnut leaves. (Constable might profitably have painted here if he hadn't been so busy watching Highgate from Hampstead Heath.) The path curved down the hill past a sculptural, sensuous tree whose trunk dipped towards the ground, tempting clamberers of all ages, and he wished as he often did that Molly might come back to him for a few hours, keep him company on his constitutional, provide the philosophical companionship of an ambling, snuffling, four-legged creature.

He was walking, Peter knew now, partly to prove that he could. An interior part of him, unidentified, protested and suspected that he should stop. *This may clear your head but it is not helping your body.* How was that possible? Walking helped everything. When he learned first of Graham's young existence, Peter had walked with Molly all the way across Oxford to Port Meadow, the wide undeveloped stretch on the far side of the canal, and then across the meadow's marshy, horse-spattered expanse to the riverside pub called the Trout. There Molly slept, exhausted, while he drank a pint of bitter slowly, listening to the parabolic cries of the peacocks and the yeasty mumble of pub-goers and trying to take in the magnitude of this information. He had thrown a few crust-bits to a frowning swan, then risen and took Molly the same miles back. By the end of his excursion, he had come to believe that it was true: he was a father. The belief was the first step in making the rest, the enactment of it, possible.

It was no use. He had to sit down. He approached the row of green peeling benches placed at intervals along the park's downslope path like stations on a game board, where the watery sun drizzled through the high leaves onto the cool and curving slats. A young couple entwined on one. An old man asleep with his newspaper on another. Peter shuddered at the sight, seeing himself in that state in fifteen years or so, prideless, asleep and adrool in public, leg twitching to a dream like a dog's. But what was the alternative? To be dead. He might be ill, it was beginning to seem more than possible, and he might never reach that man's state of decrepitude. (His stomach clenched and his bowels loosened in primitive fear at the thought.) Was that to be preferred? People should either be young or dead – it was Dorothy Parker who had said that, his friend Andrew had quoted it to him in a morbid moment that had once fed Peter's suspicions about Andrew's own health. (He had stopped worrying about Andrew.) Peter was not young. Did that only leave the other possibility?

An empty bench at last, just beyond one occupied by a solitary woman, reading. A fall of silvered hair around her pleasant face. The chilled presentiment of his own future death – it would either be now, soon that is, when he was still able and alert, or later, when he was decrepit, but either way it would come. *The readiness is all*, Hamlet pointed out, but Peter was not ready and did not know how he ever could be. He had a strange urge to sit next to this reading woman, to seize her, to begin to speak.

She sensed his hovering and looked up through the sundust and noondamp at the gentleman who could not quite make the decision to move past her.

Her face changed: light came to it.

'Is it – Peter? Peter Braverman?'

As if he were dreaming. He did not know this woman. Though her face – perhaps – a different life – he felt confused, suddenly—

'It's Helen Glidden – Forster now. Do you remember? I shared a flat with Lydia.'

'*Helen.*' Yes, of course. He did remember. He wasn't senile, yet. Different then, younger obviously, very pretty, a green dress: long ago he'd had the regretful thought that it was Helen he should have been going out with, not Lydia, but since he was with Lydia, though unhappily, the possibility retreated. It would have been too cruel, to court the flatmate. And then, after the pregnancy – 'Of course, yes,' Peter said. Helen had laughed a lot, he remembered. He put a hand out, and took hers. 'May I?' He gestured at the place beside her.

'Of course.'

And what to do then but share one's paragraphs: Yes, teaching at the Poly now, have been for years, live in London though, come down on the coach; wife a psychotherapist there, her practice in London. And hers, Helen's: still in Oxford, never left, taught at Oxford High for years, the girls' school, husband was a don at Wadham, died several years ago (yes, thank you, one finds a way to go on), two children, grown up, one in America doing something with computers, the other married and living in London. Three grandchildren. Another on the way.

'Yes.' Peter cleared his throat in the space opened after the grandchildren. 'I don't know whether you know—'

'About Graham?' she smiled. 'He's a lovely man. Terribly handsome.' Seeing the disarray on his face, she clarified. 'I still see Lydia, you know.'

He had not known. How could he? His muscles shifted. 'Ah. Yes, I haven't seen her since Graham's wedding.' A small service in the registry office in Bath followed by a party at Clare's parents' home. He and Mira had found one of Clare's northern uncles and concentrated on talking to him. It had been a difficult day. 'How is she?'

'Well, I think. Still at the OUP.' Helen's envelope smile sealed that subject, and suddenly Peter's tiredness was absolute. *Lydia*. Surely in his state of exhaustion he needn't ask further about her? Apologize somehow to her, by proxy? Helen, as flatmate, must have known the whole sordid story, and in her good-humoured way given some counsel. What had she told Lydia? What would her advice have been?

But that, as Mira would say to him later, was the virtue of being English, not to have to ask or pursue. It would be rude to walk away, to find another place to sit having sat beside Helen initially, but Peter could lean back against the bench as he now did, his face a mask of serenity, and take in the bird-decorated air, deciding to leave that tangle of difficult histories to one side of his attention.

'Isn't it a wonderful morning,' he breathed, allowing himself to become a near parody of an old geezer. Mira would have laughed. 'Such a pleasure to have a bit of sun again after that terrible grey period.'

'Yes,' said his benchmate, closing her eyes too, to take in the rationed warmth. She knew these social rules. Everyone did. She would not intrude or violate. 'Isn't it?'

The Mourning Madonna always came in apologizing and often, though not always, weeping. If she wasn't weeping when she arrived she generally was within five or ten minutes after properly beginning. Some sense of manners – or perhaps simply pride, to prove that she could – made her want to open with general conversation, as if Mira were not a doctor and this were not an office, as if Kate, a well-placed and educated woman who had once worked for a housing charity, had social reasons for coming weekly to Camden Town, to take tea with an older Serbian lady. So, 'It must be difficult for you,' she attempted today, 'to watch the news from here. Being so far away.'

'Thank you,' Mira said, her hands clasped on her lap. 'Yes. It is.'

'Is quite a lot of your family still there, in – what used to be Yugoslavia?'

And for some reason, her guard down, Mira yielded. 'All of them, yes.' She blinked. 'Apart from my husband. And stepson.'

'How awful. I hope they're not—' She had a beautiful scarf about her neck, silk, that made her seem French rather than English. One forgot what elegance looked like; so few of her patients had it. The Aristocrat was smart, but aggressively chic, to go along with her pointed nose, her brittle limbs; the American a disarray of slapdash boyishness. 'I hope they're not in any immediate danger.'

'Thank you,' Mira repeated, her hands holding each other more tightly. 'I do, as well.' To her horror she felt a sting behind the eyes, as if this butter-voiced woman might do something no other patient ever had – draw her to tears. (She had stayed dry-eyed through the hardest of them: the Failed Suicide, the Tragic Adolescent, and even the Bigot, though Mira knew perfectly well he had tried to break her.) She must not let it happen. 'How are you, Kate?' Mira said. She knew that she could make her voice resonant when she had to, sonorous, and she could not help knowing that the accent affected people. Differently, of course. To some, Americans or the occasional Australian, it had the sound of old European wisdom; for some, particularly she suspected the more aristocratic, it made her seem Jewish, which then connoted a specific, Austrian-influenced intelligence (the ironies of which were not Mira's affair). Occasionally, to people of prejudice, it made the therapist sound less intelligent than she was, given that she was liable still to drop her definite articles and make certain grammatical errors. With the Mourning Madonna, Mira guessed, her voice carried with it the sense of safety and sympathy and *it's all right now, to this woman you can admit anything*.

Kate felt the need and repulsion simultaneously. The moment she came into the room. It was the reason she so often apologized, with foolish, small pretexts – I'm sorry, did I close the door with a bang? I'm so sorry I'm a tiny bit late – when the real content of her apology was something quite different: I'm sorry, I don't like having to come here, I wish I didn't have to, and yet all during the week I think of this hour as the one hour that will save me. The lifejacket. The oasis.

The pain overwhelmed her. What could either of them possibly do for the pain? So Kate instinctively tried to turn the focus, learn something of the other woman's trials. The worst of the warring in Yugoslavia was over now – Bosnia and all that – but new trouble was brewing, Kate knew very little about it but William said he thought it might turn vicious once again. He followed these things. Though when he had spoken of it to Kate she had, she remembered with some shame, started to shout at him, she was able since Cassandra died to shout in ways she never had imagined before: 'How can you *possibly* read the newspaper? How can you fucking *care*? We've lost our daughter and there you are discussing the news as though it were any ordinary bloody day.' She had pounded something. What was it? The door – the table – *him*, possibly. For those minutes she had considered her husband the most heartless, unforgivable man she had ever known in her life, and she wished bitterly to God that she might never have to see him again. Reading the newspaper like some fucking minister of state, when their child had just died. What could any news matter? How could anything in the news matter at all to them now? Blair, Milošović, Spice Girls, World Cup. What the fuck did any of it *matter*?

And here she was playing the news game with the therapist, or trying to, to divert attention away from herself for just a moment because the light of enquiry, when it fell on Kate again now (the therapist had turned the tables back, inevitably), would finally show all the ugliness that was within Kate, the hatred and rage. How she *hated* people now, all sorts of people, everyone, strangers and friends and family members, people who had the gross insensitivity to issue some trite comment such as Time will heal the wound, Perhaps you and William can try again, Have you thought about adopting? Most especially she hated the pregnant, most especially those smug bloody mothers with that pride in their eyes – hated them with a drunken abandon she had not known herself to possess. And behind the hatred, obviously, grief. It was bottomless. Bottomless.

'Yesterday,' Kate began, and it was like a balancing beam, walking this narrative. How far would she get? 'William and I drove out to the crematorium to pick up Cassandra's ashes. They were in a small box . . .' There was a place she had wanted to get to, the point at which the woman, the functionary, had said unthinkingly, 'It must have been a young baby – that's a small box.' But Kate did not get that far today, she couldn't, because just then she felt a ghostly movement within her. This happened to her still, one of God's cruelties, a sensation as if Cassandra's limbs were still punching and kicking inside her, and Kate, silenced, was all but winded by the impossible, unreal exertions.

The people she had helped. Mira made herself remember. She was trying to read Marjorie's paper, she had promised to read it, an article about dissociation, the separation of self from trauma that occurred in a protective psyche. Her thoughts wandered. How could Mira help the Mourning Madonna? Nothing she could do would restore that woman to the simpler self she had been before her loss. Restoration was not the point. This Mourning Madonna was indelibly altered by the mark of grief, and any work they did together could not be an effort at erasure. Rather, Mira had to find a way to give Kate a place within herself to hold the child that she had lost. Others would tell her to move on, to put it behind her; to go on a holiday, or buy a dog, or take up gardening, anything to move her attention from the loss at hand. Some might urge her to try to get pregnant again, thinking that if she had another child she would be all right. Mira knew her role in the cacophony would be to give the woman space and quiet and to let her know, gently, that it would never be *all right* again. Something had been taken from this woman – a child – and she must learn to allow a place within herself, Cassandra's place, to remain, lined with the love the baby would have known had she lived. Only once the Mourning Madonna had made this nest within herself for her absent child would 'moving on' (or moving anywhere – down the street; to the shops) begin to make any sense at all. Mira would have to find a way to teach her to take Cassandra with her wherever she went.

Mira had spoken of Kate to Marjorie a few days before. Mouse-faced, keen-minded Marjorie, companion over a couple of decades: sympathetic, unsentimental, light-handed, necessary. One clung to colleagues so – other members of the therapeutic fraternity, friends in whom one could ethically confide, fellow travellers along this strange march in the interior. Marjorie had offered her views on Mira's hollowed-out Madonna, then shared her own unenviable list over a pot of smoky Chinese tea of the kind Mira only tolerated in her friend's book-crowded sitting room. Marjorie had an adulterous narcissist, and a self-righteous ex-wife. ('Wickedly, I've a mind to introduce them.') She had a triumphant defeatist, a man who seemed to nurture and celebrate his ability to turn every promising prospect into failure. And she had a composer, a vain and talented man critically hampered by the sour backwards glance, the reflexive comparison of his lot with others', the perpetual sense that he was not being recognized. *Performance envy*. Mira had had a similar patient years before, a playwright, she remembered. Just after the playwright allowed Mira to return his focus to his work rather than his competitors, he stopped coming to see her, leaving her to follow his fortunes in the papers.

'Do you think sometimes of Sisyphus?' Mira asked Marjorie. 'As I do?'

'Rolling the stone up the hill again and again? Oh, yes. And there will never be a shortage of stones. – Though some, it must be said, are heavier than others.'

'That is Peter's joke: *you'll never be out of work.*'

'Medical doctors must feel the same way. They set a bone or cut out a tumour one day, good; but other bones will break and tumours grow back, or move somewhere else.' Marjorie sipped her tea. 'How are you getting on with that man I sent you, Howard Beddoes? Have you forgiven me?'

'He is a test of character. He tests – perpetually. It is like arm wrestling.'

'And which one of you is stronger?'

Mira smiled. 'It depends on the day. And – it depends on the news.'

'He's still baiting you?'

'Always.'

'Have you worked out why? What his motivation is?'

'I am trying to. Trying to.'

Mira remembered the conversation now as she waited for him in the post-Madonna quiet. When the buzzer rang, no part of Mira felt able to get up to answer. The Bigot. How could she help him? What could she do for him? What was he after?

It rang again. Wasn't that like him. Pay attention to me NOW.

'All *right*,' she had called into the empty flat, in a voice that surprised her. She raised herself up, disgruntled. 'All right, Howard. Yes. All *right*.'

Four

June

You started reckoning, Peter supposed: he would need to start reckoning. He wanted more than anything to walk and think, but by now he recognized that if he walked, all he would think about was how long before he tired, and that would detract and discourage. He had to think on the bus instead, watching the countryside, and so Peter found himself going to Oxford more often now to give himself added time to think. Term was nearly over. Where would he go then?

You started, even before you knew whether this was really happening or not – your decline, your slow slide to the inevitable – to look back and evaluate what you had done. A bit like going over the exam paper before turning it in. (He told his students: Always re-read the paper carefully, take the time to reconsider what you've written, make sure you can stand by what's on the page.) It did not promise to be an easy or comfortable task, if you were honest with yourself, and if you could not be honest with yourself now, then when? What point could there be in holding on to one's self-deceptions to the grave? They would not be of much use to anyone there.

And so. He allowed himself to look. The years did not record glorious victories in battle, or moments of great moral courage. At no point had Peter been required to make a stand, be a lone voice in the wilderness. He had never been asked to sign a declaration for rights which might have risked his livelihood or his family. He had scaled no great mountains, crossed none of the world's animate, deep rivers in some slight craft that might testify to his adventurousness or physical prowess. There was not even the writing of important books; there was the translation of the work of others. And though much of Peter's teaching rested on his conviction that it was important to recognize worlds other than one's own – and translation made that possible for readers – he had always been aware that no libraries contained any original Braverman. Peter had produced a serviceable, lively version of some late Turgenev stories, and a lesser known work by Goncharov. He was best known for a trade translation he had produced of Solzhenitsyn's *One Day in the Life of Ivan Denisovitch*. And while he was proud of those volumes, he remained conscious of the fact that none of those reflections on God or morality or death or marriage were *his*. He had spent his life passing on his second-degree thoughts, his thoughts about thoughts.

It was not easy or comfortable, looking back. But it was better than looking forward. Peter did not just now want to see ahead of him the snake-shaped question of which precise disease might be hobbling him; which monstrous treatment might be suggested by doctors; how futile or not that treatment might be, as he wended his way through the cycles of optimism and discomfort, despair and pain that he had seen in acquaintances and colleagues. (Cancer. Some form of cancer. Must be.) It was easier now to look back.

Peter searched for something notable, colourful, in the heap of days he had stacked up behind him that were beginning already to seem taken for granted. Toast and tea in the morning, reading the newspaper (the *Guardian*, through its redesigns and font changes). Was he glad now to have spent all those morning hours reading? Had the cultural minutiae enriched his life, actually: this champion of Wimbledon, that surprise Grand National winner, another controversial choice for the year's Booker Prize? Dutifully Peter had followed the endless bleak intricacies of Middle East hostilities and peace talks, the partisan killings and abrupt explosions of the Northern Ireland stalemate, the bloody transitions in various African nations, the massacres, the wars, and finally the fratricidal dissolution of his own wife's country. And for what had he done so? Was this the right way to have spent all those hours of his life, acquiring information to develop opinions on global crises that would evolve in their ways regardless of what view he, Peter Braverman, Englishman, happened to take on them? That information, too, he would take with him to the grave. None of those consumed pages of newsprint had given him anything to leave behind for his nearest and dearest.

Peter thought of the elections he had lived through. Weeks watching Kinnock build false hope of a victory for Labour; that early startling landslide by Thatcher's Tories; the surprise victory of Wilson's Labour in 1964. And Ted Heath. (How he had despised Heath, the sight and sound of the man, that plump gullet and pompous, throttling voice. Though in retrospect, after the monstrous Thatcher, he had seemed all too calm and measured.) And feeble Callaghan – and on and on it went, he could stretch right back to Eden and there again what had been the point of it? Peter might as sensibly have gone to bed for the two-week campaigns and read a good novel. Caught up on the Americans, perhaps, Faulkner or Steinbeck, rather than follow party political broadcasts and the predictions of pundits. Or

lana had told Mira that as the wars' ravages spread through Yugoslavia, the state-sponsored television increasingly glutted the airwaves with girlie-led game shows and empty pop music programs, the Milošović mafia's efforts to numb and distract. No – there was a duty to pay attention even if one felt at times powerless. That was why one spent hours of a life reading the newspaper, it was part of one's duty towards country and yes, character. Peter did believe in those old-fashioned qualities.

Besides: what else should he have filled the hours with? Reading more poetry? Praying? But he did not believe in God, in spite of all the hymns and Lord's Prayers he had intoned as a youth. Given who Peter was – and one did have to acknowledge one's own virtues and limits, even at this stage, perhaps especially at this stage – it never *would* have been Peter climbing the mountain, writing the symphony. Even if he had cashed in every last one of those newspaper hours. He would probably just have used them to walk, or to talk to Mira, or to talk, perhaps – possibly – to Graham.

Peter winced. He was tired now, quite tired – as if he had been walking, after all. He shifted in his seat as the bus approached Headington, once a drab though endearing village, now a meaningless strip of cheap chemists and off-licence chains. Perhaps the pain he had been feeling lately had not been from walking at all, perhaps it had been from thinking. That's it, Peter. You've a brain tumour. If you can only stop yourself thinking, you'll live another ten years, easy. Think of all the papers you could read then.

He dug himself into his seat, trying to burrow his way out of the recognition he had found uncomfortably before him. What was it? Oh yes. Graham. In the end a person must, minimally, be able to say he had done right by one's children, if he had any. And that was the thought that made Peter writhe in his seat as if he were already in treatment, as if poison were already being leaked into his veins to counter whatever tumour his body unwisely nurtured.

Had Peter done right by Graham? Of course he hadn't. How could he ever forgive himself, or be forgiven, for that first crucial absence? It was not enough to plead, 'I didn't know.' He should have known. He should have felt it in his bones, that a child of his had been born and now lived. Failing that, he should have *asked*. Tracked down Lydia and found out. How could you not ask? – A question his son had been too fearful, or angry, or considerate to put to Peter directly, though with indirections of glance or gesture he had asked it over and again.

I was not meant to be a father, Peter thought. They got it wrong with me, the gods. They should have picked someone else. I'm a kind man and a decent teacher, I'm a good friend and a loyal husband. I am not incurably selfish, and I am quite a good cook. But I have not been the father I should have been to Graham. It has not been enough.

The bus slowed along the London Road. 'Anyone for Gypsy Lane?' the driver called, and Peter uttered a hollow assent, raising himself wearily, as if already he were on the vehicle that was to lead him from this life and deposit him in the next. Ah well, he thought, defeated, his customary irony deserting him. If it was his turn to get off here, then so be it.

'We've heard from Josip.' It was Svetlana's voice, and she sounded twenty years younger than the last time Mira had heard her. 'He's in Trieste. Trieste! He's not fighting at all. Never was! He's fine. He's all right.'

So, as an aunt too your heart swelled with relief, with joy. Then – rage.

'Why didn't he *tell* you? Why hasn't he been in touch with you?'

'Yes, I know.' Mira heard a forgiving exhalation of cigarette smoke. 'We've been through it all. The best you can say is he wanted to kill me, slowly, painfully, inch by inch, and that was the best way he could think of to do it.'

'What did you say to him? How did he – did he call, or write, or—'

'Telephoned. Jasna was here, and said I screamed as though it was the devil on the phone. She thought it was Dušan.'

Dušan *was* the devil. By now Mira and Svetlana agreed on that point. That he was still in name her husband and the father of her children was an added misfortune.

'I didn't know I was screaming until I stopped and thought, God, God, who's making all that noise?' Svetlana laughed again; she was giddy as a teen. Her voice was more serrated each time Mira heard her: the catches and scrapes of years upon years of cigarettes, alcohol, coffee, privation. 'Then I suddenly stopped, like turning off a tap, and there was a silence, and I thought, my God, Svetlana, shut *up* or the boy won't call you again for another five years.'

'It hasn't been that long. Has it?'

'It has been twenty years,' she exhaled again, 'since the wretch fed his mother any morsel of affection. He was five, I think, or six the last time he turned those beautiful blue eyes on me with total adoration, as though no one could be more per-fect or divine than I was. I had probably just given him an ice cream.'

Mira remembered those blue eyes and remembered the boy, too, when he was sweet and playful and contained hope and mis-chief and affection within his small self. Gradually, inevitably, he acquired the sullen hostility and impenetrable anger of an adult. Children always did. Their earlier exuberant selves, a mirage.

Svetlana had not sounded this high-spirited in years. How long had Josip been gone? The years passed at different rates for the sisters. War years, mother years, had a different density and duration than Mira's childless London years. In fact Mira sometimes had the impression that Svetlana had gradually aged beyond her, becoming the older sister: she seemed to have lived so much more, and through so much more, leaving Mira feeling doughy and undeveloped by comparison.

'Is he coming home? When will you see him?'

'Coming home?' She could imagine Svetlana's melodramatic shrug. 'Why would my son do something simple like come home? No, no, he says he's going to Kosovo. He has business in Kosovo.'

'Oh no, Svetlana. Not now. He's not going *now*.'

'Of course he is. "I know how to look after myself. Don't worry." *Don't worry!* "I just have some business there. I won't get in the middle of all that crap. I'm not stupid." '

And again, even as an aunt, Mira's heart constricted around worry like a snake around its prey. How could Svetlana bear it? Why couldn't the idiotic boy just go back to Beograd, where the worst he would face would be rifle-armed men guarding nightclubs and a city poised for war? Or if not Beograd then stay in Trieste? Mira almost said this to Svetlana. (Those eyes, she remembered them, and the boy's carved, beautiful face – though he had always looked a little too like Dušan for Mira to trust him entirely, even before he was a spectacled smoker, like his father. But the fundamental sweetness he'd had, she remembered it; she had loved him.) Mira did not want to voice the worst of what she was thinking. Svetlana was high still from the knowledge that her son was alive. Why draw her into the next round of fears and anxieties?

'Did Jasna speak to him?' Mira asked. 'She might be able to talk sense to him. Older sisters often can.'

'Jasna!' Though the name was inflected by the same sarcasm, Mira could hear a change in her sister's tone; a creep of sobriety. 'She started yelling at him worse than me. She's so angry all the time now, Mirka – "It had better not be drugs, Josip. Is that your very important Kosovo business? Don't tell me it's drugs." I grabbed the phone away from her, God knows who listens to telephones now, but of things to talk about—'

'Is it? Do you think—?'

'I don't want to know. *I do not want to know*. Then the baby started crying, and what with the shrieking and crying I'm sure Josip must have thought he'd reached a madhouse, and that Kosovo sounded positively serene by comparison. Finally Jasna handed Marko to me, took the phone back, and said, "It's true, little brother, I've become a mother since I last spoke to you and you didn't even know it. Live long enough to be a good influence on your nephew, will you?" and then he asked her something, the baby's name, and she teased him, "Gavrilo Princip, of course. Our Serbian assassin. What did you think?" When I spoke to Josip after he said, "You must stop feeding her raw meat, mama. It only makes her wilder." ' Svetlana exhaled again, then said emphatically, '*Mira*.'

'Yes?'

'You must come to visit. Come before – before whatever comes next.'

'I would like to.'

'Don't *like to*. Just come. Come this summer with Peter. How is Peter?'

'He's – I'm not sure. I'm concerned – there seems to be something—'

'Yes, I'm worried about Jasna too.' Mira had noticed this before, even before the wars had given further licence to Svetlana's self-absorption: her sister seemed constitutionally incapable of allowing Mira to finish a sentence on the subject of her own life. 'Joking aside, she is quite depressed. It's the baby, I know. I remember that, I had it myself – but it's Zoran, too. The brute. God knows what he's doing.'

'He's still in the army?'

'One of the loyal barbarians. Fighting for the glory of Serb people everywhere.'

'Where is he?'

'We don't know.' Svetlana's voice had flattened again. 'What is the use of all these men, Mirka? Whose idea was it to have men running all the countries and bankrupting them with their battles? I'm becoming quite the bitter old feminist. Hate men more with every passing day. The Women in Black are still organizing their protests in Beograd, you know. I go along, occasionally.'

'We'll come. If we can.'

'Don't *if we can*. Just come. Come to our madhouse. Before one of us kills the other.' She laughed again so that her sister would know that the dramatic tone was deliberate. 'And bring cigarettes, will you? Silk Cuts. They're murderously expensive here, and I'd love to have some kind of luxury to keep me cheerful as we all take the next slow boat to hell.'

The light went on, and Mira had no idea where she was. She had been dreaming. She was somewhere very cold, icy – Russia, perhaps – branches were falling and a horse was down, struggling. Someone was beating the horse, cruelly. The figures were shadowy. She heard a noise. A cough, or a heave, and the room had strange dimensions in the diagonal fraction of escaping light, and she could not say where she was.

Peter. Must be.

'Peter?'

'Sorry, love. Did I wake you?'

Peter. Of course. 'Are you all right?'

'Well, I'm . . .' His voice, from the bathroom, was dampened by the sound of running water. 'I'm all right. Sorry.'

Mira lay in the compromised darkness waiting for him to finish. Unusual for Peter to get up in the night. More often it was her awakening with one of the pre-dawn trains – you could feel them as much as hear them, the night-time leviathans out of Euston, carrying their heavy urgencies northward. She was frequently taken from sleep by their noises, to be thrust into the spiritual drear that stretched from the last of the night till the first of the morning: that close, poisonous time in which there was never enough air to properly breathe. (There was a biochemical reason for the mind's emotional fall just then, but it did not help Mira to know that; like telling the Mourning Madonna that her unleashed hormones added a maddening edge to her distress, a useless knowledge.) In those small insomniac hours all was stark and unsolvable: patients Mira was not reaching, the conference paper she was meant to write and could not, the unspeakable fact of her distance from her collapsed country and family. The only thought that calmed her then was *Peter*. And though he might have drifted sideward in his sleep and be snoring, heavily, she would approach him, move close to him, with the intention not of making love (it wasn't often, now) but of comforting herself, of reminding herself of the good, right piece of her life, which was him. Peter. Life without him did not bear thinking about. She would reach one arm around the soft slopelet of his chest and unfailingly, even from the deep thickets of dream, the voice would murmur, 'All right?' and one of his hands would press her arm close to him and tell her with his touch that he was there, that he loved her, that he always would.

The door to the bathroom flared open, a blind of light which abruptly ceased. 'Sorry,' he said again. Peter was always, ubiquitously, sorry. When Mira had first known him she found it so foreign, all the apologies, many of which could in no way be sincere or meaningful; but gradually she had come to understand the word was her husband's passport through the world – as if 'sorry' were a set of skeleton keys that could open any door, or some social oil that allowed the mechanics of any engagement to work more smoothly. Sometimes an empty, reflexive punctuation. Sometimes, as now, his gesture of regret at any of the ways he might annoy her.

'Are you all right? Peter?' she repeated.

'Just a bit of – tummy trouble.' That he patted his stomach instructively as if she might not know what he meant, seemed to Mira a symptom of some deep nervousness. Peter was distracted, almost as though he, like Mira a few minutes earlier, did not know where he was. He climbed back under the duvet and onto his back. She could tell from the alertness of his body that he was nowhere near sleep.

'You're worried about something?' Mira asked at last. She did not know whether or not this was an intrusion. Peter's insomnias were so rare that Mira was not sure whether they were best aided by solitude or company. In some night troubles the last thing a person wanted was conversation.

Peter heaved an exhalation of some weight, a dread breath, a sick sigh. This too was unusual: usually it was Mira who took the part of the melancholic, the existentialist. 'I've been thinking about Graham,' he said. 'I must speak to him.'

'About having a child?'

'Sorry?'

'Do you mean about their having a child?' When Peter didn't answer, Mira added, 'Did Clare speak to you?'

'No. She didn't.'

This derailed Peter's neatly trained thoughts. He had planned to tell Graham something about the past, about his own life, why it had the shape it had – he wanted to *explain* it to Graham, You see, this is where I took this turn, and then that turn, and this happens and that happens and here we are in 1998 and I am walking in the park with your wife and you with mine and then we have tea, talk a bit of Blair and a bit of Europe but not, evidently, of what at heart concerns us.

'What do you mean? What did Clare say?' Peter asked then, reluctantly, and he puzzled to hear Mira's story of Clare's distress, the ferocity of her longing for a child, and of Graham's resistance on the point. 'But of course they'll have children,' he said. 'Why wouldn't they?'

'Graham has hesitations. She is still young, he says.'

'That's absurd.' Peter found himself angry, suddenly. 'What's the matter with him? They have that nice little house in Bath, they both have decent jobs, they're married a year – of course the poor girl wants a child.' He was agitated now. 'I'm sure he'll come round. Why wouldn't he?'

'She would like you to talk to him.'

'What?'

'She thought you might talk to him. Encourage him.'

Now that *was* absurd – the idea that he, Peter, could have some father–son conversation that would make a difference to Graham. Perhaps Clare had an inflated sense, dear girl, of Peter's importance in Graham's life. In Peter's view Graham considered him a bit like a wayward uncle: the boy could be affectionate, nicely so (more, in some measure, than Peter had any right to

97

expect), but it seemed clear he did not take Peter seriously. Did not take him to be a *father*, truly. Peter could not imagine the expression on Graham's face if he tried to give the boy something like advice.

'I can't see the good of it,' he said finally into the dark.

'Yes,' his wife replied. 'I know.'

What did she know? To what was she assenting, exactly? Peter was not sure he had finished his thought and felt a rare spasm of irritation at Mira's assurance. She reached over to hold him and he turned his back to her so they could fold into one another – and so that his face could be, even in the darkness, turned from hers. He held her arm close against his chest as he often did, their customary evening embrace, and soon he heard the steady fall of her sleep breath, slow and underground-sounding, as though she had fallen into a well. That was good, that she slept. His reckoning would not allow him to, not for some time. It was a few hours, nearly dawn, before his own mind relaxed, releasing him once more to his uneasy dreams.

She must do something about the Bigot. She must work on him and on herself, bring them closer, so that engagement was possible. Otherwise his continued visits would have no purpose.

People had the idea that the job was simply to sit still in a room and nod and murmur tactfully, then collect one's fee at the end. 'I could do what you do,' Svetlana had said to Mira often enough. 'Sitting about listening to people complain about their husbands and their children. I do that myself in our apartment block, every day. I should set myself up like you do, and charge money for it.'

At her worst, after a bad week or a bad day or a bad hour, Mira could share her sister's scepticism. But she knew otherwise, when she had the time to think. Then she knew why she did what she did, and how. Other people did not know how she worked on her patients when they were apart from her, that these were some of her most inspired moments, when all she had was their voices in her ear, the brush of their lives on her fingers. She saw the patients' difficulties with sudden noonday clarity, and their troubles would become transparent to her – or, rather, the surrounding murk, excuses and apologies, rage and distractions, would become transparent, and Mira would see through to a line, or an image, that made sense of the people and their self-deceptions. Those illuminated moments, when Mira's perceptions offered themselves, like gifts, to her, lent her the impression of being a visionary – a seer, almost, as she might have been in another time or place – and the confidence that she gave her patients something essential they could not find on their own. It was, she had once told Peter, something like the way she imagined solving a mathematical problem must be: the sudden appearance of the equation in your emptied mind, the solution so sweet you could almost taste it.

The challenge then was to allow the patient to find the line for him- or herself. One had to tease the patient along, encouraging dreams and fantasies, self-exposures, self-discoveries, with the gentlest of urgings and directives. The psychotherapist, like a priest or a teacher, a captain or confessor, was a little like those clever, subtle sheepdogs they showed on the television here. (It was something that could, even in bleak times, make Mira love England, a nation that would put those crouched, uncanny sheepdogs up on its television screens, along with a lone jacketed whistler off to one side.) Mira felt like one of those corralling black-and-white creatures, chasing the thoughts and complexities of a person in a particular direction, into the tidy pen.

She had to do something about the Bigot. The trouble was, when a patient stirred something within the doctor, that transparency became near impossible, and instead what surged out was a cavalcade of one's own demons that obscured the patient's. It was all Mira could do not to greet the Bigot at the door with a long, bitter poem about Serbia – one of the original folk poems on the battle of Kosovo Polje, or some words of Desanka Maksimovič. Or like any nationalist, she could simply recite all the instances through the ages of the oppression of her people, the fears and terrors visited on them by a series of foreign savages (Turks, Austrians, Nazis). Thus Mira, triumphant, could tear apart this travesty of a story now circulated that Serbs were ruthless to the bone and always had been, had no cause for their actions other than their own stark, intrinsic wickedness. With the Bigot Mira's heart hammered with the desire to lecture and correct. Something similar happened, she realized, with Graham, though he was quieter with his slanders, more smug, quiet in his judgements. (More like Blair, perhaps, that morally satisfied face, believing *I am English and as an Englishman I am Right*.) With the Bigot, Mira could hear herself transmogrify into some frenzied, irrational creature she preferred not to be: she started to sound like Svetlana after a drink or two, and especially when the sanctions had been biting hard and she, hungry and furious, was wild as a dog. Even hating her government as she did, Svetlana hated the withholding West more.

This was one of the relational ironies of life, that Mira tried on the telephone with Svetlana to tone her down, to offer another view, to counter the rage of Beograd with some rational London line (It will be over soon; the Europeans do want to make peace, if not necessarily for noble reasons), only then to turn around in an English conversation and become Svetlana herself, speaking with bitterness of the former sanctions and the ways America and the West could carelessly choose to tighten the screws, unthinking of citizens' distress and deprivation, making the tightening all but invisible as they shepherded the press to one pre-selected conclusion or another – because journalists, too, were sheep and were herdable. Where were the stories about children dying in Beograd because basic medicines they needed had become scarce? Had anyone mentioned that the Croats hired a Washington public-relations firm in the early nineties to help recast their image? Was it possible that American presidents sent armies or did not in response to their own sex scandals, the need to divert attention from their lowered zippers?

Mira breathed. She made herself breathe.

He must not speak to her of Kosovo. If he spoke to her of Kosovo, she would not be able to contain herself.

Think, Mira. *Think.* Why does he come to you? Forget the politics – yes, forget the politics, forget Svetlana, forget Jasna, forget *yourself* – and think of him. This angry man. Early fifties now; fifty-two, let's say. The world disappoints him. *Remember his voice.* Two years past a divorce that still fills him with bile. His wife left him, though he has done what he can to wrench the story around, as people do, to make the rift more flattering to himself: his boredom with her had become so evident that they had no choice but to separate. How relieved he was no longer to have to live with her lists and complaints, those tiresome years of it, all the shoes and shopping and gossip – that was all she was made of, so much rubbish, and she had shaped one daughter the same way, the middle one, Alison; though, thank God, not the younger one, Jane, whom he surreptitiously adored. This teenaged daughter, the 'marriage saver' (only she hadn't, but someone, must have been the wife, had the idea when the others were quite a bit older that a baby would be just the ticket, just the thing to keep them all chained together), the Bigot clearly had hopes for her. There was a spunk and spit in Jane that he liked, and, he had said this to Mira, if there was one bloody thing about the divorce, apart from all the money squabbling and pointless flurry of accusation it engendered, it was that he no longer saw as much of Jane as he would like to.

There was something there. Something in the daughter that Mira would need to discover, or she and he together. Some link even, possibly, between this younger daughter and herself. The man allowed himself a warmth in relation to Jane that gave the lie to the ogre persona he otherwise honed so carefully.

Because the other real puzzle about the Bigot was why he came to Mira at all. Yes, he was a refugee of divorce as so many people were, each staggering through the acid-flinging ordeal of it and emerging blind, scarred and worsened, after – if free. Mira had seen dozens of victims over the years, all altered and bittered in their ways. But why did they come, once the initial venting was over? That was a question, men often didn't, of course, went the more familiar routes of drink or women instead. (He wasn't bad-looking, the Bigot, he could have had a girlfriend of some description by now, and yet he did not.) And why did The Bigot stay with Mira, given his views, real or invented, about the Serbs?

Mira sipped her tea. She listened to the curves and repetitions of one of Bach's violin concerti, hoping it might open her to something.

She made herself think. She had to find the line.

It had been Hampstead Heath on a salty afternoon, gulls in the air, children underfoot, as they climbed their way towards the view and the kites. Peter would not forget it.

Today was a humble echo, a solitary excursion. He had cancelled his meeting at the Poly without telling Mira. He did not want to worry her. Yet. Later he had an appointment with the doctor, the GP for now, to see whether the blood tests he'd had

– he hadn't told her about those either – pointed in the direction that had begun to seem likely. (The GP did not like the look of the swellings he had about the neck – the lymph nodes, apparently.) Peter was reminded of the times as a boy, as a young man, he had spent waiting for exam results. The different places in his life he had had to stand bare before the panel of judges, head dipped, awaiting the assessment that would shape his sense of self and his prospects. The eleven-plus: a place in a good grammar school. School certificate: might do well in the future, and university depended on it. Oxford degree: a First, which might allow for further academic work; or merely a Second, which would more likely lead to teaching Russian to schoolboys in stripy ties and grey shorts who would call him, with varying degrees of irony, *sir*. Peter had done well at each reckoning, and each time had known it, in spite of superstitions and second guesses. His internal examiner told him so, so that while he sweated and waited along with the others for the day of envelope opening or notice posted, a sureness had set in him, solid as earth, and he felt no surprise at the eventual news.

Now, too. Peter tried to smother his ongoing anxiety about his health and kept track of tiny diversional instances of normalcy or improvement. He had gone shopping for supper the other day without feeling terribly tired. He had eaten a sandwich at lunch, just today, and it seemed to him that he ate the sandwich because he was actually hungry and not merely to prove that he was. Yet all along he knew that some rot had set in. The internal examiner could tell that he was failing. Something within Peter was decaying; he could almost smell it.

Up the gentle slope of lower Hampstead to the initial benchy stretch of heath, where all was ducks and lunches and signs by the water stating the rules about fishing. (Did anyone fish, apart from the sleepy gulls? And for what?) Across the little bridge and, though it wearied him undeniably to do it, up the hill to the height of the kites: the view of Highgate, the clearing of light and sound, the tidy metal plaque-map. A place which invited revelations.

Peter had recognized by the time they walked there together that he was falling in love with Mira. He could feel the fall. Their conversations, shape-changing and meandering as a river, and his ability to speak to her with a freedom he had never experienced with anyone other than a dog (he had confided in Molly, occasionally, in the old days, counting on her discretion). Her lovely, tawny face, round and grey-eyed and shaped by an elsewhere that spoke in the thick unfamiliarities of her voice, which by then he heard in his mind even when they were apart. He heard Mira's voice in his ear all the time. He dreamt of things he meant to tell her. He wanted and waited only for the next time he would see her.

Had she felt those things for him? Peter had not been certain. He saw the colour in her eyes when she caught sight of him, that twitch of pleasure at the edges of her smiling mouth; and she held him, his arm, his hand, as they proceeded with near virginal caution towards the physical intimacy both surely, by that stage, anticipated. But something, too, was holding her back, he'd thought; and something was holding him back; and that day on the Heath would have to be the place to admit it.

They had walked towards the top of the hill, slowly, and as they did, before they got there, Peter decided to stop.

'Mira,' he said to her then. Suddenly it could not wait another minute. He did not know why he had withheld the fact. It was not as though he was ashamed any more, and he got along all right with the boy by then (Graham was fourteen: spotty and sarcastic, but he read, at least). All Peter could think of as a reason for his own reticence was that he felt so much for this Yugoslav-

ian woman – he'd known her for a month or two, several din-
ners' worth – that he had been frightened to tell her the truth.
But it must come. All at once. 'There's something I must tell you.
I – I have a son. Graham. He's fourteen.'

Mira had paused too. A wave broke over her and she teetered,
briefly.

'A son,' she repeated. Why had she not guessed? A divorce, of
course, London seemed to be full of them. Half her work even
then seemed to knock into divorce, one way or another. 'You
were married? Or' – this too was possible – 'you still are, perhaps?'

'No, no,' he said hastily, relieved now to tell his story. 'Neither. Never married. It was – I wasn't with Graham's mother any
longer when he was born, and she didn't tell me. About him, that
is. Till he was seven. It was all – it was rather . . .' He couldn't
find a word for it.

'Novelistic.' She was proud of that. Her English was coming
along well. She was breathing more easily now. Would it be all
right? Something in his eagerness towards her made her hopeful.
The next question was crucial. She tried to make her voice neutral. 'Does he live with you?'

'No, no. With his mother. He comes to see me alternate
weekends. We – we go for walks, play chess, or – but no, he lives
with his mother, in Oxford.'

It did break something in Mira to learn this. She had wanted
to give this man everything. Everything within her: every story,
every grief, every joy, every pleasure. She wanted to cover his
body with her own. She had wanted to be next to him. Always.
And now: now: she would have to preserve something. Hold
something back. There must be privacies. He had a son. The son
was not hers. He had a child, and the child was not hers, and she
did not want a child, and she did not want his child.

They waited still, just below the kites, whose darting colours zigzagged overhead like drunken diamond-shaped flies.

'I suppose I could meet him.' The tongue stuck in her mouth as she said it.

'Yes!' he rushed, eagerly. 'Some time,' he had added, seeing her subtle recoil. 'If – when you'd like to.'

She turned from him and thought, almost, that the turning was absolute. What a lovely man he was. The first since . . . perhaps the first ever, with whom she could imagine beating a true and companionable path through the world.

'I've never wanted to have a child,' she said, her voice rather hard (she heard it), her hands fisted invisibly in the pockets of her cardigan. 'It is not what I want.'

'I know that.' And, because love made him brave, and reckless, and because if he did not do it that very moment he might lose the possibility, the courage – he touched her, reached into her pocket for her hand, found her fingers, entwined them in his own.

'I understand,' he said to her that afternoon on the Heath, and Mira, bewildered, had wondered what it might mean if she chose to believe him.

The earth comforted her fingers. It was dark and soft as coffee, and rich with nutrients she could feel seeping into her hungry fingers. Potting soil. Always made regular dirt – the stuff that lay about the garden nurturing worms and stones – seem degraded by comparison. When Clare's father first took her into the garden and showed her how he was planting a new bed, she found the idea of soil in a bag a bit ridiculous. Wasn't packaging up earth like selling people vials full of air? There seemed to be plenty of it around. Clare's father explained to her that the soil in the bag was a special soil, rich, *smell* it (he urged her), touch it, do you feel the difference? And often when you're putting something new in, you want to give it an extra lift, a leg up. Like the milk programmes they used to have in schools, a half-pint in the late morning to keep the young ones going. Like that, Clare, you must think of these plants as children who need all the care and help you can give them. When he put it that way Clare found herself more interested. These greeneries ceased to be merely leafy bits and stringy stems, petals shaped this way or that, thorns or not, depending. Her father's words helped individuate these scatterings of colour and texture throughout their garden at the Willows and allowed her, too, to see the gruff chemist – whose face she mostly saw mottled with the flickering television light, or twitching at the newspaper, or jowling over dinner – as a man who believed in raising things. He brought the plants up. He talked to them even, a bit, with impatience and with affection (You'll like being over here much better, you old fussbudget, this corner will suit you down to the ground). Clare loved to listen to him. Washing up at the kitchen window (as a teenager, or later, visiting, after cake and tea) she heard the low flat rumble of his conversation like a train's soothing rhythms, and the sound allowed her to discover a heart in her father she had not known him to have.

Now, her hands in the earth, delving, tidying, children's voices came flying over Clare like birds. The neighbours. A boy and a girl, Simon and Martha, sweet little things on the whole. Calling loudly, ordering each other about with the authority of small people as they established the routines and rules of some new game. Clare listened as she troweled and spaded, feeling something like a child herself, making sandcastles at the seaside. 'No, you stand there. No! *Martha* – you stand there, and then I'll throw it – like this—' And more discussion, and Martha, a strong personality in her own right, engaging in a debate about some finer point of the invented rules.

'Would you like some tea?' Graham appeared at the door, a rumpled late-morning look about him though it was after noon already, Saturday sleep sticking still at the corners of his eyes. He had been reading probably, or watching Wimbledon.

'I'm all right, thanks,' Clare called back, waving a trowel. Then, while she still had his attention, she tilted her head towards the neighbours' fence, made a comic face. Eliciting no response from Graham she amplified: 'It's quite funny – they have a complicated game going.'

Graham nodded, shrugged; turned to go back inside. As he did, a ball went astray, or hit someone, *surprise*, on the cheek; or a rule was broken, or an injustice detected; or someone, simply, lost the game, whatever it was, and could not bear to lose. In any case the air filled suddenly with a siren of grief and anger, a wail that cut the cloudless sky and was not kind to the ears. Illusory, elusive residential peace torn to pieces. Life revealed as what it was: a long blind march of pain and conflict.

'Christ,' Graham muttered, hovering on the edge of the kitchen doorway, shaking his head.

Clare's stomach clenched as if the children were her own. *I'm terribly sorry. Simon, will you be quiet, stop making such a dreadful noise . . . I am sorry.* She had been trying to get them to behave, show this man how lovely children were, encourage indulgence of their strange but endearing habits. Aren't they sweet? They normally get on so well, the two of them – wouldn't you like one of your own? And then this, the peal of argument (it was perpetual: they were siblings), the keening of regret, the adamant I'm NOT playing any more! The cry, the slammed door, the instant dissolution of laughter and pleasure. Brisk summary of any human relation going wrong.

'Bloody hell,' said Graham. 'That always was my hesitation about this house – the banshees next door.'

And he turned back in to make his tea. 'Do you mind if I close the door?' he added politely. 'I can't bear that racket.'

Clare shook her head and huddled back into her planting task, willing the door to close swiftly, her husband to disappear. She wanted him gone.

She did not want him to witness her own grief, which followed hard upon the other's, as she sniffled into her soil-darkened hand, longing for a banshee of her own.

PART TWO

The Blood

Hurts! He wants to know if it hurts!

Beckett, *Waiting for Godot*

Five

July

Once the diagnosis was in, the narrative began. Illness and its treatment made a story, any literature professor knew that, and the time before the diagnosis was an antechamber, a waiting, a spell of vagueness when all the edges were soft and shapes unclear and Peter found it impossible, after, to remember what that had been like. Hadn't he always known he had cancer? Would get cancer? It seemed inevitable, scripted in his blood and bones since the early days (and weren't scientists saying as much now – genetic predispositions – bad lines of code on the helix?), holding back only until Peter was old and brave enough to admit it.

His was a soft word, though, not like the hiss of *cancer*, and if you didn't know better you might think it meant a flower or a pillow, *Lymphoma*, a breathy cushion, you might land on it, mightn't you? And yet its delicacy shrouded a deep misfortune, an insidious mistake, whereby what had turned cancerous against you was not just an organ, the liver, the lungs, the breast, the skin, but rather what was most essential to your life, to who you were. Your *blood*. Lymphoma, the doctor explained to Peter

113

in the tone of a person who thinks explanations can diminish fear, the inescapable, gut-loosening fear of death, is a broad term referring to any time there is a compromise of the lymph nodes. Your lymph nodes have become swollen and exaggerated as they try to fend off the alien cells circulating in your blood. It was *blood* Peter heard. There was something wrong with his blood. He had bad blood, apparently.

How – how does one get it? Peter had asked nervously, foolishly. It wasn't a sensible question, he knew (what did it matter, after all, now that he had it?), he felt like a nervous student who wanted to fill the air with his voice but had not read enough of the course material to ask something relevant. The point was not *how did I get it* but *how will you stop it*, yet the doctor, graciously, looked serious and thoughtful as he considered Peter's question, as though it were a reasonable line of inquiry.

It's unlikely that the lymphoma has any relation to anything you have done or not done, he said, and his tone remained calm, as if this should be reassuring to Peter, almost as reassuring as if he were saying that Peter did not have the disease at all. We know little about causes or risk factors. We know the rates of incidence are rising in industrialized societies, and particularly among younger people, but this is true of many cancers. (Peter winced at the word *cancer*: he wanted to keep it at a distance. He preferred, certainly, *lymphoma*.) There are the usual theories: environmental causes, diet, stress . . .

Peter lost interest in this part of the lesson. If they did not know, he did not much care for speculation.

How do you treat it? Now Peter tried to mimic the man's tone, the conversational, Open University tone one might use to ask about the Napoleonic Wars, or the proper declension of *hominus*. He thought it might calm his nerves to do so. There can't be anything to remove, then? His only thought of cancers were of the things one took out or irradiated. How could they irradiate his blood, or his immune system? Wouldn't he begin to glow green with it, or thinly waste away, like the early Curie experimenters who did not know the dark side of the magic they handled?

If the disease spreads secondarily elsewhere, we may remove a tumour or mass at that time. However, judging from the results of tests you've had so far, we will advance quite quickly into a significant level of chemotherapy. It appears in your case that the lymphoma is an aggressive one; they do vary. It may surprise you to know that with some lymphoma patients we do not immediately treat at all.

Peter heard the word *aggressive*. He knew enough not to like it. Aggression was never what one wanted. Not on the other side, that is.

We can discuss the details further, but I will initially propose a biweekly treatment for four months—

Do you mind, before you go on, if I ask my wife to join us?

Not at all. Of course. The doctor half-stood, gestured. He had seen this before – patients who preferred to be alone to receive the first blow, thinking perhaps it would make them braver. Others clutched their spouses to them to ward off the words. Thomas Mellon could understand either desire – the role of discussing mortality with his fellows had long since broadened him to accept almost any reaction – but he did feel badly for the husbands or wives left outside. This man's wife, for example, round and solemn when he saw her in the other room, had seemed already to be in a state of shock, and though she had a book with her, she would not, he imagined, read it, but would rather look around at the mute sage walls (they did their best to make the waiting room neutral, soothing) and wonder what secrets they contained, and what information was unfolding behind one of them, where her husband sat to hear his verdict.

Peter had waited to tell her. He must have waited and waited to tell her. Mira sat in the dull room holding her book, as if it could help her (it couldn't; nothing could), and counted the privacies her husband had stored while his body slowly brought him down. Down to a knees-bent confession he finally had to make in their bedroom, divided in pain, that something was wrong, and he could no longer keep it to himself.

They had always kept quiet with one another about their bodies. Was that it? Strange itches and uncomfortable rashes, the odd wart or growth, even her murmuring heart questions (her father had died of its failure, as had his father before him, and Mira had not forgotten that) – these were not the subjects of conversations between the two of them, much to Mira's relief. Their side-by-side companionship had been one of mind and spirit and less of body – was that it? But Peter and Mira were lovers, too, twenty-five years it had been now, more, of loving one another's bodies, and yet that, too, had been one of the wordless territories between them. They had loved each other and found comfort in each other without feeling the need to voice or catalogue. Mira had never told Peter that the pattern of hair growth along his legs reminded her of a man she had known when she was twenty, her first lover (a Croat, not that it mattered), and that stroking him there as she sometimes did brought on some unspeakable nostalgia that only added to her passion for Peter. She had never told him that she found the hair in his nose distasteful, but the hair in his ears endearing. She had stroked his calves, reaching under his trouser leg when they sat side by side in the park. She had held his ankle, his heel, his toes in her hands and rubbed them, massaged them, knowing how much of the

116

soul falls down and settles into the feet, waiting there for comforting attentions.

Nor had Peter spoken much to her, even gallantly, of her body, its potato shapes and the full breasts that drooped over the passing years. He had adored her, in his murmuring way, and his touch and nuzzle had told her as much as she needed to know of her body's ability to arouse and satisfy him. Beyond that, she wanted nothing from him, no lyrics or nicknames or compliments, all of which she associated with a man she had known once who had taken her body from her in a way she could never forgive. Had never forgiven. If Mira had worried, as she had, that marriage might compromise her deep sense of protection of her body, it had soothed her to discover in Peter a fellow hoarder of somatic secrets. They had developed, over the years, a hushed code for referring to disturbances of their internal working orders, in which little explicit had to be said, and questions were mutually agreed upon not to be asked. And that was how – was it? – he had nurtured this descent so long in silence.

How long had he known? And why had she not asked him? Each question made Mira angry, as if a better answer to either one might have forestalled the calamity she now knew was taking place behind the large dark door. Her husband was being told that he had cancer. The doctor was an oncologist. Given that he had not waved at both of them cheerfully, saying, 'No, no, it's all right – it isn't cancer at all, you can go home now – ' there was only one possibility that remained. You have it. It's got you. You, too, are going to die. Surprised?

Why had she not asked him? Mira had seen Peter weakening, had noticed his lack of appetite, had watched him holding his lower back and speaking evasively of a new and difficult stiffness. Why had she not asked him something more than *How are you feeling?* And why had she accepted his clearly understated reply,

'Not too bad, thanks. A little tired'? 'You should see the doctor.' Had she not said that to him? What had Peter answered? 'Yes, I dare say I should,' or some such deferring Peterism, and like a coward, like a fool, like an English person, she had nodded and retreated, thinking Well, after all, he probably knows best; or thinking, perhaps, I shouldn't bother him with my questions; or feeling, most basely, I don't want to know what it is, either. I am afraid to find out.

And so on he had gone, alone and uncharted, to the GP, for his first conversations and his secondary blood tests and it had only been last week that he had asked her, awkwardly, to accompany him to the hospital off Gower Street, where the doctor had ordered a spinal sample to be taken from him for a further examination. And even then the shared reticence had been a kind of conspiracy between them. Mira had asked, 'What is it? What are they looking for?' And he had said, 'There's a list. It's a sort of MOT test, they're looking at all the different parts and how they're working.' And Mira had allowed this answer to stand as though it were plausible, as though she did not know Peter well enough, as she did, to hear the quiver of anxiety in his voice and know that the joking was merely bluster and there was something he concealed from her, a tumour of information.

'Mira?' The voice came from a pale planet of a face that floated for a moment there by the night-dark door. The room was a coffin. So lost she felt, suddenly. *Where was she?*

'Da?' she answered in a voice from a choked throat, and it had been years since she had uttered that simple syllable of dislocation.

And once inside the room, seated next to him in a surprisingly soft chair, as if this were an interview they could relax into, rather than one that prompted a rigidity of posture and a shortening of breath, Mira held Peter's hand tightly while watching the doctor's creased and practised face. She noticed a great deal about the man – that his head was slightly sunk back into his neck, like that of an abused doll; that he had a large liver-coloured mole squatting plumply by his left ear, which she had a mildly savage urge to remove; that his eyes were dark and his skin sallow, as if there were something other than the sunless Anglo-Saxon in his blood. She watched Mellon wondering if his were a face, like a priest's, that she would come to know well as it guided them along this ash-scattered path. She took in little of what the man said.

Mira had the sensation of being underwater. It seemed to her that Peter and she, hands clasped tightly, were slowly drowning in front of the sallow man's heavy desk, his endless meaningless flow of language inexorably filling the overlarge room and removing from both of them the possibility of breath. Looped and distorted like the water-heavied words heard by a swimmer, snatched, empty phrases reached Mira – 'T-cells', 'lymphocytes', 'genetic mutations' – followed by a soothing-voiced cross-current: 'I know this is more than you can take in just now. The important thing for you to know is that we shall begin treatment as soon as possible and do what we can to slow down the growth of these destructive cells, which have been making you feel so unwell.'

This was the point when some listeners asked the raw, flayed question: 'What are my chances?' 'Are you telling me I have a certain number of months left? How many?' 'What are the survival rates with this kind of cancer?' Some version, direct or not, of the question mortal wanderers had asked mystics and fortune tellers always: When, sir, is my time to die? Can you tell me the length of my remaining lease on life?

When faced with such questions Mellon had a variety of

choices, and as elsewhere in the interview had to gauge the nature and tone of his reply by the degree of tremor in the asker. For some, an equally roundabout response was the right one: if they had had a hard time phrasing precisely their question, he found it best to avoid the blunt, undecorated answer. *We'll do what we can to slow the disease's advance, and have a better sense of our progress when we're some way into the chemotherapy. Everything will be done to have you feeling better and stronger, and that will be the first step towards making the disease recede.* With some patients there was simply no point in making them aware of disaster statistics and mortality rates, it would only suppress their clearly compromised immune response further as depression and resignation set in, leaving no room for hope or for fight.

Such had been the general philosophy until quite recently. Why tell? Poor buggers, keep them in the dark. In France, he had learned, the doctor's withholding of full knowledge was still the norm. But now, even in this underspoken nation (which did not altogether share the open ethos of the Americans), there was some quarter given to the idea that patients did have the right to know what lay ahead of them. Particularly if they asked. To those steeled and certain – one might imagine men would more likely be in this category, but he had encountered equal numbers of straight-speaking women – Mellon had other sentences. *There is a percentage of patients for whom the chemotherapy proves effective. If the therapy is successful, you may have more than a year, several years, though some return is most likely within two to three years. For others, the cancer progresses in spite of our best efforts against it, and may spread to other organs, in which case it can pose a very serious and immediate threat.* For this man here, benign, frightened academic in his sixties, the prognosis was not good. He seemed weak; his lymphoma virulent. *If you were to ask me, Mr Braverman, I'm afraid I'd say in all likelihood you'll be dead within the year.*

days with her New York friend Lisa, who had a one-year-old, about Jess's own baby yearnings and what to do about them. For a regular old married person Lisa was admirably tolerant of some of Jess's wilder flights of fancy. ('I'm thinking of cooking up a journalistic reason to go to Siberia, where I figure HIV rates are low, then drinking a quart of vodka in a bar and getting knocked up by some chisel-featured blue-eyed Siberian. I'll call the baby Nikita and he'll grow up to become a famous astronaut.') But Jess suspected that Lisa did not really believe Jess would go through with any of her schemes, thought she was just talking and joking, filling the international airwaves. The other person Jess spoke to was her gay friend Sue who lived in Northampton Mass. and, having just broken up with her lover of eight years, was planning to go to Guatemala and adopt a poor orphaned baby. Sue was a hardliner. 'Don't you think there are enough abandoned children in the world that you don't need to go to extreme measures to produce one of your own? Why don't you take those maternal feelings and divert them towards some disadvantaged child who really needs your help?' Which was all very true and worthy, of course, but didn't do anything directly to answer what Jess called, to Mira, the 'cry of the womb'.

'I swear to God,' she said to Mira now – she hadn't cancelled, something always drew her there, it was a compulsion – 'it's like I have a lost puppy in there, or – no – a wolf, a hungry wolf, howling. I don't know. People talk about biological clocks, as though there's just some little metallic mechanism that issues this discreet BEEP BEEP BEEP at regular intervals, or a BUZZ, which maybe becomes louder after you tap it, put it on snooze, you know – Aaah, stop, let me sleep another two years, will you, and wake me up then to see if I'm ready to have a baby?' Jess paused. (This was quite a funny image, actually; too good to waste or forget. She'd probably end up using it in the column. That was the other point of these sessions, she sometimes felt – even when Mira said little, as today, the intelligence of her presence inspired Jess to work up some good material.)

'Anyway, it's not like a clock, the womb. That's what I've been realizing. It is alive, I mean this makes sense, we're animals, the womb is somehow alive and asking, demanding, that you not ignore it any more. You know, *Pay attention to me, goddamnit.* What am I here for? What do you think I've been waiting for all these years, while you frittered away your time working out your precious career and travelling to interesting places and embarking on a series of more or less monogamous relationships none of which were ever deeply promising and so were ultimately a waste of time except in that they generated good copy for your wretched columns?'

Jess paused, but only for breath.

'I know this sounds crazy. And not just crazy – but a little as though I'm some mad fundamentalist anti-feminist zealot who thinks women's only job is to procreate. I mean, if you'd said exactly these words to me about ten years ago – five years ago, maybe even – I'd probably have called you a reactionary, or said, "*Jesus*, what kind of weird throwback attitude is that?" And here I am saying it myself. I've become this bizarre Stepford Wife, internally, not that anyone knows that about me – ' Mira wouldn't understand 'Stepford Wife' probably, but Jess was on a roll now and could not interrupt for cultural translation – 'you know, because on the outside, on a good day, I still seem like a relatively hip Londoner, with my big trainers and black trousers and my ability to drink with the best of them, and being smart and irreverent and all that. And secretly, underneath the Camden Town exterior, I'm slowly evolving into a fundamentalist Stepford Wife who'd give anything for a makeover and an hour or two's shopping in Mothercare.'

There was another pause as the girl exhaled, evidently with some sense of satisfaction. Mira was not surprised: it had come out with considerable fluency, this 'rant' as the American herself would call it. Mira waited one beat; two; three.

'*Jessica*,' she said then, her voice slow and thick, a coagulant, a brake. The younger woman looked up, her eyes bright with the adrenaline of her oration. Oration is all very well, Mira wanted to tell her, but it won't protect you from anything. It is a false sheath, a thin wrap. It can become, all too easily, a shroud. 'What are you talking about?' This was a simple, important place to start.

'What do you mean?' Jess looked impatient.

'Why are you talking about this?'

'Why?' Her tone one of irritation. 'Because – because it's what's on my mind, obviously, I mean I think about having a kid all the time, you know, it obsesses me. I've told you that.' Her face suggested that she found Mira's question absurd, but Mira declined to respond. She sank back into her self-as-owl expression: the wide-eyed, silent attender, emanating wisdom. It was something of a gimmick at times, and easy enough to resort to when her heart, mind, thought, were not fully in this room at all but were elsewhere, with Peter. Nonetheless, with the American more than with many others, the owl-self was appropriate as it stopped the woman in her own eloquence, which had in itself become a burden and a trap: she took such gratification from her own speeches, from her facility with the language, that she often forgot to stop and hear what her words actually said. To do the hard work of self-listening.

Defiant, though. Defiant, this time. The American had enjoyed this latest delivery.

'What are you asking me?' she said stubbornly, determined to make Mira work, too. 'What is the question here?'

'What is the desire you are talking about? Why are you speaking of this?'

'*I want a child,*' she said, and her voice took on an acrid edge. 'And if I didn't tell you about it, who would I tell? Who else wants to hear it? Who cares? There are thousands of women without children, it's the female condition of our time, there's nothing particularly special about my case.' Hearing herself say that, the American caught a glimpse, perhaps. Would she allow herself to see it? 'There's no one else I can say this to. It's too humiliating, and too much of a cliché,' she said more softly, and where she had been hard and glittery and oddly triumphant she was now, a moment after, flat and defeated, hearing the genuine poverty in her comment. Mira remained silent.

'So the point you're making is, how pathetic I am here because I have no one. Is that it?' Frustration in her voice now and Jess wondered, not for the first time, whether the ultimate goal of these therapy sessions was to make her feel terrible, to force her to realize with a clotted heart how many incurable mistakes she had made in her life; how she must have wandered and failed, to have wound up here, in this room, saying what she said to an older Eastern European woman. Who, apparently, found her pains fundamentally trivial. Next time, Jess thought, she should just stick to telling Mira her dreams.

Mira found all the time now that everything seemed unfamiliar. Her own room – this room, she stayed in it after the American left, feeling the hollow echoes of their conversation against her skin as if she were a blind, wings-folded bat listening for sound waves. She did not recognize it, this room. She was not comfortable in it. She had an inclination to move the furniture, perhaps sit facing north rather than south, feel a different slant of grey sky on her cheek. Would any of it make a difference? She could not feel less at home than she did now. Could not feel more restless and wrong. And it wasn't even she who was ill. Her hands and knees itched as if it were.

She sat, mute and unmoving, for an unmeasured time. Perhaps she slept; perhaps she imagined. Eventually the clock arrived at one of her allotted times and her body, used to its rhythms, tensed and wakened. More stories. Other people. Be ready for new material. Protect yourself, cover over, lose your own griefs in another's.

The clock ticked, silently. Had Mira forgotten the day? Was she so confused that she had muddled her schedule? The next patient was usually quite regular. Had she telephoned, and Mira had slept through it? She was still unable to work the answering machine properly, machines of that kind had never made themselves legible to her. She left it to Peter. She was not proud of her incompetence, but she had accepted it. As Mira waited in her chair, she found in herself a hard kernel of dread: this was one of many things she would, in all likelihood, have to learn to do by herself. This working of machines.

When the buzzer finally came Mira jumped up, as if the sound signalled the arrival of the first person at some jolly party. She smoothed down her skirt, checked there were no stray grey hairs coming out of the bun at the back of her head. She felt crease-faced, uncertain, as if she had just woken from a deep, disorienting sleep.

'I'm so sorry,' Kate said, on entering the narrow carpeted hallway. 'The trains were running very slowly. Man on the tracks.'

'Come in,' Mira said, though she turned her back on Kate as if to hide her face, which was not characteristic.

'It's such a horrible euphemism, "man on the tracks".' Kate settled herself into the chair, careful as always with her things:

sleek brown leather bag, sunglasses, novel. She still made the effort. It made her feel better to start these sessions with some semblance of ordinariness, now that she was past the point of breaking through the doors heaving with sobs.

The 'man on the tracks' had drawn out Kate's journey, making it an odious underground odyssey, soot settling blackly in her nostrils and down her throat as the minutes dragged on and they extricated some suicide's mangled body from under a set of murderous wheels. Kate had once read an account of a Tube-driver's trauma after the train he'd been driving had killed a young man in his twenties. The driver had seen the body fall half-seconds before the train had struck. There had been no time to slow or to stop. The driver could not get the image of the falling body from his eyes, nor the feel of the train's shudder on impact from his own hands and feet. The memory haunted his dreams, dulled his days, made him distant and short-tempered with loved ones and friends. He had been given medication, finally, and an indefinite leave of absence from work.

'I did think of that, at the beginning,' Kate said softly. 'Horrible and bloody, obviously, but so quick. So easy. Wouldn't have required any preparation.'

'You thought of—'

'Jumping in front of a train.' She was ashamed to admit it, though in the first of these sessions she had spoken often enough of wanting to die. And again, none of this could shock Mrs Braverman – she had heard all of it and worse before, surely. The therapist did have a rather stricken look, however. 'Sorry,' Kate added.

'For what are you sorry?'

'Oh . . .' She tucked her skirt under her legs; a lick of hair behind her ear. 'I don't know. It seems so melodramatic. Even after what happened. It just seems – you shouldn't multiply life's

127

cruelties, probably. Much as you might want to, initially.' She had been so enraged then, especially the first weeks and months, she had no compassion within her for William, nor her mother. It had not been the thought of them that had stopped her. It was, actually, thinking of the poor driver. 'What a thing to do to people,' Kate said, shivering. She could not help imagining, over and over, the falling body, hear the crunch of bone under train.

She looked out the window at a gloomy, watery sunlight. It was trying with scarce success to insinuate its way through thick banks of cloud. A squirrel stopped on the balcony in an uncanny stillness that was near photographic.

'I had a letter this week,' Kate started in a different tone. 'From someone I hardly know. A friend of my mother's who lives in the Hague.' She thought the European reference might interest the therapist. It wasn't the Balkans, but at least it wasn't England. 'It's so odd how the most comforting words come from the strangest places – you know, a neighbour on our street I've hardly spoken to dropped off a Japanese poem, simple and beautiful.' She paused to find it in her purse and read:

> 'An autumn night –
> Don't think your life
>   Didn't matter.'

She replaced the card. 'Or a cousin of William's I've never much liked, a Hooray Henry type who works in the City, wrote a lovely note about a school friend of his who was killed on a climbing expedition when they were thirteen, and his sympathy for us. Then these words, in a fax from a friend of my mother's I've met just a handful of times.' Mira did not reply, so she continued. 'It was so wise, and good. It really – helped. It seems so curious that someone's words can actually help.'

'How did it help?'

Kate sighed. 'She didn't try to make me feel better. Do you know? There are so many people who would like you to say that it's less than it is. I've had people say to me, "Well, at least it wasn't an actual child, that would be worse," or "Perhaps it was better that she died before she was born – I know someone who lost their baby to cot death and that was *so* awful" – as if – you know, as if it's important to set up some sort of order of suffering, and firmly establish that *you're not on the first rung, Kate.* All right, it's very sad, yes, poor you, but it could be worse.' Her voice was dark and bitter now. 'As if that would mean anything to me, to be told that. As if these people had even a shred of understanding of what this is like. They don't. They don't want to. They don't want to know what it's like. It's too ghastly. It's better if they can reassure themselves. *It could be worse. Terrible, yes, but—*' Her voice had twisted in mock sympathy. 'It's as though these people have no idea what it's like to lose someone. Perhaps they don't. Perhaps they never have. Or they've forgotten, if they did. People are so weak.'

She looked up briefly at Mira to make sure the therapist was still there, and awake, but she didn't really want her to say anything. Kate just wanted to speak, freely. 'You know, I've started to hate people. I never used to. William was always the misanthrope, and my role was to persuade him that people weren't as bad as all that. But they *are* as bad as that. They don't know a bloody thing. I mean friends, even, as well as strangers. People who write or say something idiotic. People who ring up and want to talk about something else. I know, I'll distract her with my very tedious story about the latest row I had with my husband, *that* will help. – Then there are the friends who never wrote or sent anything at all. Nothing! Just never wrote – anything. Don't they know? Hasn't anyone ever told them? Don't they know that you must write something to someone, even if it is feeble and inadequate? That's the only thing you can do. People do want a card or a letter – anything – they want every card they can receive, they want the greatest number, a number commensurate in some tiny measure with what they've lost.'

Mira was perhaps starting to comment, but Kate couldn't stop. 'I must have told you about my friend Charlotte. An old friend, known her since school, also married late, also going to be a late mother – our babies would have been nearly the same age.' And here the tears came again, but Kate was too angry to spend time on them. She swept them away from her cheeks impatiently. 'And bloody Charlotte, a *month* after Cassandra died, sent me the announcement of her daughter's birth. Can you imagine? A little footprint – "Sophia Antonia".' Kate's face was livid. 'What does it take to do that? What sort of incredible blindness? You just want to – you want to smack people. Pick them up and shake them. I wrote her a letter. *How could you fucking dare.* William wouldn't let me send it.' She shook her head. Her pretty mouth was sour and compressed. 'I'll never see her again. I couldn't.'

And here Kate paused, giving Mira time to ask, after allowing the pause, 'What did the other letter say? From your friend in the Hague?'

Kate cleared her face, allowed the rage to drain a little. And in fact she felt the tautness loosen and change as she thought of the words from this woman she hardly knew. Margaret. Kate's voice became a hush, a dove.

'She just wrote about Cassandra. Not about anyone else, or anything else – just about Cassandra. That she had been shadowed by this story, and how strange it was that from so many miles away she kept imagining this little girl, Cassandra, and who she might have been. And she said—' Here again the tears started, but how could she help it? When would she ever be done weeping? 'She said she realized she didn't know Cassandra as I knew her, that I would always be the person who had known her best and that no one could know what I did. And that that must be very difficult, because I'd never be able to tell anyone fully what she was like; but that – that I must hold on to what I had known, and who she was. And that in that sense I'd never lose her.'

Kate's eyes were closed, and her hour was over. But Mira did not hurry her. She wanted Kate to have the time she needed there, her eyes closed, collecting herself. Mira's discretion was for the Madonna's sake, but not only hers. Because if Kate looked up now she would see the face of her therapist also streaked by a silent, furtive wetness. And that was, professionally, considered a weakness one ought not show.

It couldn't be helped. One could not cancel selectively; the whole structure would collapse if one started down that road. Today you might feel able to manage the Widower and the Sulker, but not the American, the accent would grate and you would fret to hear the underground arrogance. Cancel her. Tomorrow – yes to the Mousy Student and the brittle Aristocrat, but not the Mourning Madonna. It's too terribly sad: her grief would overwhelm you. Another day? Oh all right, yes to the American, she's the only remaining superpower after all, you should take pity on her, it's lonelier than you know; and perhaps the sadness of the Mourning Madonna might feel apt today with the worries and war weariness of your own. But God protect you from the Bigot. You will not have the strength to manage the Bigot.

No. One was not permitted to select. Mira's was an ironic work, shaped as a response to human frailties and confusions, in which the practitioner was not to be seen having either. In

131

accompanying patients through their demands and inconsistencies one had to be silent and consistent, the trust necessary for the patient's unfolding depending largely on the therapist's perceived selfless stability. In that sense, too, Mira had the feeling that being a psychotherapist was like being a parent. Children will have tantrums and stubbornnesses, unreasonable requests followed by warm gusts of affection; adults and parents will, ideally, not. (Mira's worry over Svetlana as a mother had been that, starved of the stage, she enacted her dramas and tragedies – with Dušan, primarily; though there had been others – in front of Jasna and Josip; and she felt that you could see the afterlife of these dramas in the sag of Jasna's now-grown shoulders, the twitch of her cigarette-seeking fingers. It was not entirely a surprise to Mira that Josip, overly loved, required after Dušan's desertion to stand in as Svetlana's main companion, her one faith, her beloved – might, when older, flee his mother's embrace. Might not call for years. Might try to escape the gaze, the too-strong press of flesh, the parent turned child in her insecurity and need.)

The buzzer rang. *No.* Mira did not want to see him, she wanted to lurk, to hide in her hold, her confessional. She spent longer than needed raising herself from her chair, making her way over to let him in. She expected a second buzz. The Bigot was impatient; you had the feeling not so much that he was eager to begin, but rather that he was counting his minutes by the pounds and pence, wanted to get full value for his money.

He did not ring twice. Mira buzzed him in, heard his recognizable weight in the hallway and, an inadvertent gesture, crossed herself before opening the door. Where had that spontaneous prayer come from? Was the Bigot, too, the devil? Was he a harbinger of death? She would have to ask herself later.

He came in calmly. Oh, he still hated her, but today he felt

132

that she would not be able to get to him, burrow under his skin, bringing on rash and rage. He felt protected. Besides, he was halfway through, now; it was July. There was some comfort in that.

Howard sat on the familiar chair and waited. He looked out the window. Who, he wondered, had first devised this strange system, two people sitting in a room together, one of them paying for the privilege of being able to speak without interruption and without the need to apologize for his complete self-absorption? He knew it had to do with Freud, of course. But could one man, even an Austrian (perhaps they were all megalomaniacs, in their ways), have foreseen the vast global industry he would spawn? Howard had seen pictures of him, the spectacles, the beaked nose, the cigar. In his way he was like Henry Ford, or the man who invented steam engines. A captain of industry. Howard liked that idea. He would tell Jane later. She might find it amusing.

He would see her later. That was what made Howard safe today. He would see her every day this week and the next: she was staying a full two weeks with him. Not that it should be such a bloody miracle, two weeks with his own daughter, but this was how the divorce had weakened and unmanned him, taking from him the people he loved. All right, Monica, leave me, I shall manage without you and with some relief, let me tell you. But don't take the others, for Christ's sake. Oh, all right, take Alison, Alison has left home anyway and has had her suspicions of me for some time, never really recovered from various adolescent catastrophes, eating problems and all that. And bloody Richard – that had been a bitter pill to swallow, seeing how quickly the boy snapped up his mother's version of Howard's long list of failings and errors. But don't take my Jane, Monica. Don't take from me Jane.

'My daughter is with me this week,' he thought he might as well say as an opening. He didn't have the spirit, today, to launch in about the Serbs, though the news from Kosovo was gorier by the day.

'Ah,' she said, or perhaps 'Oh.' It was such a quiet, unconfident sound that Howard looked at Mira more carefully. Was something the matter with her? He looked her in the eyes, something he did not do often, and was surprised to see how little defence there was in them. Had he caught her unprepared? Had she not readied herself to see him? She often seemed steeled against him, he'd noticed.

'Is something wrong?' he asked bluntly. 'Are you all right? Or is that one of those questions I'm not allowed to ask?'

She folded her hands in her lap neatly, over one of her full corduroy skirts. (Someone ought to help her with her wardrobe, really – couldn't the husband give her a suggestion or two? She had a husband, obviously – *Braverman* – not a Serb name, that.) She looked down so that her eyes were no longer available to him.

'Thank you,' she said, in her obscure, obscuring voice, and he could see that was all he was going to get from her. Generally this would have aggravated him, and he might have pushed or prodded to try to learn more. But he did not have the heart, with his own temporary happiness. Mira looked different to Howard today. She was not a Serb monster at all. Not now. She was a sad older woman, heavy in her chair, to whom someone had recently delivered some sort of terrible news.

Dear Graham

Peter had been staring at the two words for some time without any inclination to add to them. Every time he picked up his pen with half a phrase in his mind – I thought this would be a good time . . . I wanted to write you a note, to . . . You may be surprised . . . – his eyes would wander across the desk and on out of the window, against which tapped a thin, plaintive rain. July rains: warm and troublesome, dashing hopes everywhere for nice wedding photos, or picnics.

He'd had some idea, had he not, that he would send Graham a reckoning letter. Was that right? Or some full discussion about having a child, that's right, how it had gone wrong in his own case, and how distressing that had been, along with an exhortation to Graham not to disappoint that lovely young woman he'd married. Good Lord, son, he would have said if he'd been a figure from some not very good post-war novel, the girl wants a family! Who can blame her? Do the right thing, boy, give her what she wants.

Now the thought of saying anything so specific or directive seemed exhausting to Peter. Trying to have an influence on someone else's life or decisions: what a tiring prospect. He had so little energy himself, and he had not even started the treatments yet, which he knew would be debilitating and awful. Hence a letter rather than a telephone call: it was such a greater effort to speak than write. He must save what energy he had for himself. For his own wrecked body, his own harried deterioration.

They were starting next week. No time to waste, Mellon had said, we must start work on this right away, with the determination one might use in reference to a building project – fixing a leaking bath, for example, or replacing the roof. If there was some implication that Peter might have submitted himself to tests earlier in order to have caught the disaster sooner in its trajectory, Peter made an effort not to hear it. The etched acid of the word *cancer* was such that other words faded beside it, and there was a way in which every other sentence of the doctor's had been a wasted emptiness, released into an unlistening air. It was Mira who had told Peter when the treatments were to start, though she too had been vague about how often he would go and what was entailed in the sessions. They would have to ring, as the doctor had suggested, for clarification. There was a telephone just near Peter on the desk; he considered it, then looked away.

> *Dear Graham,*
> > *I remember*

He did remember. He remembered seeing Graham for the first time. He'd seen Lydia first, the boy's mother, differently hairstyled but recognizably the woman he had found modestly attractive eight years earlier, at least until he had discovered in their stuttering conversation how hard it was to talk to her. Lydia was nervously helping the boy out of the Mini as Peter watched from the steps outside his flat. He had expected – what? A miracle? A revelation? Some thrill of recognition, blood from his blood, self from his self? He saw a boy with a slight cold, nose pinched and runny, dark hair in a child's approximate haircut, face cautious and half-averted from this mythical figure, the Father. Lydia led the boy by the hand across the road, a rushed and distracted expression on her face. Playing god had, it transpired, required a dignity and largesse she found difficult to muster. 'That's him, love,' she said redundantly to her son. 'That's Peter. Your dad. Say hello.'

And he did, a small mumble, not quite looking into the face of the man he had spent various hours and evenings and dreams imagining. He did not seem to feel a lightning strike either. *That's my dad?* Peter could hear him thinking. *That's it? That's him?*

Peter crossed out 'I remember'.

He put the pen down and ran a hand over his face. Perhaps it would be better to begin on a new sheet.

Dear Graham,

He wrote more confidently now. It had occurred to him, finally, what he had to say to his son.

I'm afraid I have some rather bad news to tell you. I have been diagnosed with lymphoma. It is a form of cancer, a cancer of the blood, of the lymphocytes. The doctor recommends I begin treatment next week.

As I have been feeling unwell for some time, it is in some measure a relief to know what is wrong. I believe I have a good doctor, he seems experienced in this area.

I hope you and Clare are well. Do keep in touch.

with love from

'Peter,' he would normally have written, but in a surprising flourish he wrote, instead, 'your Dad'.

Six

August

There was no way to make them seem other than they were, these rooms. No number of posters or magazines – not that any of them tempted, they were out of date and dust-eared and thickly oiled with the sweaty fear of distracted fingers. It was an antechamber, this room, and Peter had already in this short journey known too many of those. Already realized that each stage of this ending (No, no, he tried feebly to urge himself, don't think that way, mustn't think that way; but his body spoke its bleak certainties above the clamours of false hope) had a wait before it. If death was a series of steps down, of trains heading deeper underground, each one seemed to have its own platform with reading matter and advertisements – Eat healthily, here's how; Interested in meditation? – its chipped chairs and poor lighting, lighting designed always, apparently, to draw out the greenest and most morbid shades of one's complexion.

They would call him in due course, he had been told, and then he would go through, for his first infusion of corrective poison. He sat deafly, considering the word *chemotherapy*, a sinister sound he had heard over the years in association with friends who had 'successfully' battled cancer, forestalling its triumph, or else who had submitted ignominiously to defeat. 'Yes, the chemotherapy was dreadful,' they always said, 'but it did the job, she's better now, they seem to have got rid of it,' or alternatively, 'and all for nothing, can you imagine? The growth came back, and she died a year on anyway, bald and ravaged by the so-called medicine.' He shuddered. Whose notion had it been to attach that bland palliative 'therapy' to the prefix? Therapy was massage, or conversation, the work Mira did speaking and listening and urging and comforting – surely 'therapies' were not meant to contain toxins, even toxins thought to have grim benefits? He must ask Mira about that. Mira was beside him now, but would not come in with him for the treatment itself. 'I wonder – ' he turned to her, but he was unsure whether he could summon the spirit to engage with her here in one of their old, familiar kinds of conversation, a word and its resonances. She looked up, startled, from the book she had brought with her.

'Mr Braverman?' came the dull summons from the hushed half-open door. A nurse stood with a kind expression sketched professionally across her features.

That was true of the platforms, too: just as you settled into the reading material, or began an interesting conversation, the train arrived, cutting off talk with its noise.

Mira clasped Peter's hand before he stood. He tried, as he'd watched others try before him, to maintain a no-nonsense bearing in the face of this promised therapy.

'I should take a walk if I were you,' he said brightly. 'Do something cheerful. They said it would take a couple of hours.'

'Perhaps I will. Do some shopping.' She tried to smile, as if this were a pleasing prospect, a jolly outing to Tesco's or Habitat. 'But I'll be here when you're finished,' Mira promised him, her voice thick enough to touch, and it was a protection Peter planned to take with him as he went into the next unseen room to whatever chemicals awaited him.

She was noticing her dreams. They seemed at times, like this morning, to continue even into wakefulness. She was in a terrible hurry to get to the bank. Must get to the bank, withdraw money. What did she need so much money for? To pay for his grave, Peter's grave. He had already died and Mira must bury him, but it was a Friday, the Friday before Easter, and she had to get the money out and then get to the cemetery to buy the grave before the holiday weekend. But it all took too long. The bus wouldn't come. The cemetery closed and so his body would remain unburied, slowly spoiling in a back room, while she went to her church for the great Orthodox Easter service. She needed it this year more than ever. The deep music, the gratitude for the miracle. Christ, yes. The hope for resurrection.

This coffee was tepid and she did not know why she drank it, except that it was a gift from Peter and she had not wanted to refuse it. A sign of Peter's disorienting nervousness, that had him rushing Mira out of the flat impatiently, only to arrive at the hospital three-quarters of an hour early, a stretch of time filled by a stop in one of those colourful new coffee emporia where he bought a pallid, distressed croissant he didn't touch and a coffee drink for Mira though he knew she generally drank tea. Tea was her English comfort, her stewed brown sustainer; coffee was a drink of journeys elsewhere, France, Italy, countries that had believed in it for years. *Yugoslavia*. Home. The drink thicker there, Turkish some would call it, dark and true and bitter, nothing better. These new American cafe chains dispensed a different sort of drink altogether, milky and emasculated, the way Americans had previously dispensed beef burgers and blue jeans, defying the rest of the world not to share their tastes and proclivities. The bronzed cafes had proliferated suddenly, even in Camden Town, making London less the London Mira had once known and loved. (There was a time before Peter, when the city was like a lover for Mira, she was passionate for its textures and scents, its sounds and its humour.)

When the paper cup (paper! that was all wrong, too) was presented to Peter at the cafe he had handed it on to Mira as if it were a gift of jewellery or flowers. Recognizing the faded gallantry in the gesture, Mira took it, keeping a neutral face. Her professional techniques were already proving useful in handling her ill husband, though Mira was splintered by the realization that Peter was becoming a patient as well as friend, companion, husband. She knew about patients. There were rules and principles for dealing with patients – their abrupt vulnerabilities, their irrational outbursts.

The coffee was cool now and she was not going to drink it. Neither was she planning to walk. The effort of movement was beyond her. She looked for a bin, and in casting about allowed herself to look for the first time at the other sitters in this grim room. Singles and pairs: a lone, neatly dressed man in his late forties, reading from a business folder (civil servant? solicitor?); a couple in their fifties or sixties, holding hands and looking abstractedly at the wall posters. Two middle-aged women talking. Mira was reassured by the general calm and normalcy of the group's appearance: with the pairs, it was not even easy to say which of the two was likely waiting for treatment. So cancer was a scourge, yes, but as one had known already, a universal scourge. It chose the weak and strong alike, the fat and the thin, the old and the less old.

One figure, a plump, sausage-and-chip-faced man, made less effort than the others to play the stoic. His lion head was hidden in thick-fingered hands, his shoulders drily heaving. His straining shirt suggested to Mira a pounding, unhealthy heart, reminding her of her father.

Mira traveled home inwardly, to Nikola; thought of her father's blue-veined eyes, his creviced skin, the brown on his teeth from the cigarettes and the angled illogic of his laugh, when he laughed, because he always stood to one side of the subject at hand – had seen too much the dangers of standing square in the light to risk directness. He had never been the same towards the two girls. Mira he treated as the one who knew and understood him better, but that knowledge brought with it greater responsibility, a greater cost for crossing him. He was, on the whole, doting and gentle with Svetlana. Of Mira he expected more. She remembered him watching her once, when she was sixteen and questioning him over something – whether she might go to the cinema with a boy he did not care for, whose family he distrusted. The look of bewilderment and nascent rage in his eyes had stopped her. *You?* his face said, accusingly. You would do this to me?

A door opened from the chamber within. A pale scarved woman emerged, grey under her eyes, hapless and weary and thin. A patient. She looked, Mira thought, like a creature from the afterworld, come to warn the room's inhabitants against sinning.

Immediately the large man stood, brushing his thick hand across his damp face. He approached the waif. Not husband, surely, though such was possible? Mira read the eyes, the heavy arm that wrapped itself, a sturdy mantle, around the young woman's brittle frame and in the shattered blue of his too blue eyes Mira read who he was, saw his swallowed greeting to the young and obviously dying girl. The father. They were father and daughter.

Mira wanted to speak, to give a hand, to give them help, but this was not the place for it. She had nothing to do in this room, nothing, but wait for her husband.

She should not enjoy it, but she did. If only, primitive thought, he were willing to do his share. If only he were willing to be a *husband*. She was ready to be a wife.

You could not say as much to anyone without fear of sounding like some pathetic creature who had missed the main events of the twentieth century, and failed to notice that women were not now what they had been once. Her sister Sara, for example, still fiery with university certainties (she was twenty-four), would heap scorn on Clare's efforts to prepare for a *dinner party*. Either because she thought dinner parties were so middle class (as if Sara and Clare were anything but), or because if Clare and Graham were to engage in such a thing Clare should at least insist on a reversal of roles, with Graham the sort of modern man who cooked and sweated in the kitchen while his wife offered wine and conversation in the next room.

Such was not their structure. The ugly truth was that Clare took a real, if guilty, pleasure in planning a menu, shopping for it, preparing it. There was more of her over-floral mother in her than she might earlier have guessed, when she was at university and shared those certainties of Sara's. Not that Clare felt this was her duty or her destiny, but it gave her something, in her under-furnished interior, to cook well for others, to provide, to satisfy. Furthermore, it hastened and enhanced her sense of having embarked on a proper, adult life with Graham. And – Clare admitted this only in a hollow pocket of herself, the hollowness that pushed and ached against her – if the two of them could master this stage of a marriage, wouldn't the next stage become unavoidable? Wasn't this elaborate meal-making a rehearsal (and who could she confess this hope to? nobody), for the meals Clare more fervently wished to make – a simple roast chicken and potatoes, pasta with tomato sauce, even perhaps, on a tired evening, beans on toast for smeared small mouths and greedy hands, loud and high and demanding voices?

'So who's coming?' Sara, though sceptical, was always good for a gossip. She liked to tease her older sister about her life in Bath – whose 'a' she insisted on drawing out in mock-Southern languor. Sara lived in Brighton, where she had been a student and still had the borrowed furniture, unemployed boyfriend and vegetarian diet to show for it.

'Graham's friend David, who's also a solicitor, and his wife Anna. She's a journalist – writes a column in one of the papers—'

'The *Daily Telegraph*? The *Financial Times*?'

' – About life with small children. You know, sort of jokey, isn't it all very difficult and chaotic, but aren't they sweet little monsters really.'

'God. Put her on the other end of the table. She'll only make you depressed.'

'I'm planning to. She's a bit flighty in any case. Likes to flirt with the men. And his friend from work, Mark. The one with the Saab—'

'Does Graham still go on about that bloody car?'

'A bit. When he's not moaning about how expensive our holiday in Italy's going to be. He'd rather spend fifty quid walking in the Scottish Highlands, I think.'

'God, the dilemmas you two have. *Italy this year, darling, or Scotland?*'

'All right. I'm not finished.' Clare was chopping onions now, her eyes tearing. 'Mark was going to bring someone, a girlfriend, but it fell through. She's chucked him, apparently. So he's coming on his own. I'll sit next to him, and he can console himself by talking about the Saab.'

'Is that everyone?'

'No. Another pair – Hugo, an old school friend of Graham's he thinks I won't much like. And his wife. They don't have children, which is supposed to make me feel better, I suppose. He hasn't said as much, I'm left to work it out for myself.'

There was a pause.

'Clare, why don't you just lie?'

Clare stopped chopping, brushed the tears from her nose. 'How do you mean?'

'I would.' Clare heard the telltale exhalation. Sara was always quitting and starting again. A vegetarian who smoked: Clare thought it comical, but Sara did not see any contradiction. 'I mean – just tell him you've taken the pill, and stop taking it.'

'I don't take the pill.' Clare lowered her voice, though she was alone in the house.

'You don't? What, then – a cap?'

'Yes.'

'There you are, then. Stop wearing it. He'll never know. And then afterwards, tell him it must have torn. They do tear. I know someone that happened to. She had to have an abortion.'

Clare winced. 'Could we—'

'Sorry. I'm just saying, you don't have to sit back and wait. If he's being so bloody-minded, just lie to him and get on with it.'

'But—' The onions spat and sizzled as they hit the pan. 'What sort of basis is that – I mean, a child born out of a lie, how could that work?'

An even louder exhalation. 'Oh, Clare, don't be such a—'

'Such a what?'

'You sound like Mum.' It was an effective conversation closer. They both stopped over the injury: Clare, stung; Sara, guilty. 'I just mean—'

'Look, I'd better get ready. Graham's back in less than an hour.'

'Sorry. I'm sorry. I was just trying to say – I was just trying to help.' Her sister sounded apologetic, but also defiant. There often came a point in the conversations between them when the subject of Graham became a minefield. 'You want a child, Clare. It's the least that bloody man can do for you. Given everything you do for him.'

Had she done so much for him? Clare wondered. Yet even as she chopped and prepared, she felt her sister was right. *It's the least that bloody man can do.* She could not say as much to Sara, of course. She could only allow the shallower of her difficulties with Graham into the conversation with Sara at all, lest a deluge of sororal criticism of her husband overwhelm Clare and her fragile contentment. She was not always sure that she would be able to argue back, defend Graham and defend the two of them together. Were all marriages like this? Thin skins of peace stretched tight over drums of doubt and uneasiness? There was no one for her to ask. Sara didn't know. Her own boyfriend was useless, she often said so, but she had not yet got round to splitting up with him.

It's the least that bloody man can do. Perhaps Sara was right. But what sort of beginning would that be to a child's life?

Graham opened another bottle of the burgundy and poured it round. He was at that expansive point in the evening when everything merged: he was no longer seated at a table with separate elements, colleagues, school friends, wives; drained, crimson-stained bottles on the table; plates half-cleared of ingredients he recognized and some he didn't, lamb smothered in something that left a pleasing richness on the tongue. He felt rather that he was not at a table at all, he was carried along on a current,

146

buoyed by the flavours and noise and stories. Graham could be funny with the right company, and Hugo and he had always made each other laugh, something about having been at school together, fished together, gone to a few moderately painful parties together as teenagers – made them able to carry on a routine of sorts that had everyone at the table going, even Clare, though she was of a bit of a blur at the far end, across from Mark, keeping the poor lad company.

Graham knew Hugo was probably a bit of a bastard, and not in the technical sense. He had hinted to Graham once a year ago or so about an affair he was having with a research assistant at the House of Commons. Graham felt mainly fascinated, and oddly jealous. And yet the marriage had survived it. In fact you had to say that Hugo had found a good match in Caroline, who came from the political as well as social aristocracy. (Graham hoped Clare had not recoiled visibly at Caroline's upper-class bray; it took some getting used to.) Caroline had a savage sense of humour, and she and Hugo performed a sort of hilarious daredevil act together of mutual insult and exaggeration, decorated with emphatic *darlings*. Though tonight Caroline seemed a bit subdued –

'More wine, Caroline?'

'I won't, thanks, Graham. Lovely burgundy, though.'

– and talking seriously to Clare. They were engaged in some line of women's talk – *All men are bastards. How do you cook duck* – but no, Graham was trying not to differentiate pieces of the evening, he was too much enjoying the sensation of oneness with his company, of the night's essential coherence; and yet he did catch the phrase 'IVF' from that end of the table, an unpleasant pebble of a harder reality, and he remembered now others of Hugo's lines from that lunch they'd had last year, 'spending quite a lot of time at the baby lab these days, filling vials, it's pretty grim, actually' – which had perhaps led to the revelation about the research assistant. Graham shuddered. The mechanics of producing a child in that way – he could not bear to think about it. Producing a child in the ordinary way was nerve-racking enough, but *that* . . . Clare was fascinated, evidently. God. Let them talk. Keep him out of it. Closer to hand, David and Hugo were going at it about Blair and Europe, whether Labour had pulled a fast one on the electorate, trying to walk both sides at once, and that was more to Graham's taste, a bit of seriousness, the argumentative stretch, Anna coming into it as well, all to the good, she was attractive, Anna, ample breasts and long dark hair, a self-conscious pout or giggle. She had a full, appealing mouth and she knew it, pursed her lips suggestively, why not? He made sure everyone had enough wine and he picked up the conversation at his elbow. 'Yes, but if Gordon Brown genuinely thought . . .'

And on it flowed. Clare clearing away the plates, he and David and Hugo in the thick of it now, murmurs of appreciation about the food from Caroline, she had impeccable manners, and Clare disappeared for some time into the kitchen only to emerge again at last with seven bowls and a bowl of lightly dressed berries, it may have been August and autumn threatening (first a holiday, though, he was strangely fearful of it – Italy) but there was still summer to be had. And she had made a fool, sweetly, a dish from which Graham was instructed, a bit briskly he thought, to serve. Gladly he did, while continuing in a quieter tone now with David and Hugo, David launching into a long story about a client of his who did business in Germany, how it was for British businessmen to negotiate around their nation's loudly expressed ambivalence towards a federal union. Balanced against the loss of sterling, national sovereignty, all that. Whether NATO supported the arguments for or against the European Union, finally, and then a solemn nod to NATO's idiotic dithering over the Balkans, the uncertainty of how to respond to a civil war tearing apart some non-member countries down the road.

Anna drifted at that point, Graham noticed, the political conversation wearying her, fair enough, he was getting a bit bored by it too now, frankly, what could you say about the Balkan disaster after a certain point except that the Serbs should have been kept in line long ago, but then David turned back from the Balkans to Frankfurt, trade barriers, and it was at this point that Graham noticed a warm blush suffuse his wife's cheeks: someone must have paid her a compliment. Mark, evidently, judging by the way Clare shyly kept her eyes cast away from him. What on earth could Mark have said to Clare? Evidently something delicate, as he saw Caroline turn and exchange looks with Hugo; though Anna, quite drunk now (Graham could suddenly see it), was keen on echoing whatever Mark had just said to Clare. Graham leaned in, slightly, while nodding still in the direction of Europe and the Union, listening for the content of Anna's echo.

'It's true,' Anna said with a burgundian sincerity different from the tone she had taken earlier with himself and Hugo. 'It's true, Clare. You'll make a wonderful mother.'

But it was Mark Clare had listened to. Mark! A different girlfriend every month and he had softened her, Graham saw, Clare was beautiful in the pleasure of his remarks and attention, and there was Mark looking pleased with himself at having drawn her out, the host's lovely if rather shy wife. Her secret passion. Her throaty longing. He had touched her.

'Fantastic dinner, darling,' Graham called to her now over the din, borrowing the 'darling' from his old school friend (it did not suit him or his voice) and interrupting David in the midst of some other interminable sentence about Germany, but Clare scarcely looked up at him to acknowledge the praise, so absorbed was she by the deeper, more important appreciation of the man across from her at the table.

She had bought the tickets before they knew, but it still seemed like a good idea to go. Mira felt it was important for both of them. The excursion taken now not merely for its own sake, but as proof and as testament. We are not going to be turned away from living. We are here, in spite of the disease. *We are not going to speak and think only of the war.* Mira remembered Svetlana saying that a few years or so before. We can talk of things other than the wars. *Please.* Tell me about London. Tell me about a play you've seen recently: who was in it, was she good (would I have been better?), did you howl, was it laughter or the other kind of howling.

Possibly a sheer comedy, a farce, would have been a better choice, but Mira could not have known that when she bought the tickets. And it wasn't *Medea*, it wasn't *Lear*. They would not be compelled to watch a person tear himself limb from limb on the stage in grief or madness. It was one of those clever, living playwrights' latest offerings and it would have humour and ideas and characters, she hoped (she hoped the ideas would not over-whelm the characters). One of their favourite older actresses was starring and it would take them somewhere else, as the theatre always did or promised to. Somewhere else was beginning to seem a good place to be.

Peter had faintly suggested he was all right to take the Tube, and Mira was glad she had not believed him. (He had become more optimistic after that first round of chemotherapy, briefly. They were beginning to cure him, weren't they? Sicker though he felt?) Even in the taxicab Peter's frame seemed pressed against the seat back as if he were an unwilling passenger in a demand-ing space pod, and his face looked unhealthy in the orange of the

City's lights as they blurred through the cab's rain-mottled window. 'Shame – I always like walking across the bridge,' Peter said, and as the cab rattled towards Waterloo they each thought of it and whether, perhaps, they would ever have that together again, their customary walk from Embankment, the rushing feet, commuters and culturalists alike beetling towards the South Bank, and then the cement walkway on the other side, annotated by the circling, scraping rhythms of furtive skateboarders.

They arrived, finally, without time for the pre-performance drink, a ritual enjoyed by the suited and scarved and skirted and animated. Not that Peter could drink now in any case. And he was as glad not to watch them all milling about, it was tiring even to look at them, the standing and healthy, those who were not planning to die, any of them, who had every intention of living and staying. Not for them the humiliating journeys into a room of tubes and toxins and benign nurses and less benign nurses.

'We must find our seats,' Peter said to Mira.

And as they seated themselves – Mira had found a good place for them, not so close that they would be splattered by the sweat and spit of the performers, but not so far that they would be more aware of the chocolate-unwrappers and tense coughers than of the drama unfolding – Peter felt a wave of new panic. The proximity to other bodies made him nervous. What if the blond-bobbed woman on his right had flu, or even a cold? That ancient gent was pulling out a handkerchief, did that not signify sickness? The doctor had impressed upon Peter that he must be especially careful now about exposure to germs. Why had he come out at all? Why this false and damning confidence, after one round of treatment?

Peter was empty entirely of the familiar sense of expectation as the lights dimmed, the moment previously when he would release himself into the great vaulted chamber with other strangers and

151

await the actors' hands and voices, ready to lead the audience deep into the ground of some new story. It had been one of his truest pleasures, going to the theatre. (Theirs together: more characters to share.) Nothing else could touch it. Film had always seemed so thin and watery to him by comparison. *Filmy*, as the name suggested, moving pictures merely. Actors who could do this, throw themselves at you, night after night, had seemed to him in a minor way like gods. In another life he might have known one. Might have married one.

The scene opened and Peter had nowhere to look but *there*, no one to listen to but *her*, and so in spite of his doubt and his building resentment (how angry he was at Mira, now, for not knowing that he couldn't do this, for encouraging him in this exhausting ordeal), Peter unwrapped himself and let the voices in.

When he did, he was suffused. By her. It was she, and she was divine, crop-haired and not beautiful in a conventional sense but possessed of a humour and a resilience that gave her eyes a light he could see even from a distance. One felt instantly close to her; one *knew* her. She was playing an actress, and Peter soon involuntarily lost the distinction between person and role as he watched the woman move through the challenges and crises of her life, as though there were nothing separating him from her. She had a wayward son who had lost a good deal of money and had inadvertently helped her to lose hers, too. She was ageing, and there were the attendant embarrassments (how Peter sympathized!). Acting was an unkind profession for anyone who had the audacity to age. Another child, a daughter, had married unwisely, and the son-in-law appeared to make remarks that were topical and political but Peter did not pay much mind to them or him. Above all he felt for the actress, who had recently broken off an affair she was having (with a politician; Peter had

152

no interest in him, either) and was choosing now to go through these crises alone. What courage that took! To be sixty, perhaps, alone. He admired her. In one scene she sat backstage having a conversation with her son, as she slowly stripped herself of gloss and mask and returned to the naked expressive pallor of self outside performance. The son stood behind her, arguing that the losses had not been deliberate or foreseen, that he was not in fact responsible. Across the imagined mirror the two exchanged looks of scepticism and frustration and, above all, in spite of everything, love. She had that light in her eyes. She would forgive him. She could not help but forgive him, her son.

It ended, finally, on a note of surprise and acceptance and by the time it did Peter had no idea where he was and had forgotten the body that encased him. Nothing he had been thinking of before mattered, now. He was filled with the spirit of the actress (his hands could not applaud enough) and if he placed a palm on the shoulder of his female companion – at whom he had been so angry, hours before – it was perhaps less a gesture of affection for the Serbian therapist he had made his life with than it was a silent communication with the woman he had just watched on the stage, who'd had the supreme generosity to take him somewhere else. He adored her. She was, in Peter's view, an angel.

As she packed, she hesitated. A darkness had stirred in Clare since that conversation with her sister, and since that confusing dinner, and she no longer held her marital promises quite so certainly. Look at that troubling couple Caroline and Hugo, who in some ways seemed to loathe one another, or at least find each other ridiculous; and yet as the evening had worn on their mutual teasing had developed a momentum, and the stories they told were very funny, if generally demeaning to one or other of them (Graham had laughed uproariously), and by the end of the evening Clare had come to believe they were perfectly matched. (Graham told her later that Hugo had had an affair, and to her surprise Clare found herself saying with conviction, 'He's had more than one.' You could see it in his vulpine features.) There was some question in Clare's mind about their not having children; Caroline had turned abruptly away from the subject, Clare noticed with the sharp eye of one for whom that question – children, or no children? – was the defining, essential one to ask of any person, of any couple.

Sara had suggested she tear it. Clare stood holding the plastic box and staring at its contents, the earplug-coloured disc that reminded her of one of the outer planets. It had a cosmic function, in its way, this barrier between Clare and the children she wanted to have. This piece of rubber – it was rubber, she was fairly sure – represented an agreement between herself and her husband, on the launching of themselves or not into a future with a family. To tear it would be to tear some crucial fabric between them, wouldn't it? Trust, for instance, or understanding, or the sense that they were sharing their lives and their intentions, all those worthy words they had intoned that day in the registry office in Bath.

Yet Clare did not share the intention of this bit of rubber with Graham. *It was not her choice.* She did not agree with this piece of rubber, with what it meant and what it promised. So then what did one do, in a marriage, if the two disagreed on such an essential question – children or no children? How could that be reconciled? It was not the sort of issue open to compromise. Clare could not have a little bit of a child; she could not have a child half the week, leaving the other half free for her and Graham to be alone. Would she leave Graham, finally, if he refused to have children with her? She didn't like to think of it, but yes, she probably would. In which case wasn't her sister's suggestion perhaps the right one after all, since staying together would be better than separating and in fact he probably would come round in the end, if presented with the reality of Clare, pregnant? She looked around for something sharp, a safety pin or earring end. Would a pin-sized hole be big enough? It couldn't be too obvious (not that Graham had ever looked at the disc, nor was he likely to). And sperm were very small, weren't they? Couldn't they wriggle through a hole the size of a pin?

But what of the child, Clare? Was this a story you would want to tell your son or daughter, one day? I'll never forget the morning I was packing for a holiday in Italy, sweetie, it was a few hours before we left and I took a safety pin I found in one of my new shirts and I pierced a small hole in the device your father and I had been using at the time to make sure no one like you came along. I pierced the rubber (and so she did) and as I did it I thought, here is a step I am taking to move in a different direction. And it led me to *you*! Isn't that wonderful, darling? Isn't that a sweet story? I know it's a bit sad that your father ended up leaving me when I finally confessed later what I'd done (Clare hid the safety pin, guiltily, in her toiletry bag), because he himself was the product of a split just like ours had been, one parent wanting the child and one parent not and finally, as your father said rather bitterly, it was in the woman's hands these days, wasn't it, the men did not have the ultimate control over the question of life or no life, children or no children, that they had once had. And your father did not want to raise a child like that, a child he had not agreed to, had not wanted, and so there we were, sweetie, doomed to repeat this piece of his history, a child raised without a father because the woman had gone ahead and made the decision on her own. And the irony, love (Clare said this to her future child), is that when I was younger, at university, I made the other decision altogether, when I was with a young man, a young idiot, in fact, who fancied himself a poet, who could never have been a father, not then—

'How are you getting on? All right?'

Clare gasped, as if Graham were a strange man suddenly entering their bathroom. Someone who had no right to be there. Someone she did not know. She dropped the plastic box.

'I'm – ' she said nervously, picking it up – 'there's a tear in this. It's been torn.' She offered her husband the box with its disc of rubber and then placed her hands behind her back like a naughty schoolgirl.

Graham took the box and looked at its contents with a strange, gentle expression. As if she had just proposed to him, and the box contained not rubber but a ring. He placed it on the counter near the sink and put an arm around her shoulders.

'Come on. Let's sit down a minute.' He led her to the edge of their bed. How skittish she seemed, like a deer, as if not knowing what to expect from him. He had frightened her somehow. His own wife! How had he done that? He had frightened her and had taken something from her, some strength, some knowledge she used to have in her hands and her eyes. (He remembered it.) Still, she was lovely: the lake-blue eyes, the high, stern cheeks, the dawn mouth that opened willingly into his. There was always something of the morning in her, the time of day Graham, fisherman, walker, had always been happiest. He was more easily aroused in the morning than at night.

He kissed her, brushed a few hairs away from her eyes. 'I've wondered,' he said awkwardly, holding her hand, as if he too were making a confession, 'whether perhaps we ought to leave that box behind on our holiday.' And then, because he could not bear to see the expression on Clare's face – surprise, understanding, and, most painfully, a shattering gratitude – he kissed her morning mouth more passionately, a kiss that made its intentions plain.

Graham had always wanted Clare – that essential desire was for him the core of their marriage – but it seemed to him that he became hard even more readily that day, and harder, and the fact brought with it the unnerving possibility that he had been aroused by his own suggestion. That the idea of unprotected sex with Clare, after all this time of rubbers and discs and the occasional risky use of the calendar and its promises, was an exciting one, as perhaps was the notion (was this possible?) of making a child with her. Their lovemaking was fast and fervent – each, perhaps, making a silent calculation of how much time they had actually before they ought to resume packing – and urgent in a way it had not been for some time. More like their early days together.

Afterwards they lay flat on the bed, scarecrow-clothed, a sweater astray, trousers down. Graham restored himself to order first; he never felt comfortable with the half exposure of afterwards. He rebuttoned his trousers, then reached for Clare's hand.

'Clare,' he said to her, and her hand felt warm and true in his, 'I wanted to tell you. I've had a letter from my dad.'

Seven

September

She liked to meet Eleanor for coffee in Primrose Hill, either after or before her session with Mira, but recently it seemed there was a new outbreak of babies in the neighbourhood and often Caroline found she could not bear it. Eleanor had children herself, but she had been clever, had them early, so they were seven and nine now, Theo and Emma, and Eleanor told pleasingly awful stories about their character flaws (Emma, an attention-seeker; Theo, prone to whingeing) and how horrifying it was to have to deal with schools and school choice and in any case it was Eleanor, they had been friends from school and she had tact and sense both, and hers sometimes seemed the only voice other than Mira's that helped keep Caroline sane.

It was nine o'clock and she was risking it, a cappuccino in the little Polish cafe where the servers were sullen and blintz-plumpened and the cafe-goers routinely discussed their new plays or contracts (Primrose Hill had become that kind of enclave). She was waiting for Eleanor. The Polish cafe was a place Caroline never used to frequent as they did not allow smoking, which she had considered fascistic until her doctor told her that to be safest, she ought not to smoke any more or even be around smokers, in the run-up to their next IVF offensive. It will do you good, he said, in the smug tone non-smokers always used when telling you how much *better* you'd feel once you'd quit.

Her mobile rang. Scotland the Brave, in the diminutive robotic tones of the tiny silver device. Caroline had always had a soft spot for the Scots.

'God, I'm so sorry.' It was Eleanor. 'We're having the *most* ghastly morning. Theo had a vile stomach virus, which he seemed to be just about recovering from, but now of course Emma has it. We have become the house of vomit. I can't come to see you, I'm afraid – too busy holding children's heads over the loo.'

'Oh!' Caroline must not mind. The people without children must never mind. 'Never mind. How awful for all of you.'

'Honestly, I'd come if I could – I'd like nothing better than to get out of the vomitorium, believe me.'

'It's all right, I have to leave in a bit anyway. Madame Freud calls. Give me a ring when the plague has passed.'

'I may have lost my mind by then. Two down at once, it's too much. The gas oven's looking better and better.'

'Bye, darling.'

'Speak soon. Theo, *no*! DO NOT—'

Snap.

Now just herself, exposed; she always felt more protected when Eleanor was with her. Nothing now between her and Mira except for this scattering of coffee-drinkers: a millennially slow-moving old fellow with a metal walker, edging his way towards the marble table by the window; a lone scribbler in the corner, woman, her table a collage of typescript pages reddened by pen-edits; a large unshaven man noisily reading *The Times*. It was possible to look at such a gathering of the lonely and decrepit and pause, ask oneself, Might that not be my child one day, if I were ever able to have a child? Ungroomed, unshaven, struggling with a walker? Is there much point in this perpetuation, after all?

A woman came in with a pram, inevitably, from which issued unnerving complaints like a cat's. The woman had a distracted, harassed look, and her clothes were what Eleanor called 'maternal resignation wear', the I-can't-be-bothered slouch of sweatshirt over jeans, and comfortable shoes. Face without make-up, or the softening touch of sleep. Nonetheless, her eyes were proud. She had about herself that unassailable bearing that new mothers had. *What I am doing here is the most important thing that there is.* I have created new life.

Caroline dipped her head. The ugly bristly man lumbered up to leave, generously abandoning his newspaper, which she grabbed rather desperately. It was not time to leave yet – her appointment was in half an hour, the walk would take half that – so Caroline spent the rest of her time filling her yawning mind with newsprint, what chatter she could find scattered across the paper's crackly metropolitan pages.

He was every day weaker. He was every day weaker and the medicine made him sicker and there was no question, now, of his teaching this term. The decline seemed measurable, daily. Did she imagine it? Or was it simply the case that every morning she woke hoping to see Peter, and was faced instead with a wan, worrying impostor, whose skin seemed grey, whose hair was falling out, whose eyes did not, around her, always disguise their pessimism and fear?

The buzzer rang. She did not hear Peter stir. He was either sleeping or reading. He had gone in yesterday for his second round of treatments and always, she had to remind herself, he was particularly bad in the days just following. The medicine

160

dealt an emotional strike – she knew he dreaded the room, the tubes, the attempts to mask pity – and a physical one, too, of course, a new circulation of poisons to counter the poisons generated by his own body. The treatments also triggered a depressive reaction, some cruel biochemical trick. Like the unneeded hormones that had tormented the Mourning Madonna just after her baby died, or like the days during the Aristocrat's fertility attempts when she came in frantic and impatient, her body overstuffed with specially prepared eggs and shot up with hormones to help bring them along into life.

Mira must open the door.

'Good morning,' she said, and to her own ears her voice, generally languid, was positively stagnant. She had no intention of explaining the cause; she must not speak of Peter. But the Aristocrat was unlikely to ask. She was not one of the curious.

'We're having another round of treatments next week,' the lean woman began, once seated, and Mira noticed her face was flushed, pinkish, healthier-looking than usual.

Treatments. Mira nodded sombrely, but was confused for a moment. Was the Aristocrat ill as well? Or no. Of course. *Treatments.*

'So I am on a sort of purification course in the run-up. No smoking or drinking. Only good thoughts. This is the third time. I think—' With effort, she kept her voice steady. 'I think it will be our last. It's become terribly expensive, apart from anything else.'

'Is money a difficulty?' Mira had never heard that it was.

'When you're not doing it on the NHS, it becomes rather deadly. My mother suggested we go privately after the first effort didn't work. She offered to pay for one of them, which was very good of her. But this last one is coming out of Hugo's pocket, or should I say his secretly hoarded resources, the extent of which have never been made absolutely clear to me. But judging from the way his face constricts when we discuss it, I take it he has the sense that he's throwing away money he'd hoped one day to spend on a pile in Tuscany.'

Mira listened. This was surface still, obviously. There were times when Mira suspected the Aristocrat would be content with an entire hour of surface. But if silence, with the American, sometimes forced the latter to dig deeper for the better thoughts, with the Aristocrat Mira knew she had to help. The Aristocrat could not do it on her own. It was not in her blood, the tendency to burrow within.

'Are you angry at Hugo about the money?'

'I'm furious with Hugo all the bloody time,' the Aristocrat said, inviting laughter with her tone. Mira did not laugh. 'But not, actually, about this. Not about the money.'

She could carry on now on her own, could she not? The squirrels performed their dance on the railing. Mira could see the silver distractions moving across the green Aristocratic eyes.

'I suppose there is one thing Hugo and I agree on. Amazingly. (So perhaps there is hope for us, after all.) If it doesn't work this time – if one of those little eggs doesn't hold – well, at a certain point you have to be willing to accept your fate, don't you? All right, I understand, I'm not meant to be a mother. My mistake. I'll give up the test tubes and the injections, I'll stop subjecting myself to mad-scientist medical interventions, I'll accept the fact that my womb must contain pebbles not eggs, or that Hugo's sperm, bless them, have all the speed and drive of a Yugo. Or that in any case the race of Hugo–Carolines was not meant to go on, that we'll die out just as we are.'

The squirrel stood still; the woman's eyes did, too. Her face came the nearest Mira had seen to gentleness. Gentle, she was beautiful, had a stately, noble bearing. She might have been painted by Reynolds: Mira could finally see it.

'Hugo would never use that word – *fate* – he doesn't believe in any of that. Thank God, I suppose, as with that wretched woman Miranda he never tried to pretend it was fate that drew them together. I did appreciate that. I know some men like to glorify what they do. He was quite straightforward: "She was a bit of a predator, and I was rather bored" – even if it was probably the other way around. He was probably the predator, of the two of them.'

This would lead the Aristocrat back into Hugo's perfidy and infidelity, a subject Mira knew was inexhaustible, unless she was diverted.

'Is that how you see fertility treatments? As battling your fate?'

'It doesn't make sense, does it? If I were truly able to accept my fate, I wouldn't have all these doctors swarming round me with their injections. I'd leave it all to its natural course.'

'But as you say – perhaps one must sometimes make interventions with fate.'

'Yes, though . . . I don't know. Do you read *The Times*?' Mira smiled noncommittally. 'Well, there's an American woman who writes a column in it, has for a few years, "A Broad from Abroad" – it's a pun, obviously.' Mira was amused by her patients' uncertainty with the dimensions of her English. Not that she did not understand their doubts – every day she had reason to comprehend newly the vastness of the language, see illuminated some obscurer recess of it, admire its openness to play. 'A Broad from Abroad': yes, she knew it, though she gave the Aristocrat an encouraging nod, merely, that might mean anything.

'It's usually just a funny sort of description of some absurd episode in this woman's life, you know, the hazards of being single, all that, her observations as an American – it's not Proust, obviously, it's sort of sub-Bridget Jones but it's a good laugh, and quite clever. Ten minutes' entertainment, usually.' Her eyes narrowed. 'But recently she's begun to veer off and write about wanting a child. What she might have to do, as it were, to "get" one. I read the column today, it was supposed to be amusing, about drinking in a wine bar with a group of Russian journalists and finding herself wondering whether any of them would make a good father.'

Mira kept her face quiet. She knew of that evening; she had not read the column.

'It was just so *grotesque*. I didn't find it at all funny, I know you were meant to, and perhaps I'm just suffering a sense-of-humour loss because I haven't had a bloody drink or a fag for weeks, but . . .' She shook her head. 'It seemed to me either it was all a great lie for the sake of the newspaper and the column, which is possibly rather offensive for those of us who really *are* trying through madly extreme means to have a child, or – worse – possibly it's true, and this pathetic woman is looking at every man she meets now as a possible donor of sperm, which is – which is, as I say, grotesque. And pathetic. And – and stupid.'

It was an uncharitable description.

'I mean at a certain point, this is what I was thinking, shouldn't she just accept her childless state and get on with it, rather than subjecting these hapless men to her mercenary examinations? Not that I feel terribly sorry for the men, I mean, but – you know what I mean.'

Again, Mira allowed an ambiguous nod.

'But then when I finished reading it, I thought, God, is that Hugo and me? Or what I really mean is, Is that *me*? Am I that pathetic character, essentially just using Hugo as a sperm donor, at this point, to satisfy my terrible craving for a child?'

And now the Aristocrat looked at Mira directly, her intelligent eyes seeking in Mira's something she rarely wanted: a judgement of character. She wanted Mira to answer her question. Is that me? Am I that?

'Do you think that character is you?'

Answering the question with another bloody question. Wasn't that always the way of it: just when you wanted the therapist to tell you something straightforward, helpful, issue some pronouncement, she would retreat into the Freudian evasions. Trained to do it, presumably; she couldn't help it. Caroline sighed. Well, the woman wasn't a friend, was she, someone who could tell you what was what without mincing words. Caroline would have to go to Eleanor for that. Once the vomit had been cleared up.

'I don't want to become that character,' Caroline said softly, with dignity, wondering with a piece of her mind how much longer she would make these excursions to Camden Town. She gathered her coat and her bag. 'This round begins next week, of treatments. And this, I've decided, is going to be the last one.'

It was not the conversation she had hoped for. Mira had hoped she might, in hearing the voice and the language, have the sense that a homecoming might still be possible. That *Those are my people, and I am theirs* might still be possible. There had been times during the worst of the wars when Mira could not bear the distance and the not knowing, and wanted to be with them there, in Beograd, even during all the horrors, the sanctions and hardships and posters of him everywhere, Milošović, our man after Tito, our hero, even during all the horrors she had wanted to be there and the phone was one of her only lifelines to the place, the sounds, her sister. Yes there were Serbians in London, of course, Mira knew a few of them but they were all stranded, removed in their ways. They did not satisfy her. The people she wanted were the people who could speak to her from there. From Beograd.

But this afternoon, hearing Svetlana's voice, Mira had the shock of not feeling comforted. It was only her sister. Yes, it was the language (*Buna ziua, ce mai faceti? Ine, multumesc.*) She knew the voice and its patterns as well as her own. (Dušan is having trouble at the university, and I want to be glad about it, that the bastard is being hounded, but I hate the other bastards more.) But they could not, those tones, pull Mira away now from the land she inhabited. She was in England, London, Camden Town, but more than anything she was with Peter and he was ill, and she loved him and wanted to protect him from pain and could not now, could only be beside him. That was the only place for her to be and the only conversation that mattered. There was no other home, after all.

She had thought to tell Svetlana immediately, but Svetlana was a life force, unstoppable, engaged in that other crisis which she laid out for Mira as soon as their initial greetings were over.

'All the talk here is of war again. The country is headed right back into war. Dear Slobo will not let us be pushed around about Kosovo.'

'Does he—'

'And the NATO threats! It is sounding like Bosnia again. "Do what we tell you or there will be dire consequences . . ." If there are sanctions again – you have no idea, Mira, we could not go through that again.'

Mira did have an idea, but only from the stories Svetlana had told her before. The blackouts, the lack of food, the lack of fuel, the lack of hope. The black market oozing up through the cracks, mafiosi all over. *Punishment.* The concept had lived on to this end of their century, after all.

'It is making everyone so tense. So frightened. People begin to have that grey look that they had before. It is affecting Jasna terribly. I am worried about her, Mirka. She is depressed – she is not herself.'

'How so?'

'I worry about her. I worry about Marko. He's not yet two and he spends most days at a crèche in a horrible damp building with a handful of lice-ridden children while she works at the cafe. He looks depressed too, poor little fox. When I see her she is so lifeless, do you know? Hair lank and heavy, no light in her eyes. Mirka, what should I do? This is your line of expertise. What can I do?'

So Mira offered suggestions, she could not help it, the voice on the line, the knock on the door – *Help is needed, there are always others who need help.* Mira told her of the medications, if it came to that, though was unsure how readily Jasna would be able to find them. She urged Svetlana to find Jasna someone to talk to. It was important that Jasna not be too much alone.

'But that bastard Zoran isn't anywhere about. She should move back in with me if she wants someone to talk to. Zoran hardly appears. God knows what he is doing. Probably in Kosovo, not that he'll say. Too much of a sadist to explain where he's going or say when he'll return.'

And more on Zoran, and the evils he may or may not have committed. Svetlana allowed herself to make of Zoran an architect and executor of all the wars, each new campaign and invasion and terror. About Kosovo she said little more. Mira had read reports in London newspapers here ('police forces' driving Albanians from their homes, torching villages), but such tales were unlikely to be circulating in Beograd. Should she tell Svetlana what she was reading? But today she did not have the heart. Not for Kosovo.

'A friend of Zoran's saw Jasna recently – he was drunk; they were in a bar – and said to her did she know Marko might have a baby brother somewhere in Bosnia, a few even, Zoran was that kind of soldier, did she know? Can you imagine? What monster would say this to the man's wife? Even if it's true, which it probably is.'

'*Svetla*, there's something else—' Mira had somehow to interrupt the endless course of her sister's voice. 'I have something to tell you.'

'What?' A pause, at last. 'What is it?'

'Peter is ill. He is quite ill. He has a kind of cancer of the blood. They call it *lymphoma*.'

There was a silence. Mira had finally found something to quiet her sister. She could hear Svetlana smoking. She wished she could see her sister's face; there were times when the voice, the bodiless voice, was not enough.

'I'm sorry,' she said after a long minute. 'I'm sorry, Mirka. That is horrible. What are they doing for him? He has a good doctor?'

'How can one tell? They seem good, I suppose, but—'

'He'll have good doctors there in England. Medicine is so advanced in England.'

'Yes – we're on the National Health Service—'

'I'm sure they'll treat him well.' So that was to be Svetlana's line – You live in England, the doctors are good there, you can afford good medicine? 'They'll give him the best treatment. Cancer's not always what it used to be. People live for years now—'

'He did not look optimistic, the doctor. He tried to – I'm not sure technically of everything he was saying, but I could see his face. You know how someone looks when they are covering over their pity.'

'There's hardly any pity left in Beograd. I can remember it only faintly. Now there's only fear. And anger.'

Now? She was going to talk Beograd now, how terrible life was there, how much easier it must be in England, how glad Mira should be to have left?

'You and Peter could not come to see us now even if you wanted to. Did you know? The European Union has banned all flights. We are pariahs again.'

'I did read that. But in any case Peter is far too ill to fly. He is having chemotherapy treatments, which are making him very weak.'

'I understand. I was just using that as an example. We expect the war to come here this time, you know. NATO may bomb.'

'They will not bomb,' Mira said impatiently, though for a moment she found herself indifferent as to whether they bombed or not. *My husband is ill, Svetlana.* Can you no longer remember life on the human scale? Your daughter is depressed; my husband is ill. Can we not leave the war, just now, and converse?

'It may be easy for you to feel sure of that where you are,' Svetlana said coolly. 'Here we are not so sure.'

'They will not have the European support to bomb. There are limits to what they will do. Europeans will not bomb their own.'

'They have in the past,' said her sister. And as the money drained Mira felt her fight die down. She did not, today, know how to speak to her sister.

'Would you like me to send you medicine for Jasna?' she asked dully. 'That I could do. An anti-anxiety medication. I could find a way to do that, if you think it would help. And perhaps you should think of having her come back to live with you. She should not be alone.'

'If you could send medicine, I'd be grateful.' Her sister's

warmth still at a distance. Svetlana's angers never faded quickly. 'I am sorry about Peter,' she said again, formally.

'I should say goodbye. I must go and see how he is,' Mira said, the sort of attention-gathering remark more characteristic of her sister. Just now there was no voice Mira wanted to hear, ever again, other than his.

Another day, and they kept coming, of course. She was powerless to stop them. Peter, when not recessed in his own inaudible thoughts (he spoke his mind less to her now, which induced in Mira both a shamed relief, as she was afraid of what he might tell her, and an incipient panic, as it made her feel she was losing him already), told Mira that her continuing to work was important. Not just for the money, which was taking on a new significance, but for her spirit. He was still able, good man, to concern himself about that. 'You need them, Mira,' he said. 'You always have.'

However. *Him?* How could she face him? Her fear was, she knew, irrational and wrong. The patient could not hurt her; he was the one seeking help, remember. And she had determined to find their commonality, to make the work possible. Yet she could not escape the odd primeval dread that there was something of the devil about Howard. He had been sent to torment her. (Why?) He was her punishment, perhaps – that word, again – but for what? For what was God punishing her?

The buzzer rang. She heard Peter from the sitting room, where he was half-reclined against the vinyl nightmare. 'It may be—' he called, to which she responded, 'Don't get up, Peter. I have it.' Mira stifled in herself the same urge she'd had last time – to cross herself before opening the door.

Bewilderment met her at the door of the flat, in the shape of two men: the Bigot, yes, but also someone else altogether, a handsome, tall man in his forties, dark hair and with a pleasing elegance about him. The Bigot looked positively shabby by comparison – his black corduroy trousers sooty, his pullover unravelling. Was it possible, could it be, to pity him?

'Mira, hello,' said the handsome man, extending a hand. 'It's Andrew. I've come to see Peter, I was up for a conference and he said this might be a time to come by. I seem to have arrived at the same time as . . .' He gestured towards Howard, who was trying not to look short.

'Howard Beddoes,' supplied the Bigot, and he, too, extended a hand to Andrew as if they were being introduced. His embarrassment was evident and seemed poised to turn into hostility. 'It sounds as though our errands are rather different.'

'Yes,' said Andrew and with a discreet smile he murmured to Mira, 'I'll just go up, shall I?' Mira wanted to call out to the other side of the flat, 'Peter – your friend Andrew is here,' but could not bring herself to speak such a simple spousal intimacy in front of the Bigot.

She waited another moment, heard the men's subdued greeting from the sitting room, then said with what dignity she could muster, '*Howard*. Come in.'

The Bigot settled himself in his customary chair, his body ready for battle; hands empty and searching, as if for a knife or a rifle. The mildness that had temporarily inhabited him in the summer had long since expired.

'So your husband is ill, I understand,' he began, with a tone she could not read. Was she wrong to hear a smirk? 'I'm sorry to hear that.'

Not half as sorry, Mira thought, as she was that Andrew had relayed this piece of information. To the Bigot, of all people. One of her women patients she might have coped with: they would have been sympathetic, at least. With the Bigot she did not know what to expect.

'It must be very difficult for you,' he said, reminding her of nothing so much as a politician issuing hollow regret on the television screen for a botched policy, a caught piece of fraudulence.

'Thank you,' Mira said, folding her hands in her lap, waiting, and Howard knew the procedure well enough by now to know that that signalled the subject was over. He did not intend to let it rest, though.

'What with an ill husband' – the chap hadn't said how ill, but from the hushed, portentous air Howard surmised this was not a mere flu or cold. Something fairly horrible. Cancer, probably. Wasn't it always? – 'and NATO rattling its tomahawks in the direction of your native country, I should think it must be a bit of a stretch to feel interested in the tedious outpourings of someone like myself. Oh God, here he comes again, that bloody man, stopping by to moan about his evil wife and ungrateful children.'

What would she do with that? She couldn't deny it, but even to acknowledge its truth, as he felt her slow, blinking eyes did, was to give away more than she ought.

'Do you consider your outpourings tedious?' Mira asked flatly.

Yes. He might have expected that. Well, why not be honest, for a change? Life and death were at issue, after all.

'I do consider my outpourings tedious, yes. Don't you? – No, no, I know you can't answer that. But if I hear myself say one more time, "That bloody Monica, she's such a bitch, this is what she's done this week" – I'll shoot myself. It *is* bloody tedious. *I* find it tedious, and it's my life: horrible divorce, children scattered bitterly about, only one of them left, Jane, to hold on to. So what can you possibly make of it?'

Wouldn't it be delightful if she could give him a straight answer, for once?

'Why is pain tedious? What bores you about distress?'

172

Howard uncrossed his legs and sat forward. He might as well keep at it; he was paying her, after all. It was up to him where the conversation went.

'Yes, I know, I know that's your technique, your game strategy, I've seen it a dozen times now, turn it back to him, make him look at what *he's* saying, don't let him get through to you. Don't let him get *you* talking.'

She sat still, silent.

'But doesn't that – honestly – strike you as an empty, pointless way to talk to somebody? This is what I don't understand about this therapy farrago.' He sat back, folded his arms, gazed out the window. 'I don't, actually, in spite of what I sometimes say, think you're bad at your job, Mira. I just can't quite see – I honestly wonder – how you can find it a job worth doing. Especially now. I mean there you are, an ill husband somewhere in your flat here – terminally ill, for all I know. A terrible thing to go through, obviously, and a reminder of how bloody *short* life is – we could any of us go at any time, this is what I told Janie in the summer, that if anything happened to me, suddenly, she'd be the only one of the lot of them who would be able to go through her life knowing she had known her dad at least, beyond the party line on him, and the rest of them would go to their graves knowing me only as an enemy of the state. Exiled for his crimes.'

Howard trailed off for a moment, looking at an incommunicable image of his daughter, his children.

'The point is . . .' He turned back to Mira now. She was fat as ever, but he had not been able to shake that sense he'd had of her a few weeks ago, confirmed now, that she was not as untouchable by life as she liked to pretend. It was oddly aggravating to know of the therapist's vulnerability, though it had been for confirmation of this that he'd poked and prodded her for almost nine months now. 'Aren't you tempted, ever, to say

173

what you bloody well think? Especially now? Your country might have a few tons of military might dropped on it in a week or two, before your fellows succeed in "cleansing" any more Albanians, and here you'll sit, trapped with various middle-class English people nattering on about their annoying spouses or their quests for inner truth. Their laundry lists of failures and complaints. Doesn't it seem a bit ridiculous to you, at times? Come on. Admit it. It must.'

You couldn't put it fairer than that. How would she answer him? She kept her face sphinx-like. That must take quite a bit of self-control. Admirable, really.

'Howard,' she said to him, her voice resonant – he sometimes wondered if she dramatized the Serbian accent for effect – 'can you tell me why you come here? What you are hoping to find, here?'

A reasonable question, if an evasion, if one he had no intention of answering.

'Too much to hope for a straight answer to mine, then, is it?' he asked in reply, and what he wouldn't know, wouldn't see, because Mira managed to maintain a stolid face over the course of their session, was that his speech had set her shaking, and it was only by holding her hands taut together that she could keep it from showing.

Reading was no longer what it had been. Still he read, and still it could remove him, on a good day, from the worst of the nausea and, worse, the thought of what the nausea meant. Previous to the treatment, Peter's stomach had been pained and indifferent; now it positively recoiled at the possibility of any food other than babyish pap, digestive biscuits and very weak sweet tea. He wasn't really supposed to drink tea, but it was one of the only liquids his lips would allow. Even water seemed sour and sinister to his tongue.

Company was a welcome distraction. Today had not been a good day. His skin chafed, and each of his attempted books seemed inadequate. Unlike Mira, Peter did not find poetry helpful; the light of any of his old favourites (he'd tried Rilke; Pushkin) was too bright, too strong, and he was not adventurous enough to try new voices just now. Best were irrelevant narratives that tugged him along powerfully. Mysteries and thrillers.

'Hello, Peter. May I . . . ?'

It was Andrew at the door, he had thought it might be, and Peter was surprised by the pleasure that washed over him on seeing his colleague.

'Sorry, I won't get up.'

'Good Lord, don't. Your leather nest looks far too comfortable.'

Andrew sat down on Mira's armchair, looking well and groomed and utterly unperturbed by Peter's altered appearance. How good of him. Had he practised that? Or did the tact come naturally?

'I've brought you this.' He handed a book to Peter across the frayed carpet. 'I didn't think you'd be wanting grapes or teddy bears.'

Peter looked at the book. Zola. Clever choice.

'Thank you. This looks possible. Not everything is.'

'No. Well, as you know, the French aren't exactly my chosen people, but a friend of mine at Leeds was just teaching Zola and she was quite convincing on his virtues. It seemed to me that Paris a hundred-odd years ago might be just the place to be.'

'Notre Dame, yes,' Peter said, locating an irony he had thought he'd misplaced. 'How one misses it.'

'The stench of the Seine, the gay chatter of market sellers.'

'And Madame Defarge, dear old thing. Oh no, different book, that.'

'Yes, that's one of mine. Along with Sydney Carton, bless him. *It's a far, far better thing I do now* – the undergraduates do love Sydney.'

Why was this, Peter wondered, that Andrew could inspire him to something ever so slightly like play, whereas with Mira he was only gloom? Because the two of them together were frankly afraid, whereas Andrew could afford to act a little, in the most considerate fashion, as if the ending were still at some distance?

'It's a bastard, chemotherapy, isn't it?' Andrew said.

Peter suspected his own smile was wan; reclining in this way did make him feel rather like a tubercular poet. Perhaps this would be his moment to write something original, after all. A late hymn to life. To love. 'You've had other friends who have gone through it?' Peter was beginning to loathe the word *chemotherapy* almost as much as *cancer*.

'Well, yes. I have.' Andrew nodded. 'But also I went through it myself. Years ago. When I was a child.'

'Chemotherapy?'

'Yes.' He looked so well, it seemed to Peter: lean but strong, a man in his forties who swam or played tennis, perhaps, to keep himself young and healthy. How could he ever have been ill? And how could Peter ever have imagined him to be ill? He remembered some notion he'd had – a fantasy, Mira would consider it – that this fit, trim colleague of his had been wasting away with some plague or other. Projection? Another of her technical terms. 'When I was ten,' Andrew explained. 'I had a tumour removed from my intestine – it proved malignant.' His face struck an ironic pose; an old injury, half-masked. 'I never liked that word, *malignant* – seemed to assign so much agency to the wretched tumour. As if it were deliberately after me. Not that I understood all that at the time.'

'Were you hospitalized?'

'Yes, for a bit, in one of those terrible wards for sick children. There's nothing more depressing, even for the child. Especially for the child. All the adults wear tragic expressions, more even than in the regular wards of hell. The hovering sense, *all that promise lost*. Some of the children are in there for broken limbs, you know, and yet all of you end up feeling blighted. Doomed. You're quite conscious of yourself as an object of extreme pity.'

'Was it – how dangerous . . . ?' Peter could see the problem people were having with him; he was having the same problem, even retrospectively. How did one find a way to ask about the severity without seeming bloodthirsty, or unduly pessimistic?

'My mother thought I'd be dead within the month, that was *quite* clear from her harrowed face, riven with tears. She could not remotely disguise it. I'm sure the doctors constantly pulled her aside to say, "Do buck up, Mrs Pullman. For the child's sake." She couldn't manage it.'

'And yet . . .'

'And yet. Here I am. A medical miracle. Months of chemo-therapy, becoming a bald, shrivelled creature, eminently teasable in the shark tank that is a boys' grammar school—' The ironic mask again. 'Yet I survived. And the world of Victorian scholar-ship is the richer for it.'

'Indeed it is.'

'I imagine that's what drew me to the Victorians, in any case. All that sense of pathos, the beleaguered Nells and Janes and Pips. They're my people.'

They heard a sound of opening doors downstairs – that ner-vous, rather sweaty man he'd come in with was making his exit, probably. 'I'm afraid our time is up, Mr Braverman,' Andrew quipped riskily; but he did feel the worst thing to do was act as though the invalid had lost his sense of humour. He could see Peter was tired already. 'I hope this session has been helpful.'

'Oh yes, Doctor,' Peter replied, closing his eyes. His smile was stronger this time, Andrew noticed. 'Your comments on my dreams were particularly helpful.'

'Let me know if that one about the hamsters recurs. We might want to delve deeper on that one.'

'I'll keep you informed. At our next session.' Peter's eyes remained closed, which liberated Andrew to move stealthily closer. They had been colleagues, primarily, rather than friends, but Andrew had always liked the stuttery professor of Russian. He gave Peter a quick embrace.

'I'll come again,' Andrew said quickly, not wanting to worry or bother him, though he could see before he turned away the eyes fluttering open again, and the warm, liquid gratitude that filled them.

She could not have said why the room was as comforting as it was, but it seemed to have become the only safe place to go. That worn, sunken sofa and armchair facing it, that soothing soft-coloured print on the wall. And her presence, too – that must be part of it – the plump, doughy presence of an older woman with a complicated voice, who came from war and bloodshed and tribal hatreds (so it was said) who would not therefore desire a pretty picture of the world and its griefs. This was what Kate could not bear any more, anybody who wanted things to look better or nicer than they really were.

It was a perspective she now shared with William. He used to be the dark-spirited one, speaking (privately, to her; you wouldn't know if you met him) of life's pains and degradations, how bloody he found people. Kate had been the lighter one. Oh, come on, William, look here and look there – there is goodness about. There is kindness. Look for it, for God's sake. The flowers for Diana, for example. Kate had been astonished – moved – when she walked by Kensington Park Gardens near the palace, to see the ground covered utterly in flowers and flowers and soft animals and notes and more flowers. Yes of course it was sentimental rubbish, but the sight was nonetheless extraordinary. All that love and wailing, the concern for the children, the sense of loss, the sense that the nation had let go of someone important. This in a country famous for the interior coolness of its citizens, who were thought to be better at joking than taking seriously, better at tipping the cap than embracing, better at soldiering on than shedding tears. Yet how they wept.

Nonsense, William had said. Pure media-driven hysteria, all over a person who was more doll than human, an invention, a creation – a rich, unhappy woman with an eating disorder and a miserable marriage, neither of which made her a saint. The flowers were, William found, an enormous piece of hypocritical theatre, common people duped and diverted, as they always had been by royalty, into thinking they cared passionately for some figure who neither knew nor cared about them.

Kate had fully expected, once she was sentient enough to have anything like a rational thought or expectation, that William would be scornful of her journeys to Camden Town to see Mira. He wasn't beast enough to stop her going, or probably even tell her if he thought it ludicrous, but she knew she would sense his judgement or his scepticism if he had any. He didn't, however. He was in such distress himself, difficult though he found it to say so, that he seemed to think anything Kate could do to lessen her own grief was a good thing. Anything that helped. Nothing would alter Cassandra's death, but any palliative substance – therapy, films, work, alcohol (he had been drinking a lot lately) – that could make a dent in the excruciating pain was worth a go.

William was also intrigued by her therapist's being Serbian. Half a year on, Kate no longer flew into a battery of rage if William mentioned the news, though she still could not find it in herself to pick up the newspaper and care about any part of it. But William fed her morsels now, like a mother bird feeding her chicks, mostly about the building war in Kosovo, and he was curious, though delicate in how he expressed it, about how this changed and mattered to the woman whose job it was once a week to cast out the worst of his wife's persistent demons.

Kate sat down this morning with some of those morsels in her mind, a less particular, inward expression than she sometimes wore.

'Good morning,' she began, always polite. 'It's a beautiful morning, isn't it? You can tell it's autumn, suddenly. The air is different.'

Mira nodded. 'Yes. The light, the colours change.'

There was a silence, as there often was at the beginning with the Mourning Madonna.

'Do you know – ' she said at last, and her voice was full, as though she were catching herself in mid-stream, mid-thought – 'William occasionally says something to me – he reads the newspaper, which is littered with horrors, of course. Child snatchings. Bombs. Kosovo.'

The patient looked up cautiously; Mira kept her face still, nodded faintly.

'And I think he feels, in some perverse way, comforted by how terrible it all is. "Well, we wouldn't have wanted her to know all that, would we? Isn't she better off without it – given how bloody awful the world is?" '

She looked out the window as people so often did, across the railings and roofs and rain puddles on balconies.

'As though the worse everything gets, the better it is that Cassandra didn't live. Perhaps – one of my mother's friends said this to me – she was "too good" for us. Too pure for this world.'

Mira allowed the silence its due. Much of what the Mourning Madonna needed, as she had said herself, was a sustaining quiet. An acceptance.

'But the fact is, no matter how terrible the world is – and it is terrible, and I'm sorry for what is happening in your country, and I hope the fighting ends, and I hope they don't resort to bombing. But the fact is . . .' She turned back to Mira, this lovely, deprived woman, and her back was straight, and her eyes were dry, and her face had across it the poetic depths of old Englishness. 'The fact is, I would rather the world had Cassandra in it. I wish she were with me in this world. No matter how terrible a place it is. No matter how full of brutes and hypocrites and tyrants and fools.'

The woman cast her eyes again across the London air that was still there for her to breathe. For her and Mira both, alive, to breathe.

'It would have been a better place, this world, if Cassandra were still in it.'

Eight

October

When she began to feel sick she could hardly suppress her excitement. This must, then, be real. She had stepped across a line that had previously marked off territory that was fantasy, a fantasy that had begun to seem unrealizable, like winning the lottery. Of course she had already known, there were signs and portents: two matching pink lines in the doll-sized windows (she had done the test several times to make sure); the subsequent booklet from her GP that carried soft-toned, optimistic pictures of loving couples, gently remonstrative instruction on the new need for purity (good diet and no alcohol), and avuncular advice on how to make this transformative period easier. There was the vial of large, veterinary-sized purple pills she had immediately bought from Boots that were hard to swallow, making her feel like an unruly animal. And Graham's green-edged nervousness – that if nothing else should have reassured Clare this was really happening to her. But it was not until her body confirmed the news with a land-bound seasickness, a drug-like lethargy, and a veering vertigo, that she was willing to believe. When the debilitations arrived, she could only be thrilled.

It seemed strange to her that such a significant piece of news – *your life may, in nine months or so, change beyond your most fanciful expectations; you are on the verge now of beginning the adventure you had always hoped to begin* – should be delivered in such an artless, mildly degrading setting: sitting on the loo, doing what the thin printed directions told you precisely not to do, namely staring fixedly at the white plastic messenger for the long minutes it took for the pale colour to come through. The thing looked like an ice-lolly stick, something you'd find in one of those colourful Wall's freezer bins in summer, or from the tinnily ringing ice-cream van that circled the park on hot afternoons, wise vulture seeking its prey.

She had not even told Graham she had bought the tests. She locked herself in the bathroom – the room for make-up and ablutions, magazine readings and secretive evacuations but not, generally, spirit-shifting news. Would it have seemed more appropriate had she been sitting in a doctor's office with a benign older gentleman telling her, as happened to her own mother, 'You and your husband can look forward to a tiny bundle of joy arriving next year, Mrs Cox'? Should she have received the result alongside the man she married, putative father of the bundle? Clare rather enjoyed her few days of privacy with the fact, which she waited to share with Graham, the secret nestled within her like its subject, turning and growing and evolving away from public view. She surprised herself by her ability to conceal her joy, her anticipation, her disbelief. (She had always harboured an uneasy fear about her ability to bear a child, after the other – and you read so much about infertility, these days.) She was calm around Graham, and if he had been paying attention, Clare thought, he would have noticed the calm, the new lack of vibration about her. *They had started. It had begun.* But Graham did not notice. He was distracted – by work, by the flurry of new autumn exchanges, and of course by the letter from his father.

When she did tell Graham, he behaved properly. He embraced her, kissed her, told her how pleased he was. But his voice seemed to come from elsewhere. He was not beside her as he delivered the necessary sentences, though he seemed to be. (Where was he?) She felt nearly as alone with the news after telling Graham as she had before.

Nobody asked Clare – it was unclear who could, apart from Sara – whether it reminded her of the last time she was pregnant. Graham could not ask; he did not know of another time. Clare had hoped it wouldn't remind her, that this would be entirely different, the hope for rather than a dread of the parallel lines, her greater age now, the marriage ready and waiting, the father in place. It was entirely different. Not the same biological process at all, surely. One, a mistake of timing and carelessness that could be corrected (had to be) by a brief, bleak excursion to a dingy clinic where she spent several hours in a young-women-filled ward, endured a minor procedure, and was allowed afterwards to recuperate with biscuits, weak tea and a novel. The other, this time, a possibility, a hope – a *life*, actually. A wanted life. Clare had never thought of the other as a life but only as a mistake, as a fault, as that boy Derek's foolishness and her own. Clare wasn't sure whether or not she believed in God – her mother did – but since August she had spent some time during the nights in whispered, cloistered conversation while Graham slept. Praying and explaining to Him, if He was there. I am sorry. Perhaps I was wrong. *Please let me try again.* This time I will be a good mother. *I promise.*

When the nausea hit her, she remembered. She lay down in the bed she and Graham shared in the small Bath house (the marital bed, that resonant phrase), after calling in to say she could not come to work. She lay in their bed in midmorning dimness, the shades drawn, feeling the pleasure and displeasure of this sickening sickness. And she remembered feeling it before. The rage when the nausea struck her that other time, the sense of doom and cliché, when the possibility cradled within her seemed nothing more than an inconvenience, a cruel joke, a crisis that would send her clinicwards on a spike of dismay and fury at her body's stubborn intentions to thrust her into a role she was not then old enough, brave enough, to assume.

Initially Graham had written. It was easier to write than to speak – than to imagine speaking – and besides, Peter himself had written rather than called. Perhaps that was how he preferred it. How would they speak of this?

Graham had written from Italy, one morning when Clare had gone off to find presents for her family and friends. He had ambled along to a large cafe on the plaza and sat with stuttering pigeons and phrasebook tourists in the cool shade of ageing ochre buildings, trying to think clearly, with the help of a cap-puccino, about his father who was ill.

Dear

Absurdly enough, Graham had had to pause there for rumi-native minutes. How should Graham address him? He had noticed the 'Dad' at the end of his father's letter; it had troubled and moved him, seeming as it did like a subtle, slightly pathetic plea for sympathy. *I am your dad, after all.* Yes, of course, they had both learned and accepted that in their ways years ago, but – wasn't he Peter, primarily? When Graham himself called the man 'Dad' it was usually in implied quotation marks. He did not know that he could write 'Dad' sincerely. And yet now must be the

185

time, if any, to call the man by that short familial endearment. Why not simply pretend? What harm could that do?

Dear Peter,

    Thank you for your letter, which I received just before we left for Italy.

    Of course Clare and I were both distressed to hear your news.

He needed Clare next to him, rhetorically at least, to feel up to this task.

But what else was there to say, finally, other than that? Graham sat at a bronze-rimmed circular table letting American, Spanish, Japanese voices break into his hearing. Against his red lids, if he closed them, a slideshow of images from the past days: Donatello's pained, thin, pitiable Christ; Uccello's fat elegant horses and riders stampeding across hills; Madonnas, of course, with their children, but also Mary visited by the Angel, who arrived in mid-air to bring her the surprising news. (Me? I'm to bear the child of God? But I'm reading! – She was always, admirable woman, reading when the Angel found her.) And on through the Pietà, all that joy and struggle over his birth only to have to hold the grown man in her arms at the end, son of hers and son of God, brutalized by those who did not understand Him. Dead.

He started on a new sheet.

Dear Dad,

    I don't know what to write about your difficult news, except that Clare and I send every wish for your recovery and improvement. I'm glad to know you trust your doctors, and I am sure they will do everything they can, but do remember to ask questions. Make sure you agree with what they're doing.

I know you'll have Mira helping you through the ordeal –
I'm sure the chemotherapy won't be pleasant, though it's clearly
necessary – and that you have close friends around you in
London. Clare and I will try to come and see you as soon as we
can when we're back in England.

Florence is extraordinary. I remember your telling me that
years ago; it's taken me this long to find out for myself. I have
heard that there is a fever that sometimes afflicts visitors here
who become overwhelmed by the stupendous beauty, the power of
the art, and have to take to their beds to recover. I can
understand how this could happen to people. I feel rather faint
myself.

Look after yourself. I'll save the other platitudes for another
time. Meanwhile, from Clare and from me –
*   our love*
*   Graham*

He did feel faint, actually, that was not an epistolary flourish.
In rubbled Italian he asked to see a menu again. The pastry from
their hotel breakfast was not, apparently, enough to hold him.
He would need something more substantial to sustain him
through a last late wander in this city of countless glories.

It alarmed Peter to discover how quickly one could be led into
the temptation of self-pity. He was shrouded in the stuff – it was
sticky, clingy, like spider's webs, which made him weak and not
admirable. One only ever heard stories of the heroes who fought
their cancers, whose spirits remained indomitable, who retained
their senses of humour, who became positive, ennobling forces in
the lives of friends and relations. Less was written about the
legions of inferior beings who must exist too, people who became
impatient and unpleasant, or hollered with fear, or those like himself (Peter did not believe he was the only one) who simply

became resigned, passive, gloomy, discouraged. How did the heroes pull it off? Peter looked around, he scavenged, sometimes desultorily and sometimes with genuine effort, for optimism, for the confidence that he might triumph over the disease, fend off the invader and emerge all the better, purged of evil and contaminants. He had no such confidence, and he could not manufacture it. He felt only defeat, panic, irritation. Ultimately, his cluster of unworthy sensations led to self-pity. No one, not even Mira, understood how purely awful he felt, physically. Pain, weakness, nausea. Material degradation. The body conceding.

Peter lay in the sitting room, as he did more and more now. The bedroom he found too depressing; in the sitting room he could lie on the vinyl nightmare, which had begun to take on his shape and yield some of its brash, tactless shininess to a softer matte as if in deference to his oversensitive eyes. (Light now hurt him; one more new symptom he had not even mentioned to Mellon, it had been lost amid the rest.) Lying there he was surrounded by their books, their photographs, their haphazard lamps, the shelves of dictionaries – English, Russian, Serbo-Croat, Italian – and of Mira's people – Klein, Freud, Winnicott. He did not find the titles tiring. Rather, they gave him the soothing sensation that even if he left right now (and sometimes he imagined that, the departure forced on him suddenly, his heart stopping, a crucial organ abruptly failing, giving him no time to register or comment) the great works would remain. They would speak better than he ever had. Oh yes, he had made his translations, but it was a far, far better thing that there be Tolstoy, Dostoevsky, Gogol. Their existence comforted him. Helped him not to think of empty sheets, Mira's sleeping alone, the half-empty flat; the clichéd image of the clean, remade hospital bed, if it happened there, fresh again after the latest fatality.

He avoided the bedroom now. Even retiring there each night

to sleep with Mira had acquired a certain horror, and not just because those hours brought with them insomnia and night-terrors. He preferred to stay alone on the vinyl nightmare. His and Mira's bodies had started to inhabit distinct regions: for him, the cool, ghost-filled hallway of the ill, for her, the heated, rosy-hued corridors of the well.

The telephone rang. Mira was seeing patients – was she? Or perhaps she was out shopping, he could not remember. He answered it.

'Hello. It's Graham.'

'Ah, Graham.' That's right. His son. All of *that*. There had been a letter. 'How are you? You enjoyed Italy, then?'

'Yes, it was great, thanks. Wonderful. I sent you a letter—'

'Yes. It came. I read it.'

'And. How – are you?' The voice hesitant; not necessarily seeking a real answer.

'I'm all right.' So there was no need to give one. 'Tired, quite a lot of the time, and – the treatments do make one sick. That's unpleasant.'

'Yes, Clare . . . reminded me that was one of the side effects. Sounds horrible.'

'I have another session next week and two more after that, and then they'll stop and see what effect it's had. If it's beating back the cancer or not.' I suspect not: but one did not want to say that. Don't be defeatist! 'They tell me this particular combination is the most effective against lymphoma, that in some cases it can make a real difference.'

'What is it they're giving you? Do you want me to – I could do some research on the Internet for you if you like. Why don't you tell me the name of the treatment?'

'Oh yes, the Internet,' Peter said vaguely. There had been a time when Peter had thought he might become quite interested in the Internet: its broad promise of infinite, immediate information; its omnipresence; its universality. It had struck him as being a little like God. When he had come to it, however, he had found that its democracy allowed plenty of room for banality and repetition, that its brash promises of possibility were not always kept. Over time he had come to use the machine in their flat chiefly for e-mail correspondence to do with work. 'Do you know,' Peter said, 'I don't find myself terribly able or even – this is terrible to say, perhaps – *interested* to take in all the facts about lymphoma and the treatment they're giving me. I have been urged – they do urge you – to find groups of people, other people who have had it. There's a Society.'

'I know. I've looked it up.'

'Have you?'

'It seems useful – other people writing their stories, their questions. You might find—'

'But I don't have questions. That's the point. I have decent doctors. They're doing what they can. That's all I really want to know.'

'But perhaps reading other people's accounts might reassure you.'

'About what?'

'About . . .' Graham faltered. 'The fact that others have been treated and have done well. About the efficacy of this particular treatment, the one they've chosen—'

'But I believe that already, Graham. I know that others have survived – not a high percentage, perhaps, but some – and I believe the doctors are treating me as they think they ought. I imagine they're doing their best.'

Even to his own ears, his voice sounded passive, feeble. He had flummoxed his son. The boy wanted to talk about the Internet. The idea wearied him. 'Look, it's kind of you to offer. I don't

– I am just telling you that I don't, myself, feel the need for a surfeit of information. It makes me a renegade patient, perhaps. We're supposed now to want to know everything. But I don't.'

'I see. Well.' Poor Graham. That had been his best attempt. What else could he say now? 'On a different subject, Dad – ' and Peter heard the cough of embarrassment – 'I don't know when the right time would be to tell you this, but' – I'm gay, actually? Or – Lydia finally told me that you aren't my father at all, it was the milkman all along, she just went through the rest to punish you? – 'Clare's pregnant.'

Pregnant. That other kind of news. Good news, in this case, wasn't it? There had been that scene, months ago. The girl crying on Mira's shoulder, wasn't it? Wanting a child. Peter had still felt, then, able to engage with other people's troubles, desires, joys. He lacked the ability more and more, now.

'Congratulations,' he managed. 'That's what I'm supposed to say, I think.' (As if he were speaking to himself.) Then, making an effort, with a counterfeit heartiness, 'Congratulations, Graham. That's wonderful news. Please send all my good wishes to Clare. How is she feeling?'

'Not too badly.' This was untrue. Clare was nothing if not green, constantly, about the gills. She could not be near Graham eating anything with meat in it as the smell sickened her; the other evening he'd had to retreat to the guest bedroom to eat a beef stew he had picked up at Marks and Spencer. Furtively, like a teen trying cigarettes. 'We'll come and see you soon.'

'Yes. Do. Don't come straight after the treatments, I'm at my worst then. Come a week after that. Mira can tell you the schedule. And don't come if you've any suggestion of a cold – of any illness at all.'

'I'll have Clare set it up. She's best with the arrangements. And we'll be sure to be healthy when we come.'

But how cruel that sounded, that throwaway line, as if he were thumbing his nose at an ailing man, flaunting his youthful ability to make such a breezy promise; or as if he sat smugly at home with his pregnant spouse, placidly anticipating the joy of their new arrival. When in fact (had Graham successfully disguised this?) the only panic that matched his rising anxiety about his father's health was that which bit Graham late at night: about his future, and Clare's, when they would be joined by the unimaginable figure produced by that late unsheathed morning some months before, the fruitful embrace he had allowed himself to share with his grateful wife.

In her own country, in such circumstances, they might have hired a cook. There had been a girl who came in when Mira's father was ill, to make soups, clean sheets, keep him comfortable, as comfortable as he could be with the knowledge that he was dying. The girl helped Mira's stepmother (also her aunt; Svetlana's mother) who was overwhelmed. What was her name? Radmila. Yes. Soothing Nikola's brow. The soups she made were too thin, but her presence had helped. The proximity of her warm young body.

People did not have cooks here unless they were very wealthy, which Peter and Mira weren't. Mira always sent money whenever she could to Svetlana; and they travelled; and, truth be told, Mira was disorganized with her patients, neglected to bill them, did not always successfully collect her dues. A century earlier they might have had a cook. Now, instead of cooks, the culture provided Marks and Spencer, a short walk from their flat. The company (with its mysteriously religious brand, St Michael) must have cooks itself, people who toiled invisibly in some anonymous kitchen in an outlying suburb, producing palatable, nicely packaged dishes along nationalist lines – French, Italian,

Chinese, Indian. Not so long ago Mira would have scoffed at buying soups from such a place, when five minutes further along Camden Town's sooty beer-flecked back streets one reached the fruit-and-veg market on Inverness Street, where the man in the tweed cap sold potatoes and other earth vegetables ('Much obliged,' he always said after you paid him, a phrase Peter had explained to Mira), and a dark-haired lady with a small rheumy-eyed dog dispensed the season's bruised but edible fruits. Mira had formerly taken her string bag to Inverness Street several times a week, collecting carrots, onions, potatoes, parsnips. Soup materials. Essentials.

Now it was all the bright and easy Marks. Tired, dispirited, conscious of the fact that many strong smells – sautéing onions, any kind of fish – turned Peter's now delicate stomach, Mira brought home Bistro Selections and, for herself, the grimly predictive Meals for One. They had marvellous sweets. Mira became in this period helpless as a naughty child when confronted with the tantalizing boxes of sponge cakes and trifles, the jolly jam roly-polys. It was only the cheerful banter of one of the shop's Irish clerks – a woman her own age, with bird-bright eyes and face, probably a grandmother to half a dozen lively children – that relieved Mira of her guilt. She took her expensive collections to the checkout area in the upper back of the store, where bras and pants stood delicately on guard around biscuits and snack packets, and experienced a shiver of affection for a people who could proudly sell underwear and food in such proximity.

'The doctor did say you're to have protein,' Mira called to Peter now as she huffed up their few stairs like a burdened bear preparing for hibernation. 'I've found something very simple, plain, a piece of chicken. I'm sure you can manage it. It's a Café Favourite.'

'I'll do my best.'

'There is also a Taste of the Mediterranean – some sort of bread with toppings.'

'The Favourite sounds more likely. The Café.'

'Good.'

It was, after all, the chief desire when someone one loved was ill: feed him, sustain him, keep him strong. Though a good part of Mira was rational enough to understand otherwise, in her heart she believed that Peter's difficulties had begun when he stopped eating properly. Months ago. (She should have noticed. She should have urged him to eat more forcefully than she had.) He had allowed himself to get weak, and once weakened it had been easier for the cancer to attack him. Why had he not kept himself strong? Why had she not kept him strong? She blamed them both for their failures. It had been up to both of them, they had vowed to one another, publicly and privately, to keep themselves whole. I will look after you, yes, in sickness and in health – the line from the cool March ceremony at the registry office in Kentish Town (Peter could not abide the possibility of a church). Didn't the line also imply, I will be looked after: I will agree to get better? It was entirely wrong for Mira to be angry at Peter, helpless as he was, yet at times she succumbed. She could not stomach the idea of his leaving her.

'Before that though, love, before the Café offering' – Peter called to her from the vinyl nightmare. The couch seemed, blackly, to have become his home. The word 'nightmare' no longer to Mira seemed as inappropriate as it once had – 'could we . . . ?' He gestured towards her chair. As she approached, it occurred to her that they had contrived to arrange their furniture in an uncanny echo of the analytic setup: here was she, Mira, on her armchair, while Peter, the patient, lay across the couch.

She took her seat. Waiting, as she knew well how to do, for the other to start.

194

'I don't want to be gloomy,' Peter said, not looking at her directly, 'but there are certain things I have to put in order. There has been something on my mind that I wanted to discuss with you.'

'Of course.'

'It's Graham.'

'Graham. Yes.' Not yet, then, the burial arrangements, whether or not there should be a memorial service. How many of these conversations must they have, sketching together the shape of a future that would lack him?

'I'm not quite sure how to say this, Mira.' The wince was either from bodily pain or the difficulty of the subject. 'But will you – in some way – look after Graham, when I can't? And Clare?'

'Look after them?'

'I don't mean – obviously they're perfectly independent, and don't need – and it's not as though *I* have . . .' The sentences were too hard to finish, evidently. 'I just mean I wouldn't want you not to see them. I wouldn't want that connection – broken.'

But this was not a patient. This was Peter. Mira was expected to reply. She could not take shelter in a resonant silence. She could not hide in the comfort of a question. She was supposed to speak. Could not.

'I know you and Graham haven't always been close,' Peter said, as an odd new pain in some unnameable part of his body distracted him from acknowledging the dimension of the understatement. 'He's not – I know he isn't . . .' But how could Peter express it? Mira had been stubborn. Perhaps that was a fair comment. Beneath the passion and devotion she had shown to Peter, there had always been a hardness. Hadn't there? Towards his son? Peter had not allowed himself to recognize it completely before. Curious how much clearer matters became when one's time suddenly grew small and countable: whatever comforting myth Peter might have harboured, as everyone surely did, about time's infinite stretch, had now departed, along with his sense of the geographies within reach, the books he might still read, the people he might see. Peter was London-bound now. Gone from him was any rest of the country. Gone France, Holland, Italy. *He could see the point.* That was his son speaking absurdly of Florence, and the sudden spasm of love Peter felt for that man, his son, shook and surprised him.

'Peter, of course. It doesn't matter,' said Mira, incomprehensibly. 'That is, it doesn't matter what arguments Graham and I have had. Of course I will – whatever you would like—'

'Clare's pregnant.' He needed to get this said. 'Graham called to tell me earlier today.'

'Pregnant,' his wife repeated blankly. 'That must please her. It is what she wanted. When will she have the baby?'

'Due in May.' And Peter knew that the same thought travelled across their minds: he might not be around by then. 'So you see – all the more reason—'

Bloody hell. What was the point now of tiptoeing and side-stepping?

'I want the child to have you as a grandparent, Mira, since in all likelihood the little boy or girl won't know me. I want you to be there with them. Can you do that? Will you do that?' He did not keep the edge from his voice.

'Of course,' Mira said. Her voice solemn. 'Peter – *ljubavi* – of course I will.' She came over to him then, to embrace, to soothe.

Was she sincere? Could she do it? But that must be the impulse at this stage, wasn't it – promise the poor fellow everything. He'll never be able to check, will he? Unless Peter had been wrong all this time, and there was an afterlife, after all.

He allowed himself to be held. Peter had nothing to do, now, but believe her.

There was a man, an American, named Richard Holbrooke. He had been involved at Dayton, and in his well-fed body he carried the inflated pride she remembered Owen and Vance having before their earlier plans for peace had been shredded by the innumerables who would not go along. (Karadžić, Milošović, Izetbegović, Tudjman, the Americans . . . The blame could be placed all over.) Holbrooke clearly felt he had fixed it, finally, this intransigent European problem (the Europeans were too damned inept to take care of it themselves); he had brought Milošović around, he had made of the tyrant a peacemaker on those cold Ohio morning walks. And if Holbrooke had done it before, he could do it again. He knew how to talk to Milošović. Kosovo was getting out of hand, from the American and European points of view. A national army (still called the Yugoslav army, even in the absence of a coherent Yugoslavia) was responding to a terrorist group (the Kosovo Liberation Army, which had vowed to take Kosovo back for the majority Albanians and had renounced pacifism as a means of doing so). But the Yugoslav army was behaving brutally, as armies are encouraged to do, driving people from their homes, terrorizing citizens. This could no longer be tolerated. *We will not allow Bosnia to happen again.* This was said as if it were self-evident what it meant; and from that all-confident place where 'we' make such decisions on behalf of other people.

In the sitting room Mira watched Richard Holbrooke, the volume turned low. Peter was dozing. She sat near him on the nightmare, stroking her husband's lately departed hair, facing the screen and its heads and voices, not hearing every phrase and every nuance and not sure whether she wanted to. The

American confidence and imperiousness was intolerable. The self-appointed bosses of the world. Holbrooke was saying now, in an interview with the suave silvered English reporter who asked questions always with a satisfying scepticism, that NATO (by which Holbrooke seemed to mean he, personally) had made it clear to Milošović that bombing of Serbian targets was imminent unless Milošović pulled his troops back from their aggressive activities in Kosovo. Holbrooke was in Belgrade. And what response do you expect from the Yugoslav leader? I think, Holbrooke responded, Milošović knows the risks in the game he is playing, that he understands the international community is watching him and cannot let this aggression continue. But does NATO have credibility at this point? Might Milošović not look to the disagreements among NATO members – over the deployment of ground troops, for example – for some comfort? Clinton has emphasized that America is unwilling to commit ground troops. Ah but he, Holbrooke, had made it crystal clear to Milošović that there was absolute resolve on the part of NATO members to bomb Serbian targets if the Serb leader did not immediately comply with their terms. And Holbrooke expected a positive outcome from this? Oh, yes. He fully expected Milošović to recognize that the time was over for his latest campaign of violence in Kosovo. It wasn't worth it for him to suffer the rain of NATO's most powerful weapons on his forces. As happened at Dayton, Holbrooke felt sure a ceasefire was possible – indeed, imminent.

Hitler had not announced his plans to bomb, beforehand. Hitler had not bargained or made deals. (None that he kept.) The Yugoslavs – Serbs, specifically – had balked at the fascist government the Nazis had installed with full Croatian participation, and had rebelled; to this rebellion the response was swift, merciless, absolute. *Punishment*. The Germans did not pretend they had a moral reason for their attack. They were honest about war being war. You defy us? We will crush you. That was always the message of war, and the hope of generals, whatever else they might latterly have been trained to say. We will crush you. Do you doubt that we can? Allow us to show you.

The Americans had their own habits of war, however, which consisted in taking the pained, paternalistic attitude that they would only unfurl their appalling weaponry when it was clearly for the greater good of mankind. This was what itched and stung Mira as she listened to the man, Holbrooke, discuss even-handedly his conversations with Milošović. He wanted, Holbrooke, to be seen not merely as powerful, as having the machinery behind him to make good his threats (and Mira had no doubt that the Americans did have the very best in the machinery of war, while her people made do with their Russian hand-me-downs). But he also wanted to be seen as resolute, and right. Milošović is a tyrant who must be checked and we – NATO, but Mira felt as Svetlana did that NATO was a shield for the Americans – are the ones who will stop him.

Mira turned the television off. To do so she had to lift Peter's heavy head and place it gently on the softer pillow, then lumber over to the box, as Peter called it, which stood rather precariously on a narrow wooden card table. The remote control was another device Mira had not mastered. She was the master of so little in this world.

Svetlana told her they had been clearing out bomb shelters from the Second World War, that people were panic buying, that there was a deep feeling of dread and pessimism and rage in Beograd. Svetlana herself sounded weary and resigned: there was nothing to do but hate NATO, if they intended to punish people like herself for the actions of a tyrant; but it was impossible, for Svetlana at least, not to hate Milošović, too, a brutal, greedy man who had reduced their country to a place of gangsters and bankruptcy. And fear.

Had she told Peter of this latest? Mira returned heavily to the sofa, but now he was lying full along it, and he looked comfortable, and she did not want to disturb him. Instead, she found herself – thick knees and all – kneeling beside him, watching his face, at rest.

Peter had been so good to her, so strong during the earlier horrors: Bosnia, the shorthand for the worst of it (Sarajevo, the city a late-twentieth-century icon of gruesome violence and destruction), though in truth vilenesses had erupted all over, the body politic thoroughly contaminated. Peter had remained astute in his reading and listening all during those years, and his humane intelligence had helped Mira keep hers. He was able, unhypocritically, to grieve over the end of a dream that had probably never had longevity in it. Brotherhood and Unity; it had been tried elsewhere in the world as well and who anywhere had been able to stay with it? Peter could see the pointless devastation of the wars without resorting to simplifying stories of ancient ethnic hatreds or the mysteries of tribalism. (The press made the Slavs sound like the Rwandans, for ease of reference.) Peter loathed Tudjman and his obvious fascist sympathies, distrusted Izetbegović, and darkly regretted Milošović, who he thought had the mad, marbled eye of a megalomaniac. Not that he was Hitler, Peter felt, the comparison was crass – Milošović had neither the territorial ambition nor the frenzied charisma of Hitler, though as with the Führer, perhaps, you could sense a twisted, collapsed ego under the layers of uniform. Peter had helped Mira to understand all this better than she might have on her own, with only her instincts and frustrations to go on. And Peter had never stopped loving, for his wife's sake, Serbia. So few others still could. There were times when Mira herself could not.

'Your people,' he had once said to her, 'have tried for so long to find the right home for themselves. Living with others, living ruled by others, scraping out life alone – nothing is quite right. They cannot find the home that suits them.'

Mira kissed Peter's deep, ever deeper forehead now. There was so little hair left; and she had so loved his hair. The longish dark brown that had slowly, over time, discoloured to ash. As she loved his forehead, his closed eyes, the slope of his nose, his just-open lips.

What would Peter have said, had she woken him, about the spectacle on the news she had just watched?

How would she get through Kosovo, whatever new hell awaited, without him?

Graham had tried to tell Clare, and more importantly himself, not to be shocked by Peter's appearance. Clare had been warned by Mira, when they spoke of the best time for a visit, that the treatments had made him weaker, and of course that he was losing his hair. Peter had never been a great, strapping man – an average Englishman's height, tending towards lean, with a modest desk-sitter's paunch that gathered or not, depending on the numbers of walks – so Graham could not see the likelihood of a truly drastic transformation. His father had always had a slightly watery appearance, which he himself had inherited, in part. The hair loss would be odd, though he might wear a cap of some kind as people did; but the man was in his sixties (what, sixty-three? sixty-four?), and men of that age were often bald. It wasn't as though he were a young woman or even an older woman, for whom the hair loss must be a stark, distinct mark of affliction.

And so when Mira welcomed them in at the bottom stairs of the flat, Graham held his volume of P. G. Wodehouse in a careless hand, joked with surprising ease with his stepmother about Clare's pregnancy and made his way up the few stairs unguarded. Entered the sitting room all naked, as it were, and unprepared.

Graham took in a swift scoop of air. He could see, as if he were not there, as if he were God, a scene of some pathos: his father slowly manoeuvring himself to his feet from the leather couch, newspaper scattered at his slippered feet, bony fingers knuckled against the seat to propel himself upright, the entire act one of precariousness, pride, difficulty, defiance. Graham wanted immediately to retreat, to allow his father to complete this movement on his own, as if without a witness the action might not cause his father as much shame. Hapless wish; Graham's animal presence had been felt, and Peter looked up with haunted eyes, tried to say, 'Ah, Graham,' in much the tone he would usually have used; but as he spoke and looked up he lost his balance, so that Graham had to lunge forward to grab his father's elbow, saying, 'Steady on,' as he helped right the man to standing – an awkwardness that soaked them both in embarrassment, that in turn could only be covered over by the clucking of females.

'Hello, Peter,' Clare said, her voice warm and untroubled, and, 'There, are you all right?' murmured Mira, though Graham continued, as unobtrusively as possible, to gulp in air as he took in the sight.

For there stood the man who was his father, depleted, yellowed, battered, altered. He was not the man he had been whenever Graham had last seen him. How many months had it been? How long did it take for this to happen to someone? Was this, already, what dying looked like? Peter had the look not just of a man ill, it seemed to Graham, but of a man who had begun a journey to another place. Some of Peter was already gone. His face – Graham tried to remember it, a face he had somehow never thought he would need to know, keenly, in the way he had his mother's. (As a child, he remembered, he stood by his mother's bed and watched her sleep, taken with the familiar shape of her face, expressing a wordless, boyish prayer that she might never desert him, for she was all that he had; beyond her – should she disappear, as people might and did – a chasm of solitariness, like all those children in stories whose parents were lost to war or to cholera, leaving them unprotected and alone.) Graham's mother's face had been known and necessary, and contained half of him within it, leaving him to speculate idly about the other half. People had always said Graham looked like her, and so he believed until he finally met his father, whose face carried within it echoes of his seven-year-old own. He had been fascinated by his father's face – the long sloped head, the full brown hair a bit like his, the long jaw. But it had not seemed to him as frighteningly essential as his mother's. He had done without his father before; could, if he had to, do without him again. That was always the equation in the relation. The man had never been a given.

But *this*. Peter's face all but broke Graham. He had to stop gulping, stop wanting to flee, stop his heart beating as it loudly was, in fear of the general evidence: good God, people die, this is someone who will soon die (there hadn't been many, before: the suicide at his boys' school; one of his older clients felled by a stroke in her sleep; his mother's father, when he was young, Graham had hardly known him). There was, as well, the specific fear: this bald, deteriorated man has been your father, but you will in the next months have to lose him. Again.

They spoke of Clare's pregnancy – the nausea, the exhaustion – and Clare and Peter even managed a jokey nod in the direction of their similar symptoms. Clare told stories of their time in Italy; she had brought photographs to show them, a pleasant diversion as Italy had been one of Peter and Mira's shared geographies, and Mira had occasionally taught seminars there. Peter enjoyed a long, gentle reminiscence about a train journey he and Mira made on New Year's eve some time in the early eighties, an adventure that involved late overcrowded compartments, families sharing panettone, guards mislaying passports and gesticulating in comic denial over their incompetences; and some glorious New Year's morning on a coast, finally, the air clear as it ever would be, their hearts full, young, hopeful, content.

Clare managed so beautifully. Look at her facility, her instinctive, relaxed warmth around Peter that helped put him at ease in his uneasy skin, not by pretending that he was not ill, or that there was a great subject Not to be Mentioned (this was Graham's frightened inclination), but by accepting that he was ill, that it was bloody awful, but that it was not all. There were other events, stories, dreams, jokes to be told and canvassed. Clare was helping Mira as well. Graham could see, even through his fog, that Mira was overwhelmed, felt pressed in by all that was asked of her now and would be asked of her in the weeks to come. She was scared and drained. Clare, calmly, helped.

Graham scarcely spoke. He did not accurately listen. His thoughts darted, nervous, from corner to corner, looking for an exit. Then, in the interval of a neighbour's visit – puffing, voluminous, clearly fond of Peter and Mira but made anxious, as a woman in her seventies, by the unmistakable scent of decline in the room – Graham allowed his mind to settle on a possibility, for himself and for Clare. A relocation, temporary at least, to somewhere closer. Closer to here. If his father was planning to die soon – and to look at him, it was hard to imagine otherwise – then Bath seemed more absurd than ever. Pointless to spend hour after hour eating up motorway. Their small comfortable house was too far.

Wasn't it his place as a son to be near his father?

Wasn't this Graham's bitter opportunity to take up residence in London, at last?

In a thick, soaked atmosphere Mira made her way to the Tube. Had to start early on the weekends, to avoid Camden's packed eager throng of pierced and stapled Sunday shoppers, who swarmed up the High Street like crowds at a rally. All of those massed people, Mira sometimes thought, gathered not to protest or celebrate ('Slobo! Slobo!) but simply to shop. To eat, wander, browse. Capitalists all, even with their big rebellious boots and defiant, improbable hair.

Sunday-morning Tubes often had the sweet-wrapper-scattered morning-after feel about them. A few sleepy passengers, some possibly churchgoers like herself, though it was not a very religious country. Mira had noticed it when she first settled in London – the dearth of crosses and saints, of symbols of belief. Mira had heard it said about the English, though it still surprised her, that they did not much feel the desire for God. Their desires were social, literary, conversational: for a quiet home, a nice garden, a cup of tea. Was that it? Even after years here Mira found herself, at times, unable to distinguish stereotype from fact, myth from reality. They were not cold fish, the English – and yet they were, shunning physical contact and turning away from parades of emotion. They were not inverted and depressed – and yet they could be, Mira had seen it often. They were largely godless, with Queen and Shakespeare taking precedence over Christ or the Virgin – or did the outpouring over the stricken princess show a nation's needs for saints and icons, after all, for a belief in someone higher than themselves, who strove for a greater good, who was capable of miracles?

Tottenham Court Road. Mira changed lines, to the straight red Central.

But Peter was the only Englishman she genuinely knew, the others would always be a mystery. Even her friends, even Marjorie or the Epsteins. Mira could read them, watch them, listen to them; heal them, even, bringing particular individuals towards some greater peace with themselves, some relief through the pain. But they would never be kin. They could not be. (Look at Graham, his distance from her. Did Graham believe in God, or gods? Mira had not the slightest idea.)

Peter did not have a god. He did not know Christ or the saints, he was untouched by Christ's supreme act, by His humility, by His wisdom, by His love. This was not something they had spoken much of, because it was so hard to face the man she loved with her fear for him, knowing that he would not understand or share it, that it might offend him, even. Peter was not a bullying atheist, he was far too gentle to want to persecute others who had different views from his own, but neither would he welcome Mira's concern for his soul. Not expressed in Christian terms, that is, which were the truest terms she had.

Mira emerged from the underground into another grey slab of the city. Ladbroke Grove. She was early. Yet in the rain she had no desire for an ambient stroll, a weak Sunday coffee somewhere, if there were even anywhere open. She made her way directly to the church. She could light a candle, kiss the icon, pray quietly until the others came. She could read the stories of the few frescoes (St John the Baptist, and St Sava, for whom the church was named), waiting for the simple room to fill later with the voices she craved, their ancient melancholy chants, the haunting, mythic music of the priest's blessings and the choir's solemn replies. *Lord, have mercy.* The priest would share his spirit and incense, he would take her and all of them through the necessary words until he reached the point when they would share Christ's body and His blood. Mira's home, her interior self, would know then its only serenity, its only sense of rightness, in a long, dark week. She would cease to distinguish between wars and peace treaties (Holbrooke had his way, it seemed; there would be no bombing, not for the moment); between sickness and health, between solitude and companionship; between England and Serbia. She would be suffused at last with Christ's suffering and His boundless love, and that was, after all was fought and won, or lost, or forsaken – the only good. His love was all there was.

Nine

November

He lived near Baker Street. An odd, nondescript part of the city that confirmed for Jess his bachelor status: who but a single man, or an unknowing immigrant, would live so near the character-free clog of the Marylebone Road, a few blocks from the tweedy actors who stood outside the fictional residence of 221B Baker Street, where tourists were invited to enjoy some Edwardian-styled kitsch to do with the famous sleuth?

Yet the flat itself was nice; it did not, as she put it to him rather bluntly – but knowing her as he did from her columns, he'd be expecting the bluntness, she figured, would be disappointed if she didn't deliver – have that depressing sterile stench of the newly divorced. The furniture was new and Habitatish, but looked like it had been chosen with humour and care rather than in desperate haste. Maybe he was the sort of man who had been waiting for years to get divorced so he could finally buy a gleaming, high-end sound system and that reclining armchair his wife had found so tasteless. (It was comfortable, Jess had to admit, though an awkward place for the complete act; good only for foreplay of a leathery kind.) He had taken the trouble to set up several shelves of his books already. And if the kitchen was under-equipped – though he said he cooked – the refrigerator was stocked with actual food and not only pre-prepared meals and half pints of milk for tea or coffee. Was all of it an elaborate set, a lure for the eager ladies? Jess was willing to suspend her native cynicism. Nick was a good man, maybe. Alone, but catchable. Couldn't she allow herself to think so, for a few minutes at least?

Jess left the flat before he did, to make her appointment with Mira. She did not explain where she had to go, and he was curious. 'I thought the freelance life was spontaneous and unscheduled?' To which her response was a mysterious smile, as if her morning assignation might be something rather interesting and character-enhancing rather than the dreary, American-seeming fact that she had to talk to her therapist. She could not let him know everything right away, obviously. She was too hopeful about this man to trust him with any difficult truths just yet.

November stretched across Regent's Park like a damp cloth, bringing out the soaked green in the lawns and the paper whites of the swans. A few lonely bread-feeders huddled round the fake lake and Jess passed the occasional bundled shape pushing a pram. She moved onto the great flat stretch of grass, colour-blurred on weekends with teams of footballers, playground on a stifled weekday morning like this one to stuttering black crows, the odd dog and a solitaire or two like herself.

She decided not to tell Mira about Nick. Her nascent passion was like some delicate fledgling creature that might die if exposed too soon to sunlight and air. It could not yet breathe on its own. She wanted to keep it inside, nurture it, give it the dark-ness and privacy it deserved. She wanted to go home to her own flat and think about last night, remembering his touch and hers, his moments of eloquence, and hers. Nurse away the embar-rassments until they disappeared, hold on only to what was most promising and, yes, romantic about their encounter. She wanted to be a girl, goddamnit, giving in to girlish fancies, and to tell Mira she had slept with someone, a guy who worked in the sales end of the paper she wrote for, would suddenly make ordinary the whole prospect. Oh yes, here's Jess again, throwing herself at some other new prospect, getting ready to put all her eggs, so to speak, in one apparently available, recently divorced basket.

'Good morning,' Mira said to her, and Jess noticed that today the round face looked rather haunted and weary. The voice – that dear, accented, near-fictional voice – was hollow, as if something had been carved out of her, reducing her density, shifting her solidness. Mira always seemed so sturdy and present to Jess, even when Jess suspected her rambles were boring or aggravating the poor woman. Mira seemed, like Europe, to have been around for long enough not to suddenly change or dissolve.

Today, however, not. Today she had an alarmingly transient look about her. Surely that was Jess's – the patient's – prerogative, to be transient? Not the therapist's?

'How are you?' Jess tried, though she knew it was futile.

'Thank you.' Mira nodded as she always did, and waited, hands folded, patience of a saint.

Jess was adept at talking around, so she talked around. There was plenty else to mention: the status of the book, currently being fought over by two publishers, much to her agent's salivating delight; an upcoming visit from her mother, the combined irritation and affection she inspired (she also had a new boyfriend, which was good, though Jess had her doubts about him, from what she had heard so far); how Jess felt about her friend in Massachusetts, the one who had gone ahead and adopted a Guatemalan baby and brought the tiny thing back to her town of beautiful fall foliage and progressive, family-oriented lesbians. Mostly Jess was, she felt, filling airtime in a rather desultory manner and mostly Mira said little, though her few comments about Jess's mother's visit were astute and surprising, reminding Jess of that quality Mira could have, on a good day, of appearing to know you better than you knew yourself.

Then there was a moment, on the Guatemalan baby, when Mira made reference, as she occasionally did, to the people of her country. This was not entirely uncharacteristic. She never said anything about herself personally, but she sometimes spoke of her reading; if Jess talked more seriously about her work Mira might bring up Dostoevsky or Beckett, and when her fluency faltered as it occasionally did, she might say suggestively, 'In my language we have a phrase – I don't know how to say it in English—'

Jess had always refused these invitations in the past, if they were invitations, to hear about Mira's people and her language. It had been a mystery she had enjoyed, proof of the secrets that were harboured between therapist and patient, corroborating Jess's sense that their exchange was somehow free of nationality, of border, addressing only what was common and human – in addition, of course, to what was peculiar to her fucked-up self. Jess's fondest hope had been that Mira was Czech. Jess loved the Czechs, in a way that she recognized was ignorant and senti-mental, for their novelists and for Kafka and for their playwright turned president. Ruling from the Castle.

But, 'Yes,' Jess said today, thinking that perhaps now if ever was the time, 'your people?' Gesturing towards them, whoever they were.

'Serbian people,' Mira sat back in her chair.

'Serbian?'

'Yes.' The therapist looked surprised. 'You knew that, I think?'

'Right, well – right,' Jess hurried. 'I mean, yes, I'd – that was

211

what I'd guessed, what I'd thought.' *Serbian*, for God's sake. So the Balkan wars and all that. The bloody, incomprehensible dissolution of Yugoslavia. Jesus Christ. The situation had been mostly calmer since Jess had been seeing Mira – the whole Bosnia nightmare was in the past, so it seemed – but still – *Serbian*. That explained . . . but what did it explain, actually? Everybody hated the Serbs. Even more than they hated Americans. Regrettable, maybe, but there it was. This might then explain why Mira's references had been as they were – guarded, shapeless, somewhat defiant. Jess understood now. 'My people': Mira loved her people, clearly, and that must be a hard thing to admit or say with the thick clouds of anti-Serb hostility all over the place. Jesus Christ. *Serbian*. And what did Jess herself know about the Serbs? Nothing.

But she must have been aware of that, surely? Mira sat up straighter. The American could not have been coming to see her for two years without knowing Mira's nationality? She had never been like the Bigot, pressing and hounding Mira on the actions of her nation, but the American had at certain moments acknowledged (had she not?) her comprehension of what Mira was. Of what she came from. It was true that the American had been, Mira thought, discreet to an unnecessary degree, not saying much in the direction of Mira's country, language, people, because – primarily because she was the patient, of course, but also because she was the one whose country, language, people, made all the decisions and set all the rules, and perhaps she had some faint shame about that. Given other remarks Jess made about being American – apologetic, self-deprecating in her nationality as in so much about herself, though Mira knew that a bedrock of prideful confidence underlay the self-deprecations – it seemed merely like a particular kind of tact, her avoiding the words *Serbia* and *Yugoslavia*.

Yet there was no mistaking the look of discomfort and surprise on her patient's face now: discomfort about the information, perhaps, but more than that discomfort at her own surprise, which she was trying, with touching obviousness, to hide.

'That's all we have time for today,' Mira intoned, the profession's magic escape hatch, and she felt as she said it, not for the first time, that her work would always take abrupt turns she had not expected, and that this was a good thing in life: to keep oneself moving.

She was in there, seeing someone. One of the hapless and needy, one of her flock. Peter no longer felt like Anne Frank, needing to disguise his presence; rather, he felt they were the ones who ought to apologize, to tiptoe, for invading his home at a time like this. Couldn't they go elsewhere, with their germs and their problems? Were there not other Confessionals, other Delivery Rooms that could take them? If ever Peter heard a cough or a sneeze from that room – he couldn't hear anything over music, but lately music had seemed to demand too much of his ears and it was silence he craved – he shrank back against the sofa, as if the microbes might not find him if he pressed himself out of their way. He had become fastidious, irritably so, about Mira's washing her hands, cleaning the doorknobs, not allowing the throngs to linger in the tiny downstairs hallway more than a moment. He had told her, now that it was November and the seasonal ailments were gathering momentum, that she must flatly turn away any patient who seemed possibly to have flu or pneumonia.

Mira nodded and agreed but not, Peter felt, with quite the soothing reassurance he would have liked. As with other requests of his (not to cook certain kinds of meat, whose smell he found nauseating; to keep lights dim in the evening, for the sake of his painful eyes), Mira's response had a distance that was

213

new to this compromising episode in their lives together. She was acquiring the habit of talking to him as though he were a dear, troubled child and she must necessarily retreat at times into the adult world to which she properly belonged. He sensed that her withdrawal might have to do with fears of her own, but surely his fears, his death panics, should be more important now than hers? Should she not repress her reactions and tend fully to him, to his distress and discomfort? But perhaps this was Mira's method of tending. Perhaps this was the mask she assumed for her patients, and sick as Peter was now, he had become another of her patients.

Was he jealous of them? People occasionally used to ask; *she* used to ask. Was it difficult for him to know there was a cluster of paying strangers to whom his wife owed a deep, emotional loyalty that might at times take precedence over him – had, at times, when she'd had to take traumatized telephone calls, set up emergency appointments? Peter had never felt so before. He had the sense of Mira's patients being passengers in her ship, as if she were their benevolent, watchful captain and they helpless without her, and that made her admirable and noble, and made them objects not of jealousy but of pity. Poor things. They couldn't help it. They were lost and angry and troubled, and needed his Mira to steer them to safety or contentment.

Today, though, the unhearable conversation grated on him. Rarely before had Peter lain around idly while Mira performed her talking cures. He had always been working himself, reading, writing, marking papers, preparing for a meeting or course or forthcoming conference. Now the subdued exchange from the other side of the hallway caused him to itch and mutter, not that he could catch any specific piece of it, it was rather a generality, an abstraction, a murky sound signifying talk of nothing, he felt. Nothing. Who were these people to think their upsets were so important? Were any of them dying, actually? Were they not rather carping about family frustrations and employment indignities, or trouble, that's right, Mira had told him some months ago, with the pressing problem of reproduction?

Irritation gave Peter energy, a rare and welcome entity, and he stood up, reached for items he had not much use for these days, other than on his odysseys in for the treatments: his coat and hat. He could go out, still. Certainly he could. Just the other day Mira had urged him to go out with her to the park for a brief walk (a touching offer, really, as it was nothing she would ordinarily have done) and he had begged off, blaming the weather, damp and chill. He had felt as he said it what a defeat it was. They had both heard it.

Now he shuffled down the few steps towards the door, hearing as he descended a few American-accented words from the monologue, 'I just feel it's so wrong . . .' Whatever that was, whatever might be so wrong, it was Mira's task, not his, to listen, and he was free as he always had been just to go. Freer now than ever. He had no work, no obligations, no one to report to other than his illness and its attendants, and he did not intend to share comment with them today.

The air struck Peter like an unfriendly towel whipped in his face. That nasty boy at school, Martin, rugby player, who had taken occasional pleasure in tormenting Peter in the changing rooms, weak-legged teenager that he was. (Memories flew at him like birds, now.) It was colder out than Peter had imagined. Yes, he had seen the November grey from his windows, he expected it, but *cold*: he had not known it would be so cold. The air bit straight through to the bone, like a steel trap on a fox leg. Had he so few defences? Was his winter coat so negligible, or was it rather what lay under the winter coat, his no longer fatted body? Was he suitable now only for wards and sitting rooms and other interiors?

He would simply buy a paper. Not a walk in the park after all, that seemed overambitious, but a short jaunt across the railway bridge to the tiny newsagent's near the pub that sold *Standard*s and cigarettes, cartons of Ribena and tooth-rotting sweets for the children. It would still do him good, a short walk. Just getting out like this would, surely, do him good.

He saw people walking over the bridge. A young mother struggling with a rain covering on her pram, trying fussily to do it or undo it, he wasn't sure which. An older woman – well, Mira's age, his age – carrying heavy plastic bags from Somerfield. In the distance, a young Greek-looking man spitting onto the pavement.

Peter was not like any of these people, and the difference now frightened him. Their world was not his. He could see that each of them, in being distracted – the woman with her shopping, planning the evening meal, perhaps, or turning over a morsel of gossip in her mind; the mother trying to shush the cries of her child; the Greek, his mouth full of tobacco-stained spit – each of them made the primary, essential assumption of health. That was how they moved and lived, as if they were well, and he, Peter, no longer knew those moves or those lives, and in tasting this external air and seeing these people he had the solid conviction he would never again know them. He was different, now. Marked. Headed for the knacker's yard.

The ground shook beneath him and a roaring filled his ear. Sounds of the apocalypse. Was this what death would be like, he wondered? Was this death? A stampede of noise, followed by the endless yawn of silence? Or did the lights dim slowly, like houselights before the start of a play or a concert?

It was a train, of course. Familiar enough dragon. He

needn't have been frightened. It was not a bomb, nor an earthquake. Merely an intercity carrier, ferrying anonymous newspaper-reading, sandwich-eating passengers from London to destinations north.

Not death. Not yet. For now he still stood, he still walked, and he could go and buy a paper.

He felt freer to touch her now, and it had never occurred to him that this might go along with everything else. Graham had never considered, one way or another, how a pregnancy might change his marriage; he had only harboured a vague dread of his lithe, thin wife becoming fat (and of what followed after the birth, but he had scarcely even imagined much of that, beyond a loud, off-putting blur of wailing and nappies and prams in the hallway). He would not have guessed how newly wantable Clare might become at this early stage, and though it embarrassed him fully to articulate his desire, he was not too embarrassed to act on it, reaching for her in the mornings soon after they woke, urging her to an early bed so they could share an evening hour together. And she was sick, poor thing, quite often – in the mornings, yes, but at any other time of day as well – and though he had always found vomit, and digestive matters generally, off-putting, he now found himself waiting patiently until she was done and had rinsed her mouth out and then seeing whether she might be on for a fondle, after. She generally was, good Clare; thankfully the cacophony of hormones seemed to pull her that way too, bed-ward, and she was eager and attentive to him in a way she had not been in a long while. Grateful, perhaps (he knew this) for his change of heart about children, and yet genuinely hungry, too. And they both luxuriated in the freedom of making love without birth control. What a revelation that was: no equipment, no calendars, no fumbling, no hurried trips to the bathroom cupboards. He loved it. He loved her. If this was what having a child allowed and entailed, then perhaps he should look forward to being a fruitful patriarch.

They lay together one evening, a cool November a few weeks after they had visited Peter, and Graham wondered as he often had since that day when to mention it to Clare. When did one broach significant subjects? Clothed and seated over lunch or dinner, or precisely here, in the bare-shouldered satiated calm of after-love? How, when it came to it, did one talk to one's wife?

'I had a thought,' Graham began.

'Yes?' She was listening to her stomach, which was for the moment the organ that spoke louder than her womb. Impossible to know what was going on deep in her feminine interior, where cells were dividing, limb buds forming, a new heart was beating. (She had read the books, of course, and studied the diagrams: this was the initial faceless grain of rice; this, the bug-eyed Martian spawn, at eight weeks, and at twelve; this, the vulnerable twenty-week-old that begins to look like a baby but would expire, like a fish, if taken out of the womb too soon. Fascinated though she was by the progression, it seemed mad fantasy to imagine this diagram having any corresponding reality within her, and Clare looked at the pictures rather as she might a travel brochure of some exotic place she considered visiting. Interesting, and no doubt true in their ways, but not necessarily bearing any relation to her own life or future.)

'It may sound – I don't know how this will sound to you.' Graham's voice was nervous. What would he mention? Possible baby names? They had not yet had a single conversation on the subject, which Clare found odd. Her own mind rattled like a Filofax through lists of possibilities, girls and boys.

'What is it? Go on.'

He rolled closer towards her. 'I've thought – that is, I've been thinking.'

Then: silence. What was he struggling after? She had no idea.

'My father is very ill now, and it just seems a bad time to be so far from him, I mean several hours away. That this might be the time to be nearer. We could live in London for a short spell – move up there. I'm so fed up with the office in Bath. I actually spoke to Hugo, he has friends everywhere of course, and he knows a senior partner in a London firm, a decent one, where he could arrange for me to have an interview.'

What?

'And you'd be taking maternity leave in any case I thought, and we could let the house, probably for a decent amount, and – or even not, even leave it empty, but—'

'But, Graham. I'm pregnant.'

Now he was moving, though. He had momentum. 'Yes, I made a few telephone calls about that. You see, I found a flat that's available, handily enough, in Mornington Crescent, just near my dad's place. And there's a good GP in the area who could sign us on. He said at this stage in the pregnancy it would not be difficult to resettle yourself. You'd have a midwife there, obviously, and UCH – that would be your hospital – has an excellent maternity ward. Very well equipped, a great place if anything went wrong, which of course it wouldn't.'

'So . . .' Her mind was slowly catching up with him. 'It sounds as though you've had this in mind for some time.'

'Well, I've been *making enquiries*.' He used a jokey cockney accent, like a bad television detective. As if that would make this scenario more approachable. Less catastrophic. 'And I've been thinking about it. Yes.'

And what did you do, as the wife, with a conversation like this? Did you cry and protest? Did you say, What are you, mad?

We have a house, we have our lives here? Did you storm out of the room; or did you react calmly, with humour, in the hope that then it would all go away?

'He seemed very ill to me when we saw him,' Graham said quietly, and to this there could be no selfish or contradictory reply. He had seemed so to Clare as well.

'It might be the right time, finally, to be close to him,' Graham said, touching her arm. 'I don't know – we don't know – how long he has.'

Clare lay still and silent, afraid to allow her thoughts anywhere near her mouth. Should she be pleased and touched by this surge of feeling for his father, or should she view it cynically as Graham's means of escaping the reality of the baby? Death or life: which was more important, actually? Which had rights over the other?

Clare closed her eyes and groaned, felt the familiar surge in her troubled stomach. She had just enough time to make it to the loo before the latest meal heaved its way back up her burning throat.

There were days, now, that passed as other days had – before – and she was not yet sure whether to fear or welcome them. There was inevitably a sense of betrayal about days become ordinary. Kate was back at work, had been for some time, at the charity. She had intended to leave the job – had planned to leave shortly before the baby was born, had in fact been headed towards her final fortnight when Cassandra had stopped moving. It was only a few days a week and done more out of social duty to her mother's friend who ran the place than out of her own deep conviction or financial need. By March of last year Kate had been ready, frankly, to stop thinking about other people and think only about her child. But, in the event . . . Once Kate was able she returned, newly grateful to have somewhere to go, and there was a large benefit auction coming up for Christmas that had given welcome activity to her yawning mind. As all the clichés and homilies and kind older women said to one – it was good to keep busy.

Kate could bear riding on the Tube, now. Mostly. And she had come to enjoy, if that wasn't too perverse a word for it, these excursions to Camden Town, a part of London she had never had reason to go to before, that had like so many areas – Brixton, Dalston, Kilburn – hovered on the edge of her urban awareness. When Kate said 'the park' she always meant Hyde Park, Kensington Gardens; all other parks seemed peripheral and provincial. The heaths and commons were outside her experience.

But once a week, still, she stepped out into an unknown London. It was a little like seeing someone you knew very well in costume. Unlike sleek Kensington, Camden Town was fundamentally grubby, stinking of last night's beer and vomit, but it was colourful in a Dickensian way, and Kate recognized that there were more young trendies here than around where she lived. Then too she felt a self-punishing rightness about her weekly walk up the Parkway and over the car-clogged railway bridge, down Mira's one-sided, train-edged street. Kate considered it an appointment with Cassandra, she supposed, the pain and horror of losing her daughter demanding Camden Town, somehow, in return. It was fitting that Camden Town was not lovely and serene. Kate would have felt wrong taking a train to some bucolic suburb or a tiny outlying clinic and tending there to her grief and bewilderment. She did not want to feel the world was comfortable and benign. It so obviously wasn't.

Nonetheless. The reason Kate kept coming (and William had asked her, gently, why: he wondered, almost nine months later now, how long she would need to) was for the ease of pain offered once she was inside the room. There was still something there she could not find anywhere else, much though she tried to make some place similar in their own home: there was a place for Cassandra here with Mira. From their own home Cassandra remained cruelly absent.

'Often, do you know, I don't even know what to say here any more,' Kate said this morning, in the familiar surroundings. 'I can't think of anything new.'

Mira nodded. Do you have to? was the question on her face, but she did not ask it, and Kate loved that about her, the Serbian woman's rich and nuanced use of silences. There was something so full in them. They were so careful and attentive. It was a strange, uncanny gift.

'People keep assuming we will try again. William wants to, as I've mentioned. But I don't – I can't—'

'Does he understand that?'

'No.' Kate smiled. 'There has been so much he hasn't understood. And to be fair, probably a great deal I haven't understood about him, either. I think through all of this we have become quiet mysterious to one another.' She paused. 'But not in a bad way, somehow. Isn't that odd? I don't speak to him the way I did before, I don't find myself chatting to him as I used to. There are hours that pass when we say very little – we watch a film together, or something on television, and hardly speak. Yet we are so much closer in some deep way than we were. Closer, per- haps – ' Kate looked out the window at the colourless air – 'than we would have been, had Cassandra lived.'

'It can break apart or it can draw together,' Mira said. 'Grief.'

'Yes. Yes, I've heard that some couples don't survive this kind of thing. It wrenches them apart. I can see how that could happen. But now . . . I would be so lost without William. Even more lost,' she added, ruefully, 'than I am with him.'

'Yes,' Mira said, as if she knew what that meant – to feel you'd be lost without someone. That was the extraordinary thing about the psychotherapist, any reaction or thought one could describe seemed familiar to her already, as if she somehow encompassed all human emotion. Was it a trick? One could begin to think (Kate had sometimes speculated, though would never ask; she understood the rules, and in any case it would seem intrusive) that Mira had herself carried a baby once, and lost him or her. She seemed to understand from within, not simply in a textbook sort of way. Whereas there were legions of people still, well-meaning people, friends, women who were mothers, women who weren't, who could not accept the devastation wrought by Cassandra's death. A range that extended from the unspoken impatience of, *For God's sake, can't you move on?* to the hostile assumption that by now Kate was just trying to get attention; to simple bafflement. *Why doesn't she have another one? Wouldn't that help?*

'Kate,' Mira said, and in her voice the English name was thicker than usual, perhaps had other consonants secreted within it. Mira used the word, Kate had noticed before, as an announcement. Kate! This question is for you. Almost as though they were in a room with others. 'What is your hope, now?'

'My hope? How do you mean?'

'How would you like Cassandra to stay with you? How would you like to keep her?'

Because one day – was this the hidden message? – you won't be able to come to Camden Town once a week and find her here. You will have to hold a place for her yourself.

'I think—' Kate began, but stopped at a sound that seemed to come from elsewhere in the flat. A violent coughing, a painful sound. Someone retching? Possibly. Kate was startled and saw Mira's face darken, her eyes grow wide with unhideable alarm.

'Sorry – do you need to—'

'I'm sorry,' Mira said, her voice scarcely audible. 'He is not well. My husband. But someone is with him. I am sorry.'

Kate nodded, murmured, 'No, no – how awful,' and knew then that it was true. She would have to consider the possibility of not coming to Camden Town in the future. Look at this poor woman – her distress was palpable, it impregnated the air. What could Kate say? 'That must be very difficult. I hope he feels better, soon. I'm so sorry . . .'

'Thank you.'

Again, Kate sought the windowed world outside to shape her thoughts, her words. Unwell. Yes. She sensed this was an under-statement. Again, she was quiet.

Like the quiet times with William, she found these silences with Mira untroubling, companionable, even. There was no hurry or need to say anything. This had been new for Kate, one of Cassandra's gifts, perhaps. Before, Kate would always have felt the need to fill an empty space as if it were an awkwardness or a mistake: she had not wanted it to seem as though she had nothing to say, or was bored or distracted in someone's company. Silences had seemed ominous and insulting, a result of social misfire. Now they seemed merely appropriate, and somehow kind. How much kinder, finally, than talk that said nothing.

'They tell you what to do,' she said after some time. 'The people in the hospital. The Health Service, that is. Everyone is clearly proud that they manage the death of a baby quite differ-ently than they did ten or twenty years ago, when they moved you on briskly, "Come on, never mind, chin up, get on with it. Try again." ' She looked at Mira. Listening, miraculously, to every line. 'You know, probably, that very English habit of trying not to dwell on unpleasant matters.' Mira nodded. 'Well, now they have plenty of ideas and instructions. They gave us a book-let. Make a box, have a memorial service, read these books. Talk to other people, you may find it useful, here's the number of the helpline. No need now, in this more understanding age, to pretend it never happened.'

She looked at her hands folded on her lap. 'I wonder how much, though, these ideas help. I don't, you know . . .' She shook her head. She thought of the box they had, its few items – a card with the baby's footprint, a lock of her hair, the plastic band they had placed around her tiny wrist at the hospital. The very poverty of that small box, and the paucity of items within it, made the thing more depressing than helpful. Kate had hidden it finally in a cupboard in the guest bedroom. (The bedroom that might have been Cassandra's; thank God they had not yet painted it when she died, though William had had to remove the cot they had acquired.)

She continued. 'I didn't want Cassandra in a box, I didn't want, and still don't, want to stand about with a group of people talking of her. How would that be possible? I may pray, yes, but I certainly can't pray around other people. It is very quiet and private, it has to be.' Kate felt that today was a day to be gentle. Not bitter. Here was a woman whose husband was ill. How ill? 'So to answer your question, how should I keep Cassandra with me,' she said – but then the retching began again. It sounded dreadful. Deep and painful.

Mira closed her eyes for a moment, and Kate once again looked away. And perhaps, after all, she did not need to voice more of an answer to Mira. Perhaps she should simply bear in mind the question, and leave this poor woman in whatever peace might be possible for her, given the terrible sounds coming from elsewhere in her flat.

*

What would happen if she ran out of room? Mira had never had the worry before. Certainly not at the beginning of her work, when she was so energetic – Mira remembered herself, newly trained, eagerly plumbing the complications of her life in her own treatment so she could better serve the others. She was waiting then only for her hours to fill with the searching and the troubled, she sat in anticipation of meeting them, as one might anticipate a long summer's read of novels brought home from the library. What were their stories? Who would they be? How would she help them?

There had been other times, of course, when Mira was stretched and worn, and the space within her was occupied entirely by tragedy. It went with the territory. Years ago, in the eighties, there had been a suicide, a lean beautiful boy with the face of a prophet, who chose finally the long and dreamless sleep over the continued confrontation of his demons. The parents were destroyed. Mira remembered the way she had tried to make the suicide readable for them, a terrible prospect, even as she punished herself nightly over possible missed signs, her failure to have the boy hospitalized. It had been already his third, his last, attempt, and the parents were good enough not to exercise all their necessary rage on her for the death, and Peter gently reiterated that she could not have saved the boy. Yet Mira could not for months stop the wringing of her hands. That had been a time, she recalled, when she was so full of this singular catastrophe, the parents' grief and her own, all the questionings and self-criticisms – that she found it difficult to accommodate the rest of her patients and their congregations of distresses. She had taken a two-week break (Peter and she had gone to an island in Greece: the bone-white heat and too-blue sea, lean cats sunbathing along wall-edges helped still her mind's circlings), but that was the longest she felt she could be absent. Why punish the others for what had happened? She must not let her patients down, the group she had then (the Miser, the Dancer, the Difficult Daughter; the Anxious Student, the Man Who Didn't Know). She had had to dig deeper within, hack away a thick undergrowth of doubt and preoccupation, to clear the space again for the others, but she had done it. She had been young and stronger then. She had worked hard, so hard, not to let them down. To find for them, each, some room.

Now Mira was neither young nor strong, nor determined in the way she had been. She felt her imagination shrinking. There was a weariness now, a sigh, a sense of *how could she get through it?* these hours, that was wrong. It was fraud of a kind for her to think of her work that way. She would become the person snaptongued Svetlana had sometimes imagined her to be, a charlatan seer who collected people's money by putting on a wise face, who remained hollow, unknowing, within. If this happened Mira would have to cease working. She was a person of integrity, and could not bear to watch herself deceive or pretend. The prospect reminded her of a final show of de Kooning's she had gone to at the Tate with Peter. The early rooms vibrant with his controlled, dense madnesses, the power of the lines, the intensity of the forms. At the last, a lonely room of work produced once the painter had Alzheimer's and could not reliably be considered to have a mind. These final paintings were pale scribbles, empty exercises, sad shells, and they made Mira choke: why expose and humiliate the man this way? Why exhibit the mortifying, humbling spectacle of an artist losing his self? She did not want her own work, her sessions, to become like those late, mad de Koonings, gesture merely with no heart or thought behind them.

If she lost the muscle to listen deeply, as she must listen, she would have no choice but to close her practice. It would be the only honest thing to do, to stop working.

And if she stopped working, Mira feared, she would follow Peter shortly into the disintegrating hell that was now his.

There was a month and a bit left now till the end of the year and Jan One. That gave him, what, four, perhaps five more sessions before 1999 rolled in – that cusp of millennium year, when the armageddonists could issue excited warnings about *Y2K* as they called it. Computers everywhere would melt or explode. Air-traffic control would go haywire, jets would crash midair and no one would ever even hear about any of it as all radios and tele-visions would have cracked under the strain, the power grids failed, darkness descending round the globe. Howard did not take the millennial fears seriously – it was scaremongering, simply – but he knew 1999 would bring some form of apoca-lypse. Public or private. Every year did.

His bearing had changed towards Mira as the year had rolled on; now, with the days shortening, he could not bring himself to hate her quite as he once had. Jane was coming to spend two weeks with him at Christmas, and that was softening him towards the Serbian brutalizer-turned-psychotherapist. He still enjoyed baiting her, to a degree, but since learning about her ailing husband the sport had rather gone out of it. Like learning Hitler was a vegetarian, and kind to pets; it put you off your stride.

Still, as usual when he sat down, he had no great urge to start with anything close to home. What was there to say? The end of 1998 was in sight. If the Queen had had her *annus horribilis* a few years back, this had been Howard's. Monica had been monstrous to him all year. Richard had now elected to be out of touch alto-gether. Job was dreary as it always was, the department was likely shrinking and everyone was at each other's throats. Where was the interest in speaking of any of that? It was elsewhere in the world that the important dramas were taking place. He could not resist asking her. He was curious, actually, and here he had a source, a direct source. What was her view?

'Do you think this ceasefire will hold?' he asked. 'Can they keep their bloody hands to themselves, the Serb army?' It had been a recent concession to her, after he found out about the husband. 'Serb army' rather than 'the Serbs'. A change in word choice. He wondered if she had noticed.

The therapist tilted her head neutrally. Her face was careful; wary; as blank as she could make it.

'My guess is it's a smokescreen,' he continued. 'A way to give the troops a winter break, reorganize. Keep the bombs at bay for a while. Con the Americans into thinking they're fantastic diplomats and have some influence on Milošović, when in fact he's playing them like a pipe. He'll be back. He's not going to give up Kosovo like that. He's not going to give in, after all this time.'

That tempted her, he could see. She was seriously considering letting him have it. A long tirade about Kosovo, its deep meaning for the Serbian people? Howard had read enough to know that's what they said to justify the latest horrors: it's our ancient homeland, that sort of line, never mind that the Serbs were a desperate minority in the province now, outnumbered by Albanians. Or perhaps she'd jump straight in with a bitter condemnation of NATO and the Americans, their hypocrisies and inconsistencies. Howard wouldn't argue that one. Europe and the Americans had made a hash of this one right from the start, way back in the early nineties when the slaughters began and everyone shut their eyes and said, It's none of our business. Yes that was hypocrisy, and cowardice, and politicians' unwillingness to take on evil when they saw it if an intervention wouldn't play well at home. Losing troops somewhere people didn't much care about, and losing popular support as a result. These were countries, after all – Howard would not pretend the British were saints in this – who had had the brilliant idea of appeasing Hitler (that English genius, Chamberlain) or of accommodating him to save their own skins (the contemptible French). No, he would not argue for the purity and virtue of NATO. But the bomb threats had been a good thing. There should have been more of that from the beginning: you see an adder and you cut off its head, simple as that.

'Well?' he said impatiently, hoping to nudge her over the edge. Howard could sense it in her, the stored-up froth and fury. He would so love to make her show it openly. That would make the year oddly worthwhile. He wanted to prove to this woman, finally, that he was not the only one. *He was not the only one who was angry.* This was perhaps what he hated most about the structure of these sessions, about the entire rationale behind these sessions. All right, he was fucked up in his way, who wasn't? But the assumption that on one side of the room sat all the trouble and rage and inadequacy, while on the other sat calm, serene wisdom . . . that was what Howard loathed. What bloody claptrap that was, designed to keep patients humble, paying obediently, lining the pockets of the mute psychotherapeutic guru, who – as was perfectly obvious and unavoidably true – had quite as many difficulties and fuck-ups of her own. It was common, human sense. Each person had his demons. Had her demons. Look at her, Mira Braverman, Serb married to a wasting Englishman: she was positively writhing with hers. Why not, for once, admit it? Why the attachment to the unruffled Buddha pose, when it was clear from the wrinkles gashing her face and her anxiously clutched hands that she, just like Howard himself, was ready to open her mouth and scream?

'Well?' she echoed him, her face cold as stone.

'Oh, come *on*, Mira,' a sudden exhalation, like the steam from an engine, that was half-laughter, half-exasperation. 'Give me something, will you? Just something small, for my money. All right? The ceasefire. *Will it hold?* There. Just that. Can't you tell me your view about that? I am paying you, after all.'

'Is that why you come to see me?' she asked, and fuck if she hadn't managed to collect herself, after all. Merely simmering, now. 'To hear my opinions about the wars, and about Kosovo?'

'I just mean,' he said, trying to sound reasonable, 'it seems like something I could fairly ask, after all these months. I'm interested, you see' – he could not keep the sarcasm from his voice, though he tried – 'in your opinion. Your judgement.' Was she flatterable? He doubted it. Too damned canny for that.

'What would you achieve, Howard,' she asked him sternly, the headmistress, now, 'by coming here in order to talk about Kosovo?'

'Oh, God forbid,' he sighed, 'we should talk about something that interests *me*. Shall we go back to my unkind father and his experiences during the war, the other war? Fighting in Italy and all that? You like that, don't you – that's what interests you. I just thought, as the paying customer, I might try to have one of these meetings go as *I'd* like it to. My mistake, obviously. It's your bloody show.'

'Is it?'

'Well, it certainly isn't mine.'

'Then why do you come to see me?'

'Believe me, Mira, I ask myself that question every time I get on the bloody Tube to come to Camden Town.'

'And what is the answer?'

'The answer,' the Bigot said, sitting back in the chair and puffing noisily like a bull, 'is that my daughter made me promise that I would. For a year. The year's almost over. Thank Christ. We're nearly shot of one another, Mira.'

'What do you mean – what sort of promise?' Now it was Mira who sank back into her chair. She felt oddly winded.

'Jane. After the divorce. She thought I had *things to sort out*.' If it had been anyone other than his youngest daughter who had issued the phrase the Bigot's mouth would have puckered as he quoted it, but to Jane he had always, it seemed, been willing to listen without prejudice. Jane had been his lifeline. A voice he could hear.

'And so you—'

'So I promised her I'd find someone. For a year. I promised one year.'

This explained so much. This was one of those narrative details that tied everything together. Suddenly a story cohered, and the presence of this hateful, difficult man in her room, weekly, had a source she could recognize. His sense of paternal responsibility: Howard did have that, as Mira had known for some time. He had paternal feelings. It was introversion that he lacked. Interest in the inner workings.

'And,' he smiled wryly, 'I may as well tell you, Mira – this is my Christmas gift to you, all right? – she thinks it's been very *good* for me, seeing you. Jane thinks I'm much calmer now. Not as – how did she put it? Some daft piece of jargon. Oh yes, that I'm not *carrying* as much anger as I used to.'

'Do you agree?'

'Ah well, it's like taking medicine, isn't it? Antibiotics for an infection. Would the infection have cleared anyway, in which case the pills acted basically as a placebo? Or did the pills take the infection away? How can you know?'

Mira nodded.

'A year on, nearly, I've had to – I mean, you have to accept, don't you? Monica's a bitch, hates me, has for years it seems, and in her vengeance has turned one if not both older children against me. I'm left with Jane – sometimes – who's a lovely girl, a credit to her dad . . .' His small smile was endearing in its way, and Mira could see, as she sometimes had before, how women might find this ego-bruised man attractive, an unnerving thought. 'She sees the situation more fairly. I'm left on my own, which, to be honest, is a bloody relief, most of the time. It really is. We did not live well together, Monica and I.'

Mira could not speak.

'And the others do listen to Jane. Alison, the older one – she'll come round eventually. She won't feel she has to hate me so. I can see that.' He watched the window. 'Richard is gone. I'll never have Richard back.' He shook his head. 'But then, Richard and I, we never . . .'

The man paused, caught in window-light, then thought of something, something else altogether. Mira could not know what. He looked at his watch and again smiled. Mischievous rather than spiteful: it was a fine line with Howard.

'We'll have to leave it there, I'm afraid.' Parroting the therapist.

Which left her with the expression normally reserved for her patients, the startlement, the brief hurt, the sense of being abandoned. Though, too, it was hard not to see the comedy in it. Mira allowed a small smile. A first, with him?

'Don't worry, dear,' he said in mock kindness. 'It's not our last session. I said I'd stay with it for a year. Until January.'

Mira watched him, conscious of the fact that she had not spoken. She must find something to say, to assert herself, but no words came to her.

'Why don't you save those good thoughts for next time?' the Bigot concluded, ironically. He was enjoying this performance, she could see. In a strange way she was, as well. He put his coat

Ten

December

The Christmas tat had already been everywhere for weeks. Mira enjoyed that Anglicism, *tat*, a blunt, true sound to capture the empty sparkles and green and red excesses of cheap decorations, storekeepers' dutiful bowing to this season of colourful, manufactured religion and frenzied consumption. Mira had loved holidays and their rituals since she was a child, but hers was the Orthodox tradition, Christmas celebrated in January with particular foods and traditions that were meaningless here. She had, when required, given in to plum pudding and party hats on December twenty-fifth to be agreeable to English friends and family, listened to the syncopated voices of carolers warmed by mince pies singing jaunty songs of Bethlehem and merry gentlemen, and she had learned to associate the day with the dreamy, foreign hush that fell on the capital when everything, briefly, closed. The commercial perversions of the celebration, however, tended to dispirit her. December's arrival brought with it a series of necessary appointments between herself and the High Street, shops she ordinarily avoided and dreaded encountering. But she knew how much pleasure her presents brought to Svetlana and Jasna, even Josip when he had been with them, and though the prospect of shopping filled her with melancholy, this year of all years she must make an effort.

Mira left the flat on a Saturday morning, willing herself not to carry with her in every step the image of Peter as she had just seen him, asleep in their bed, mouth agape (once again she thought of Bacon, and shivered), his flesh a nameless, unholy colour in the region between yellow and grey. She had felt both guilty and frantic, leaving, the need to stay with her sick husband tugging as hard as the ignoble desire to put a temporary distance between herself and him. She wanted keenly to be near Peter, near as she could be, greedily stacking and stashing moments spent by his side, even in this compromised state, as if she could hoard them for later like a bear gorging on berries preparing for hibernation. Then, too, she wanted to leave. If Mira could leave the flat, that might be a kind of spell fending off death – it was like an ordinary day, for her to go out shopping, and so perhaps if she went out shopping their lives would miraculously be ordinary again. Besides, it had been a full day, two, since she had breathed other than sickbed air and she was close to suffocation.

Mira left a note. GONE SHOPPING. LOVE, M. She hadn't wanted to wake Peter to tell him. He had slept so poorly in the night. There was a good deal of pain now, more than either of them could stand, and the medication he had for it was inadequate. He had turned and moved and groaned through the slow dark hours in a vain effort to get away from it. (Again Mira found herself angry at the disease and at Peter's body for the unwillingness to give Peter rest: didn't that body realize how desperately the release was needed? Why resist it?) Only in the later morning had sleep finally arrived to give the poor man some relief. They must see the doctor again. Today. They must see what could be done. She should not stay out long.

Cigarettes for Svetlana. A carton of her favourite Silk Cuts separated into individual packets to be stuffed in and around other offerings. Mira did not think one was allowed to send cigarettes, but had got past any squeamishness about possible smuggling years before, during the period of the sanctions, when the West had seen fit to deprive and humiliate the people of Serbia for their leaders' policies – when Svetlana and her family were desperate not just for cigarettes, but also for basic medicines and food items. Mira's overstretched imagination taunted her with the image of an EU official coming to the door of their humble flat, urging her away to some dank prison for those who sent contraband in defiance of Western Europe's laws and regulations. She shrugged. Her husband was dying and her sister needed cigarettes. What could frighten her now?

Then – baby clothes. Mira ventured into foreign areas of clothes shops, seeking doll-like outfits to clothe the unknown boy, her niece's son. Women swooned, Mira knew, over such items. Maternal or would-be maternal hearts melted at the diminutive. A tiny this, a tiny that, how sweet, how dear. Mira did not so much soften as try to weigh what Jasna might need or want for her child. A yellow pullover with little green footballs? Pale-blue pyjamas with navy and red cars? A woman at the till tried to engage Mira in grandchild chatter, a bright confectionery expression on her face. 'Thank you,' Mira said, resisting, eager to return to the High Street and its newly welcome press of large, adult bodies. All were babies once, she sometimes reminded herself. There were faces and figures of whom it was impossible to believe.

Next, to cloak the Silk Cuts, a soft polo neck for Svetlana. She liked dark colours, claiming they hid the telling folds and wrinkles of age. 'My face I can live with – if I do well with make-up and stay in dim light you might think I was still in my forties. But the neck! The neck gives it all away.' Mira supposed the same was true for her but, at sixty, did not feel she was in the business of concealing time's passing. She was who she was and the age she was, and not interested in sleights of hand or deceptions on either point.

And feeling older now, by the day. As Mira aged, her city contracted. The familiar patches – her postal code, primarily, the dingy edges and newer-minted niceties of NW1 – became more and more familiar, until she ceased to see the bizarre giant boots protruding from the fronts of Camden's many shoe shops, or record the ever more pierced and bolted youths who came in leather and metal droves to visit the weekend market. She no longer registered with any surprise the juxtaposition of bottle-blotched drunkards propped on the pavement and impatient Volvo-driving mothers turning into the car park at Marks and Spencer's or Sainsbury's. She saw very little of any of it now, though once-bohemian Hampstead, up the hill, was still capable of lifting her spirits. Reminding her of her former consort, the London she had loved.

Mira should ideally go to Hampstead now to find a few other suitables for Jasna and Svetlana, but as the morning lengthened towards lunchtime Mira felt anxiety pulling around her ankles like a net. She needed to get home. Peter was at home, yellowing and greying, and she must be with him. Such was her abrupt conviction that she needed to rejoin him that she decided to leave for another day the ordeals of parcels at the post office, that winding, sniffling queue of patient, envelope-laden citizens urged by a tuneless repetitive voice towards the next numbered window.

No, home. Home, it must be.

The right instinct, evidently, as immediately on opening the outer door of the building and entering the tiled foyer, Mira heard an ungodly sound, an otherworldly howl, that could only be coming from her flat and her husband, and could only mean it was time, now, for some new crisis to commence, for which she would have to find some as-yet-unplumbed source of calmness and strength.

So that was what finally broke you: the pain. Not, in themselves, the fear, or the humiliation, or the anger, all those known emotions that had become nightmarishly magnified. Fear of one's own end; humiliation at the prospect of total degradation; anger at the unfairness of it, the approaching annihilation of self. You might spend a lifetime as a literature professor or a psychoanalyst considering the dimensions of the emotional life, chronicling its dips and sways, noting the different ways a person could be gripped by passion or anxiety or rage – only to discover, finally, that we are all bodies, and that the worst there can be of anything is pain. Pain swallows all.

Peter had lost track of the time. So much so that he did not know whether it was day or night. There were signs to go on – earlier, Mira's distant body had been near him (how foreign now, how impossible, the notion of touch, of communion) during one long and excruciating stretch, which must have been the *night*; its subsequent absence (a relief, if you could call anything a relief in this gnawing hell, to have the sheets empty around him) probably signified *day*. But there was no way he could sleep in this agony, because how could any part of him relax enough to release him into that longed for perchance-to-dream state? And yet he must have slept. Or he passed out. He was permitted, in any case, by whatever arbitrary powers were overseeing this demeaning ordeal, to pass into a different state of consciousness for some time, in which whatever tiny piece of him, of Peter, was left, could retire to a safer place, shelter temporarily from the battering storm.

When he awoke he was thrown back into the vat of vipers. He had some sense that this time it was bad enough, violent enough, that he chose to answer back. He shouted at the pain, was that it? He argued with it. Was that it? Or perhaps it became less adversarial than that, perhaps he and the pain came to some civilized agreement, *we must learn to live together, it is no use shouting this way; it does neither of us any good to engage in battle* and so they came to a harmony with one another instead, a cohabitation, he and the pain, they fell into a rhythm, a joint pulse or melody, and perhaps that was the sound he was making, it was a song of sorts, a song of songs, to accompany the dancing devilish pain. It was his music, Peter's, to accompany the pain's.

The sound had the effect of getting people's attention. Peter had become nearly unaware of the existence of his fellow fellows, of the other people around them. He might as well not be living in a city at all, he might as well have been in a hut on the edge of a hillside, a Norwegian mountainside, for all that he knew or cared of neighbours. (They had gone to Norway once together: how he had loved it: how the steep grandeur and cooled slate green of that landscape spoke to him.) Apparently others did not share Peter's indifference, however. At some point in this so-called day the world outside his haven, outside this flat (that's right, he was in a flat, not in a hut at all but in a set of rooms one called a *flat*), elected to make its presence known. There was a banging on the door. It might have seemed initially to be a banging on his head, but on closer inspection (he could see nothing around his head, and the banging was at a distance) it proved to be the door. Voices could be heard. *We are getting help for you. An ambulance is on the way*, whatever that meant. Oh, ambulances. Were they not loud and shrieking and alarmingly white, harbingers of doom? A way of announcing *The end is near*? Perhaps he could travel in something quieter and more discreet. Then again, need he travel at all? Where could he possibly go, from here?

Mira was near him, suddenly, and others. He was still making sound. He must still be making sound as they were trying to stop him, Mira and the rest, with the kind of placations one feeds to a newborn. *Hush, now, hush, it's all right, Peter, you're all right, we are helping you.* It didn't work on babies, did it? Why should it work on him? Peter had a late sympathy for those freshly delivered into the world, whose primal wailing so distressed parents and listeners. Why not let them cry, Peter wanted to say to all of them now, all the shushers, they are crying for a reason. They are responding to the world around them and are only speaking the truth. Can you not bear to hear it?

'We are going to lift you on to a stretcher now, Peter,' said a white voice close to him, not Mira's, and another gasped, 'Oh, God – the blood—' before the first overrode him with a gentle, 'All right, Peter? You'll be all right now. We are going to give you something for the pain. All right?'

Give him something for the pain? What could that mean? Had the pain not already been given all that it could? Had the pain not proved itself impossibly greedy already, taking everything from Peter, every piece of him, leaving him with nothing; or, at best, with a thin shaving of self left, a flake, a negligence, and how was he to carry on with just that, with nothing of himself to hold onto?

'No, no,' he tried to say, evidently incoherently, about being given something for the pain, but the shushers kept shushing him as they shunted him into the death wagon, and whether they had given the pain anything or not (he was not certain; his senses were blurring, like rainwater over a windscreen) he could feel

241

himself falling, falling into oblivion, which right at this moment seemed the only and best place to be.

'He's quite bad,' Graham was saying, and his hands did not know what to do, so they occupied themselves with putting the kettle on and fumbling for bread, an effort at a restorative tea and toast. The look on his face suggested he had no hunger, had nothing but confusion. 'He's in the intensive ward – he lost quite a lot of blood – I'm not clear how. I'm not sure Mira understands. She doesn't seem to know, or be able to explain . . . '

'She's probably in shock, love,' Clare said gently, hoping to settle him. He did not seem settlable.

'He's on morphine now. For the pain.'

And Clare did not either know what to say to *morphine*, the word calling up as it did images of addicted Victorians lapsing into states of blissful passivity, or very old, very sick people given that last tonic to ease them into the next life. Had Peter reached the end already? Was he sliding that fast?

'We must – Graham, we must go—'

'To London, immediately. Yes.' He turned off the kettle. 'Let me just—'

'I'll pack a bag for us both.'

As Clare moved around the bedroom collecting clothes and necessities, she dithered over whether to include the Christmas packages she had already wrapped for each of them. Books, and a scarf for Mira. Was it absurd to bring them still? Gifts were the last thing they needed just now, probably. And yet not to bring them suggested that you had already given up. A scarf was not offensive, was it? Books? She had chosen them carefully, as distractions that might not seem to be distractions. She packed them along with her special purple pills for the creature inside her.

Clare returned to the kitchen to speak to Graham but found him on the phone, his voice making an attempt at social normalcy, his eyes fixed on something through the window that was not their garden.

'I know it's very last minute, and I wouldn't ask if it weren't— Yes, at UCH, and he's on morphine now, apparently – for the pain— Do you really think Hugo wouldn't mind? Do you want to wait to ask? – No, right. Well, that's very kind, Caroline, thank you, I can't— Well, yes, exactly. Thanks. Right, we'll see you later, then. Afternoon, some time.'

And as he dismissed the phone-enclosed voice and replaced the emptied object into its receiver, Clare continued to watch Graham's eyes straying over something distant, unseeable; and simultaneously felt a flutter within that could have been worry, or premonition – or something else altogether. She instinctively put her hand low on her belly. Her interior was silent, revealing nothing. Had that been it already? Was it possible? She knew it might happen any time now, the first sensation of movement. They said you weren't sure of it at first, unless you had been pregnant before, but that after a few times you would learn to recognize it. A butterfly flight; an internal flicker; an odd swimming sensation. She had read different descriptions. (Clare spent so many private hours reading about the pregnancy's progress – Graham had no idea. She kept it secret from him, something like having an affair, she imagined.) Had that been her child, its insect wings flapping against her innards, already? Or was it just the morning's breakfast?

Graham did not see their house or the car, and scarcely had a memory of driving. He could not fathom the fear that gripped him. His father was very ill, yes, possibly close to dying, but why should that frighten him so? He, Graham, was healthy enough, wasn't he? Yet his entire body seemed to shake and bend like a fragile poplar in a pre-storm wind. He could not concentrate. It was all Graham could do to keep steering, his clammy hands holding too tightly the wheel.

His wife talked to him of London. She had dismissed the idea initially, he recalled, pleading pregnancy, pleading house and stability, offering ineffable female resistance to movement or discussion. But something made her change her mind, he had no idea what, and they had, miraculously, been preparing for this temporary move. In a little over a week – just in time, it seemed. For now, they'd stay with Caroline and Hugo. Clare was trying to help him. Graham had the sense she was trying to be a good wife. He noticed a maternal efficiency in her words and actions, new qualities since the arrival of the possibility within her. This was not an altogether different Clare, but it did signal to him, even in his fog, something of the Clare she intended to become more fully as she aged. As she became a mother. As the role of wife became one whose meanings, whatever they might be, she came to wear more easily.

They arrived. Must have. Must have because here he was in a hospital lift, desperate suddenly for a coffee, for some substance that would help him focus and understand. Clare squeezed his hand, and though Graham might once have found that embarrassing, looked to see whether the uniformed man had noticed (a nurse, male nurse – well, this was London), today he simply took the touch for what it was, a presence and reassurance. It was all he had to go on, in the absence of a steaming cappuccino.

The lift stopped and out they poured into the subdued density of dramas and heroics that made up this floor in the hospital. Much as the luminous fluorescence and soothing greys tried to disguise the fact, tried to stare down awareness, Graham knew it was death going on around here, death and survival. He knew there were plastic buckets filled with blood or excrement, that pieces of bodies were removed and burned here (or removed and tested and burned), and that clever architects had arranged the lit labyrinths in such a way that the building's many darker functions were invisible, as if unknowable. That, like an Escher drawing, the place held wards and corridors that were open and acknowledged, and other corners that were accessible only to the initiated and the brave.

'It's this way,' Clare said to him at his elbow, reading the runes, and he let her guide him to the right blue door, the right beige room, the right pale curtain behind which lay an improbable, sallow figure who was, Graham was told, the right man. His father.

Mira was sitting on a thin plastic chair, pale too and clearly wearied. She rose to greet them.

'Thank you—' she began, but Graham did know, if he knew anything, that he could not let his stepmother thank him for coming to see his own father, so he quieted her with a warm hand on her arm that evidently startled her. Clare embraced Mira. The woman looked haunted as a child woken in the tiny hours with night-terrors. Seeing her disorientation helped dispel for Graham a little of his own.

'What have the doctors told you?' he asked her, and it seemed the first clear sentence he had spoken all day, since receiving her original distraught telephone call.

'We're to have a meeting this evening, whenever the cancer specialist – Mellon, he is called – can come. We are waiting to talk to Mellon.'

Graham nodded and turned back to the figure against the bed. Substances were being dripped into him. He was nowhere near consciousness. He looked peaceful, at least. Graham was grateful for that.

His shaking had diminished. The sadness was gathering now

245

in his stomach; he could feel it balling there like fat, indigestible yarn.

'Hi, Dad,' he heard himself say to the body before him. No blink or flicker of acknowledgement, of course. Graham moved closer to the bed, put a light hand on his father's arm. 'It's Graham. And Clare. We're here now.' He felt his wife sidle closer to him, as if to be seen, as if to be in the picture. 'And we're staying.' He stroked the arm slightly, up to the point of the tapes and tubes. 'We're here now, Dad. All right?'

Yes, it was again Mellon. Here he was, with his sunken neck and the vile mole, and Mira did not like the face more with progressive viewings. She felt always that he was hiding something from her, that he was playing some game with her. He reminded her of one of those oily communist functionaries, back when Yugoslavia was still whole, men who would hector about the good of the state and the greatness of Comrade Tito (Brotherhood and Unity) while waiting eagerly with the bugs and handcuffs for those who dared misstep or betray. The kind of man who might invite you into his office (this had just happened to Dušan, Svetlana told her, at the university in Beograd) after your years of dedicated teaching and tell you, with falsifying placidness, that it was time for you to leave your post. Why? (And even if you hated Dušan for what he had done to you, or to your sister, or to their children, or to himself – allowing his good mind to waste its richnesses on the obsessive pursuit of the young and voluptuous – still you knew that his poetry was important and his teaching probably even now compelling, mind-changing as it had been forty-odd years before, and that to hobble him now, in his seniority, was an act of venal and petty vengeance. 'He did not have the right views, of course,' Svetlana told her, 'and he wasn't as quiet about it as he should have been.' And in spite of

246

the bitterness about him Mira could not help hating his tormentors more. 'Many people at the University are being chucked out. It's a kind of purge. Mira Marković and her people. You're either with them, or you're out.' Dark-haired wife and muse of the President, that other Mira was said to have an iron grip on her beloved Slobo and a hand in his decisions. In Svetlana's view it was Mira Marković running their country, Milošović was just her cat, her familiar, assisting her in her dedicated plans to ruin Serbia, what was left of it. The woman fancied herself an intellectual, too. And a feminist. 'My feminism disappears when I think of that woman, Mirka,' Svetlana confessed to her sister. 'I have a terrible desire to see her burned at the stake.')

Here he was, then. Mellon. Sunday morning (he had been out in the country during the crisis of the night before, he apologized), a quiet church hour when Mira would have preferred to be lighting candles and praying rather than listening to the agnostic, science-cluttered speech of a medic. Graham and Clare were on their way from their friends' flat, where they had been staying, but had not yet arrived. Mira was alone with the doctor, unable to defend herself against him, or even interpret him.

'Not a nice Christmas gift, this, is it?' Mellon began with a tone which might, in some strange account of human exchange, be imagined to lighten or reassure. Mira wanted to slap him. *Tell me how bad it is.* Mellon must understand she had no need for nonsense or pleasantries.

He wanted to talk about the body in complicated circumlocutions, and again, Mira did not want the body and did not want his circumlocutions. She did not understand them. 'Response to the treatment – one of the drawbacks,' and then some, 'very dramatic, of course, but not quite as bad as it looks,' and then some, 'immune system weakened,' and then some, when what Mira wanted to know was *How much longer do I have with him, Doctor?*

247

What is ahead of us? And, a question not for this desiccated man at all but for the priest, for someone who tended to deeper places than just the body: *What can I do for his spirit – for his soul?* Mira wanted this doctor to be a fortune teller, not a tracker of blood-cell counts and organ failures or successes. Perhaps in England the wife was expected to follow the body's minutiae, each inter-related action, and from that information make her plans about their lives and how to proceed. Mira was not equal to it. She wished – how she wished – that Graham were here now. Another Englishman. He and the doctor could speak to one another and then her stepson could translate.

She was not absorbing the information, Mellon could see that, and in all fairness he could not be sure whether the blame lay more with himself or with her. One of them was not trying hard enough. His own effort was to keep the wife calm and focused on what was closest to hand: her husband, lying here tubed and drugged, an alarming sight, he knew, which he was attempting to demystify. Explain what was happening with the illness and how they were treating it, and why (the cancer had spread to the liver, as it often did; they might have to back off from the chemotherapy if the body couldn't take it, but stick with pain medication to keep him comfortable), so the woman would begin to see this as a rational, explicable process, not simply as overwhelming chaos and disaster. People became fear-ful of course, spouses especially, and he knew from years of experience they often had an underground suspicion that all the treatments were fundamentally blind, useless gestures at a grimly impending death. On one level, perhaps, they were right. (This man, Braverman, did not have long, poor fellow, after he recovered from this shocking episode. Six months at the most, Mellon would have said. More only if there were some miracle.) But on another level they, spouses, needed to be clear that doctors did know what they were doing, that they were cautious, diligent, attentive and in a particular way optimistic: optimistic enough to make good faith efforts, even with an older man in this state, clearly weak, clearly declining, to prolong his life.

She was not responding, though. She was, Mellon understood, not *receiving*. Perhaps he should retreat. Try a different approach.

'Where are you from originally, Mrs Braverman?' he asked in a voice he tried to make amiable. Conversational.

'Belgrade,' she answered dully. 'In Serbia. – Yugoslavia, formerly,' she added, either with a touch of irony (as though he might not know of it) or defiance.

It was not an answer Mellon knew immediately how to manage. He stepped back half a foot or so. A *Serb*. Did that explain why she was so cool, so encased and unreachable? He could not help wondering what had they been like as a couple before the lymphoma had struck.

'Why do you ask?' Mrs Braverman questioned him pointedly, and Mellon floundered as he very rarely did, faced with the keen, inquisitive eyes of a woman who came from that benighted place, those unlovable people. Why had he asked?

'I had thought— One finds that different – different countries have different approaches. It can make a difference . . .' Where was the sentence? Explanations usually came so easily to him. 'People have a wide range of expectations about how doctors will speak to them,' he succeeded finally, a line he had issued often enough before. Yes. That was why he had asked. 'Illness can be disorienting for a patient's spouse as well as for the patient himself. We try to address that.' That was it. He had it now.

'Do you—' she began in a voice that sounded hostile, and Mellon began then to think of moving to his next patient. There were other people to be seen and spoken to and now it was quite clear to him: it was she, the Braverman wife, who was the problem here. Certainly it wasn't Mellon himself. He had done his best to steady her, reassure her. He had done his best.

'We know how difficult it is for you,' Mellon said blandly, invoking with that 'we' his peers and fellows, so that she knew he had the crowds of this establishment on his side. Then he prepared himself to go, after giving her certain numbers she could ring in case she should ever find in herself the need to speak, or (which he doubted) the ability to listen.

It was not pleasant to wake from the deep dream of crisis in a hospital bed; but it was better, Peter supposed, than not waking at all. He might never have come back. No one had said as much to him, but even in his diluted state he was able to read faces and voices and it was clear to him from the cobweb fears still clinging to Mira and to Graham that death had come close to him, close enough that still when his consciousness wandered he could remember its frost touch on his neck, dimly recall the oppressive sense of its presence.

He had warded it off, however. For now. He was in the hospital (grim place; they couldn't help it), had been here for a week or two, he was not sure how long. Time had altered since he had last examined it. He might be home 'in time for Christmas' as they kept telling him eagerly, as if Christmas could matter to him this year. It was a day, just that. Meanwhile Peter was mostly to stay in his bed receiving visitors, like royalty. There were flowers about, and fruit (grapes, dates, clementines; he'd always loved the neat completion of a clementine), a few sweets. He could eat little of it, but he had been attended to, which flattered him, and gave him an unfamiliar sense of his own importance. He mattered, apparently. That was good to know.

Graham and Clare were moving up to London for a spell.

This development, which might once have made him hesitate, seemed simply sensible in Peter's current distracted state. (They were giving him something for the pain, which instilled a pleasant, sleepy indifference to any sinister implications. He used to dread such states of vaguery; now his once thorough mind enjoyed them.) Graham and Clare would be nearby. Good. So they could help Mira look after him, if necessary. Good. Peter could not imagine Graham in the Florence Nightingale role but his dear daughter-in-law would fill it nicely, her pretty face, her gentle manner, her kind ministrations.

Graham, though: it was surprising. Graham's had been the first face Peter had seen on returning to the land of the living; a slow wash, a rising from the depths, the ship had almost sunk but here it was, surfacing again, and there was Graham, his son if it was to be believed, sitting on a nearby chair reading a newspaper. The boy had rattled it shut on seeing Peter's opened eyes and moved jerkily towards the bed, saying, 'Dad! Hello – hi – it's Graham—' As if he didn't know. 'How do you feel?' Too much of a question to be answered there and then, so Peter hadn't bothered. He had let his eyes reply, it was too soon for words, and also with his eyes to ask the question.

'Yes,' Graham said (so he understood, good lad), 'Mira's just popped back to the flat. Obviously if she'd known – she'll be disappointed. She has been here the entire time, nearly.'

And Graham had gone on like that, talking about Mira and the doctors and Clare too – 'she's just popped out' – his son suddenly a middle-aged lady in his speech, and not only that but reaching comfortably for Peter's hand or arm, when they had rarely touched each other much, before. Graham seemed so at ease with the motion, there was none of the embarrassment or reluctance Peter was used to nosing from his some-time son. If you saw them together here in the ward you might think there

251

was nothing out of the ordinary about this father and son at all. Perhaps there wasn't.

Mira returned later, as did Clare. The air about the bed became suffused with a female atmosphere. It had never been as clear to Peter before how warm and golden women were, but here in the hospital it was perfectly obvious, that and the fact that when they were around, the drearier objects (tubes, machines, bleeping devices of all unknowable kinds) became unimportant and translucent, strangely shedding their materiality. When it had been just himself and Graham, or on occasion himself and the cancer doctor (Peter could not remember his name), all the objects surrounding his bed became heavy and immovable, bearing down on him as though keeping him pinned to his bed. Even the blanket across his chest weighed more, took on an uncomfortable scratch. And though he had no wish to blame this transformation on the men themselves, he knew it could not strictly be their fault, still he longed for the company of women who could make the world lighter and freer, permit some wandering of the spirit.

When he was better and speaking again the other visitors started. Neighbours, old friends (the Epsteins, Mira's Marjorie), colleagues. The Gertrudes and Alans of his department sent cards or gifts but that dear fellow Andrew, a welcome soul, made the trek from Oxford and came to Peter's curtained chamber exuding some mysterious sympathy that acted as a balm, a holding. The jokes he told, or the jokes he did not bother telling. The sense of honesty about him. He had come once, and Peter hoped he might come again.

'You have a visitor,' they told him now, and he wanted the visitor to be Mira. It was all very well, other faces, the concern and fruit they brought with them alongside their good intentions, and when a quiet spell arrived he was at times bereft, wanting more of them, wanting everyone to come, everyone he had ever known, the whole parade: his parents and school friends, his earlier colleagues, the man who had taught him to racewalk, that tweedy fellow from Inverness Street market, the famous actress, a prime minister or two. At other times, now for example, all he wanted was to see Mira. To feel her near him. Her completing presence. Her deep, good voice. Her hand on his.

'It's Helen,' someone said to him, a silvery figure approaching his bed, though what 'It's Helen' signified he was not certain. What was Helen? This person, evidently, whose face brought back to him a green dress and a distant preference, the knowledge that he had made a mistake, years ago, an important mistake that had clung to and distorted everything that followed. His decisions, his sentiments, his hopes. (It was a mistake that had given him Graham, however; and he would not have wanted not to have Graham.) She had had a green dress. He had chosen the wrong flatmate. Helen's eyes had such humour and life in them, but he had been with the dimmer, more fearful girl, who could become animated in the company of this flatmate but on her own, with Peter, was subdued, faded rather into just a body, a body with which he had chosen to have intercourse. Lydia. How cynical he had been. How young. And what had happened then?

'Do you remember – from the park? We met again—'

'Yes. Lydia's friend.'

The visitor looked remorseful about that. 'That's how I heard,' she said, gesturing apologetically at him, his bed, and then 'I brought some flowers,' which was clear from the clustered colour in her nervous hands, and whatever they were – he hadn't the names – they were unusual and cheering.

'Thank you.' He was experienced now in accepting offerings. People brought him gifts: he had come to expect it. He was

253

benign and gracious. 'A nurse should be able to find somewhere to put them.'

'I've brought a vase as well. Hospitals are hopeless with flowers. I'll put them here, shall I?' She cleared a space on a side table with some efficiency and in her, too, a woman he scarcely knew, who had no reason for being here that he could see (except that everyone should come to him), Peter felt that relief and that sun, if that was what it was. She carried with her into this light-less ward something of the sun. Yet that was wrong, surely. Women were the moon, were they not, in so much fable and imagery? Not at all. Warm and golden. They were the sun.

'She wanted you to know she's thinking of you and sending all her good wishes,' this one, Helen, said to him, almost furtively. Almost as if she were on a mission, an undercover job. He might have asked *Who?* but she continued, 'If there is any-thing she can do – she'd like to help, if there is a way to. She has told Graham—'

And then, thank God, so he did not have to ask Who or try further to decipher this encoded communication, here was Mira. At last. His Mira.

'Ah,' he said, his voice all gratitude, all openness and want and his dear Mira leaned over him, kissed him, comforted him with the proximity of her alive body. He wished he could lie next to her. Enfold his thinner, foreign self in her ample arms.

'Here's Mira,' he said when she stood up again, to the silvery figure whose name he had temporarily forgotten. 'And here's . . .'

'Helen,' she supplied kindly. 'Hello. I'm so pleased to meet you.'

The slender silvered woman did not have the look of a col-league. Mira could not place her.

'I knew your husband at Oxford,' the woman explained. 'In the early days. He cut quite a dashing figure then. Quoting

254

Baudelaire. Reading Pushkin. Nobody knew anything about Pushkin.'

'I can imagine,' Mira made herself smile and this woman seemed all right, nothing the matter with her, she had a good face, not the sharp and shuttered kind worn by some English women of that age but an open, lively look. She might have a sense of humour. She might have a fine heart. Mira did not feel she would find out. Had Peter and Helen been lovers at Oxford? Such people did surface in these circumstances. Mira did not feel inclined to find that out, either.

'He does it still,' Mira said softly to whoever Helen was, and spoke a few lines of Pushkin into the airless air, drawing a smile to her beloved's lips, which started to move, silently, in the same rhythms and shapes as her own.

This was the last night she and Graham would stay with Hugo and Caroline. After this they would move to the flat in Mornington Crescent. Clare could not quite believe she had agreed to it. Both this fact and her altered physical state – she was getting larger now, a noticeable bulge – seemed unreal, as though part of a story being told about her life rather than the life itself. Clare and Graham in London. Really? Her sister, of course, thought it a brilliant idea, wilting any of Clare's fears with the strength of her own brusque convictions. 'It will be fantastic for you to get out of Bath, Clare, and away from Mum and Dad. You were on your way to becoming Mum and Dad, which is a horrible thought. No, London's just the thing for you now. Your baby will be a cool urban baby rather than some dull Bath baby. And it's much closer to Brighton, it will be easier for me to come and see you.' As if that were an uncomplicated prospect: her tattooed sister in the same room as suited Graham and his full-skirted Serbian stepmother (they were waging peace between them now, at least, since the crisis) and his dying father and her own fattening pregnant self. One great happy family.

They had been generous, Caroline and Hugo, in all of this. Well, chiefly Caroline. Hugo had been 'decent', Clare supposed, to borrow a phrase. She did not have much sense of him still, he worked a long day and when he got back he and Graham went off to the pub – one of those done-up pubs, not so much pints of lager and packets of gammon crisps as posh wines and dishes of olives and almonds, and media types all over. Very smoky. She never used to mind or notice that but now – and with not drinking – that sort of place had little appeal for her. Not that it mattered. The men preferred, she guessed, to be on their own.

Leaving her with Caroline, who was not at all what you'd first think. Away from the performative setting of a dinner party, Caroline's humour was gentler and more self-effacing, and though she still said dismissive things about Hugo ('He's a monster, I'm afraid') she had time now to tell Clare all the stories which made such jokey vitriol understandable: the affair or affairs, the general neglect, the degree of self-absorption. 'I used to think we would get divorced, in the wake of the Miranda nightmare. That we'd join the severed masses,' Caroline told her one day over coffee in a nearby pastry shop. 'It seemed inevitable. But in a bloody-minded mood I persuaded Hugo to launch on this mad odyssey, the IVF farrago instead. And that does cement a bond, in an odd way.' She chronicled for Clare, quite graphically, the unpleasantness of the IVF treatments and procedures. They had, she said, embarked on their last attempt now. Clare found herself waiting in suspense for the date when Caroline would find out whether this time, by luck or miracle, the IVF had worked. Caroline was neither hoping nor expecting, she told Clare adamantly. She was braced for disappointment. 'Always the best approach.'

And Caroline proved a good listener – selectively. The age difference between them made Clare feel like a younger sister, or a distant niece, to Caroline, and she revealed far more than she had intended. Caroline asked acute questions about Clare's marriage, and in exchange for Caroline's honesty about hers, it seemed only fair that Clare should offer up her year or more of condensed unhappiness before Graham finally agreed to having children. 'What a selfish bastard' – Caroline's assessment – 'to make you wait like that. For no good reason.' About the current crisis, however, Caroline had less to say, taking in its general shape, that Graham's father was increasingly ill with this horrible cancer, poor man, and that as a result the couple were temporarily at least moving up to London. Clare, for her part, kept mangling the details of the disease. He had weathered some devastation and was, if not recovered, at least something like himself again. He should be coming home soon. Not in time for Christmas, perhaps, but in the new year. Perhaps in time for his wife's Christmas – Graham's stepmother celebrated the holiday on the sixth of January.

'Oh?' Caroline asked idly. 'Why is that?' She was half reading a magazine at the kitchen table as she spoke, and her face seemed somewhat flushed. She checked her watch periodically, as if there were something in the oven, or she had a train to catch.

'She's Orthodox, I suppose you call it,' Clare said. 'They do Christmas differently, don't they. I don't know a lot about it – haven't asked her.'

'Greek?'

'Serbian, actually.'

'*Serbian?*' Caroline looked up sharply.

'Yes.' Clare pursed her lips. 'It's strange, isn't it?'

'Serbian?' Caroline repeated. Now she was paying full attention, and Clare felt almost guilty, as though it were disloyal of her to disclose this information. Caroline was probably horrified. Serbs: everyone hated them, of course. Clare wanted to defend Mira. Poor Mira. Each time Clare saw her in the hospital now she seemed more bereft and bewildered than the time before.

'Yes, but she's lived here for ages. She's not part of what's been happening there. She's been married to Graham's father for years.'

'What does she do?' Caroline asked. 'I mean – does she work, at all?'

'Yes. She's an analyst. Or a therapist. I'm not entirely clear on the difference.'

Caroline closed the magazine and briefly put her head in her hands. When she lifted her face its expression was one of wry surprise. 'I don't suppose you're joking.' Her tone, mildly hopeful.

Clare was confused now. Had she said something wrong? 'No, she – no, that's what she does,' she stuttered. 'Why, is there something—'

'What's she called?'

'Mira. Mira Braverman, she has his father's name, of course.'

'Of course.' Caroline was a brittle character, but she issued a laugh, now, that had some full body in it. '*Christ*, Clare,' she said, and she put the magazine down, brushed her fingers through her hair, and then looked up at Clare through fingers half-covering her face. She was laughing, as if they were old friends and Clare could anticipate the joke. She couldn't. 'In that case, I have not just one piece of news for you,' she said, touching her belly, 'but two.'

Eleven

January

Forty-five Albanians were massacred in a village called Račak. By the Serbs. The deaths followed hard upon the murder of four Serb policemen outside the same village some time before. The massacre was a vicious retaliatory crime; or it was a just act of war, as the men killed were guerrillas of the Kosovo Liberation Army. Perhaps the number was forty-five, or perhaps it was fifty, or perhaps it was much smaller, the number inflated to fan the flames of anti-Serb sentiment. The dead were guerrillas, or they were innocents. There were many stories. At this distance it was impossible to know the truth. Then again, it was probably impossible to know the truth even there. Even in Beograd. Or Kosovo. Or Račak.

She brought him soup. There was a simple pleasure in that, in bringing him something to sustain him. Now that Peter was home Mira could finally feed him, and that was a small, good deed.

'It wasn't so much that the food was awful,' Peter said. He sat up in bed, pale still but shaven (she had helped him), restored to something of his former dignity. 'Though it was. Fairly awful. What was worse was eating it.'

She did not know where to take her outrage, her repugnance. Did you believe the story as reported here? Were the Serbs again monstrous (the word coming so easily now as to be meaningless)? Or was it a set-up? The men had been shot in the back. Their blood seeped into the snow. Spilled for what?

'I came to loathe those trays. Making one feel as though one were on an aeroplane. I didn't like that idea. Travelling, on an aeroplane – to where? Where was I going? The next world, probably. Not a happy thought.'

He spoke differently now that he was home again. He sounded like Peter. A recognizable Peter, not some Tussaudian waxwork.

'And then the nurses hovering, like bored waiters. "Are you finished?" And I often wasn't, because it took me so bloody long to eat anything. But I hated their waiting, so I let them take the trays away. Just so they would leave me alone.'

'There were too many people. Too many different people.'

'Yes. Never alone, except at two and three and four in the morning when I was wide awake.' He stirred his soup, remembering the demons. He did not wish to frighten her with them, she could see that. 'They should make a set of visitors' hours then – two to four a.m. It's one of the worst times.'

'I should have stayed more often. I could have perhaps—'

'No, love.' He reached for Mira's hand. 'The place wasn't set up for that. The night or two you did spend' – Mira had slept in the hospital most of the first week, but he didn't know it – 'was terribly uncomfortable for you, clearly. It was better that you came back here.'

Where the newspaper and television journalists waited for her with their shards of stories. They were her company now, when Clare and Graham weren't. She did not care for them. She wished she could make herself stop paying attention.

Mira stroked Peter's frail head, his narrow arm, while he sipped. Let him take an hour here to finish a bowl of soup. He was home now.

'You don't like Mellon, do you?' he asked her.

'Not much.'

'I could see that you didn't.'

'He seems so pleased with himself. And – he asked me pointless questions. About Yugoslavia.'

'Ah. Did he.'

She must not tell him about any of it, Račak or any of it. There was no point. How could Peter hear of it now, any of it, the ongoing brutality, the jumped-up pretexts for war? Illness made it impossible to travel, but not just literally, physically; the mind was equally homebound. Had to be. Resources had to be marshalled for the internal battles. This was and was not the same man who had talked her through the nightmare of Srebrenica, years earlier, who had kept a tight hold of her while the outrages warred within her, as they did now: Such horrors are impossible. My people could not have committed them. It is all set-up and lies. But perhaps they did commit them; perhaps my people can be savage, and were. But perhaps they were provoked. Perhaps – round and round until Peter had finally said to her, simply as it seemed, 'There are places where evil flowers, Mira. You know it. We have all seen it. Humanity challenges itself, What is the worst we can be? Srebrenica was one of those places. Thousands summarily executed, driven out of a safe zone? There is no explanation.'

'I felt,' said Mira now, to keep away from Račak, to keep from asking for Peter's unavailable help, 'like such a foreigner there. In that hospital.'

'They are very strange places.'

'I couldn't understand what Mellon was saying to me. It was a good thing Graham was there.' She paused. 'He was very helpful, you know.'

'Yes, he seemed impressive. Quite able to manage.'

He pushed his bowl away. Three-quarters finished. Not bad. And she saw again, as she had in the hospital, the skull beneath the face, the corpse beneath the body. The absence beneath the presence, waiting, ready to supplant it. Her heart spasmed in rebellion.

'Peter, love,' she said to him, covering his body with her own. '*Ljubavi.*' As if, if she wrapped herself round him, she could protect him, and no one could take him from her. He startled at the embrace, then leaned into it. 'I am so glad that you're home.'

And still the wretches came. Would they never cease? Christmas had been and gone, Mira's Christmas too, on the sixth of January, an Orthodox date to which Peter had always mutely nodded, though her spiritual beliefs remained mysterious to him. He could see – a part of him was still capable of irony – that the timing of his hospital stay had been quite convenient for Mira's work schedule. She would have been off then anyway for several weeks, her flock of the lame and wounded carrying on without her, through the darkest Christmas carols and most offensively glittering decorations, the bickering relations and inevitable post-holiday dawn of hangover and disappointment. Mira had always said that January was her least favourite month in the professional calendar as so much of it was spent listening to the bitter, after-Christmas litanies.

And here she was, back at it. More precisely, *there* she was, in her enclosed space – the Hold he used to call it, or the Delivery Room, the place where lost souls issued their monologues, a sealed remote place, an isolation chamber. A small box near the entrance of the flat. He used to wonder what the designers of these odd living quarters had originally had in mind for that compartment: a study of some kind he supposed, but for a small and contained person. Not a scatterer, as he was. Peter had a slightly larger area for his papers, writings, scraps, dim quarters near their bedroom, a corner of the flat he rarely visited in these days. On returning from the hospital Peter had stood one day in the open doorway to his study and stared at the room's contents as if at some exotic rainforest. He had written there, once. He had thought. He had retired to his cluttered surfaces and busy piles as if to a corner of his own mind, a corner now sealed off with a velvet cordon like one of those rooms in a stately home you could gawk at but were not meant to enter. *This is how they lived in another time: isn't it fascinating? Look at the tiny beds, the family portraits, the chamber pot.* (He himself had a chamber pot now, a nasty, plastic thing they suggested he take home from the hospital.) Peter had never been much of a one for that sort of National Trust outing, though before her death he had joined his mother in excursions to such places, along with all the other bussed-in OAPs who counted the minutes till they could visit the shop and have their tea. His own mother was like that. *Doesn't the fruit cake look nice?*

'Would you like a cup of tea, Peter?'

His new angel, rising from Mira's chair in the sitting room where she had quietly been reading, exuding her restorative presence. His ministering Clare. How he loved her.

'I won't, thanks,' he said, thinking of the OAPs. Had he been sleeping – drooling, snoring – as he slid into that memory, or fantasy? He checked the sides of his mouth discreetly with a crooked finger; they seemed damp but not positively pooling. What a relief. One relied in ways that would have been unthinkable, earlier, on other people's ability still to discern one's real self through the obscuring weakness and baldness, the bodily embarrassments, the clingy flimsy bedclothes. Still, with his pretty, plumpening daughter-in-law there were certain indignities he hoped to avoid. He would prefer not to stink rancidly, as he sometimes feared he did, nor emit grotesque noises unexpectedly. He would rather not drool.

'Good book?' he asked Clare, mostly to engage her in conversation, as the question was becoming a painful one that belonged more properly to the room behind the velvet cordon. Peter could scarcely read by himself any more; he lacked the eyes and the inclination. He could be read to, and liked to be, though increasingly there was a dependence on the video. Mira had procured a set of opera videos for him, borrowed from a neighbour, and they both found, newly, that the high emotions and soaring music, which had seemed melodramatic to them before, now struck the right tone. Other times they would play old French films, softly. He could not always follow the story but found the buttered, fluttery language easy on his ear and on his drifting spirit.

'Not bad,' Clare replied to a question he hardly remembered asking. 'Canadian. My sister Sara said I had to read it, so . . .' She gestured at its cover, dutifully.

Standing, she stretched, a pleasing, cat-like move, and as she did he could see the small bulge in her belly that represented another life. Extraordinary idea. How lucky his son was, Peter felt with sudden sharpness. To have all this. He did not know how lucky.

'Are you all right? Peter?' Clare came to him, anxiously, evidently reading a spasm on his face or hearing an inadvertent exhalation of pain.

'All right? Are you all right?' It was Mira now, too, both of them, listening to him, holding out a dish, in case he was going to be sick, a damp cloth, in case that might soothe him, a hand, in case he needed steadying.

Her husband was white with bewilderment. 'But I thought – don't you—?' he asked, gesturing with his eyes towards the entrance of the flat, the room where Mira worked.

'It's all right,' she said to him in her practised tones. 'There's no one there now.'

As in fact there had not been for the entire hour. Mira had been enclosed in the Delivery Room all by herself, alone with her cliffs and hollows, awaiting a patient who never came.

The Aristocrat. Uncharacteristic: never showed, and never called, leaving Mira to wonder privately what might have happened.

It was coming up to a year. It was impossible not to be conscious of the date. It loomed, in about a month, and with it the question of what to do, how to mark it, whether to. (*Jahrzeit*: the Jews had a word for it. How right they were to name it.) Kate's mother thought they should go away, a weekend in Barcelona perhaps, or Amsterdam, a city replete with cultural distractions. William could take a few days off from work. Or they could stay close to home, keep it ordinary, make nothing much of it. Perhaps she and William should simply go to the cinema, see a wistful foreign film about an older woman, or an escapist flick about a heist gone wrong – William liked those, couldn't resist the bangs and boffs and mad car chases. They could not watch any story that featured a pregnancy or young children, and it was surprising the large number of films that cut out. Kate had discovered in herself a latent interest in war films, which suited the times: death and fear and courage, passion in extremis. She liked all that now. Life is so dark, Kate thought now, and we are dark too.

A change, this many months on, was her ability to read the newspaper. She no longer required William as a filter, she could turn the pages herself. She followed only the drama in the Balkans, though; didn't bother about Blair or the euro or the gruesome murderers who stalked the pages of the tabloids. Of course Kate had been aware of it years earlier, the terrible stories, the images (starved men behind barbed-wire fences; endless columns of battered, shuffling refugees) and the Channel 4 newscaster sternly probing Serbian officials and European politicians on death figures and tragedy dimensions. *What are all of you allowing to happen here in Europe at this late date in the twentieth century? How can you?* William had been on the side of bombing then, some form of military action, and at the time she had thought merely, How like a man, to come up with that solution, though she had not said as much to William, nor suggested an alternative herself. They had just come together in those days, and William was a blessing and a light in Kate's life, not least because she had the notion that with William, if all went well, she might at last have a child. Her fondest hope. And if they had a child, what could it matter to her whether the man advocated bombs and guns as a response to the mayhem in the former Yugoslavia?

Now – she could tell William was surprised, cautiously pleased – Kate paid attention. How could one not? The headlines were terrible. 51 DEAD IN RAČAK MASSACRE. And yet Kate knew, honestly, that she had been just the person who would have turned away from such news a few years before. How horrible, she would have thought, skimming past such a headline, taking in the basic shape of the story – people in a distant place choosing to blot out a neighbouring group of families, for reasons allegedly related to nation or religion – before moving on to something easier to take in, Tories misbehaving or a bad boy pop star in the news. *I can't fill my head with such vileness*, she might have thought a few years earlier, shaking her head over man's inhumanity to man.

Since Cassandra, Kate was newly alert to the world's disasters, and her imagination had unfolded and grown. Specifically, she paid attention to this late stage of the Yugoslavian bloodbath because a woman was helping her who came from that part of the world; and because Kate thought differently now, and living in a clean, self-centred way, with a nod to others in her charity work, no longer seemed enough to her. Why were people killing each other in the prettily named province of Kosovo? How could fifty-one people have been massacred, without cause, and wasn't it right that some brake be put on such murdering? William's view was that the Serbs were at it again, terrorizing and brutalizing, that the October ceasefire signed by Milošović had been a sham. Milošović was not a man of peace and never had been one, Dayton notwithstanding. The tyrant only understood one language, and it was imperative now that the UN or NATO be bold enough to speak it. 'The only measure that will work with a man like Milošović is firepower,' William said, 'and the sooner NATO countries move beyond their squeamishness over airstrikes, the better. Nothing else will make him stop.'

Was that how it was? Kate wondered. Was that the language that had to be used with 'a man like Milošović'? Men spoke that way to one another, Kate knew, with threats and force (bangs and boffs and mad car chases) and perhaps she was a foolish and naive woman to wonder if there could be a solution to this violence other than the threat of more violence. Kate had always instinctively believed there must be other possibilities. If you asked people 'on the ground', as newscasters were fond of saying, the actual people living in the actual places, surely they wanted peace, wanted to be able live without the prospect of flight and

267

displacement. What good would bombing do? Would it restore lost lives? Render villages amicable and habitable again? Kate could not see how it would. Perhaps she should try harder to comprehend William's argument. Violence now to achieve less violence later, that was the gist of it. Ends justifies the means.

'I used to have such a feminine view of the world,' Kate said now to Mira, here in the quiet room. She was trying to find the simpler line in her thinking, as the therapist had taught her to. Also she sought a way of not mentioning the massacre, because what could Mira possibly say about that? 'I think I used to be a bit stereotypical that way, always seeing things from the woman's perspective. Whatever that is.'

Mira looked quite grey today. The flat was quiet, and Kate felt it would be wrong, an intrusion for her to ask about the husband who had been unwell those weeks before. Was he better now? Was Mira's skin a shaded response to the horrors in her home country? Or was it something else altogether? Money worries, perhaps. Or Mira might be unwell herself – a touch of flu. There was a lot of it going around.

In any case, it seemed wrong to pester her about her wars. Not her wars, of course, *those* wars. That war.

' "Used to",' Mira repeated. 'Has something changed?'

'Yes, of course.' Though Kate wearied now of bringing everything back to Cassandra – even she occasionally felt *Can you not speak of something else? Are there not other causes, other tragedies?* Yet it was the point of her coming here; to talk about Cassandra. If, that is, there was still a point in her coming here at all. She was beginning to wonder. 'I am not the woman I was. My assumptions have changed. But more than that – ' she tried harder, 'I'm not the woman I would have been. If I had had a child.'

'Because . . .' Mira indicated, as if towards a blank line Kate was meant to fill in.

'Well, it's an essential part of being a woman, isn't it? Having a child.' It must have come so naturally to Mira, Kate thought. Look at her ample, maternal body. Two or three children, Kate guessed; half a dozen grandchildren. There had been a time when Kate thought her therapist knew what it was to lose a child. But she did not, Kate thought, understand what it was to be childless. She could not. 'I don't mean to sound reactionary,' Kate said, going gently, 'and it's not as though I think women without children don't have marvellous, adventurous lives. Of course they do – we do, or we can.' Kate had said this to herself a hundred times to try to soothe the pain. It never worked. 'But, particularly if you want to have a child and cannot, or if the child – if the child dies—' She could say it now, clearly. 'There is simply a way in which you have failed. In some primitive sense you have not been woman enough to do the thing women are meant to do.'

'To have children?'

'Yes.' There was a rather fierce, unreadable expression on Mira's face, and Kate's thoughts drifted again to Kosovo. Was that what was troubling her? And all this rest seemed foolish, beside the point? Kate did not know what she could do about that. 'I know people think this about me. I can see it on their faces. They don't mean to, they mean to be sympathetic, but they can't help it.' She paused, and added: 'Even William, perhaps. Even William.'

'Do you think it? About yourself?'

'Oh yes. Certainly I do.' Kate still thrilled, a year on, to the honesty that was permitted – encouraged – in this room. 'Yes. I've failed. I'm quite clear about that. I'm not – I'm not a real woman, the way a mother simply, essentially, is.'

'Why are you only a "real" woman if you bear a child? Where does that idea come from?'

The Mourning Madonna tsked, under her breath, and wore that look patients had when asked to explain a truth they considered self-evident. 'It's everywhere.' She waved a hand. 'Even in this culture, where women have fantastic careers and are prime ministers and the rest. You can't escape it, this sense of your feminine destiny. And in my case, it's gone awry.'

'Isn't it a choice you make to believe that? Couldn't you believe differently?'

'How?' Kate folded her arms defiantly, and this was good, Mira thought. She had rarely seen the Mourning Madonna irritated with her. It was important that the patient had the independence to find Mira's questions bothersome – it meant she was growing.

'Couldn't you, also,' Mira pressed, 'believe that you are a mother? Cassandra was your child.'

'Yes, but—'

'Is any mother who loses her child no longer a mother?'

'It's not the same. If you've had a child die in your arms—'

'Are all experiences of motherhood "the same"?'

'But you know what I mean. To *have* a child is different.'

'Aren't there women who become mothers without bearing children? And' – Mira's voice was quite stern, she realized – 'aren't there women who bear children who are hardly mothers at all?'

'You mean I could adopt. We've gone over that, William and I—'

'I am not talking about that. I am talking about your vision of your self. You don't speak of William's failure as a man. As a father.'

'No. But it's different for men. It wasn't his body – it was my body that somehow did not do what it was supposed to do.'

270

'You blame your body? And for that – question whether you are a real woman?'

'Well – yes.'

'Isn't that like blaming people who are ill for their illness?' (How angry she had been at Peter initially, for being ill. How she hated herself now for that anger.)

'Well . . .' the Mourning Madonna hesitated. 'No. No, that's wrong, obviously.' The elegant woman watched Mira, assessing her, and Mira recognized the look. The patient was trying to guess the therapist's biography. Illness: had Mira known it? And where did her views about children come from? Mira wanted to show nothing, as in the past, but she felt so much weaker than she had been. Her skin was thinner. She worried that everything would shine through, now, that her history was transparent.

The Mourning Madonna turned away and found the window. 'I don't mean to blame myself. I know, of course, that what happened is not my fault.'

'And yet you do blame yourself. Punish yourself.'

'Yes,' she said quietly. 'I suppose I do.'

'You are choosing to have this belief of yourself as a woman. That is your choice. You do not have to do it. *Kate*. You could think differently.'

Mira knew what she was saying was hard. She believed, at times, in this direct challenge to a patient's skewed views. It was something you had to be ready to do in her work, like a doctor breaking a bone to set it properly.

The Mourning Madonna was quiet for some time, battling inwardly, then made a conscious effort to tidy herself up. She faced Mira again and now her bearing was proud. Almost regal. A new side of her. This was good.

'I understand what you are saying to me,' she said carefully, as she gathered her things. 'But you don't know what it's like.

271

You can't – to feel motherhood, the possibility of it, taken away. You simply can't know,' she said with some bitterness before leaving, unwittingly sending a keen arrow into one of Mira's own hidden wounds. It was just the sort of patient comment that permitted no reply.

Mira noticed the Bigot's absence in ways she would not have expected. In none of her work now was there room for conversation about Serbia. Within those fraught and tiresome exchanges with Howard, which at times had the quality of a military engagement, had nestled some relief after all. She would not have known it until he was gone. (How often, this past year, had she wished him gone!) Easier perhaps to have the prejudice sitting before you, calling you names, than to walk dishwatery wintered streets wondering which of your fellows near you hated your people, and how much. You, sir – are you in favour of dropping bombs on my family if Milošović does not tear his men off their Albanian prey? And you, madam? And you?

Peter was no longer to be spoken to about it; Graham never had been; and Clare, sincere girl, tried from time to time, but Mira was wary of sharing with her daughter-in-law any of her native thoughts, lest they complicate the delicate balance the four were trying to maintain in the face of the rapidly approaching end. It was not the time to probe Clare on her Balkan views, or make her a vessel to contain Mira's troubled own.

Which left only Svetlana. But speaking to Svetlana now felt less like a bridge built across waters and distances, and more like shouting from one sinking ship to another. 'The waters are cold, and the sharks seem to be biting.' 'You are my sister and I love you.' What else, beyond that, could they say?

Svetlana had got a little better about Peter's illness once she had finally accepted the news. Still occasionally she made odd

272

assumptions about how glamorous cancer treatment must be in Britain (Mira asked her once: Do you think we live in America? Have you been watching American television programmes?), but at least she did not try to pretend any more that the illness was anything less than catastrophic. In fact, with blunt pragmatism, she shunned any euphemism about the ravages of the disease, and Mira appreciated that. Svetlana asked about Peter's appetite and his digestion, his stool and his vision, keeping track from one conversation to the next of advances and regressions. She always closed now by saying, 'Give your dear husband a kiss from me,' a signal of affection she had never issued before. Mira wondered whether Svetlana could allow this new, dying Peter into some rarefied chamber of suffering that Mira herself, in unbattled Britain, was barred from. Perhaps only those in imminent danger could gain entrance.

Not that Svetlana knew precisely what danger they were in, in Beograd. Beograd news was a choked and limited business, had been for years: like a blind person staggering over unknown terrain she had to ask her sister for direction.

'You must tell me what's happening when you know anything,' Svetlana urged, her voice stripped of its habitual irony. 'Here we are in darkness.'

'What do you know of Račak?'

'Little. Terrorist beasts; staged incident; international community likely to use it as an excuse for more aggression. All of you lot' – Svetlana included Mira in the conspiring Western collective – 'trying to prevent us maintaining our own sovereignty in Kosovo. Gathering your tanks and missiles again. Trying to frighten us.'

'Are you frightened?'

'I am. Jasna is. Do you know who is not? Zoran.'

'He's back from . . . ?'

273

'He was back over Christmas. Scarred, tight-lipped, ready for more. Ready for blood. "NATO's bombs don't frighten us. They're cowards who fight in the air, too scared to come and meet us, man to man. They're wrong if they think it will make us turn back." He's gone again now. It's better when he's gone. Jasna and Marko are better off.'

'And Josip?'

'Nothing.'

Each paused, feeling the waters lap at their toes.

'We were so close, Mirka,' Svetlana said, after half a cigarette or so. 'We were so close to getting rid of the bastard, two years ago. Dušan thinks that was our great failure as a nation. He is very bitter now.'

'Dušan?'

Mira had only to utter the name. Both knew what was included in the question. *The devil, Dušan? You're talking with him again?*

'Yes.' Svetlana's voice had a new timbre in it. 'Dušan has been over here a lot, lately. Yes, out of a job, so he has more time on his hands, but it isn't just that. You'd be surprised, Mira. He is very good to Jasna. And the baby, Marko. He pays attention to his grandson. Can you imagine?'

'To a baby?'

'I know. It is impossible, but there it is. Dušan has been coming to join us more recently, and – it's not a bad thing.'

A new cigarette. Mira, numb, knew there was something important in this for Svetlana, but her thoughts were too muddied to understand it.

'He is just the same in many ways, of course,' Svetlana mused, in that same – changed – voice. 'And in other ways, he's . . . older. Aren't we all.' An exhalation. 'But he's still a man who knows how to be good company.'

There it was. The 'man' jagged Mira's memory and she knew what she was hearing. Her sister was sleeping with Dušan again. She had become once more a woman in that sense. Desired. Desiring.

It was not an experience Mira would have again with Peter. It was gone, and the rest of it was going, too. Soon. The water had come over the edge of the vessel now, Mira felt. She was sinking.

You are my sister, and I love you, Mira wanted to say, but beyond that she found it hard to speak.

Serbian. She was still getting used to the news, some weeks on. It had made Mira suddenly so specific, so real. Serbia: what could be more brutally real than that? Before, the older woman had had a mythical, abstract quality that Jess had found useful. Romantic. For selfish reasons, no doubt, but then wasn't therapy a license for selfishness? Wasn't that what you paid for, the privilege of thinking only of your own needs and not the other person's? Previously Jess had travelled the few blocks from her flat to a cultural oasis, a safe haven – this little room inhabited by Eastern European wisdom and literacy. Jess thrilled especially to hear Mira speak in her thick accent about Dostoevsky, felt that she was on some snowy Petersburg street engaged in conversation belonging to the great European ages, able to escape at least temporarily the crass modernity of her own American tongue. The conversations Jess had with Mira were by definition so separate from the life she generally led, a life in which everyone drank blithely until they were willing to embark on ill-advised amorous adventures that could in turn become good column copy the next week. It was all so trivial, which Jess knew even as she was compelled to take part – like being swept into an elaborate group dance in which you had no choice but to follow the steps, or fall. Jess did not want to fall.

She had often had the impression that Mira viewed such goings-on, and Jess's evident relish in mentioning them, with mild scorn, and in a strange way Jess had understood the scorn, valued it; shared it, probably, on some level. Mira, truer citizen of an older, truer nation – a suffering, deep-souled people like the Czechs, probably – could bring Jess back from the abyss of nonsense she seemed poised over, and remind her of what was more honourable in herself: the person behind the columnist, the voice behind the story. A more authentic person altogether. That was why Jess continued to see her twice a week, in her third year now of chronicling her hopes and her discouragements. Mira promised a pocket of sanity. A corrective. Mira's stern tone interrupting some of her inaner outpourings: 'Jessica.' That 'Jessica' brought her back to Petersburg, or Prague, the snowy streets, her higher self, reminding her of God and of the Devil.

Only to discover that it wasn't Petersburg or Prague at all. It was – what – Belgrade, Jess supposed. Or was it Zagreb? She wasn't entirely sure. And perhaps Mira's scorn (did Jess imagine it? Project it? You were supposed to project onto the therapist, weren't you? that meant it was working) did not, then, come from aesthetic disappointment in Jess but rather from something more political: a disbelief that someone like Jess could consider her social flittings and maternal strivings significant, or interesting, when in other people's countries – in *this woman's* country – people were killing and being killed for all the old reasons. Hatred, fear, lust for power. Religious intolerance, 'God'-sanctioned savagery. Jess had never, in truth, followed the Balkan drama all that closely, except to be loosely appalled by it. Along with everyone else.

'It's all seeming sort of trivial to me right now,' Jess tried as an opener. She wanted Mira to know she was aware of her own triviality, but hesitated to bring up the other subjects directly (war; Kosovo; this latest horror, some vile massacre of innocents in a distant snow-bittered village). They had gone for so long without, in these sessions, it would seem false to start in on it now.

'What seems trivial?'

'Oh, well . . .' Jess waved a hand. 'You know: the journalist juggernaut. The whole scene.' She thought of the book she was producing from her columns. It excited her, she couldn't pretend that it didn't, to remember the editor's high expectations for the book. 'This could be a Bridget Jones-sized phenomenon, Jess. You'd best be ready for it.' And film rights, and all that followed. Her imagination ran away with her. This might take her several rungs higher up the glamour ladder. *Movies*. How much higher could a girl from Palo Alto go? 'I have to deliver the manuscript in about a month,' Jess said casually, as though delivering manuscripts were something she did all the time. 'After that, I'm thinking of going on holiday with a friend. To Barcelona.'

Mira waited for amplification, and after several weeks' silence Jess decided to provide it. You were supposed to be honest and all-revealing in here, and she had not been, lately, about her romantic life.

'Not a friend, exactly – a boyfriend. There's a guy I have been seeing for a little while now.'

The sex had been great. And he seemed like a decent guy. Not always the height of gentleness, and able to bore on at you a bit in that way that men did, but – a nice guy. She had become very fond of his Baker Street flat and the soulless chain stores that surrounded it: the fiesta-coloured coffee shop, the overpriced stationery franchise, the pub with a fake name, the late night mini-grocery (good source for Bombay mix, her midnight snack,

277

or a walking breakfast of flapjacks and boxed juices). Several tiny newsagents crammed with countless British candy bars, glossy publications and an overworked photocopier. Jess was coming to love all of it, not least her long ambles back across Regent's Park in the mornings.

'I'm not sure how much to say about him.'

'What seems important to say?' Mira's voice was not as resonant today, Jess noticed. This had been true several times lately. Her voice was thinned-out, hollow-sounding. Her therapist was not in the mood, Jess figured, to hear about long nights of athletic lovemaking. Not that she had ever talked much to Mira about sex in any case. It had never seemed appropriate to the whole Petersburg atmosphere.

'He seems like a good guy. But, you know – it's early days, still. And I've been burned before, as we know.' Jess smiled ruefully – complicitly – inviting Mira to cast an indulgent eye back on some of her earlier mistakes. The invitation was, apparently, refused. Mira's face was impassive.

'His name is Nick,' Jess continued, 'and he works in sales at the paper.' But she could tell this would be one of those sessions that would not go anywhere especially. They were each locked in their reticence, and it could not be Jess's job to persuade Mira out of hers. She was the patient, wasn't she? So she would toss out a few crumbs about the new lover, his age and situation, the two boys, the divorce, and the more communicable of their conversations together, while holding on silently to the most exciting and important possibility of all.

Here, at last, I may have found a man with whom I might have a child. When the time was right, and after she had spoken to him about it (but look at the devoted father he was; she didn't anticipate any problems there), Jess would say as much to Mira, her ready, loyal witness to a life thus far filled with errors and mishaps. They were in this together, weren't they, Jess and Mira? Certainly they were. No matter about Kosovo, about Serbia. When the time was right, Jess would enlist Mira as an ally, her listening ally, in whatever came next in her determined campaign to begin a new life.

He was beginning, finally, to feel married. It was dawning on him now, what was meant by that bond and that promise. (He was thirty-eight, for God's sake, but you could not always command the time in your life when such revelations might arrive.) This was not simply someone whose company you enjoyed, whom you found attractive, with whom you could look forward to a lifetime of shared breakfasts without a heavy, dread-laden heart and the wistful memory of solitude. Graham had felt all that for Clare, and during this year and more of their married life, those breakfasts and dinners and shared nights had been deeply pleasurable, but Graham had not yet felt ushered in to that odd elect sect of the *married*.

He was beginning to now. They were side by side, that's what it was. They were next to one another. Not pullable-apart. Their blood was running together. Did the feeling follow from the putative child? Odd that it should come to him just now, when they were not in residence at the proper house they had set up in Bath, which had anyway never afforded Graham the contentment it evidently had Clare. Living as they were in a rented flat (it was furnished with bland sofas, muted artworks, unfamiliar china, one of those white-and-cobalt Chinesey patterns) should have felt more temporary, as of course it was, and Graham knew this environment would not stay with him as their home in Bath was meant to do. Yet he was free here, and comfortable. Joyful, even, a piece of him, in spite of what was happening, and in this

279

state able to love Clare with greater attention than he had been able to in Bath.

And she was so good. Clare was revealing herself to be simply, unobtrusively good. She knew somehow (how? Graham himself was so clumsy, so hamfisted) how to comfort Peter, lift him and care for him while not drawing attention to herself for doing so. She did not, as some altruists did, seek recognition or applause. She acted when action was needed, and was silent when a stiller air was required. She could be concerned without seeming worried, and cheerful without seeming like a liar. Graham saw his father relax and settle into her stewardship.

She soothed Mira, too. Living this close to them for the first time in his life allowed Graham to see (too late; he did not dwell much on that) more than he ever had of their shared life together, his father's and Mira's – the common reference, the soft-souled friendship, the immeasurable affection – even as it slowly took itself apart, falling into its separate elements. His stepmother was stumbling as she moved around the familiar shapes in their flat, accepting the possibility that she would soon have the place to herself. She was still working there. Graham did not fault her on that, though at times he could see his father wanting her next to him, wanting always Mira's presence. But she needed to work – financially, Graham suspected, and for her own solidity. He knew little about psychotherapy, but it was clearly not the kind of job you could breezily take a month or two off from, while the mad men and sad women floundered and failed.

He heard footsteps at the door. It opened slowly to reveal both faces, his weathered stepmother's and his blue-eyed wife's. Graham looked up, nodded, stretched, closed noiselessly his book. He had been sitting by Peter while the latter slept for an unmeasured time – an hour? two? – but he had not been reading. He had been watching his father. And thinking. He'd had so little time, in Bath, for thought.

Mira shuffled in, gesturing towards Clare as she did so, who in turn mouthed, 'I'll wait in the sitting room,' to Graham. They sometimes dined with Mira and Peter, or near Peter, more accurately, but tonight planned to go out together.

Mira could continue the watch. She would be with Peter when he woke. How many times had she been close to Peter when he woke? They had been married over twenty years. They had been side by side all those nights and days and again, nights.

'Are you all right?' Graham whispered to her, seeing Mira's near colourless eyes. Clearly she had not been sleeping well.

She nodded, scarcely hearing the question. Her imagination was now with Peter and she had all but forgotten Graham already.

There would have been a time in his life when the neglect would have chafed Graham. From it he would have drawn various sinister conclusions about this woman his father had taken into his life. This evening Graham saw it simply as Mira being where she wanted to be – had to be. Worrying about her husband, his father, how to help him or give him solace, if she could.

'Bye, then,' Graham said softly, and he touched Mira's arm to alert her to his going. At the touch she looked up at him, startled.

It was a girl's face, pallid and frightened, whose eyes asked him mutely, *What is happening here?* and *What help can there be?* before she turned from Graham back to the mobile, rasping body sleeping in the thinly sheeted bed.

281

Twelve

February

He wished sometimes for God. He wished he had God. He had
not had Him ever, really; it was not a matter of having had Him
and lost Him during some change or crisis. For many young
years Peter had prayed daily to the Lord along with all the other
boys, *Hallowed be Thy name* (how he had loved the rhythm of that
line), intoning the collective conviction – or was it a hope? – that
His kingdom would come, His will would be done. Ration-
depleted Peter had hungered at the sound of the daily bread and
wondered vaguely which temptations he was to avoid being led
into. And he had sung, not well, with all the other reedy obedi-
ent voices, about Christian soldiers and kindly lights, Jesus
coming to show God's way and, of course, Jerusalem. He had
never engaged with or been moved by any of it, apart from the
sometimes haunting melodies.

The Blitz might have swung the young agnostic one way or
another, but Peter's experience of exile in the West Country had
been a godless adventure, and though there was talk of the deity
being on the side of the British and their allies, Peter had followed
his parents' sceptical view that this war was men again men,

people against people; God had nothing to do with it. Peter's mother had been a quiet churchgoer who quietly stopped going when the bombs started falling. She never did tell Peter what she had seen in those years while he was away, though with school-boy ghoulishness he tried to plumb her for gory detail. She had left it to Peter's evolving imagination – what she might have come across that diminished her own belief in God, or at least her weekly attendance in His house. She never spoke of the Blitz to Peter. Long after Peter's father had died, when his mother was old and frail and making her own peace with departure, Peter had listened for late-opening secrets, wartime traumas or memories resurfacing. There were none. His mother had held on to those tales, whatever they may have been, to the grave.

The grave. Yes. This was what turned people often, wasn't it – the last-minute hand-grab, *help me*, the belated desire to accept a story and a possibility that might give a person company along these ultimate steps. Peter could see the point in it. In having a God. The sympathetic ear always there to listen to you, the open arms waiting for you at the other end of the lightless passage. How pleasant to have that to look forward to, to ease the fear and apprehension. (Not that the fear would vanish entirely, but it would surely be subdued.) Mira had it – had Him. If this had been Mira instead of Peter, thinning into a bony assemblage of pain and closing-down organs, a mind beginning to drift – she would be suffused and surrounded by Christ, by His love and His faith, and her own. Mira knew a realm other than this one, it was real to her and would become realer, she must imagine, upon her death.

He saw his wife praying over him sometimes now when she thought he was asleep. There was increasingly little difference between Peter's wakefulness and sleep: dreams came to him in both states, and his eyes could be opened or closed in either, apparently. They were giving him something for the pain, he knew, and this something blurred and confused the world, making far less significant the gap between actual and imagined and remembered and hoped for. In some states Peter was entirely well again; in some, alert, himself, if speechless; in others a ghost already, waiting in the air above the bed for men in quiet uniforms to deal with and remove the body that was no longer his.

He saw her praying. Her lips moving and her hands restless, wishing for beads or relics to fondle, wishing perhaps to light candles around his bed and invite in one of her red and gold priests to officiate. Peter had never attended a church service with Mira – he felt it would be false to pay a touristic visit to the house of her beliefs, nor did she ask him to – though he did know of Saint Sava and Kosovo, the bones in the monasteries. On earlier visits to Yugoslavia Peter and Mira had travelled to see them, the extraordinary dark frescoes at Gračanica and at Peć, rooms redolent of solemnity and worship, hundreds of years of a people fighting to sustain itself and its faith against assaults of all kinds. Peter remembered thinking of Giotto when he saw those stark drawings in Kosovo, where Mira had taken him on a short pilgrimage to places he would need to know in order to know her and the place she came from. Giotto saw the terrible vulnerability of the human body and linked it with the pure stirrings of the spirit, and Peter felt in those monasteries a similar stern sense that in pain and suffering would forever be redemption. That was Christ's promise. *My suffering will save you.* What a strange idea that was. Why should suffering save anyone? How could more suffering, in addition to what there already was, possibly help? Peter's own suffering was not helping anyone and he did not feel ennobled by it, though he did notice its having raised him up in others' estimation, a lifting and cherishing he was prepared to savour. There was so little else left.

Someone was praying over him now. He could hear the tell-tale murmur, and as he opened his eyes (ah, they had been closed before, it was against his tired orange lids he had revisited the frescoes) he saw not the plump owl figure of his wife but some lighter, younger face and body, some pretty angel. A bearer of peace, a messenger from Heaven, if only Heaven existed. Ah yes. He knew who it was. He knew precisely who it was.

'*Clare,*' Peter pronounced in a voice he had meant as friendly and welcoming; yet even in his ears it was more a sound that might issue from an imperious frog. She looked up, alarmed, the customary gentleness a little slow to dawn.

'Sorry—' he started to say, wanting to continue, *sorry to interrupt you in your prayer. I do appreciate it, even if I don't, actually, believe,* but it was far too hard to say all that. And it would have opened up too much between them. Belief, lack of belief. God, no God. Too late for all that. Too hard.

Instead he smiled at her. Peter had come to know that his smiles had become beautiful (they were perfectly ordinary before) – judging by the look of wonder, the warm, wistful expressions that dawned on the faces of his benign guardians. Clare smiled beautifully in response, and for a few moments Peter was, simply, content.

It was beginning to be the time when people should not come by, and yet how could you stop them? Death was a picnic to a particular kind of social bee, the kind that came buzzing around with chocolates and conversation and a prurient, morbid curiosity as to how this individual might be preparing to meet his end.

That was the dimmer view, one that Graham took more than Clare as they watched the parade of friends and acquaintances to the flat. Clare saw also that some of the visitors felt guilty (should have seen him earlier, should have –), or frightened, or had their

285

own griefs that sought out the company of a fellow sufferer. (Misery loves company.) Some, though, were genuinely trying to help, offering love or their version of it, a kind of secular blessing.

Andrew was one of these. Clare had heard the buzzer and let him in. Mira was in the bedroom with Peter, and increasingly Clare felt that her post was to monitor and shield, even stall and entertain, when Peter was too unwell to be seen. People should not come by. Yet how could you stop them?

'Hello,' he said, dapper fellow, tall, handsome in a Heathcliffian way. A man not afraid to wear a soft lemony pullover or to show he cared how he looked. (Graham was all black, brown and navy; Clare had given up on the attempt to shade him any differently.) Clare had met this man before, she knew. Like a schoolteacher learning the names in the new class, she searched in her mind for the right one.

'*Andrew*. Hello, come in.' She was so pleased with herself when she managed it. There were those who said you lost your memory, your sharpness, when you were pregnant, but this had not been Clare's experience. Rather, she felt all her senses heightened: sense of smell, yes, and an emotional tautness, but also a keenness in her mind, an ability to take in a great deal and hold it, keep it secure. It was a time she could have planned and executed some brilliant fundraising campaign in her old job, or rationalized their filing system. A preparation for motherhood, Clare shyly thought: her mind making new room, sweeping out the dusty, unused corners of itself even as her body did the same. (Caroline, she knew, felt the precise opposite. 'My brain has completely given out,' she told Clare. 'The hormones are eating away at it like weevils. I forget everything, knock into tables, leave burners on. If it goes on like this, they'll have to put me in a home.')

286

'Mira's in with Peter just now,' Clare told Andrew. Son of an old friend of theirs? Or, no – a colleague from the university. 'Can I make you a cup of tea?'

'Lovely,' he said, though unlike most people he did not then wait for it regally but followed her into the cramped kitchen, as if reluctant to be left alone, or to leave her alone. 'How is he?'

'He's . . .' What could she say, honestly? 'He's— Well, he's—'

'Right,' Andrew said, gently. 'Yes, I thought this would probably be my last visit. Perhaps he's not well enough to see me. One mustn't be grand and insist on it.'

'But you've come all the way from Oxford.' Liking him, wishing he would stay, Clare fell into the hostess role, not wanting a guest to leave the party early.

'Yes, all the way.' He smiled. 'On the train, foolishly. I forget how vile Paddington is, in spite of the pretence at modernization. Pigeons and soot and little shacks selling stale baguettes lined with browning bits of ham. Peter always used to take – ' She heard him pause briefly over the tense, then continue – 'the coach. He was wise.'

She handed him the tea and assumed they would return to the sitting room, but the man seemed drawn to the kitchen's narrow quarters, as if the closeness of its walls were an invitation to intimacy or confession. Like Mira's little room, perhaps. What had Peter called it? The Hold, Graham told her. The Delivery Room.

'I'd see him walking down the steps of the coach sometimes, stiffly of late, carrying that old leather briefcase. It was impossible not to feel a surge of protection. One wanted to shelter him from the crueller realities: the new rules, the jostlings between departments, the indignities inflicted by the higher powers.'

'I know what you mean.' Peter had inspired that feeling in Clare even before he had become ill, the desire to mother him, shield him from harm. And this man had felt it too. (Married, was he? Or gay?)

'When I knew Peter first I imagined he was one of those distracted, rambling lecturers that people are quite fond of but who aren't very good at teaching, actually. Too digressive. Mind often somewhere else. Then I began to hear from students, and even from colleagues, who you know are notoriously tight-lipped about others' virtues, that he was very gifted as a teacher, dedicated to drawing his students into the material, generous with his time and with his mind. You know? He did not hoard them, as some reproachable sorts do, as I probably do, saving themselves only for the selected few.' He sipped. 'Nearly everyone exercises some form or other of favouritism. But Peter was deeply, old-fashionedly, democratic.' He raised a brow. 'He didn't mind the thick ones, in other words. I'm terrible on that score, myself. No patience.'

The young woman's face was hard to read. Perhaps 'thick ones' offended her – you weren't supposed to speak that way, these days. Or perhaps she was bored hearing people go on about Peter. Was that her position in the arrangement? Guardian of the tales? Keeper of the keys? She was the wife, he was fairly certain. The wife of the son. And there had been some complication with all that, had there not? A relation made awkward by factors Andrew had never been privy to. Now was not the time.

'I'm sorry, you might like to sit down,' Andrew said, retreating to good manners, when all he wanted to do was talk about Peter. *Save it for the memorial.* But what if there wasn't one? Peter was not a religious man, Andrew knew that, they had spoken of it one afternoon at the hospital. Andrew wasn't either. They had congratulated and commiserated with one another on their godless states. 'When are you . . . ?' He gestured towards Clare's belly with a slight hesitation, stopping short of the word 'due'; one had to tread carefully around women with large bellies, he knew from experience.

'May,' she affirmed, blushing and smiling. How nice, he supposed. Nice in that general way that babies were thought to be nice.

'The news must have pleased Peter,' he said, realizing as he said it the irony, the suppressed sorrow in it. Peter would have loved to meet a little one, Andrew guessed. But surely, now – May – there was not a chance of that, now. Surely.

'He's been very sweet about it. Yes.' And only now that he could see her eyes did Andrew understand that he had underestimated this woman whose name he had forgotten. Oh yes, like Hardy. This angel Clare. There was a real character there, thickening, deepening in the pretty blue eyes. (At another time, in other circumstances, he might have come to know her.) Tears came to them now. As well they might. 'I only wish . . .' she said. 'It seems unlikely, now . . .'

'Quite.' And in the tiny, inadequate kitchen they both allowed the sorrow to show through in each other's unknown company. Suspended, for a moment, the willed falsity of sickbed optimism. In another country they might have embraced one another. As it was, in England, Clare blinked away the window's watery light from her wet eyes and Andrew kept his body to himself, covering his face with one broad hand, one silent heave his subdued expression of outrage, of sadness, at the impending loss of his friend.

When first Mira had heard that Clare and Graham were planning to move to London for this period, her private heart had recoiled. Not people, not that close, not *them*, her stepson and his wife. It would be all she could do to bear the distress of Peter's decline and fall. (She knew he was going to fall, she did not hope for a miracle, yet she did pray for more time with him, as many extra minutes as God was willing to spare her.) She could not in addition suffer witnesses to her slow panics and fast discouragements. Mira did not care to be observed. Her truest confidant in this country had always been Peter – there were limits with Marjorie, and the others – and if Mira could not sit in her chair, a book in her lap, saying to him, 'Peter dear, something terrible is happening. I shall have soon to say goodbye to my life's companion,' and wait for his consolation and wisdom – she did not want to say it to anyone. Solitude suited her.

This urge went against the grain; went against the blood. Svetlana had told her briskly not to be crazy, it was a fine thing that the son was moving up to help, Mira would need his assistance and the wife's too, she'd come to be very grateful even if just now, in her stunned and stubborn state, she could not see it. Yes, but for Svetlana disaster had always been associated with crowds, with an audience: the more the better in her own life, when darkness struck. There was still that performer in her, as there was not in Mira.

The new year had arrived. 1999. It had such a sinister sound and look to it, one could only expect the worst. Apocalypse, personal or global. And with the new year came Clare and Graham as neighbours, and Mira had to settle into a new configuration, one that reminded her of a different time and place, a different ethos. Yugoslavia. Home. Beograd. Family.

In Beograd, of course, had she been living with an ill husband, it would have been just like this – people gathering around, sister and niece but also probably forgotten cousins or children of cousins, a network of soup-makers and conversation suppliers to strengthen Mira with their numbers. (As was happening now, for different reasons, to Svetlana: the war was coming possibly, bombs were threatened, and suddenly here was Dušan back, and

Jasna and Marko living there too, and in one conversation there had been a reference to a cousin's wife and their children. All clustered, awaiting disaster. Would it come? Mira still did not believe the Europeans would bomb Yugoslavia, but she could believe it of the Americans. And the Americans held the power and the weaponry.)

So here they were. Family. Behaving as family was meant to: helping, talking, cooking. Clare could cook well, something Mira had not known before, the young woman had a confident taste and touch in the kitchen that earned Mira's respect. Graham had all but taken over communications with the doctors, to Mira's relief. It was clear to all three of them that Peter would be happier at home than in the hospital for this stretch, however long this stretch might last – he had not been given long by the doctors, though 'given' was a strange verb, as if the physicians themselves were gods, marking the calendar with their cruel intentions. To stay at home Peter needed a special bed, equipment to manage some of the failing organs and the ignominious consequences of their failures, and towards the end, they were advised, a nurse – all of which Graham organized. Mira came to have enormous gratitude, as Svetlana had predicted, for Graham's diligence and clarity. That was the habit of crisis, wasn't it (she should know, given her work): it revealed undiscovered dimensions in the characters caught in its teeth. You did not know quite who people were until you had felt their hands in the hospital, trying to touch you. There were those who quailed, who fell away; and those who could muster only dutiful silence; and those who wanted to prove something about themselves when what was needed was not proof but presence. (Mira thought of the many sessions she had spent with the Mourning Madonna listening to the bereaved woman redraw her friendships, after: so many she knew had not measured up, were revealed as frauds or as philistines. *People who did not know. People who could not imagine.*)

Elsewhere bloomed surprising bouquets of sympathy. Acquaintances or lesser-knowns had stepped forward with soft offerings of comfort: unimagined gifts, words of necessary truth, competencies one could lean on. These were the heroes. Mira could not have imagined that she might one day consider her stepson – the man who had repeatedly flung *Bosnia* in her face like a bowl of acid, intending to blind or debilitate – a hero. Yet here he was, stalwart, virtuous, a mettle in him she had not in the previous twenty-five odd years ever seen.

'Will you stay for supper tonight?' she asked him now. He sat on the vinyl nightmare, a lean, healthy echo of her husband, reading a newspaper. 'I've nothing much. Just sausages, potatoes . . .'

'Sounds great,' Graham said, standing and stretching. 'I'll ring Clare. Do you need her to pick up anything from the shops on her way over?'

'No, no,' Mira insisted, wishing her mouth had words for *thank you, I don't know how to say it, but you have been kind, and dedicated, and I did not expect it.*

Soon after, they sat together under the dim orangeish shade in the huddled dining room at a coloured, intricate tablecloth that had been Mira's grandmother's. Golds and greens and stains of stews and soups of long before. Mira had set the table with care as though this were a proper, festive supper they were having and not a hastily gathered group of items from her neglected refrigerator. It was the slide into ritual, perhaps, and the grounding sensation that she was somewhere not entirely unlike home. Her original home. More and more now did London, its infinitely grey surfaces, its startling modern eruptions over bomb-damaged areas next to smoother, older terraces

– its rude thunderous trains and lumbering, air-fouling buses – seem a cousinly relation to Beograd. As Peter sickened and Mira weakened, so her two cities, as in a dream or film, became one. She lacked only those other voices and their cadences to mingle with these smooth-toned, irony-drinking foreigners; yet as the shock settled and changed her, Mira was able too to hear those voices, in her mind, those old and different voices from the other country.

'You seem tired,' Clare offered as sausages, potatoes and one of Mira's cabbage creations made the rounds. Mira did love to see the woman eat: she was feeding Clare's body and the little one within it, and took some satisfaction from that, at least. 'Would you like one of us to stay overnight tonight? Are the nights very difficult?'

'Oh—' No sound to convey it. 'Nights and days, I don't always know the difference.'

'I'm not sure that he does either, any more.' Graham's voice was subdued. 'He's more confused than he was.'

They had done this before, sat sustaining their own bodies as they discussed the deterioration of Peter's. It seemed unfair to Mira that he was not here to represent himself or to remind them of the man he had been. This depressed her. She felt the three of them contributed inadvertently to Peter's erasure by recording the stages of its progress.

'He often worked nights,' she said, thinking of the light that used to gleam late in his office from the slice of space between door and carpet. From the light and the diminutive sounds of the wireless she would know Peter was working, Radio 3 his unsleeping companion, its murmurers and its Beethoven, and she would know not to disturb him. 'His mind was most sharp then. He was best able to find the words he wanted when there was so little other noise.'

'I remember that,' Graham said. 'When I'd stay with him. It was so different from what I was used to. My Mum always went to bed early, so I had to. And Peter wouldn't even have us eating supper until half-past eight or even nine. I used to get so *hungry*.' He smiled slightly. 'And then he'd come and sit with me in my room, reading. We'd read for hours together. He didn't mind if I didn't go to sleep till eleven – he didn't notice. Then he'd go out into the other room and keep working.' If Graham woke in the night he might emerge to see his father writing or reading, completely still, a statue. Every now and then he would move – turn the page, stroke the dog, Molly lying there looking dead, the occasional heavy thud of her tail the only sign of life. (Graham could still feel the bristled touch of the dog's brisk fur under his fingertips, when he occasionally ventured to stroke her.) He remembered loving his father in spite of himself; loving that view of the man who was not aware of him looking, who had spent so many years unaware of him, unknowing, stumbling along unsonned, who nonetheless had (with that bloody dog; but Peter's tenderness towards the animal was touching, in its way) taken on a mantle of weekend father, father from time to time, cooker of different dinners, manager of different bedtimes, a strange man and yet a *man* – a quantity Graham had otherwise grown up without. His mother had not had boyfriends in those years. His friends had fathers – taciturn, often, or largely absent; or jovial, loud; or, one of them, a drunk depressive. Graham had had none. For years after the revelation Graham had reeled with the dizzy fact of this possession: he had a father, after all. This man.

And once you'd seen it sheared that way – the connection between a biological father, giver of sperm, donor of genetic content, and the figure who stood guard, who actually inhabited your life and your house, who gave you rules and clothes and a thousand threads of Hampstead conversations, none as important as their own and their own not very important after all as it was only one in an infinite series they would have (not infinite, he knew now; finite; yes, afraid so old man, *finite*) – making a dense fabric, Peter and Mira, the Bravermans, their marriage. Was that it? Marriage as a fabric? Marriage as a cloth that wrapped them together? Made one think of mummies. Or shrouds. His own, soon enough. No, no. The conversations. They had been vital. Her voice, her thought, her wit. Her voice. The sound from elsewhere.

She had touched his leg. They had not embraced on the Heath, not significantly – they were not adolescents, some of whom no doubt that same afternoon were finding cool, black-shadowed niches for eager coupling – but Mira had touched Peter. He lay half-propped on sweatered elbows (he had always been modest in dress, wearing a V-neck over his shirt unless it was positively sweltering), one hand clasping an apple he gnawed on somewhat gracelessly in the intervals between ideas. His knees were bent, exposing a white stretch of calf laid bare by the risen trousers' edge. And Mira found that stretch of calf, stroked it. Her fingers on his calf, friendly, not insistent, a quiet addition to the talk between them; a reminder that their bodies knew each other now, that the exchanges between them were more than merely verbal. They had come together. Peter's flesh was no longer only his own as it had been most of his life. As it had been all of his life. It belonged – he belonged – to this woman, a Yugoslavian, Mira, ample-selved Mira, his beloved and his wife.

There was so little of it left now. His flesh. He was aware of this, dimly; felt the melting. Was what was left now still hers? Did she want to own such a compromised thing as his cancerous body? She must be repulsed by him now, by his scents and incontinences, though she was too good to show it. Now it was all rotten, and rotten too were the tasks that went along with caring for it. How miraculous. That she had the heart not to show her disgust, that she had the manners to show only kindness. And the other girl, too. Clare. She helped, too.

But it was Mira Peter thought of. Her hand on his calf. He could still feel her fingers, the life in her touch.

God visits us with pain. (Mira tried to think her way through this.) Pain teaches, purifies – cures, paradoxically. Cures us of the arrogance we are otherwise condemned to. Look at us; look at what we do. Despise one another, murder one another. Decide that nation and territory are more important than brotherhood and unity, the primacy of our faith more important than the enacting of its principles. Power, finally, more important than peace. We put heads on spikes, we skin sinners alive, we electrocute prisoners, we rape mothers and daughters, sisters and wives. We treat other people like animals and we treat animals like dirt, and we treat the earth like a vast colourful supermarket, ours to drain of its inventory. We are greedy, demonic children and always have been, sitting in our rooms cleverly devising new ways to debase and degrade one another. (Pour liquid bleach into the rectum, watch the victim suffer slow death as the poison devours his innards. She had read of this. Yes, in Bosnia.) Some might pin the blame on men rather than women – that seemed to be Svetlana's line these days – but the fact was that women could be bloodthirsty, too. Less often, perhaps, and less pervasively, but as able when pushed to wield the knife or the rifle, twist the blade, pull the trigger.

If God visits us with pain – and He does, you don't have to look far to see it – it is to make us see this about ourselves. Perhaps in seeing it we will learn to cut out what is dark and unworthy. We each one of us have all of it within us, torturer and saint, rapist and Samaritan. Mira believed this. She did not believe some were inherently brighter or better than others – too often in her life had she seen the benign turn malignant, the calm turn to violence – and in her weekly reckonings with God, as the priest chanted the liturgy and the air filled sweetly with potent aromatic smoke, while the chorus intoned *Lord have mercy, Lord have mercy*, Mira tried to keep the gaze within, tried not to avoid what was basest in her own self. Christ had died for her. He had died in terrible pain, excruciating pain, to save her and to save all of them; the essence of His life was that pain would save and purify, transform those it touched. It could, in its way, be a blessing. We may hope the politicians will find peace, the doctors a cure, the couple its child, but if not, God is behind the pain, improving us by it. The war. The death. The vacuum.

Mira tried to comprehend this paradox. Her life and the lives of her people, *Serbian people*, made it imperative that she comprehend it, because her life and the lives of her people were constantly visited with plagues of this kind. She must understand; that was her spiritual task, this day and all days. *Lord have mercy; Lord have mercy.* If she was losing Peter, God meant for her to lose him. The loss was God's dark gift to Mira. She could not understand it but she must try to, because outside of comprehension lay the unfathomable abyss of godlessness, of life without faith.

The man she loved most in this world lived in that abyss. Mira prayed, spoke, took communion, haunted by the awareness that Peter himself did not know God, had chosen to live without Him. How could Mira save him now? She had no power to do it. They had lived the entirety of their adult lives not arguing over their chasm-separated views on God. She believed and he did not. In her view, the cruelty and absurdity of life were watched over by God, and in his view not. *God: The bastard. He doesn't exist.* A shared favourite line of Beckett's, though they had never

298

frightening than that, finally, was there, darkness perpetual and no light, no kindly bearded face, to better it. Peter would have no company with him and expected none. No heavenly host at the other end, reaching out a hand. How nice of you to come! We've been waiting for you, have the tea-things all laid out. No, not for him. All his companions were here, earthly creatures, and staying that way, so he hoped, for some time to come.

Peter was no longer afraid. He waited. If there were more minutes, days (what was the difference? Little now separated night from day, hour from hour), that would be all right. If there were fewer, that too would be all right. It had to be. He did not want pain, chiefly. They were good about that. They knew how to address the pain. When he told them or cried out they flooded him with some form of forgetful ecstasy, it was a drug, obviously, and the drug more than anything was likely to sing him to his rest as the weevils, whatever they were, did their damage, ate him through and through. Worms, was it? Not worms. Worms were later. After you'd gone. Graves and all that. He wouldn't have that, though. The worms wouldn't have the pleasure. It would be the fire for him, he had decided that long ago. Leave them with an armful of ashes. Scatter them somewhere.

He could hear her voice. It reverberated through his body as if she were speaking through him, as if his body were hollowed out, and strong and solid Mira was standing within him, bellowing out to the world. He seemed to be empty and filled only with her. There had been a child, he remembered, a son, he had not known, no one had told him. But the son, that dear fellow, was not part of the same story as Mira, the woman from Yugoslavia. They had never been part of the same story, had they, and now that there was room only for one, one story, that story had to be her, the woman from Yugoslavia. Mira. They had met over dinner with mutual friends. He could still recall the shyness in

300

her smile. He had loved her body. He had bought her scarves, cards, necklaces. A ring. He had never mastered her language altogether, but they had spoken to each other and known each other in a range of words and seasons and plays and trains. It had been good. He had felt complete. No, they were not two halves of the same soul, no, he believed none of that, he believed in that as little as he believed in the bearded man upstairs. It had been rather that they had accompanied one another. Hands held. She held his now. Did she? He could not be certain. She was speaking to him. Her voice filled his body. God only knew what she was saying to him, but he was breathing, and he could hear her, and in what remained of his fibrous, eaten body he felt her voice.

'How about Emily? Emily's pretty.'

'I went to school with a horrible Emily. She was the kind of girl who told tales.' Clare's face scrambled in distaste. She thrummed her plump belly as she remembered. 'She once reported me to the headmistress for not wearing proper school uniform. I had a denim skirt on. We were allowed corduroy, but not denim.'

'You rebel.'

'I know. Very sluttish of me. I had to copy out pages of Shakespeare or something as punishment. Not Emily. She was always in the dreadful polyester.'

'Sara?'

'Sara Littlewood flirted with the history teacher to get good marks, which wasn't very nice, as Miss Southern was a lesbian and we all knew it. Anyway, Sarah Ferguson – not a good precedent.'

'People think of her as Fergie.'

'How do you like Emma?'

'Everyone's called Emma.' A previous girlfriend or two, at least. Graham had fancied an Emma shortly before he met Clare, another solicitor who had scarcely noticed him, a woman with a long, elegant face who had seemed literally to look down her nose at him. 'Catherine? There aren't so many Catherines now.'

'I'm sure there's a good reason for that. The Catherine I knew was a great swot, always having her essays read aloud by the adoring teachers. Then in the sixth form she had a breakdown and had to be taken away. I've often wondered what happened to her.'

'Why don't you write out a list of all your schoolmates, Clare, with an asterisk by the ones who were all right, if there were any, and then—'

'There weren't very many. There was a good Jane, two of them, actually, we played netball together, and my best friend was Mary, but I can't see us having a Mary.'

'Or a Jane.'

'Let's go back to boys. They're easier.'

'Not much. You said you didn't like Timothy.'

'I do like it, but not with Thomas – you can't have a Tim Thomas, it sounds like a character from some kids' TV programme.'

'Michael's a good strong name.'

'Yes.' Clare didn't want to be difficult. It seemed petulant, not to say tactless, to mention the Michael she had known when she was twenty, a brief boyfriend. Not the boyfriend who . . . He was called Derek. She should have known better than to have anything to do with someone named Derek. Michael had been an arrogant boy with a mop of blond hair and a pop-star confidence who soon left her for a Lucy. There had always been Lucys about, it seemed, waiting to collect the handsome boys. 'How about Harry? Harold?'

Graham wrinkled his nose. 'It's a bit House of Windsor. I'd suggest William, but there's the same problem.'

'Just because you're a republican—'

'I'm not.'

'You can't rule out every royal name. Think of all the names you'd lose – Charles, Edward, Andrew—'

'George.'

'Yes, well.'

'Henry.'

'I don't mind Henry.'

'Ethelred. Richard. Louis.'

'Ethelred Thomas. That's nice. I like that.'

They were seated on a cool late morning bench near the top of Primrose Hill, the bones of a picked over Sunday paper piled between them. (NATO rattling its swords; time running out for Milošović.) Terriers, Labradors, the occasional whippet visited them along their circular excursions. Styrofoamed cappuccinos fuelled the couple's conversation, the subject one they visited more often as Clare assumed the weight and movement of later pregnancy. She was used now to the hum of limbs moving within her, though when Graham couldn't see her she indulged in quiet, fascinated watching of the ripples along the surface of her belly. The twinning of her self seemed miraculous, but it would be soft to admit as much to Graham, whose thoughts followed a different track. Clare thought she knew which but was not sure whether it was right to mention it, break the mood. Did he want this brief escape from the impending event? Or was he hoping, rather, for acknowledgement of its shadow?

'How about Peter?' Graham suggested, more towards the kettle-coloured sky than towards his wife.

'Peter Thomas?' The child would not have the same name as his grandfather, who was a Braverman. The Bravermans were leaving soon. End of the line. Everybody off the bus, please. Had

Graham ever wished, belatedly, to be a Braverman? Was it odd not to share the surname of his father?

'I like Peter,' Clare said cautiously. There had been no boyfriend Peters, no disturbed Peters that were older brothers of her friends, there were no famous Peters she worried about, Blue Peter didn't cause too much trouble and though Peter Rabbit came to mind, she'd always thought him quite sweet in his little blue jacket and shiny buttons. 'Yes,' she said, pressing closer to Graham for warmth. 'We could add Peter to the list.'

Blair was on.

She had him on low so as not to disturb Peter, though Peter was almost past disturbing now. The dose of morphine was high. A nurse had come to help them monitor it. (She had gone now, on a break; Mira had encouraged her to go.) Mira was unsure when the last time had been that she had spoken with Peter, rather than to him; his communications now consisted mostly of the beatific smiles he bestowed on her, or on Clare – or, less often, on Graham. The smiles were angel-broad and all-encompassing. They did not look like Peter, precisely; in life his smile had nearly always had something wry in it, curved more on one side than the other, a joke told, an absurdity enjoyed. It was rarely simple, as this ethereal beam was simple; Peter seemed by his smile to be seeing already something other than the world Mira saw.

Which was just as well. 'We have in this century witnessed more than once the destruction and instability wrought throughout Europe when there is war in the Balkans,' the suave, impassioned prime minister was saying. 'We cannot let that happen again. If President Milošović continues to defy the terms of the October ceasefire and the principles laid down at Rambouillet, there will be dire consequences for his country. NATO cannot and will not now shrink from its responsibility in this crisis. Let President Milošović not doubt our collective resolve. Our determination is absolute. No NATO country wants to resort to airstrikes nor would take such a decision lightly, but each one of us is prepared to do so if it is necessary to prevent more suffering in Kosovo, and to protect innocent Albanians there from the crush of Serbian military aggression.'

We will bomb you, is what the man was saying to Milošović. To Beograd – to Svetlana and Jasna and Dušan and little Marko. To Zoran and his fellows. And to Mira. To the memory of her mother and father. To the infinite dead. To *Serbian people*.

Mira heard a rattle from behind her. He was on a hospital bed, set up alongside the vinyl nightmare which had become in these latter stages a bedside table – containers of pills, a box of tissues, a bedpan, several cloths, bunched along it. A Bible in her own language, where Mira was fairly certain Peter could not see it. An icon.

She turned from Blair to him. His body was seized, his back arched as if some terrific pain were coursing through him and yet no sound or cry emerged from his open throat. This rattle, merely. Mira moved swiftly to his side as Blair rambled on in a forceful murmur from the box and no sound, no human sound, came from the body of her husband.

The arch ceased and fell. The eyelids fluttered and stilled. And Mira heard a wheeze, as of a breath escaping, a person leaving, and holding the thin loved fingers in her own she knew that they would soon stiffen and cool, leaving her with a large and emptied object, the former home of the man she had loved.

PART THREE

The War

History is written by the victors. Legends are woven by the people. Writers fantasize. Only death is certain.

Danilo Kiš

Thirteen

March

'We had to find a place for them,' the woman was saying. Her face was shadowed, yet her colour was healthy. She had a forward look about her. 'We knew this was the time we wanted to scatter the ashes, but we had to decide where.'

Her own eyes were not, she thought, visible. They were sheltering behind sedative. Mira had requested a slower-down tablet, a dampener, and though she should not work under the influence of such a drug, even in small quantities, she needed the work and the work needed her, and possibly – her gamble – the patients would not notice.

The other woman, Kate, appeared braced for narrative. The Mourning Madonna Mira had dubbed her, though now, without Peter, what need was there for aliases? Her telling today had a deliberate quality Mira did not remember from their earlier sessions. Or was that the drug muddling her hearing?

'I wanted it to be somewhere quiet. Always quiet, always beautiful. A sense of – space. A place to breathe, decent air, a view of the land. Nothing to do with London. London's so foul.

I wonder sometimes if we would have stayed, if Cassandra had lived.' She could issue such lines now salt-free. Part of the telling.

'There's a place in Shropshire,' she continued, as if to a script. 'I went there with my parents years ago, when I was in my twenties. They'd rented a house. An old farmhouse, filled with my parents and friends of theirs who had small children – sweet children, actually, a little boy named James and his sister Annabel. I was there on my own. A horrible man, my boyfriend of several years, had just left me for a very sporty, jolly girl named Lucy. They'd met playing squash. I wanted to kill myself.' She looked up self-consciously. 'The way you do when tragedy strikes.' Her voice was thick with sarcasm. 'In any case, I was *very* gloomy, and all these people seemed so marvellous and content – my parents' friends were terribly nice and did interesting work – she was a painter, he was a curator at the V&A – and their children were perfect but not ostentatiously so, just in an unobtrusive way, the girl quiet and bookish, a bit subdued, the boy loud and lively and full of stories. Very funny, he was. I adored the children. We got on really well together. And they thought I was brilliant – which I was. With them.'

Mira nodded. Kate lively and playful, dashing about with young ones: yes, it was imaginable. Mira could see it.

'Nonetheless. I did feel sorry for myself the whole time. My mother and father were very chummy together, swapping these violent thrillers they love to read, and I became the sort of nanny by default as I didn't have anything better to do – which was all right, as the general talk was of house improvements and politics and mutual friends, and there was I in my twenties, not especially interested in any of that. It was just as good for me to talk about Hook and Wendy, or Mole and Ratty and the rest.'

She paused. Perhaps she had wandered from the script.

'There are beautiful hills there. A long ridge called the Long

310

Mynd, perhaps you know it. We drove there one day, and of course James and Annabel frolicked near the stream at the bottom, they weren't able to climb far. And I excused myself from nannying for the morning and walked up to the top with my father.

'It was one of those steamy days when the sun burns more than you think it will and the air seems to be ticking. It was too hot. But my father had brought bottles of water in his pack and we traded them back and forth. We weren't talking much. He's very good to walk with, Daddy, as he's capable of being quiet. He knew about this boyfriend – had met him a few times – but was discreet enough not to ask me about him, or offer advice. He knew there was no point in saying those things parents sometimes say, you know, "You were far too good for him," "I'm sure it's for the best", which don't make you feel a damn bit better if you've been chucked.

'Anyway, we went right up to the top where there's an extraordinary, heathery plateau, from which you can see Wales, and England, and all the history, and all the future – you feel quite omniscient up there. The air is still and there is just a gentle, subtle hum at the top.'

Again, Mira nodded. She could see England and Wales. She could hear the hum. What a relief it was to be there, with Kate, and not here.

'We looked around, swapping sips from the bottle, and what my father did finally say was, "You're very good with James and Annabel. They adore you." '

'And I said, well, they were very sweet, and that *Wind in the Willows* was about right for me just then. Without looking at me he said, "You'll be a wonderful mother one day, Kate." And in that comment was somehow included Forget about whatsisname, the bastard – which I did, finally; and You'll meet someone far better one day, which I did, finally; and you'll have a child together. Which we did. Finally.'

Kate's voice thickened, and she paused. It was a full stop, and as the seconds lengthened Mira saw it offered the space for a question. 'And so you returned . . . ?'

Kate nodded. 'I imagine you remember that this month marks the anniversary of her death.'

Did it? 'Of course.' Yes. Mira did remember, once reminded.

'The scattering was our way of marking it. I decided there would be no point in trying to ignore it, that would be futile. My parents, as you know, were very keen that we should distract ourselves. My mother will not cease in her campaign to get me to stop "brooding" as she puts it. So this was ideal. I told them we were going to Shropshire for the weekend as I had such fond memories of our holiday there, and missed out the bit about the plastic box in our luggage that contained Cassandra's ashes.'

Kate raised her brow, an ironic expression.

'William and I agreed about this. In fact, it's been quite incredible how much in agreement we are, now, on so much. We talked about how to do it, how much ritual to use. Neither of us is especially religious, though I've found some comfort lately in attending Quaker meetings. I am – searching, I suppose one could say.'

Though funnily enough this part of the story seemed too private to Kate – her Sunday morning silences in a square, underlit room in Chelsea, sitting with dowdy devout others. She did not know how to speak of it to anyone, including Mira.

'We liked the idea of quiet, and emptiness, and we thought we would each say something to her once we were there. We would not be completely silent. I was thinking of that Quaker notion of giving witness, I suppose. So we got up early that morning, had our *b* at the B&B, then drove straight there and started walking. Hardly anyone was there yet. It was Sunday. I wanted us to be the first ones up on the Mynd, to have it to ourselves. And we did, apart from the sheep.'

And now Kate slowed. She had nearly run dry of things to say.

'It's beautiful at the top. As I said, you can see everything. And she wouldn't be bothered there – she'd only have sky and rain and cloud and the occasional walkers. So – we took the box. And—' Kate focused at last on Mira, whose eyes seemed pooled: dark and liquid in an unfamiliar way. Was she listening? The therapist looked so solemn. So *sad*. 'I don't know if you've ever scattered ashes . . .' But perhaps hers was the sort of religion that kept and revered the body? Open-casket funerals and so on? 'They're different from what you'd expect. Just a fine dust. I suppose one imagines the ashes one sweeps from the fireplace.' Kate could feel still the tickling sensation of her daughter's dust on her fingers. What remained. 'William spoke to her first, very simply and beautifully. He told her how we'd wanted her . . .' But why repeat? Why repeat all of it? She knew what William had said, and Mira wore on her face such a funereal expression. Appropriately, Kate supposed, but still. Why draw it out further? And there was something else she must leave time to mention, as well. 'And then I spoke,' she concluded rather briefly. 'And we prayed, each in our way. Then took handfuls of her – there wasn't much, she was so small – and scattered her over the Mynd.'

A cool, dark morning, threatening rain. It started to fall on their way back down; by the time they reached the car again they were soaked. They had spoken little on the walk, and Kate had never felt closer to William than on that day. She loved him so, felt more viscerally than she had when they married that life would be unbearable without him. She was pledged to him, deeply, and more so than on that bright, ignorant day of church and flowers and broadly slanted hats.

'I'm afraid the time . . .'

'Yes, yes, I know,' Kate said quickly. 'But Dr Braverman – there is something else.' She had practised the speech, yet was still nervous about it. It felt like finishing with someone. How odd. As if this were a romance. 'I think – now that it's a year on – I think I should stop coming to see you. It seems to me – not to parrot my bloody mother, but it really does seem to me that I must move. Not "on", exactly, not move *on* as I don't believe that is possible, but simply *move*. Perhaps continuing to talk with you would make moving difficult.'

Mira's face contracted to an unreadable immobility. She reminded Kate, strangely, of the way she herself must have looked when she first came to see the therapist: numb, angry, speechless. Or was that what they called projection? Kate had never much understood all that.

'William and I,' she said carefully, 'have been talking very closely about the possibility of adopting. Specifically, a child with Down's syndrome. A child rejected by its parents. Obviously loads of people do the various tests while they're pregnant, and if they find Down's syndrome they just remove the blighted creatures from their bodies. Heaven forbid they should have a child that was less than perfect.' Kate did not disguise the harshness of her judgement. 'But there are others who don't test, who don't know, and when they see these different little faces or bodies, rather than feel love, or welcome – some parents want to hand the children on. Let someone else cope with this. How embarrassing to have one that looked like *this*.' She pursed her lips. 'And we would like to help a child rejected in that way. Raise him, love him, give him a home and a family.'

'I'm very sorry, Kate. We should speak more of this, but—'

314

The therapist eyed her watch, flustering Kate, who said, 'Yes, of course, I just thought you might like to know.' She collected her things. There had been more to the speech. She had wanted to mention, at least, the possibility of war in Mira's country. But how to, now? The moment had passed.

'Thank you. Thank you,' was all Kate could say, clasping Mira's hand before leaving. Was this the first time they had touched? After all they had spoken of? 'You've been so good to me. I don't think I could have got through this without you.'

'It's all right,' the therapist said. 'But we should speak further of your decision. You may change your mind, Kate. Please do call, and come back to talk about it.'

'Yes, of course, yes,' Kate said again, gracious as she could be, feeling like the abandoning boyfriend, knowing that she would not call, would not come back, would choose not to speak further with Mira. That this awkward encounter in the doorway of the airless little room would be their last.

It was only after the door closed that Mira realized her mistake about the schedule. The poor woman was gone now – Mira had named her the Mourning Madonna, and yet over the course of the year Kate had developed a strength, a kind of defiance, that might have earned her a different moniker, had she lasted. She mourned still but would find a different expression for her grief. She would find kindness to help her. Charity. A hampered child, turned away by its parents. Yes, Mira could imagine Kate thriving in the role of rescuer. Some people were capable of this kind of transformation. Had Mira enabled Kate to do it? Perhaps she had. Hard to know for sure.

Mira did not mind Kate's leaving, for this reason: it seemed, in this case, a good sign. She would have liked to talk to her more about it, but Kate had left no time for the conversation. This was probably deliberate. The nicer patients did not always know how to ease away from the relation. Still, Mira should have probed her for some emotion or reaction about the change – and would have, had she not been so conscious, in her internalized calendar, that she needed every minute of the gap between sessions to prepare for the next patient. Could not let this one run over. The next arrival (the next assault, as Mira thought of it) required every atom of her stilled and disciplined presence.

But he was not coming any more. Mira had forgotten. Was that the drug, blurring her? Or her grief? And what knife-turn of irony was it that she wanted him here now, that savage man who had lacerated her so often and with such little contrition? Yet here she was, eagerly awaiting the Bigot. The alternative to Howard's presence was this – this blackness and chasm, the yawning shock of absence dulled only in a sleepy, loose-muscled way by the medication. The drug was not an amnesiac, however; it did not make Mira forget Peter's last breath, his death, what followed. The sudden, absolute solitude in the flat. The thunder in her ears, the tearing at her throat. This drug acted only as a kind of barrier to the worst of it, a thin wedge diverting the river of thoughts and memories from the most painful places. But more effective at this diversion would have been the voice of a patient. The demands, the rage, the self-concern. The fifty minutes just spent with the Madonna, her ash-scattering story, had oddly comforted Mira. Was comfort permitted?

But the Bigot wasn't coming again. He had told her so. She had met the news calmly enough. (Peter was dying then, but he had not yet died, he was still there to be spoken to, tended to, stroked and loved.) She had told Howard simply that she would leave his appointment time open for a while, should he change his mind. He had barked with laughter at the suggestion that he would willingly return.

Weeks ago now. A month or more? Mira had lost sense of time. She saw that the two had been so twinned in her mind – the Mourning Madonna, wringing her hands over her lost baby, followed by the heavyset Bigot, jabbing and sneering; the difficulty of stalled, intransigent pain giving way to the difficulty of condensed aggression – that she had shooed the Madonna away in order to wait here in an empty office (the Delivery Room, Peter had called it) for the not-appearing Bigot. Mira should get up, make herself a cup of tea, ring Clare even, find something to occupy herself with. She could not move.

He had begun the final session, characteristically, with a taunt. Quiet first for a few full minutes, not his usual style, allowing her to watch his stubbled, obstinate face, the too-small eyes, the smug, sunken neck. Porcine altogether. There had been occasions Mira had found Howard attractive, she recalled. That morning she could not see it.

'I could just sit here, couldn't I, for our last session? Fifty minutes of silence and then I'd be free. We both would. What do you reckon?'

Mira had smiled. Made herself smile. *Try to find him amusing.* 'As if today is the day of your release? From prison?'

'Exactly so, Mira. Exactly so.'

They did sometimes understand each other, in spite of everything.

'But,' he said in a hearty voice, 'that wouldn't be *me*, would it, to keep quiet? Waste of money. Don't want to let you off that easy. So my thought is—'

'How are your children, Howard?' A strategic interruption often worked well. And she did want to earn Howard's last fistful of resentful cash, actively rather than passively.

'The children? How should I know?' A practised, bitter laugh.

'Richard doesn't call. Alison is in France. I am not encouraged to enquire.'

'But you could.'

His lips soured. 'Remind the old bastard of his paternal duty before he leaves? A final shot? You should watch it, Mira, or I'll bring up Serbian atrocities again and where will that get us?'

'You talked of Jane recently, her hopes for you in these sessions. You have not mentioned Richard or Alison. Have you spoken to them? Do they know about your seeing me?'

'I shouldn't think they give a toss. Sorry.'

'Have you spoken to them?' she persisted.

'Ah but Mira, wouldn't I have mentioned it if I had? Something that significant? Even if it were in some backhanded, reluctant reference?'

She answered that one with a stare, a slight arch of the brow. He was sharp, Howard, he knew himself better than he often let on. This had been the challenge of him that Mira had come lately, guardedly, to savour.

He sighed with exaggerated volume. 'Dear oh dear. Richard, is it? We're going to end on Richard. It would make him happy, if only he knew. He never felt I gave him enough attention, of course. Thought I was more interested in the girls.'

'Were you?'

'What do you think?'

Again the stare, the eyebrows. She would not take his bait. Not today.

'All right.' He laughed, abruptly. 'You're right. I was more interested in the girls. No, not interested, I just – I liked them better. Isn't that permitted, in a parent? To have preferences? There's some idea that you can be like God and love everyone equally, but you can't. It's not realistic. You love them all, obviously – ' here, an eyeroll, acknowledging the piety – 'but you don't always like them. They are not always likeable. Sometimes they are loathsome.'

'Was Richard less likeable?' Make him work, this last hour. He was capable of it, despite the bluster.

'Richard?' Howard shrugged. She watched his memory set to shuffling about in old, closed boxes. 'He was a baby, that's all. The first. You know babies: scream a lot, make a mess, drain their mothers dry, rob the parents of their sex lives. The usual.' He looked at Mira, seeming to expect an indulgent feminine smile, *Yes, I know, babies can be a handful*. He was imagining her and her children. Or perhaps trying to offend her maternal self. 'I don't have much feeling for babies, to be frank. I suppose he was all right. Then, early on – ' he folded his arms – 'I don't know when exactly – Monica had a call in the middle of the night. Her father had just had a heart attack, come at once. I was to follow in the morning, join her at the hospital, or she would come back. She left the baby with me – it didn't make sense to bring him.'

Another deep, distant breath.

'He had been a little – well, he'd seemed a bit fussy in the night, but in light of the father's heart attack that was forgotten. Then once Monica had gone he started to make very strange sounds, a sort of grunting, painful sound. Not that I felt like much of an expert but it didn't sound right. When I went to the cot to give him a little shake, even I could tell that he was very hot.

'I didn't know how to reach Monica. This was before mobile phones, obviously. So I rang my own mother, who said, "Take him to the GP straight away," which seemed sensible. So a few hours later we were in the GP's waiting room, morning surgery, everyone snivelling and hacking and generally scattering pestilent germs far and wide, and the receptionist takes one look at Richard and says, "I don't think you should bring him in here, sir.

Let Dr Green see him straight away." And within minutes Dr Green was shunting us off to the hospital. Not the same one as Monica's father, of course, that would have been too simple. And by now the little bugger was practically *limp*. I'd worried about feeding him, but he was too bloody tired to be hungry. He just lay very still, grunting. It was – it was terrifying, actually.'

In the pause Mira could see Howard's eyes travelling across the inner story. Recalling the scenes. The stopped heart of fear for a sick child. Mira remembered it over Jasna, a pneumonia once, when she was a year old. Svetlana's face streaked with terror, the clutch in her urgent hands. *Pray for her, Mira. Don't stop. Pray and pray for her*, and she had. Mira saw that the Bigot, whatever his posturing, had not been immune.

'Meningitis,' he said crisply. 'It was. Meningitis. By the time Monica finally found us the baby was in an emergency bed, hooked up to a hundred tubes. Very still but breathing – just about.'

The tubes. The hospital. The breathing. Mira had turned her face from the man across from her, trying not to inhabit her own memory. Trying to inhabit his.

'All that gear looks particularly obscene next to a baby. The tubes and wires. It's bad enough for anyone, but for a *baby* . . . Monica spent the entire time white as a sheet. Couldn't eat. Couldn't sleep. Had to be forced to have a little tea, to keep her going. Just sat there keeping vigil over him for three days, until he finally turned.'

Stay with him, now, Mira. His hospital. His vigil. It was a baby, years before.

'He got better, obviously. You know how the story ends. But he always seemed a sickly child after that. Colds, stomach problems, one thing after another. And I'm quite sure Monica thought I'd given him meningitis – that she somehow thought it was my fault. It only happened after she'd gone.'

'Although, in fact,' Mira said, 'you saved his life.'

Howard slapped his knee, almost jovially. 'Well, that's what I always said, Mira. But Monica couldn't see it. Never did see it that way.'

'What happened to her father?'

'Oh, he was all right. They put a pacemaker in and he lived another ten years, the cantankerous old sod, making my life miserable.'

Howard's story had brought them to the end of their session, and Mira could see that she had used it as a lure. Surely he would not stop coming now, having just rediscovered such an important episode? A life-threatening illness in his first-born: might that not explain some of the willed distance between him and his children?

She underestimated him.

'And that's where we'll have to leave it, I'm afraid.' The Bigot's voice heavy with irony. 'But what a fascinating note to end on! Leaves all sorts of questions unanswered, doesn't it? Good heavens. A veritable trove of possibilities in that story.' His exit had been quite friendly, quite light-hearted, after that, perhaps simply because he was relieved it was all over. Though he hadn't resisted a parting shot: 'There's going to be war in Kosovo yet, Mira. Mark my words. Think of me when it happens.'

January, that had been. And now it was March.

The room remained empty for fifty minutes, empty of all but Mira. It was some sense of ritual she had, not to leave, rather to sit here, remembering the Bigot and his infuriating hatreds, and his walled, pitiable griefs. The rage certain men clung to with a fierce pleasure, like terriers, savouring the growl and bite of it. Mira wanted to talk to Peter about that last session with the

Bigot. Peter had always been rather interested in the character of the Bigot, more so than in some of the softer, gloomy female patients. He seemed to want to crack the case, as if Howard were a mystery novel and there were a culprit somewhere, an explanation. He might have made much of this infant meningitis story. But Peter had been too ill already in January, just returned from his hospital stay, for Mira to burden him with it. She was increasingly left on her own with the multifaceted cacophony from her office. Voice after voice, tale after tale. Hers and hers alone for the listening and for the internal replay, after.

Where was Howard now? (Arguing with his family still, or not. Reconciled at least with Jane. At least with her.) What would he have said to Mira about the showdown with Milošović? She imagined having to fend off his crowing over NATO's resolve at last to fight the tyrant on his own turf. *They're going take Kosovo out of his hands, Mira. Precious Kosovo. He's gone too far now, you know, he can't make laughing stocks of us any longer.* She was relieved not to have to hear that, surely, as she surely would have – and not to have to endure the man's uncannily sharp eyes searching for her reaction. For her grief. The Mourning Madonna had noticed it, Mira had seen that, though she did not properly know the source and was in any case too polite to ask. Howard would have asked. He would not, at this late date, have resorted to tact or discretion.

And yet. The silence swallowed her. How she missed him.

The bombing started. Under shelter of a euphemism – 'airstrikes' – to nurture the illusion that this was not a war under discussion, as sanctioned by NATO nations. That, rather, military planes were simply and cleanly 'removing' strategic elements of Milošović's arsenal, of his military structure. NATO allies were not speaking of death. They were not speaking of killing people – certainly not *Serbian people*. It was all morality and correction and the righteous, humanitarian prevention of more suffering. The puffed-up, self-satisfied language of parents. About Milošović: he could choose peace at any time. We are not fighting the citizens of the former Yugoslavia; we only wish Milošović would choose the road to resolution. Just like parents. *I don't want to beat you, darling,* as the cane smacks the backs of the knees, *but you give me no choice. This is your punishment. I hope you will learn by it.*

Mira could not contain her fury, and she had no reason to. The flat was empty now of a dying body, empty of solace or companionship, cluttered no longer with hospital supplies and plastic bottles but rather with a dead man's lifetime of possessions. Mira was free to fill the rest of it, every available corner, every square inch of shelf space, with her fury.

'War is war,' she said to Svetlana on the telephone. For once Mira spoke first; Svetlana was subdued. 'Why can they not at least call it what it is? Have the integrity to say "We are declaring war on Serbia"? This language of evasion. Tony Blair: the man is a monument to hypocrisy. His moral tone, his oozing assurances, his weak-shouldered effort to sound like a leader. Here they call it "spin", how the news is presented to the willing, stupid public.'

'We're used to that,' Svetlana said dully. 'It used to be called "propaganda". Do you remember?'

'Of course. But in Britain they don't believe they are distributing propaganda. They believe the television is telling the entire story. And if it is, then Blair must be right, and it is time to attack Yugoslavia. There are no protests here to speak of. No one is against the bombing, except a few old-fashioned pacifists. It is seen as necessary. Good, even. They have all convinced themselves that Milošović is Hitler.'

'Yes, and so they play into Milošović's trap. *Stupid.* He wants them to attack: that way he will stay in power. The country will rally round him.'

'But they don't care what happens in his own country,' Mira said. 'They don't give a damn what happens to Serbs. They just don't like to be shown up by a minor European leader. *Eastern* European leader. It offends their pride.'

'It isn't Blair behind it, Mirka,' Svetlana asserted. 'It's Clinton. He is the one trying to distract people from his sex scandal. That is what American politicians do when they are in trouble – drop bombs on other countries. It is Clinton telling the others what to do. The planes – they're American.'

'But Blair goes along. Stirring speeches in Parliament – I couldn't listen. Had to turn it off. But I saw the glint in his eye. The thrill of war. They all want to be Churchill again, finally. Thatcher, too, with the Falklands. I remember Peter's outrage. He used to shout at her, Thatcher, on the television.'

'At least you *have* news,' Svetlana said. 'Here we have nothing but lies. There's a radio station, B92 – you know, a music station, but also it made some attempts at giving us information. Dared to question Milošović. Jasna was almost religious about it. The thugs have shut it down again. Half a dozen times in the past years, but this time I don't see how they will come back.'

'How is Jasna?'

'Frightened. We all are.'

'And her family?'

'She worries for Marko more than for Zoran. She hardly speaks of Zoran. She doesn't hear from him, doesn't even want to, I think. He is there, in Kosovo. Beyond that – God knows.'

'*Kosovo*, Svetka.'

'Yes. I know.'

'Do you remember when Father—'

324

'Of course. I've told Jasna the story. I think of it often.'

In the span between girlhood and womanhood, Mira sixteen, Svetlana ten perhaps, eleven, their father took them to Peć, in Kosovo. The seat of the Serbian Orthodox Church. For their father the place was not just the heart of the country: it was God's own heart; one of the earth's most sacred places. His face, when he listened to the archbishop officiating there in Peć, withdrew from the girls, leaving behind it a pale mask of faith and humility. This devout man, so different from the boisterous, confident, imperious character they knew as their father, alarmed them almost. The gentleness. His heavy head beautifully still, lids closed over fervent eyes, lips moving silently in prayer. (How much more serene than in death, years later, his stalled face trapping still its pain, its rage.) Later, when he and Mira fought terribly over her decisions – she did not marry as she should, she chose studies that were unfathomable to him – Mira shuddered with anger at her father, her entire body shaking, and Svetlana sometimes would say to mollify her, 'Remember how he was at Peć, Mirka. Remember him there.'

'I wish I could be with you,' Mira said now, her voice fierce.

'Oh, no, you don't. Every evening the lights extinguished in Beograd by seven o'clock? Air-raid sirens through the hail? Worry all over? Faces sewn shut? No you don't, Mira. No you don't. And we don't want you here. It's hell. Stay where you are.'

'I have to. The airports are closed.'

'It is just as well.' In this crisis Mira's sister was able to step outside of herself. If she were playing a part now, it was a noble one: victim of war, made stronger, better by the experience.

'It is *not* as well,' cried Mira, erupting abruptly. 'I don't want to be in England. *Now.* What is there for me here now?' She wept into the phone. How cold was a telephone for weeping. She wanted her sister beside her; it was all she wanted.

'I'm sorry, Mira,' Svetlana said. 'I am so sorry. Your husband – he was a man to cherish. I went to the cathedral yesterday to pray for him. The room was alive with candlelight – so many lit for peace, or for the soldiers. I lit one for Peter.'

Mira did not speak for a few minutes, could only hold the phone in one hand and wrap the other one around her belly protectively, holding herself in as well as she could.

'Besides,' said Svetlana, 'you must stay there. The baby. Your grandchild – you must be there for the birth.'

'It's not my grandchild. They are not my family. Graham is not—'

'*Mira.*' With both sympathy and authority. 'Think of Peter, of what he wanted. They are who you have left of Peter – his son and the wife. They *are* your family. I never understood the lines you drew. Why draw them? Dušan brought a woman to the flat the other day, distraught, pale, empty-eyed – she'd just learned that her brother had been killed by one of the bombs. This was an old girlfriend of Dušan's, certainly. I could tell. I took her in, we all did, she played with Marko, somehow the baby made her feel better, and do you think I worried over her being one of Dušan's girlfriends? It's not the time. It is not the time to draw those lines. Graham is Peter's son and they're having a child soon, and that child will be yours, too. Peter's and yours.'

But Mira was so far from believing it. When she thought of Peter all she felt was hollowed out by his absence; that, and an incipient fury at him for leaving her here alone, in Britain, declared enemy now of her people. If she could have left that day she would have, turned away, gone back to the people she came from, even in their darkness and cold and sirens.

She would not have looked back.

★

'God,' she said, watching the television. 'It's like a video game.'

Clare was folded into Graham on the couch, back in their house. They had returned to Bath for the weekend, guiltily measuring their need to be away from London after Peter's death against the knowledge that they must not leave Mira too much alone.

'I hope Mira isn't watching this.'

'But she must want to know what's going on.' Graham jutted his chin towards the packaged war footage. 'She wouldn't want not to know.'

'But can you imagine? Watching those jets circling your country? It would be surreal – terrible. I can't imagine it.'

'Kosovo isn't her country. It's a province, with a majority Albanian population—'

'I don't want to argue all that.' Clare pulled away from Graham slightly. 'You know what I mean. Besides – it's not just Kosovo they're bombing. Look.'

It was a brief report, a few grey-green images of struck targets, a talking head or two from the NATO command. Making the first airstrikes seem clean and efficient. The story was followed by an account of thousands fleeing the province, Albanians and Serbs alike, in an attempt to escape the latest heaven-sent terror.

'That's very clever.' Clare shook her head. 'Drive out the people you claim to be trying to save.'

'Well. They always knew there would be some problems like this. But in the long run it will make Kosovo safer.'

'So they tell us.' Clare stood, stretched. How round her belly was now. There were times when Graham saw her and he could not quite believe it. Since his father's death he could believe very little. Everything seemed, as she had just put it, surreal. And much of it terrible.

'I think Ethelred and I are going to retire. It can't be good for him to hear about all this. Dropping bombs. He'll wonder what sort of world we're bringing him in to.'

'You sound like your sister.'

'No, I don't.' Clare allowed herself an older-sibling eyeroll. 'I spoke to Sara today. She's in a proper rage. Thinking of storming Ten Downing Street to make her views known.'

'She should talk to Mira, perhaps. In sympathy.'

'Mmm.' Clare moved her fingers through Graham's hair, leaned over heavily to embrace him. She kissed his head and very nearly toppled. 'She sends *you* sympathy, love. She's very sorry about your dad.'

'Thanks.' Graham returned her embrace but turned his head. He didn't want her to see his eyes. 'I think I'll stay down here for a minute, if you don't mind. Watch the end of the news. I might stay up to see who Paxman is going to badger about it, later.'

'All right.'

He pressed her hand before she left. *That is my wife.* He made himself say it internally every day, now. *She is carrying our child.* The most ordinary thing in the world. But it was happening to him. To him! He was never have supposed to have been a father. What did he know about it? So little. *So* little. *Do not feed your son fish. It is wrong to feed your son fish.* But that story, those memories (puking in his dad's ghastly green bathroom; Peter's self-deprecating telling, years later), would only be useful when the little blighter was older. What was Graham to do before then?

It was not fair. He indulged the childish thought while holding a pillow close to himself for comfort. Or did he want the feeling of fullness in his belly that Clare had? With the kicks and movement inside her it would surely be impossible for her to feel empty in the way that Graham did now. The news spooled uselessly on. Robin Cook issued a statement. France urged

Germany . . . Manchester United at Old Trafford . . . President Clinton denied . . .

He was old enough to know that fairness was not inherently part of the story. He was thirty-eight, for God's sake. Graham did not have a father, then he did, now he did not. His father had not been there when he was born; he would not be there when Graham's child was born; nor had Graham been with his father when he had died. It all fitted. Mira had rung them straight away, but by the time they saw Peter he was bluish, a waxwork not a man, and Graham had to look away. He poured himself into the technical unpleasantness that follows a death, which Mira was not equal to: ringing the doctor, then the coroner, alerting the nearest neighbours. How grateful Mira had been. She and Clare sat close together, hands clutched (with the belly slightly intervening), tears on Clare's cheeks, shock on Mira's. The tableau of mourning. Graham could still see it.

His mother Lydia had asked him awkwardly whether he thought she might come along to the crematorium for the short, secular occasion. He could not imagine why she wanted to. When was the last time she had seen the man alive? Graham and Clare's wedding, probably. What would it mean to his mother to stand in a drably appointed, noise-smothered chamber in North London near a box containing the heavy dead weight of a long-ago boyfriend, before the container and its occupant were ramped on up into the flames? 'Of course,' Graham told his mother. 'Though I should probably just check with Mira.' This was a new delicacy on Graham's part, but in fact Mira was far too numb to voice any surprise or objection. And so it had been the four of them, himself and Clare, Mira and Lydia, along with a friend, Marjorie, ostensibly there to help Mira (though her own skin was ashen and frightened), and a tall, handsome man named Andrew about whom Graham was rather vague. Graham passed the morning in

329

a dull-stomached awareness of the finality of this departure of his father, and a queasy sensation, pitched somewhere between thrill and discomfort, produced by his standing at equal distances from his mother and his stepmother. The one, with his father, having stubbornly, unheedingly produced Graham himself; the other, with his father, having lovingly produced a marriage. Mira was the woman who had made his father content. She had accompanied him.

And here are the main stories again. NATO planes continued their air bombardment of Serbian targets in Kosovo. NATO commander Wesley Clark said—

And now that NATO was acting, at last, Graham did not have the justified satisfaction he had expected. It was, looking at the television screen – it was hard to say, simply, Yes, this was right.

He found the phone and dialled.

'Hello – Mira? It's Graham.' He cleared his throat. 'Yes, we're in Bath. She's fine, thanks. No, no news. I was just ringing to make sure that you were all right.'

The telephone had caught her staring at the urn they had given her. (She'd had to turn off the news.) It was balanced placidly on a shelf, promising some later significant day on which they would scatter what remained of him. She still found it hard to believe Peter had refused to allow himself to be buried; burial was all Mira knew and understood. There were rituals to be observed. Food and prayers at the graveside. What was she to do with this ash? How was she to learn a new way, this late, to honour her dead?

'Thank you.' Mira was glad, yes she was, to hear his son's voice. In its tones, in its kindness, the remembered tenor of his father's. She was glad to hear him. 'Yes, Graham, I am here. And thank you.'

*

Her eyes burned from lack of sleep and from upset. Jess had not stayed with him the night before though she had expected to, so she did not have her usual morning thought-path across Regent's Park. Only the familiar, short, traffic-clotted leap from street corner to street corner in Camden Town.

It was so fucking *tragic*. The moment Jess was awake again, fully, and rehearsing the telling of the tale to Mira, disappointment slapped her down again and bitterness overtook her. The more so because she could not help, given her mental habit of finding the situational punchline, seeing the comedy that lurked here. There was an absurdity about it. A *vasectomy*. It was like a bad joke. Not at the time, of course, nothing especially comical about it at the time, when it was probably frightening and rather painful – but now. How could she fail to appreciate the irony? She, Jess, the Broad from Abroad, chronicler of her sperm search, had finally met a lovely man, generous, kind, sincere – so it seemed, though with an Englishman you could never be altogether sure – and a good father. It was obvious that he was and would be a good father, had already tried his hand at it: had two boys, Alex and Theo, nine and eleven, whom he clearly adored and by whom he was clearly adored. And she, Jess, liked the boys – the older one had a bit of an attitude, but that was to be expected, he was nearly a teenager. When they had all gone to Madame Tussaud's together, her idea (their dad lived so close and the boys had never been), they had had a good time with the waxed pop stars and Battle of Waterloo, the stiffened, lifelike Royal Family and, best of all, the Chamber of Horrors. So successful had that day been, that Jess had allowed herself with the unguardedness of love to indulge in a fantasy with Nick afterwards, late at night in bed together, after a hushed, passionate entwining of selves and limbs. Perhaps, she had whispered, they could, one day – her heart loud in her ears with the importance of the moment –

331

think about having a child of their own together. A little brother or sister for Alex and Theo.

That was when he told her. He'd had a vasectomy.

'But, but,' Jess had blurted, a little too loudly (the kids were crashed out in the bedroom next door), 'that's reversible!' – Which was true, technically, she had just had a conversation with an English friend of hers about it, but bringing it up was a bad move on Jess's part as it visibly tensed the muscles in Nick's neck and made him sit up in the bed rather than lounge across it. His body moved out of the post-coital posture of warmth and relaxation and into battle-ready station for conversation.

What followed was a long, earnest, boring account of Nick's marriage and its dissolution, how difficult it had all been, blah blah blah, and an intimate detail she could have done without – how the vasectomy had come about as the relationship with his wife faded and weakened. It had been Nick's desperate effort to rekindle their sex life, as his wife claimed that dealing with birth control and the fear of another pregnancy hampered her desire. In the event, their sex life remained terrible and she began to have an affair with one of Nick's old friends. This speech included a retread over his many shocks and disappointments, how he had not been the kind of person who expected divorce in his own life (but really, who would admit to it, even if they did?); how he had wanted his children to remain in a stable home (yes, well, welcome to the real world); how he did not want any new child to come along to threaten his relationship with Alex and Theo, or, for that matter, his own perilous sense of stability. So that even if he hadn't had the vasectomy, he wouldn't be interested. Wasn't that excessive, to say all that to her? But Jess could tell that her assigned role in this conversation was to listen silently, saintfully, nodding with deep sympathy for all that he had gone through, suppressing any of her own reaction as the loyal friend and lover of this sad and wounded man. If she had managed this muted response they might have got through the night all right. And who knew? Maybe it was just too soon for Jess to bring the matter up and if she had let it rest, lain low for a while on the subject of children, shut up during Nick's whole long litany of marital betrayal, she could have swung him back around, in time.

But God forbid Jess should be able to keep her mouth shut. She would have to talk to Mira frankly about that – her inability to stop herself from sabotaging something as promising as this, even though she knew as she did it that it was sabotage. It was as though a demon possessed her. Jess could not just go to sleep and hold him, relish the beautiful feel of his arms containing her after they made love. No, no. She could not let it be. Could not simply enjoy. Had to pummel the man with questions and accusations and inquisitions, until the poor guy was defensive and furious and she was a mess of tears and hysteria, and she'd had to sneak out of the flat, trying not to wake the kids, the incipient love between her and Nick ground underfoot like a crushed, vulnerable snail.

Love as a snail. That was a weird image. Maybe she'd ask Mira about that, too.

The face that greeted Jess at the door was peculiar and haunted. Jess took in a sharp breath. In her sleep-starved state she felt suddenly chilled, and decided against taking off her jacket as she sat on the familiar chair, huddled, ready to start.

But, Jesus. Mira looked terrible. Stricken. The war, of course. Don't be an idiot, Jess, she's Serbian, her country's just about to get the shit bombed out of it by NATO, you probably would look none too perky either if all manner of firepower were aimed right at your capital. She ought to say something, probably, before they got started.

'I'm so sorry,' Jess said, making a vague gesture, as of guilt or regret, 'about everything that's going on. The news, I mean.' How awkward this was. What were you supposed to say? 'It's terrible, that they've started bombing.' *They* not *we*. Well, she wasn't NATO, was she? (On the other hand did she, Jess, think the bombing was terrible, really? Sure she did. Bombing was always terrible. Who could be in favour of bombing? She had never bought the whole 'saving more lives' argument. They said that about Hiroshima, too, for God's sake. Saving more lives. Try telling that to the Japanese.)

The instant she opened the door on the American, Mira knew she ought to have cancelled this appointment. She was not yet ready. Not for this. She would not be able to do her work properly. It was not the drug this time, nor even the grief behind the need for the drug. It was not the blood moving too slowly for her to formulate the right questions, deliver the crucial truths; rather the blood was moving too quickly at the sight of this American here, her dishevelled appearance, her well-fed mouth, the apologetic wave of the hand when she mentioned the war. For a blurred, furious minute Mira could not see her patient. She only heard the voice, and thought of war.

'If it's Kosovo they want,' Mira spoke in a thick, curdled voice she scarcely recognized herself, 'they won't get it. Not Kosovo. Do you know what the place is, in our history?'

The girl shook her head, bewildered by Mira's tone, the just-suppressed ferocity. She clearly had no idea. Stop, Mira tried to tell herself. You must stop. But she could not. She wanted to give the American some idea.

'It is the seat of our church, the Patriarchate. It is the heart of our country. There was an epic battle in 1389, the Battle of Kosovo Polje – Tsar Lazar was defeated by the Turks, and my people were led into a long, dark period of Ottoman rule. But Lazar chose the nobility of defeat and a place in heaven rather than turn away from God. He was given a choice. The grey falcon spoke to him in the dream – our poems talk of this, the great poems of our country. "The Tsar chose a heavenly kingdom, and not an earthly kingdom, He built a church on Kosovo . . . And his army was destroyed with him, Of seven and seventy thousand soldiers." That is how it has always been for Serbian people. Blessedness in defeat. But we cannot always stand by.'

'Right. I knew Kosovo was important, but I didn't realize—'

Of course she didn't. What Americans knew history? They hardly knew their own, let alone anyone else's. Scorned the stuff, did they not, believing that with enough money and technology and weaponry they had not the need for something as petty and old-fashioned as history? They were the writers of it, these days. They contrived the story line.

A torrent flowed from Mira, an angry one, a bitter river, from her own surprised mouth, as she told this American girl some of the stories about Kosovo, tried to explain that it was not simply a bit of territory under threat, some acres of land, but rather poetry, God, a people; her people, *Serbian people*; the monasteries, the relics, the bones of the saints. Could she make this girl understand? *Kosovo*. You can't take Kosovo. Take Slovenia, take Bosnia, take, yes, Croatia – we did not trust them since the war, their slaughter of us at Jasenovac, their murderous Ustaše – but do not take our heartland. Do not try it. We will not yield.

The river was fed by the streams of outrage that had flowed from Mira these past days, now that they had started in on Beograd, watching NATO 'take out' (that efficient euphemism) pieces of her city. Fed by Svetlana's voice on the telephone, reduced by exhaustion and neighbouring deaths – Svetlana had lost a friend already, in another town; the woman left a motherless daughter, grandmotherless granddaughter. Mira did not know where to turn with such information. Had nowhere to turn.

Nonetheless. Mira wearied herself in the recitation. Gradually she felt her blood slowing down. Her vision cleared. The fire fell from her eyes and, grief-depleted, she could see again, and what was left before her, as always, always in her work, was someone in trouble. The American girl. Still today what she had always been: smart, funny, wealthy, alone. Fractured. Not whole. Seeking wholeness, wanting to find peace.

She, the American, was not there to soothe or to answer: that was Mira's position, wasn't it, no matter the month or the hour, no matter what death or what war. Mira had shaken the American with this outburst. This was evident from the patient's startled face: apologetic, fearful, bewildered. She had the appearance of a student who had stumbled haplessly into a class for which she had not done the reading. It was not right for the therapist to speak this way and Mira knew it, and yet it was only now, emptied of Kosovo and of her rage about the air attacks, that she felt able once more to resume her professional role. The American could not, herself, stop the bombs. She could not help Mira. But Mira could help her.

Mira collected herself. Smoothed her skirt out beneath her. 'I apologize, Jess, for taking your time,' she said, in a voice more closely resembling one the patient would recognize. The American's eyes were wide. She was listening. 'Tell me now: how are you? Are you all right?'

and craters in their lives, solidities replaced by their crushed opposites. And Peter: Peter was gone and not returning. Without him Mira felt exposed, naked, sensitive to the slightest look or touch. Flayed, like a barkless tree.

On this day Mira found her way to Hampstead Heath and a bench nearish the famous hill of kites and views. Where one day, years ago, Mira and Peter walked, talking of their future . . . Mira tried not to replay it all constantly, but the mind spooled its stories over and over again, one could not stop it. It was a comfortable bench with a pleasant prospect, and it reminded Mira of the discussion she had had with Graham over the possibility of such an object to memorialize Peter. The English did this with their benches, apparently – she had seen it before, but never thought it an eccentricity she would encounter in her own life. They christened them, slabs of wood, for dear departed walkers or sitters. This one she was on was named for a 'John Tucker, philosopher'. If you had not known John Tucker, the thought must be, you could spend a minute wondering who he might have been; if you had, that minute could be spent in fond recollection of the man he was. Mira did not understand it. She thought of Peter constantly, everywhere, on the Heath or off it, and she always would. If there were a place to visit Peter she wanted it to be his gravesite. But Graham – round-eyed Graham, struggling still like a fish out of water with the oxygen-depriving fact of his father's death – clearly wanted to do something for Peter. He had spoken to Mira about choosing a place along one of his father's oft-walked paths to mark with his name. 'You should do as you like,' she had told the lost boy as gently as she could. In her mind hung the admonition, *We should have buried him. No matter what he may have said he wanted, everyone needs a place in the earth to rest. I could have visited him there, spoken to him, prayed for him, broken bread by him. My husband needed a grave, not a bench*. She had told Svetlana how terrible she found the occasion when they consigned his cold body to the flames, robbing her of the only ritual she knew to honour her dead. Mira had leaned heavily on her friend Marjorie, blind to everything else about that morning except the wrongness of it, and her inability to make it right.

Mira's hands held a letter. Her eyes moved back and forth between the desultory late morning heath, its lemon light, its investigating dogs, and a rounded, childish script over two sheets of paper.

Dear Mrs Braverman,

I am writing to say that I was very sorry to hear the news about your husband. My father showed me the article about him in the Ham and High, we hadn't known of the work he did and actually I read one of his translations at school. The Solzhenitsyn book about the gulags. My dad and I both thought that a coincidence.

In any case I also wanted to thank you for helping my father. He only went to see you because I asked him to, and he never told me anything about it really except to complain about the cost, but I know you helped him. I can tell. He doesn't stir everyone up as much as he used to. Even my mother has noticed, though I haven't told her why. I wanted to write to you because I doubt he ever will. He hasn't changed that much!

He doesn't know I'm writing you, but if he did he might ask me to send his sympathies about your husband. He did tell me that the illness seemed very difficult. From the article Mr Braverman sounds like a lovely man who will be much missed.

> *With good wishes*
> *Jane Beddoes*

The article had appeared a few weeks before – Marjorie had seen to it, with the help of that colleague of Peter's, the kind young man Andrew, who filled in the details on Peter's scholarship. It had been one of the few obituaries, along with a couple from Oxford publications, and it was surprising how one clung to them, thin flags of print celebrating, or simply acknowledging, a life. Mira had read them repeatedly. 'Peter Braverman was a modest, hard-working scholar, whose boyhood interest in the Soviet Union led him to an expertise in Russian and his position as a prominent translator of some Soviet writers, as well as lesser-known nineteenth-century Russian authors.' She fingered the dated photos of Peter at his desk until his hair blurred and he seemed to acquire a dark smudge of a beard. Warm, comradely – even in a newspaper, even thumb-smeared, even when gazing into the cold eye of the camera (he had not had much patience for photographs, had rarely allowed himself to be captured). She read and re-read, to confirm each time that Peter had lived, that he had been important and that others had thought so, too, even though what was most important to her about Peter – that he loved her, and how he had – was scarcely noted in these few posthumous paragraphs. Reduced to the shorthand, 'He is survived by his wife, Mira, and a son, Graham.' How little that explained. How much it missed.

It was good of the girl to write. That she had written indicated something to Mira, the kind of thing she could never have known from Howard directly, though she had latterly suspected it. He had raised his children well. (Or Monica had.) The grace of it, writing a note to Mira about Peter, the evident care in the writing (finding her address, setting the record straight about her father). A girl's sensitivity, perhaps? But that depended on the girl. Mira had had no letter from her niece, Jasna, just a telephone call which had upset more than soothed. 'It just seems that everything terrible is happening now,' Jasna had said. 'Peter being sick and dying, and the bombs – I think it is because it is 1999. The world is getting worse and worse. Perhaps in 2000, as they're saying – some great disaster throughout the world. Who *knows.*' The girl had inherited her mother's sense of drama. But nothing, from either mother or daughter, in the way of a card about Peter. It was wartime, of course. They would not, though, Mira guessed, have sent one anyway.

It was terrible how one counted. As if the number of cards – and there were many, it was England, people did write and they knew how to, just as that girl did, it was an art for which one could love the English – stacked up against the significance of the soul they mourned and feted. The Epsteins had remembered, eloquently. Marjorie had been brief and philosophical. Even the Aristocrat had written – as one might expect, with her good manners. Very sorry to hear about your terrible loss. Greatest sympathy. Had felt it time to cease the sessions as the pregnancy was distracting and tiring her . . . Mira hadn't properly read the rest, she only wanted the part about Peter. She wanted more cards. She wanted them daily. *Words helped.* Which patient had said as much to her? One of the very English. Kate, it was. (One learned from them, constantly. As with children: helped them, raised them, and was helped by them.) The necessity, the sudden blessing, of another's writing about the one you had loved.

And now Mira stood slowly, leaving John Tucker and his bench. She felt a pull inwards – out of the optimism of a park. She would find her way back to the black and airless Tube and from there to the other place she could go to remember Peter and hold him sacred: the stark hushed dusk of her church.

They had taken to meeting at the Polish place, once a week or so, for pregnant person commiserations and to test the waters for a future friendship. There was something unlikely in the alliance that they were both aware of – a question over their class compatibilities – though only Caroline was bold enough to allude to it. 'You probably think I'm a frightful snob, but I can't bear the idea . . .' she would say, and what followed would, often, be something Clare did understand, perhaps even had some sympathy with, 'of spending the next two years in and out of Mothercare buying primary-coloured plastic crap with bells on it for my baby, because some early development expert has determined that primary-coloured plastic crap with bells on it best stimulates their tiny little brain cells.' Clare felt much the same, though from a different angle, perhaps. Caroline continued. 'Flavia can manage perfectly well with a wooden spoon and a bucket, as far as I'm concerned. That's all we used to have, and, all right, Hugo and I may not be the most inspiring examples, but it didn't hold William Shakespeare back, did it? Or Darwin? They seem to have got on without lurid jingly spiders and hideous plastic saucers that play "Für Elise".' *Flavia* was the complement to Clare's *Ethelred*, Caroline's nickname for the being she also termed 'the alien within' who drove her to do terrible things, like buying chocolate Aero bars, when everyone knew Aero bars were the lowest of the low. 'The newsagents see me coming and they just put an Aero bar on the counter without saying a word. They know I'm beyond help.'

There was a nervousness in their laughter, Clare knew. The women shared an illicit fear of the eruptions to come. (Clare was due towards the end of May; Caroline in late July.) 'You're not going to try to do it without drugs, are you?' Caroline asked. 'Don't humiliate me and tell me you've got a *pain strategy*. My pain strategy is: give me the morphine as fast as you possibly can, you bastards. But you're probably one of these strong sorts who'll give birth at home in the kitchen with just a cup of tea to keep you going.' Clare played the role up for her friend's benefit, thickening her northern accent. 'Aye, I expect I'll be mucking out t'stable half an hour after birthing the little bugger' – glad that her sister couldn't hear her indulging this game. If Sara heard for five minutes Caroline's accent, or some of the harder to swallow stories of Mummy and Daddy's house in Chelsea, she would have been merciless. Clare's sister would not have seen the point of Caroline at all.

It was a relief to have somewhere to go apart from Graham and their oddly impersonal home away from home. Peter's having died in March made this let of the London flat in some measure pointless, and there were times when Clare wished she could be back in their house in Bath, appointing Ethelred's bed-room-to-be as someone in her position was supposed to, mooning over pastel paint colours for the walls and lampshades decorated in cows and sheep. She needed the prospect of the new child to hold up against the melancholy of her bereaved husband, who, it seemed, was both taking comfort from their proximity to his father's long-standing home and using it as a means of helping his new friend – his stepmother. For her part, Clare was trying in her ever-heavier hours to make sense of London, or at least this patch of it. Caroline was good fun in this regard, trading notes on the organic shop along the Parkway that was busy with progressive well-off mums and skinny, juice-fed backpackers, or the Japanese noodle bar with its long communal benches and fashionable fish-green fluorescence.

'I'll be so relieved to see the back of this bloody top,' Caroline said to Clare this morning, standing to kiss her before sinking clumsily back to her frothed decaffeinated drink. She wore a simple black maternity shirt, generous at the belly. 'I liked it once, but thirty wearings later I'm beginning to tire of it.'

'Well, you see me,' Clare gestured at a button-down robin's-egg blue. 'I'm just borrowing Graham's at this point.'

'Yes. I can't do that. Hugo's far too fastidious to let me near his wardrobe. God help me if I lay a hand on the Paul Smith's, which are the only ones that would really tempt me.'

'I don't think Graham even notices. He's so distracted.'

'Is he very low still?' Caroline shook her head. 'Poor fellow.'

'Yes, of course. But it seems odd to me.' Clare's lips touched the cinnamon-speckled foam. 'You know, since I've known Graham he's been so distant from his dad – treated him almost as though he were doing Peter a kindness by coming round at all. It always seemed to me that I was the one who actually liked him. We didn't see them very much, you know. I had to be the one to arrange visits, Graham never bothered. Then, when he got ill – I suppose it's that classic thing. Graham suddenly realized he didn't have time to muck about. And now – he's wrecked.'

'There was very little time, was there? Wasn't it all brutally quick?'

'Six months or so from start to finish.' Clare shook her head. 'It seems so cruel. He doesn't know what to do with himself. And I don't know what to do with him.'

'The baby will help,' Caroline said. 'I know that sounds very trite and granny-like, but it's a fact. Your lives will change, the adorable Ethelred will be howling at all hours, Graham will be changing nappies – you must get him on to changing nappies, so I can browbeat Hugo into it. All of that will take him out of himself.'

'That's what I hope. But what if it goes the other way, and he infects young Ethelred with his melancholy?'

'He won't. Ethelred will resist. He'll be his own man.'

'I hope so.' Clare sipped. 'In any case, Graham's helping Mira clear things out of Peter's office. I'm hoping that might help as well. You know,' she slipped into a cartoon American, 'to get closure.'

'I thought you said he used to have trouble with her? With Mira?'

'Yes.' Clare shook her head. 'That's one reason we didn't see as much of Peter. Graham and she did not get on particularly well in any case, and then during Bosnia and all that – Graham had very strong views about what was happening, and I think they had terrible rows. She got very offended by what he said about the Serbs. Not surprisingly. He always thought they were to blame for the whole mess.'

'Right.'

'I mean, to me it always sounded bloody on all sides. Not that I followed it very carefully, but I don't see how it could just have been one country responsible for all of it. It doesn't make sense. But I don't know how to talk to Mira about it. According to Graham, she can go off on how wrong everybody is about the Serbs.'

'She never said a word in the sessions. And it didn't seem appropriate for me to mention it.' Caroline raised a brow. 'Though one did feel rather trivial at times with one's tiny predictable marital woes set against this vast, gory background of ethnic hatreds and perilous struggle. *God, poor me.* Terribly sorry about the war, of course, dashed unfortunate – but can we get back to me?'

It had been one of the reasons Caroline stopped going, actually. It seemed so out of scale, somehow, her Flavia or her Bertrand lined up against the outright waging of war. Even if it was all that mattered to her, her Flavia or her Bertrand.

'I do miss her, though. In a funny way.' Caroline still found the connection with Clare and Graham unnerving. Hearing domestic stories about her therapist was a strange unmasking, like seeing one's Latin teacher in the pub after school. The authority out of role. And it was equally odd that her friend's – what was it, stepmother-in-law, was there such a thing? – should be the harbourer of Caroline's year's worth of laments about infidelity and infertility. Not that Caroline hid the fact that Flavia was a *test-tube baby* – she was trying single-handedly to revive the phrase, she felt that like flared trousers, its time had returned – but still. There were other things she had certainly told Mira in confidence. Mira would never pass any of it on, of course, but the fact that Clare saw Mira regularly made the therapist's hoard of confessions seem uncomfortably close to hand.

'What was she like?' Clare asked, suddenly. 'To talk to?'

'Mira?'

Clare nodded.

'She was – ' Caroline's gaze moved from table to table, and out onto the flagstoned pavement outside, where a small boy – one? one and a half? she'd learn these things – was kicking up a terrible fuss about a hot chocolate. Too hot, too small, spilled some – hard to say what the problem was, exactly. Caroline could watch such scenes now with equanimity, neither summoning up a false smugness that she did not have such tantrums to deal with, nor sinking into a mournful self-pity that she didn't. She would, soon enough. Caroline felt confident now, though she patted her moving belly unthinkingly for reassurance.

'She had a gift. I don't know how else to put it. You know, I would never have imagined myself holding forth as I did to this quiet, grey-haired European woman. A *Yugoslavian*. A Serbian! It seemed a bit like a bad joke.'

In truth Caroline had never been bothered one way or another about Mira's being a Serb. That made her sound shallow, which she probably was, but she felt it was important to separate

346

people from their nationalities. You were not your country, necessarily. (She knew people who were the children of Nazis and did not hold it against them, either. Her own grandfather had had dubious politics during the war and had always defended P. G. Wodehouse and the Duke of Windsor for their choices. One didn't always want to delve or blame. The Balkans were such a disaster entirely, it had always seemed best not to touch the subject with a bargepole.)

'Mira was so good, though. Clever, and subtle, and – difficult, as well. She didn't just coo and say, "Oh you poor darling" – ' Caroline smiled – 'as Mummy did. If you'd asked me before, that's how I would have imagined a therapist. Holding one's hand, saying, "Never mind the bastards, I'm here now." '

'But she's quite formally trained, isn't she?'

'I suppose so. I was always a bit vague about all that, to be honest. I just wanted some *help*, wasn't too particular about what sort. She used to ask me about my dreams, of course. I was constantly giving birth to chickens or hamsters, so that gave us plenty to talk about. But she wasn't the *tell me about your childhood* sort. Not with me, anyway.'

'But she helped you?'

'Oh, God, yes. Well, look!' Caroline gestured at her protrusion that jutted up against the marble table edge. 'Worth every penny!' She waved the joke away with a hand. 'No, but she was kind about all that. The IVF treatments, all the humiliations. Or, as I say, beyond kind. She was able to make you see what lay under your problems – it's difficult to explain. I still say all the same things about Hugo – that he's a monster, and a faithless hound – but I don't mean them in the same way that I used to. Then again, that might be because I got pregnant at long bloody last. Might have very little to do with Mira at all. We'll never know.' She stopped, then buttoned herself back up. She had gone a bit further than made her entirely comfortable.

'*Now*, Clare,' she said, in a more theatrical voice, 'can I get you some sort of oozing, sugar-encrusted delight? We may as well enjoy the freedom while we can. After all,' Caroline stood and made a move towards the glass case that displayed a tempting array of pastries, 'between the two of us, we're eating for four.'

She rang expecting one of the women, and heard his voice. It startled her into putting the phone down without speaking, as if the receiver itself contained the cold touch of his hand, the dark dregs of his remembered sediment. Yet why should it surprise her? It shouldn't. She knew he was there again now, the devil in her ear, the devil in their home. Svetlana said that he had changed. Didn't women always say that about men like him? No, no, you don't understand, Mira. The wars, the years of Milošović, have changed him. He never used to be afraid. He never used to need us, Jasna or Josip or me. Now he does. Something has left him now, you would have to see him to understand. A life force has left him. Do you remember how much noise he used to make? Now he's quiet. He spends a lot of time reading and staring out the window.

She rang back.

'*Da?*'

'Dušan. It's Mira.'

'Mira.' Immediately he started to cough, a thick, husky, gathering cough that had in it the sound of a lifetime of cigarettes. Hearing him, Mira could taste the tobacco on her tongue again. It was years since she had smoked.

'I'm sorry,' he said at last. 'I have these attacks – unpre-

348

dictable. *Mira*, hello. I'm glad to hear your voice. Svetlana told me about your husband. My sympathies.'

'He was a good man,' Mira said stolidly, her practised response. 'He fought the disease, but it was stronger than he was.' This, too, a line she had spoken often, though it concealed a different conviction. *He should have fought harder. And so should I. He and I should have defeated the cancer together.*

'Cancer is the plague of our century,' Dušan said. 'Cancer and war. Though war is eternal, perpetual: the plague of all centuries. Cancer is our own.'

She recalled this, his grand rhetorical style, and almost smiled at the memory of how it had impressed her when she was young. He continued on with a litany of colleagues and friends lost recently to cancer and she stopped over one or two of them, names she knew, faces she could still see. A woman who had taught her, several decades previously, at Beograd University, mediating Mira's first encounter with Freud. Throat cancer, ironically, for her too.

'But enough about death,' Dušan said finally, in a tone that was almost cheerful. 'Let's talk about war, eh? You picked the right side, didn't you? The side with better weapons is the side to be on now.'

'This is not my side, Dušan.'

'And we Serbs are never on the right side, are we? There is always someone ready to crush us. The Turks, the Austrians, the Nazis. Now NATO. We are like the Jews: always blamed for other people's disasters. The world won't rest until we have been annihilated.'

'It is Milošović they're after. Not all Serbs.'

'You believe that, do you? Is that what your "free" press tells you?'

Mira did not know whether she believed it or not; did not,

these days, know what to believe. NATO, and Britain, and the US, tried to assert loudly that the Yugoslav leader and his army were their targets, not the citizens of Serbia generally; but in dropping bombs across a city, as they were, did that not become too fine a distinction to sustain? People were dying in Beograd: was that to be seen as an accident?

Arguing against Dušan, though, was an old habit with Mira. 'I don't imagine the press in either country tells the whole story. Papers here chronicle savagery in Kosovo – retaliations against Albanians. The news is full of it. You must hear less about that.' The words sounded strange coming out of her mouth and not Graham's. Not some BBC presenter's. She felt like a ventriloquist's doll.

'Savagery in Kosovo? Yes, we have heard about that. Did you know they killed Zoran?'

'Zoran? Jasna's husband?'

'Killed in Kosovo. Thanks to NATO's humanitarian mission. Jasna had confirmation last week of his death. Marko now left without a father.'

Mira had met the man a handful of times. She had never liked him. He was neglectful of Jasna and the child, abusive to one if not both. The kind of man who becomes a soldier to give himself license to be the brute he has always wanted to be, who in civil society would simply be a criminal. One of the JNA's finest. Yet the death appalled her.

'But what happened? Where was he?'

'In the wrong place, obviously. At the wrong time.' His voice poured bitterly. 'In fact we have been told very little.'

'And how is Jasna?'

'Shocked, and brave. Staying strong for Marko.'

'Can I speak to her?'

'They are none of them here now.' He coughed again.

350

'They're dealing with the military authorities about Zoran's body. What remains of it.'

The image sickened her. It did not end. There was no end to it: horror breeding horror. When, how, could it end?

'You were right to leave,' Dušan repeated, though now without the shrapnel of irony sharpening his voice. 'This country is finished. Milošović brought us to our knees, and NATO is finishing off the job. You were wise, Mira. To have seen all this would have wrecked you. It wrecks all of us.'

'That is not why I left.' Dušan knew that. If he was trying to bait her into saying more about it, she would disappoint him. 'I left for other reasons. I did not know then that I would stay here, in England.'

'Of course. And then your man. Peter, wasn't it? He was always one of my favourites. The fisherman. Svetlana says your Peter was a good man, too.'

She had no wish to talk to Dušan of her husband. 'Yes, I stayed for Peter. But also for my work. I studied Klein here, you know.'

'Of course, yes. Your work. Giving aid to the enemy. That's treason in wartime, isn't it?'

'Don't joke.'

'Why not? Joking is all we have left.' Dušan paused. 'How is your work, Mira?'

The edge in his voice put Mira on her guard, and she remembered this, too. The warm, philosophical expanse, the fluency, the intelligence – and then, the barbs. Dušan could charm a woman until she was eating out of his hand. Then: bite.

'My work is fine. I have an interesting group of patients.'

'They lie on your couch and complain about mummy?'

He had always had a poet's disdain for psychotherapy. Mira had not forgotten. It was the novelists, she had come to believe, who could see the point in the process: those who had an ear for

351

narrative and an acute sense of the importance of telling stories. Poets, with their brief and fragmented lyricism, their wilful rages, were deaf to its call.

Nonetheless. Mira could not resist the futile urge to defend herself. And her patients. 'They tell me of their griefs. They try to understand why they are paralysed, and I try to help them to understand. They describe the hollowness they feel . . .' But she did not want to be too specific. She would not tell Dušan the stories about children.

'Griefs. Ah. Hollowness. *Yes.*' The sneer was audible. 'I feel sorry for them. Their lives must be hard.'

'You needn't mock.'

'Compared with explosions every night – a city blackened by fear and distrust – deaths mounting, here and elsewhere – people stashed in our flats like frightened mice—'

'It is not a contest, Dušan. I know it is hell there. Svetlana has told me.'

'No, you don't know, my dear. You could not know unless you were here. And felt the floors shake, the dogs howl and hide, sirens call, alarms ringing everywhere like the ringing in of Doomsday. You don't know.'

'I was there in 1941.' The familiar fury rising in her. The man's inability to listen to others. Always, always the conviction that he and only he was right. 'I don't need to prove to you that I know what it's like. I am sure it is terrible. I am disgusted by what NATO is doing – of course I am.'

'Bombing a television station, an embassy? Killing journalists and ambassadors? Proud of that, are they?'

She could not answer that one. Those headlines had been her worst days. She had actually caught sight of a tabloid one afternoon on Camden High Street in April after the station bombing: *Destroyed: The Ministry of Lies.* The smugness sickened her.

352

'I agree,' she said, subdued. 'The hypocrisy is beyond belief.'

'And yet – there you sit, holding the hands of the English people as they tell you of their problems. Do you not find it ironic, at least?'

'Hold their hands? Hold their *hands*?' Mira's fingers gripped the receiver like a weapon. 'You must remember that half of these people view *me* as the enemy. They think I come from a tainted race. The news here is full of nothing but Serbian torturers and executioners, and these people come to me anyway with their confusions and their desires and their dim hopes to get better. It is an act of faith on their part. Mine too. The wars very nearly destroyed my practice. The worst years – 92, 93 – Sarajevo, Srebrenica – I am lucky still to be working at all.'

'So come back. Work here. God knows there are enough human wreckages here to keep you employed into the next millennium. Though no money to pay you, of course. I'm sure you are used by now to a certain elevated standard of living.'

How Mira wished that she had not rung him back. She should have waited, spent this telephone money speaking to Svetlana, not Dušan. She was not as rich as they all thought. Her heart hit her chest in frustration. Rage. The uselessness of explaining to him: *My belief is that people deserve to be freed of their entrapments, whether they are English or Serbian. Or American. Or Croatian. Pain does not discriminate on the basis of religion or race.* Mira had always believed that. Tried to, at least.

Yet her head pounded too with other unspoken thoughts. Chiefly the deep, shaming sense of agreement she felt with Dušan's blunt words, a fear she was scarcely able to touch in herself that she was, as he said, on the wrong side now, and far from those she most loved in this time, the worst time. In war.

*

353

It surprised her to realize she was looking forward to his visit. 'Visit': as if it were a social call, which it was not, it was for the practical business of helping her sort through Peter's things. A task Mira had been unequal to for the first months that now, as the days lightened and lengthened, started to seem more pressing. She had begun to feel haunted by the presence of all these belongings that no longer had a person to belong to.

Mira was conscious of the imminent arrival of the couple's child. After the baby was born it seemed unlikely that Graham would have time to help her. The death had gentled Graham towards her; or perhaps the war had. His jaw muscles did not tighten as they used to when he greeted her, and there was a liquid in his eye that made Mira realize, for the first time, that he was a handsome fellow. More and more she could see the relation between Graham and Peter she had previously found difficult to discern. Graham asked her questions, shyly, about his father – here and there, not all at once – and Mira took pleasure in answering them. In telling him stories.

'I feel a bit like a vulture,' Graham said now, standing at the door of his father's office. 'Picking over the bones.'

'The man from the Polytechnic – Andrew – has said that he'll sort through the papers if we like, if we box them up for him. He'll know better than I what should be kept and what might usefully go to one of his translator colleagues. And there is someone up at Leeds who has said he'd like to continue on with one of Peter's last projects and publish it jointly, under both of their names.'

'I'm glad he is doing that,' Graham said, hands on hips, staring at drawers and files and the still paper-cluttered desk. 'That's kind of Andrew. I wouldn't know how to begin sorting, to be honest. But putting things in boxes – that I can do.'

'I shall have to go through the books eventually. But that can come later.'

'Right.'

'I suppose I shall have to move into a smaller flat – I won't be able to afford this one. The pension from the Poly won't be enough.' Not enough, given the money she would be sending to Svetlana and Jasna. 'My niece, you see – ' Should she tell Graham? Was it safe? – 'lost her husband a week or two ago. In the war. And they have a little boy, nearly two.'

'Oh, God. How awful. I'm sorry.'

'Yes. It was – well, he was in Kosovo.' That name. She spoke it.

'Ah.' Graham looked down. 'They're very careful in the news not to discuss casualties – the other side's, that is. I have noticed that. They make it rather easy to forget that people are – are dying.'

'They are. Yes.'

'Please send your niece my sympathies – our sympathies. Will you? And if we can do anything to help—'

She nodded. This was the same man: her stepson. Speaking to her in a fashion that was strangely, unnervingly empathetic. She must not draw attention to the fact. 'Of course, the economy is a shambles. So I must send them whatever I can.' Money was an unpractised topic between them, but it was a relief to say this to someone. She had so much stored, these days. Long and Peter-less days. 'I have to help them,' she explained. 'They have so little.'

'I understand. Look—' He sounded almost bashful. 'I could go through some of that with you, perhaps help you manage the funds, if you like. It's the boring sort of thing I do quite well. I've had experience – if this doesn't sound too odd – I mean, with my mother. I've been helping her for years. It wouldn't be a trouble.'

'Would you?'

'Absolutely. Of course.'

'Thank you – oh, Graham. *Thank you*—' She stuttered, tripping over her gratitude. 'Because you know, Peter used to—'

'It's not a problem.' That beautiful English ability to smother excess emotion. 'I'm happy to do it.'

Hovering on the edge, each of them, of an outpouring about Peter. But Mira, taking her cue from her stepson, repressed the urge to howl out loud, and asked Graham instead about Clare. How she was feeling this late on, how they were managing with the preparations. Graham, reminding Mira of herself, answered the first few questions as if from a script. 'Fine, yes. Uncomfortable now, very, finding it difficult to sleep, but it will be soon . . .' Then, as he shuffled around his father's office, tidying and organizing, he moved a little deeper, told Mira something of his and Clare's inconclusive discussions about names, their guesses as to whether it would be a boy or a girl, and finally something about Clare herself, how the pregnancy was changing her, how she already seemed older and different than when Graham had first met her. How complete she seemed now: how she was both profoundly excited, he could tell, and at the same time sleepily serene. Far more than he was. (You'd almost, Graham joked, think I was the one who had to go into labour, given how nervous I am, and that she's the one who will be hanging about in the waiting area smoking cigars.)

As he spoke on about Clare and the baby, with more ease around his stepmother than he had ever felt before, Graham could see that she, too, was changing around him. It was like something in a film – a special effect, almost: Mira's face shifting and dissolving until her aspect was quite transformed, not what he was used to. She was softer-looking. Pretty, almost. Now, this late, Graham saw the woman his father had fallen in love with. Mira.

She cleared her throat. 'You know, Graham,' she said, and he was sure he heard her say both syllables for once, rather than the usual *Gram*, 'I might have had a child, once.'

The sentence confused him. 'You mean – ' he said awkwardly – 'you thought of having a child? Or—'

'I was pregnant.'

Oh. Graham's stomach clenched, as though he were a boy again. He remembered Clare asking him when they first met whether his father and stepmother had other children together, and his horrified *No. Of course not.* The idea had seemed obscene. Not possible.

'Did you have a miscarriage?'

'No. I ended the pregnancy. I had,' Mira clarified, 'an abortion.'

The word, ugly, fell into the empty space between them. It shocked Graham. *Abortion.* Good God. It seemed so violent to him, word and act both; and with the comprehension of it came an even uglier recognition, that Mira must have made that decision with his father's help, that Peter would have wanted the abortion, too. How he must have hated the idea of a child! Of him, Graham, even. For it was one thing for Peter to have been in favour of abortion before Graham was born, before he knew the boy – but after, as well? Had the existence of Graham been such a blight in his life, after all?

'Was it a difficult decision?' Graham asked, gasping slightly. Meaning: did my father really have no hesitation or regret?

'No,' Mira said her face retreating into its past, and though the word was blunt and defiant, it was at cross-purposes with her tone, which was low and strangely forgiving. 'Perhaps it should have been. It might have been later. I was so young.'

357

Young? 'This was—?'

'In nineteen sixty-one or two.' She calculated. 'I was twenty-two. It would have changed my life – destroyed it, I thought – to have a child. I would never have worked, never have been able to do this work.'

'So the man wasn't – wasn't my father?'

Mira looked bewildered by the suggestion, then as the misunderstanding dawned she reached and clutched Graham's arm. 'Oh, no. *No.*' Her accent sounded heavier than usual. 'I'm sorry, I should have made that more clear. No, no. Not Peter. This was in Yugoslavia. Years ago. A poet, a man older than I was.' She continued to hold his arm. Graham felt the need in Mira's grasp. She must miss having someone to hold. 'But he married my sister a year later. They had two children together. So—' Her smile had some complexity in it that was beyond Graham; bitterness, regret, acceptance. 'I could not leave him behind altogether.'

What a tale to tell him. Graham tried to imagine his stepmother at twenty-two. He had never before conceived of her as a young woman, as someone who might once have been uncertain and in trouble. Frightened, probably, as a woman must be when those changes started to work themselves within her when she wasn't ready for them. Was not ready for *that*: for bringing a new life into life.

'Do you know,' he said, wanting to trade a confidence for a confidence, 'it's very odd. A similar thing happened to Clare. At university. She – well, she made the same decision, obviously. She said it wasn't difficult at the time – that the bloke was a prat, not someone she could ever have been with or had a child with – but that afterwards, for years, she had odd pains and aches. She thought she might never be able to have children. That she had ruined her chances.'

'Poor girl.'

'Yes. And she only just told me this a few weeks ago. She had seen the midwife and the midwife told her she must tell me before the birth. That the birth might bring up – you know, might bring it all back.' He recalled the scene at the Greek restaurant, Clare's face pale with apprehension, her food untouched. Graham with no idea what she could have to say that was so dire. 'It was difficult for her to tell me. I think she was worried I might react badly.'

'I never told Peter this story, either.'

'Really?' Peter and Mira had seemed so united to Graham. As if they told each other everything. Perhaps, after all, there had been patches of significant silence between them.

'I did not like to recall it. And I think – I thought – it would have upset him. Very much.' She looked at Graham levelly. 'If he had known, he might have tried harder to persuade me to have a child with him. And I did not want to. I did not want to.'

'But he wouldn't have wanted to either. I mean, he wasn't . . .' How to put this? 'He never meant to be a father himself. Obviously.'

'Perhaps. You don't know. It was one of his great sadnesses,' Mira said, her voice rather fierce, 'not to have known you as a small child.'

'Do you think so?' Graham was sceptical, even as some small, intensely greedy part of him wanted to hear more.

'Oh yes. He told me so.'

'He never gave that impression.'

'It would have been unfair for him to. There was nothing you could have done about it. Nor him. To fill you with his regret over all of that would have been unkind.'

'I suppose so.' It had never occurred to Graham to see the

story this way. This was, perhaps, why Mira's patients valued her so. This human understanding.

'It is one of the most cruel things about his dying. Now. It is one of the worst . . .' Finally, her language faltered. She was not going to remain intact for much longer, he could see that. 'It is so unfair. He would have loved to know your child.'

Graham leaned in to Mira then, unable to think of anything else, and did something he had never done before. He embraced her.

The silver-haired woman walked under the warm dappled shadows of the chestnut leaves, hardly seeing. The route was so familiar to her, she took one of these walks nearly every day, looping through South Parks and Headington Hill Park, or up near Oxford Brookes University (it had been a poly, once, but one had to keep up with the times). Walking was good for one. They said that, the doctors, the magazines, but in fact it was the sort of thing one shouldn't have to be told. It was so obvious. Helen had a new Scottie to accompany her on her travels – Bertie, a sweet black fellow with a cheerful disposition. Her daughter was needlessly wary of him, anxious that he might snap at the children. Absurd – he was a gentle, happy little thing.

She made her way along the lower path where one of the benches was newly bright, just installed. This was a good idea, to replace the old ones that were splintery and worn. And dedicated, even. *In loving memory of Peter Braverman*, Helen read, carved neatly into a back plank. Good heavens. Peter. Who had put this here? Lydia? Graham?

'Bertie!' Helen called, as if she could show the dog this inscription, but he was off chasing a squirrel and did not heed her voice.

She knew that Peter had succumbed. He had not been far

from it when she saw him at the hospital, and Lydia had told her briefly of going to the cremation. Said it was rather awkward, and that the wife, the Serbian woman, had given her peculiar looks, but she felt it was her right to go with Graham and Clare and wish Peter off in her own way. (Lydia was capable, Helen knew, of a certain self-justifying blindness to the responses of other people. 'The wife': Helen was quite sure that Lydia knew she was called Mira. It seemed petty, after all these years, to feign forgetfulness of it.)

Helen had liked Mira when she met her. Though what could that mean, in the circumstances, when the poor woman was evidently hobbled by bewilderment and panic? Mira had distrusted the doctors, clearly, and yet in all likelihood found the return from hospital equally fearful, when the care of a dying man would be in her hands, when the strange yet comforting sterility of the ward would be replaced by the known but transformed aspects of their once-regular life at home.

Helen remembered all of that. She had been through it with Charles. Some years ago now – eight – but one did not forget. One adjusted slowly, out of necessity, to moving through the world singly. And the grandchildren were a help and a distraction. (In the autumn she was planning to visit her son and his family in Seattle, Washington.) But she had resisted the so-called kindness of other people who urged her to get out and about, perhaps even meet a new man. Helen had no interest in having another husband. She had had Charles, and he had died, and that was that.

One could have a new friend, though. Helen would like a new friend. Perhaps she could go see Mira, but under what pretext? She suspected the woman was still trying to find her balance, and probably, if she was anything like herself – Helen did not know why but she felt a kinship with the Serbian woman, sensed a warmth and an intellect under the disease-numbed exterior – might need the acreage of solitude suddenly opened around her. But there would come a time when Mira would want company, too. She would want conversation. Perhaps the two women could have that together, at least. Conversation. Helen intended to try it.

Helen called Bertie to her, prepared to put him back on the lead as they crossed over the London road. It was the subject of murder mysteries and farces, wasn't it, widows befriending one another. They always seemed to end up scheming and plotting. Why? It could be a route to survival, mainly. One could pass on what one had learned about continuing, rudderless. An alliance that might help both sides.

Besides, Mira was Serbian. Her country was destroyed, was under constant assault from within and without. Helen was a Quaker, had been for years, but had attended meetings more regularly since Charles had died. She knew acts of friendship were important. Particularly in wartime. The need was all the greater now of holding other people in the light.

She allowed herself to dream. She dreamt of him.

Mira had not expected Peter, or had expected him only in anxieties and fears. Stop, help me find him – where is he? – it is too late – there must be some mistake – *I must see him.* That sort of thing. Like exams relived for years afterwards in the unravelling imagination. The nightmare repeated.

It wasn't like that. He took her places. (To Prague, to Florence.) He spoke to her. He cooked for her. Watched the news with her, told her *This will pass;* and *They will endure, the Serbs: they always do,* though this may have been more willed, a waking dream, his intended presence next to Mira on the couch, his wanted-into-existence voice in her ear. Elsewhere, he touched her. Once, he prayed with her. That was wrong, she knew, but she was so glad that he did. He kissed the icon and her spirit soared.

I will never leave you. He did not say that to her, had not said it to her and could not say it now but she could say it to him and, nightly, she did. I will not leave you, Peter. I found you, some-how – how are such findings possible? – sitting at the dark end of the table in a tattered red pullover and we shared oddly easy banter about communist threads and the uniforms of noncon-formity. The Epsteins, generous. Did they make a match of us? My language was not as good then but we managed. You asked about my scarf and I told you it had been given me by my father and already, then, I saw in your hidden eye the desire to stand next to him in my affections, the man who had given me that scarf, who did not want me to leave Yugoslavia.

You were my Englishman. You gave me your body, yes, and beyond that you gave me your country. Your foods and your words and your faces (their tea-mottled teeth, their summerless skin colours), the whole grey street after grey street of it, the park after park of it, the sheepdogs on the screens and the knickers by the biscuits. Notes of condolence, and wet mackintoshes in the hallway. Other passengers to be let off first and gaps to be minded, two fares to Aldwych, and a tip of the tweed cap with the song-toned *Much obliged*. Summer puddings and bread pud-dings and Euro-puddings, a joke. Newspaper writers' verbal vaudeville and, as a reminder that sentiment is permitted, the bucolic melodies of Vaughan Williams and the lines of John Bet-jeman. This was your country, Peter, and you gave it to me. What greater gift, finally?

The bed remained cavernous without him, and yet Mira filled it as she could. She allowed her rage to expire. She made herself settle into the fact of his absence, wrapped the sadness round her like a blanket. And, as a kindness, she allowed herself to dream.

The baby was breech. The midwife had felt the head up near Clare's breast, near her heart, a week before, and made a tsking sound. 'Why don't you do Mum a favour and turn around?' she had admonished the mobile bulge beneath Clare's skin, and it made Clare shiver to hear the midwife refer to her as *Mum*. There was still only one Mum in Clare's life, her own, and the notion that the name would soon attach itself to her as well remained bizarre. 'Many babies do turn right at the end,' the midwife told Clare. 'But if not, and the doctor thinks a vaginal birth would be difficult, there's a chance that he'll want to deliver the baby by Caesarean section.'

This seemed ridiculous after all the preparation Clare had done. She had gone to the classes with a wan and elsewhere Graham (they started two weeks after Peter had died). She had been performing the exercises, stretching those improbable muscles and putting herself in odd positions when alone in the flat. She had practised her breathing. She had even, though she would not admit this to Caroline, come up with a 'pain strategy' – words to concentrate on when the pain threatened to overwhelm her. They were not going to take all that away from her, were they? 'They' the doctors, 'they' the gods who watched over childbirth? Simply because the baby was right side up, which in this case meant the wrong way round? Graham's view was that neither Clare nor the doctors should try any heroics. If the general view was that it was safest to deliver a breech baby by Caesarean, he was willing to accept that wisdom and thought Clare should too. She should not spend days quizzing the midwife about the possibility of a vaginal delivery of a breech baby. (He avoided the word *vaginal* out of squeamishness, or out of courtesy to Clare: the word he used was 'ordinary'; Clare guessed that even a baby emerging in the 'ordinary' way sickened Graham – he'd had to turn away from the video they showed in the class, she had noted it at the time. Perhaps he found the prospect of an operation altogether more sanitary.)

So it happened that when Clare lay down on a heavy, breathless evening, tireder than usual, and on laying down felt a great surge of fluid flood from herself and seep into the bed, she called shakily to Graham that they had best get to hospital. *It was starting.* Excitement and fear vied for position within Clare, but in Graham, who was calm, methodical, and ashen, she could see that the fear handily smothered everything else.

A short drive to the hospital, and her solitary entry as Graham parked the car; the lights and bright faces of those who welcomed her there; the first bands of pain encircling her groin as they hooked her up neatly to the appropriate wires and tubes. There was some concern about when she had last eaten, and how much – a few Hobnobs at tea time, evidently, might be enough to make the anaesthetic slightly riskier, but the baby was still breech, ultrasound determined. It was not a question of whether there would be an operation, but when. Nurses continued to speak to Clare in kind voices, though she became less sure what they said: they were trying to explain to her various orders and procedures, when all Clare could do was to retreat, deeply, into herself, where her baby still lodged, and wait there with him or her until the others, the adults, came to fetch them. She had an image of herself playing in a corner with her child – handing it a rattle, touching its fingers to hers, kissing its cheek. She hoped Graham was listening to what all the white- and green-uniformed people were saying. It was no doubt important. And now she was leaning over, as asked, her hands were being held tightly, and they were jabbing her spine with a needle.

Labour was progressing quickly, so they could no longer wait for the Hobnob problem to go away. An operating room was found and cleared. The obstetrics surgeon, a doctor she had never seen before, a man with dark eyes and red lips and too-pale skin, began to talk to her, along with an Asian anaesthesiologist who tested her responses and reflexes. There was a general air of hurry and suppressed alarm – or was it only Graham who was alarmed? Graham was holding her hand and standing behind her head, and now here she was splayed on a table, yes, an operating table (you saw this all the time on the telly, all those medical dramas) and the thought that came to her was that she was being crucified, actually. She was told to hold her arms wide and still and soon, it seemed, they would be slicing into her, and everyone wore masks around her and the air was white and cold. The fluorescence was fierce. The voices were businesslike and also urgent, alternating with cheerful and falsely high-noted comments to herself and Graham. Graham's hand was on her arm. He was told to sit down in a chair. She heard someone say, 'You might want to look away now,' to him. As for her, she could not look down at her bloody, exposed innards even if she wanted to, as they had thoughtfully installed a small fence just under her breasts to prevent her from peeking.

Perhaps they explained what they were doing to her, or perhaps they didn't. The people with gloves on were evidently reaching within her, and in spite of the anaesthetic she could feel hands tugging at pieces of her, rearranging the internal Clare until it was as they wanted it to be. She felt pulling, pushing, as if someone were trying to squeeze the life out of her. She started to cry. 'Are you all right? Clare?' said the anaesthesiologist gently, and she nodded politely as it seemed best to say yes. She did not want to make a fuss, nor distract them from whatever it was they were doing. She could not believe that this operation could have anything to do with the birth of a human being. Nothing in this frigid, arid room suggested the beginning of life. She wondered if, in fact, she would ever see or touch or hold her baby.

There was a phenomenal amount of blood. It was as well they had told Graham to sit down, because even sitting down he felt the muscles in his legs jelly, and a dizziness buzz about his head. He must keep holding Clare's arm. He must not pass out. She was being so brave, had been since the waters broke, helping him find the car keys when he was frenzied and blind, and being perpetually agreeable, even in her pain. Only as they wheeled her into the operating room had he seen Clare's smile thin and fade, and he realized she was afraid too, that she was very afraid, and that therefore he, Graham, must assemble his own strength and carry them both through. It was the least he could do for her. For his wife. How he loved her! Seeing her sprawled and opened, he felt a painful, passionate admiration for Clare for enduring this ordeal. And to what end?

He stared at the doctors fumbling about in her belly and he made himself say, 'It's all right, love. They're being very careful' – when what it looked like to him was two people struggling with slippery hands to catch an unwieldy fish they had landed, a rather larger one than they had anticipated. He half expected to see a silver streak flashing in their gloves and flipping over the edge of the table, but while he watched, a blood-and-muck-covered mess was removed from Clare's body and held up briefly. 'Ah, she's a girl! Isn't she beautiful!' as the cry, the girl's first thin cry of protest, entered the room.

Where am I? the small voice asked, and *What world is this?* And Graham understood that these were the first of uncountable questions his daughter would ask him.

'Would you like to hold her, Graham?' a nurse asked a minute later, handing him the newly wrapped red-faced bundle, and he said yes, in that bloody, light-drenched room, and drank in a long look at the tiny creature, before holding her in front of the stunned face of the just-become mother.

Epilogue

The bombing stopped June the tenth, after seventy-eight days. Penelope was two weeks old. Mira had forgotten how very small and, yes, miraculous they were at the start. She had never been one to coo over little dolls, real or plastic, but one did not need to be overly sentimental to feel simple amazement at the infant. It – she – was so animal, young Penelope: she slept and slept, she screamed, she drank, she expelled. Her singular knowledge and instinct was directed towards the breast. So much of Mira's reading and theory had to do with the breast, it was fitting irony that after so many years she welcomed one at last into her own home, a milkful breast, source of maternal nourishment, life's first gift.

Milošović claimed victory over NATO as only a madman could, though Mira awaited news of his dramatic exit by suicide or execution, which would have been in keeping with the gory history of the region. There was none; the end was surprisingly anticlimactic, and the fiend somehow managed to hold on to power. Mira did not know, no one did, how or whether her country could ever recover. (As for Kosovo: it was impossible to say what that supposedly rescued province had ahead of it.) She intended to travel back there as soon as she could. To help, if possible. She recognized, in the post-bombardment quiet, that she would not return to Beograd to live. The balance of her life had been and still would be in England. She would, she could see, remain more useful to her people there at this distance, and perhaps by staying in London – who knew? – she might open up the possibility of movement to her niece and to little Marko.

Mira sat in her office, waiting. There were new patients to replace the old, as always. A young man in his twenties, musically gifted and chronically depressed; a jocular lesbian who had trouble staying the course with jobs or with lovers. Mira had begun to care for them again. Yes, even this one. The American. Foolish girl; she would see herself, one day, and Mira would help her with the seeing. Mira often sat in her office now, alone and waiting, as she never used to, because the living room offered too many familiar stations of hard memory (the vinyl nightmare, the bookcases). Her office – the Confessional, Peter had sometimes called it, and the Delivery Room, too, how apt – was wonderfully quiet, and she could remain calm in the oasis, reflecting on the patterns and urges of those who came to see her, and of herself. She was stronger now than she had been. Better able to stay separate, as was necessary for her to do her work, and to keep free for others the empty rooms of discovery they required. Prayer helped. Mira prayed frequently, and displayed an icon more publicly than she had before, to give her solace and because there was no longer someone in the flat who might object. Mira spoke to her saints again and more freely now, fearing no discouragement or distaste.

Thank God the war was over. For now, at least. There would be more wars, no doubt, and other places in the world where Jess's blighted, blighting country would throw around its weight and righteousness and impressive military hardware, but for now this episode was over, and Jess no longer had to wonder how much her therapist must hate her as a symbol of the wretched oppressor. She had recovered from that weird morning when Mira had lectured her about Kosovo. It had been clear that Mira herself was somewhat embarrassed by the outburst, though god knew you could see how such a tirade would build up in a person. It wasn't entirely professional, Jess supposed, but it had certainly made her think. And that wasn't such a terrible thing. Jess paid closer attention than she had before to the progress of this 'campaign'. (That bombing of the Chinese Embassy, for instance: Christ, what a fuck-up.) She kept better track of the different arguments. She knew that in Priština, in Kosovo, many Albanians thanked God for the interventions of the US and of NATO. There were people there who were slavishly grateful to Bill Clinton and Madeleine Albright, while in Belgrade those names would forever be curses or insults. Which side was right? The answer was beyond Jess. To some people, Milošović was a war criminal and ought to be tried in the Hague. Then again, to others, so was Henry Kissinger. Who got to decide? The men with the most weapons, that's who. You didn't see Bill Clinton lining up to turn Kissinger over to Dutch halls of justice, did you?

By mutual if unspoken agreement, such subjects were not broached in the sessions between Mira and Jess. Mira had been ever so proper since the Kosovo litany, as if on her best behaviour, and Jess thought it most tactful not to mention any of her own clouded thoughts on matters of war or of justice. She and Nick had good conversations about all that, now – he was smart, smarter than Jess had realized at first, and he had pretty coherent analyses that were slowly becoming hers. One of the conveniences of being in a regular couple was that you could borrow the other person's opinions on matters you hadn't had time to read up about yourself. Jess did not want to be some bimbo parroting her boyfriend's views, but Nick was bright and humane and he read the paper with some subtlety. She loved him for that.

There was more and more that she loved Nick for, and as Jess approached the familiar buzzer on the steel-grey street by the trains she considered her probable topic for the day: becoming a stepmother. Jess had been thinking a great deal lately about what it would mean for her to be a wonderful stepmother to Nick's kids, to abandon the idea of having a child of her own. Perhaps it would be enough. She wanted to convince herself that it would be enough. This was a momentous shift for her, obviously, and she hoped Mira would have something helpful to say about it. Something wise.

Jess entered the office, nodded to Mira and to the annoying Japanesey print – she would miss it, though, if it suddenly disappeared – and noticed something new on Mira's desk. A photograph of a baby. It was flat on the desk, not meant for public view, but Jess's sharp eye caught it at once. The whole problem of saying something about the peace immediately fled Jess's mind. All she could think of was the fact that her therapist had a photograph of a baby.

'Is that your grandchild?' Jess asked, nodding at the colour photo. It seemed a safe enough question.

Mira started rather guiltily; obviously hadn't meant for the baby to be seen, but did not want to make even more of it now by hiding it. She hesitated. She must feel a little guilty about Jess, with all her motherhood traumas, having seen it. 'Yes,' the older woman said then, with a faint, mysterious smile. 'That's right.'

'What a cutie-pie,' Jess said, because you had to say that, though it struck her, not for the first time, how fundamentally ugly and alien-looking babies were. Maybe Jess lacked the right kind of maternal instinct after all. Maybe it would be better this way. Nick's boys were fun, living characters, and they had liked

371

her immediately. She could joke around with them, take them to movies, help them with homework. But she could skip the dreary parts: doctor's appointments, hygiene issues, shoe fittings. And this way she would never have to change any diapers. Her nights could remain relatively inviolate. She need never spoon strained mush into a wordless face, waiting for the reward of a stew-stained swipe at her nose or bat of her head. Nick's kids were all right. Jess would have fun with them. Still, she could not ignore the needle of pain that shot through her at the thought of someone else's new baby. It was probably Mira's tenth grandchild. She had probably lost count. She looked fairly blasé about the whole thing.

'Thank you,' the therapist replied, typically, her hands folded together, her face that of a sphinx. The words signalled the end of their non-conversation, and Jess settled down into the chair to begin telling her story.

Thank *you*

for thoughtful words from the other side of the couch: Nancy
Chodorow
for being so damned smart: Ayelet Waldman, Peggy Orenstein,
Susanne Pari
for humanity and skill in matters of life and death: Dr Katarina
Lanner-Cusin
for medical notes: Liz Park
for years of hard questions: MR
for stories and lore: Jasna Stefanovič, Jelena Petrovič
for kindly lights amidst the encircling gloom: Ann Packer, Pam
Thompson, Anita Feferman, Edie Meidav
for that bench, among other things: Judith Tucker
for the London eye: Simon Firth
for support on the ground: Noemi Curiel
for good will and good readings: Sam Humphreys, Andrew Kidd
for delivering, and more: Pat Kavanagh
for the lifeboat: Michael Chabon
for urging and encouraging: Linda Brownrigg and Philip Lewis
for love, faith and patience: Sedge Thomson

Remembering David Lewis, and Sarah Pettit; and Linnaeus